G000075255

STAND BY
THE COLOURS

NICHOLAS CARTER

STAND BY
THE COLOURS

THE
SHADOW
ON THE
CROWN

Book 5

MACMILLAN

First published 1999 by Macmillan

an imprint of Macmillan Publishers Ltd
25 Eccleston Place, London SW1W 9NF
and Basingstoke

Associated companies throughout the world

ISBN 0 333 67707 2

Copyright © Throwaway Classics 1999

The right of Nicholas Carter to be identified as the
author of this work has been asserted by him in accordance
with the Copyright, Designs and Patents Act 1988.

1 3 5 7 9 8 6 4 2

A CIP catalogue record for this book is available from
the British Library.

Typeset by SetSystems Ltd, Saffron Walden, Essex
Printed and bound in Great Britain by
Mackays of Chatham plc, Chatham, Kent

DRAMATIS PERSONAE

King Charles I.
Prince Rupert of the Rhine, his nephew.
Prince Maurice, Rupert's younger brother.
Charles, Prince of Wales; James, Duke of York: His Majesty's
sons.
The Duke of Richmond, a friend of Prince Rupert.
Mary Villiers, Duchess of Richmond, a very good friend of Prince
Rupert.
Lord Falkland, His Majesty's Secretary of State.
Patrick Ruthven, Earl of Brentford, commander of His Majesty's
forces before Gloucester.
Sir Jacob Astley, commander of Royalist foot.
Sir John Byron, commander of Royalist cavalry.

Sir Edward Massey, Governor of Gloucester for the Parliament.
Robert Devereux, Earl of Essex, principal Parliamentarian
warlord.
Oliver Cromwell, MP and rising Parliamentarian warlord.

UNMENTIONED IN HISTORY

Parliamentarian:

William Sparrow, former officer of militia and cavalry cornet,
now captain, Mercer's regiment of foot.
Colonel Archibald McNabb, Scots professional soldier serving
with Waller.
Colonel Tobias Fulke, a gallant but rather elderly gentleman,
acting commander of Mercer's regiment of foot.
Henry Mercer, cheesemonger and colonel.
Colston Muffet, sergeant, serving with Mercer's regiment of foot.
Hereward Gillingfeather, an agitator, William Butcher,
sharpshooter, Caleb Cruickshank, orphan and pikeman,
presently serving with Mercer's regiment of foot.
Shem Bentham, John Ruell, Bob Riley, London riff-raff.
Gallen Fey, captain of Parliament's ship the *Conqueror*.
Nathaniel Hawker, captain of Parliament's ship the *Honest John*.
John Grey, his mate.

Royalist:

Sir Gilbert Morrison, disgraced MP, former colonel of militia,
wool merchant and turncoat, Governor-in-waiting of the Royal
Westward Society of Oceanic Venturers, presently awaiting
assignment.
Maynard Morrison, a West Country miller, Sir Gilbert's brother.
Captain Jamie Morrison, Sir Gilbert's son, recuperating from
battle vapours.
Bella Margueritte Morrison, Sir Gilbert's daughter.
The Earl of Dartland, known as 'Black Bob' Dyle, Royalist
magnate and justice.
John St John Dyle, Lord Clavincale, his son.
Mary Keziah Pitt, Bella's maid and confidante, William Sparrow's
sweetheart.
Master Algernon Starling, clerk to Sir Gilbert.

Captain Hugo Telling, Prince Rupert's regiment of horse.
Colonel Michael Slaughter, an officer recently returned from
service in Ireland.
Valentine Cruikshank, captain of the King's privateer the
Messalina's Purse.
Edward Callow, his mate.
Terrence Gable, captain of the King's privateer the *Blue
Doubloon.*
Colonel Scipio Porthcurn, Cornish officer of foot.
Major Brinks, Captain Took, in command of the Royalist
garrison of Penmethock.
Compton Speedwell, captain of dragoons.
Henry Graves, Auld Guppy, Martin Pike, Royalist dragoons.
Margaret, Lady Ramsay, widow of the Royalist squire Sir
Marmaduke Ramsay.
Anneliese Ramsay, her daughter.

STAND BY
THE COLOURS

FARNHAM CASTLE,

William lad, I send these lines in the fonde hope they may yet find you (which I gravely dowt) well, aye, and tolerable fit after your misfortunes at the hands of those damn fine anabaptists presently cokking theyre beevers at Westminster.

I am handing this letter as you can see to a cornet of mine name of Carter, a mickle grate pock-pudding who has recently transferred hisself (if you please) to yr old friend Colonel Cromwell's fine regiment of horse up by East Angyla. I have tipped him a shilling to drop this in to you, but no dowt he'll drink to me with it first.

Well lad, it woonds me deep to report our divers misfortunes outside Bazing House, that pit of popery I wrote of in my last dispatch. Many's the good man I've seen fall beneath those walls and in all truth I have never yet cleered the reek of their smoking flessh from my nose trils. Three storms close, and yet the malignants who serve Charles Stuart in that place bid us do our worst, saying further that it would never fall as long as they had theyre breath. You will have red of the man: John Paulet, styled fifth Markquis of Winchester, a Catholic Gentleman mark you, as rich as Krusus and as stuffed full of vile Jesuit imaginings as can scarce be credited by honest men. As unrepentant a papist and malignant as ever drew breath or sword. He has fortified hisself up in his great manshun place on the London road, and billt walls and entrenchments around besides from which he offers us defyance, strangling the wool traid to the harm of our Godly and humble merchants in London.

Three times we did dispute those walls, and as many times were cast back in bloody and bewildered ruin, some crying out our Lord Jesus had forsaken us at the hour of our most urgent need.

When our generals urged this Paulet surrender the place, he replied to them that if the King had no more ground in England than Bazing House, he would adventure as he did, and so maintain it to the uppermost, damn his black heart.

I was there William, when owr friend Sir William Waller made fast the siege in November. I had no service as there was precious little for horse to do and besides Argyl had taken lame and so William, I volunteered (if you'll credit it) to serve with Master Cook's company in the Yellow Auxill-hairies of the London Trayned Bands. Godly sober boys William who I chanced to meet up with during our last visit to you. Now maybe our God in heaven was about other works that day, I cannot judge, but suffice to say he smiled not upon us.

Our first attack took in some outhouses and a porshun of a wall, but the enemy, having espeshall skill with match and brimstone (as can well be imagined, given theyre masters serve the Great Satan hisself) burnt those poor brave fellowes back out of the works, taking them much by surprise as they refreshed themselves with pies and sweetmeats they had by chance discovered in those sheds. Next (and it was a Sabbath Day besides) our Major Strachan, as brave a Scotch man as ever drew sword, took our men in from another angle. As it happened, a spy had told our general of a place where the wall was but one and a half bricks thick, and Major Strachan took with him skilled fire men and a petard, resolving to make this breach that we might get in to the pile. Our men pressed in with great energy and singing of psalms, and got them to the spot where the spy did assure us the wall was barely strong enough for a henhouse, leve alone a fortress. But he was a thrice damned liar or his memory mistook him, for tho our petard blew up a great stink of smuts and chips it did not trouble the brickworks at all. And as if to tread our faces into the dirt, (and the telling is almost as bad William as the act itself) further damnations overtook our brave brothers in the Westminster Trayned Band. They had come at another porshun of the walls as a divershun to Major Strachan's attack, as neat a body you could wish to see with their musketiers commanded in six ranks and packed right close upon one another in the open sward. Whether the fault were with their chief leeder, or through want of courage or discretion I know not, but the front rank fired before it was in position to do any execushun upon the walls. And for want of intervals to turn away speedily, the second and third ranks fired on our own men. We had seventy or eighty slain or hurt in that disorder, and afterwards the remains of our trayned bands cried Home Home, and would not serve another minute under Sir William, who had no choice but to get himself off to rest his men and write of his woes to the House.

Well William, we have presently marched back on Farn-Ham castle, where the Colonel I told you of (you remember the fellowe now) has taken the bloody flux and shites his bowils out before his eyes. I need a new man for Carter here, and would look no further than you yourself, if you have the mind. This being no time for wallowing in cold pity and warm pish, as I found you in London lad, you would do well to find me here with Waller, and as God's my witness I'll make you captain, aye.

You'll get no better offer, sir, now's the chance to rejoyn the colours before this wretched war is done. Your obedient friend, sir,

Archie McNabb.

The Royalist dragoon scanned the closely written letter, wondering if it might be some valuable piece of intelligence for his captain back at Alton. Ah, the fellow hadn't looked much like a messenger, the dragoon reflected. He had been riding this slow, clumsy horse for a start, and hadn't looked likely to outrun a three-legged badger, let alone the squall of well-aimed musketry he had wandered into. The man had been weighed down with a bulging sack of spare clothing and personal effects, as if he had been off on his travels despite the ferocious weather. The dragoon shook his head at this conundrum. He had already taken anything of any use from the corpse, stowed his pipe and baccy into his pocket for a sly smoke later. The blizzards had given out now, but there was barely a road, house, or hovel to be seen, and it was most likely the unfortunate fellow had gotten himself altogether lost and wandered by mistake into Royalist territory. Whatever had happened, the fellow was lost now, right enough.

'What is it, Samuel?' his colleague called, peering over the drifted snow at the downed rider, the wounded horse shivering like a dogfish in the slush. 'One of Waller's?'

'Oh, he's a Roundhead all right. Tried to turn about and kick him on,' the sharpshooter called, reaching out to take the dead man's panting horse by the bridle.

'Dead, then?'

'You wouldn't chuckle.' The dragoon poked the dead rider with his boot, wondering if the rogue's buff would be worth washing off. It might at that. He glanced at the scrawled letter which had been torn from the owner's pocket by the passage of his ball, rubbed a speckle of blood from the signature. Archie, was it? That didn't sound much like a high and mighty Roundhead general now, did it? He dropped the letter into the snow and regarded the trembling horse with gruff pity – he'd been a farmhand before the war, and disliked seeing animals suffer unnecessarily.

'We might jus' 's well shoot this bliddy horse now, Eli, he ain't goin' be any use to us like that.'

The dragoon's companion clambered down the snowy bank, cocking his pistol as he came. The horse stared at him through its bulging brown apple of an eye, its chest black with steaming blood.

'Ah, might as well. Cut off a haunch and we'll have it back to the camp,' Eli Pitt suggested easily, bending down to retrieve the stained paper his companion had discarded. He had no idea as to what was written there either, but he tucked the lost letter into his breeches as if it was a saucy love note from his favourite sweetheart.

It would do to wipe his arse later.

PART ONE

WINTER QUARTER

'Sir, we are all lost and spoyled if we have not commanders.'

John Ashe, Parliamentary Commissioner in Somerset

WAREHAM FOREST,

DORSET, CHRISTMAS DAY, 1643

T he forest sustained the strongest of them like a snow-
mantled mother. It wrapped its chosen men in its fragrant
embrace, warmed and even fed them – after a fashion. The
starving survivors of William Sparrow's hotchpotch war band
burrowed through the drifts after the frozen remains of woodcock
and moorhen; torn stiff, kite-winged rooks from the coiled brambles as if the rank meat would be fit for Charles Stuart himself.
They ate snow off their daggers and chammed leaves, bark, and
feverishly dug roots – anything which might ward off the angels
of death which tramped so patiently behind them.

Soon they would be forced to leave the creaking canopies
behind, trust themselves to the hideous wilderness of the coast
road. And they all knew the road was bound to be watched, after
the slaughter and shambles they had left behind them.

Their journey had not been an easy one, but toiling thirty
miles through the worst blizzards any of them could remember
had been preferable to capture at Penmethock – and almost
inevitable extinction at the hands of the vengeful villagers.
Sparrow's men had slaughtered garrison, pirate, and Trained
Bandsmen alike. They had razed their homes and wrecked their
livelihoods, scuttled their merrily painted fishing fleet in pursuit
of their main quarry: the notorious Royalist privateer the *Messalina's Purse*. The hell-spawned blockade runner's mad dog of a
captain had thrown a score of them overboard earlier that
summer, in a cold-hearted bid to throw a pursuing Roundhead
warship from his forked tail.

Captain Cruikshank hadn't expected the demented survivors

9

of the atrocity to turn up at his smugly secure base and burn the town and his precious ship from beneath him.

His legendary life savings, a fabulous hoard of stolen gold and jewels, had fallen into the bloody hands of the victors, a fortune in coin which they had taken turns carrying through the snow, even as their weaker friends lay down in the drifts to die.

But their eagerly awaited revenge and unexpected windfall had not been achieved without loss. A dozen and more rebel raiders had been killed, as many more had been wounded, and all their chief officers slain. Worse than that, the ship which had carried them into the enemy harbour in the first place had been lost in the tremendous duel with the despised *Messalina's Purse*.

William Sparrow had assumed command of the survivors; the sailors, the looters, the waifs and strays who hadn't dared remain behind with the furious fisherfolk. He had ordered the nightmare march to Poole, the nearest friendly garrison held by the Parliament. He had cursed and cajoled and bribed the pitiful bandits, promised them their fair share of Cruikshank's gold when they got home. He had joked and kicked, fetched and carried, bawled nonsensical orders at them in a bid to lift their tumbling spirits.

'Stand straight in your ranks and files!' as the shivering mob panted through the snow like broken winded nags at a steeplechase. 'Assume a lazy posture!' as they pushed and crawled and stumbled through six-foot drifts.

Some had cursed his madcap antics, some had smirked and some had ignored him altogether, lost in their own private purgatory. But the survivors had staggered on, frosted weapons clutched in their frozen fists, another mile more. And another. And another.

They had given the Royalist garrison of Dorchester a wide berth, taking to the high downs and losing themselves among the snow-heaped long barrows. They had skirted the wide white plains, bent their backs against the blizzards which raged out of the east, and finally, thankfully, reached the welcoming eaves of Wareham forest ahead of the whooping pursuit they had so feverishly expected. The filthy weather had smothered their tracks and kept more sensible men at home, so their ghostly journey and miraculous deliverance had gone practically unnoticed. For the first time in his career William hadn't minded the fact his martial efforts might be overlooked. He had been grateful enough to have reached the temporary sanctuary of the woods.

The ancient forest proved to be scored with treacherous ice-choked gullies and reamed by swift boulder-strewn streams. The gushing water turned their blood to lamp oil as they waded, teeth bared, to the uncertain sanctuary of the far bank of the little River Piddle. The dwindling band of survivors shivered in their saturated rags, steaming breath hanging in lazy haloes about their frozen heads – knowing in their bones their loud-mouthed captain had it right, but hating him a little more just the same.

'Move on, move on, you poxy whoresons! You'll freeze sitting there, you'll never wake up again! Do you want your damned share or not?'

The orphans of the forest hardly heard him. They melted away by ones and twos into the brittle undergrowth or cast themselves down in the feather-bed snowdrifts, unmoved by William Sparrow's savage encouragements and fanciful promises. Not even the prospect of grabbing their share of the treasure they had carried at such back-breaking cost could tempt them from their murderous slumbers. They lay down as if they had gotten home at last, locked their fingers beneath their cold-clouded heads and closed their eyes for ever.

'There's a charcoal-burner's hut along the way, Captain William, zor!' the half-daft herdsman who had volunteered to guide them called, gesturing towards the cold heart of the woods. Sparrow took his suggestion, urged the company to make one more march.

'Charcoal, we'll have a fire tonight!' Sparrow roared, tugging his coat about his red neck and stamping past the stragglers toward the front of the miserably chilled caravan.

The very thought of a good blaze was worth another half-mile. And then another.

'Well? Where's this damned hut?' Sparrow asked dangerously, fists clenched in the herdsman's threadbare lapels.

'Well, it was yere th' laz time I came this way, zor, by God 'twas!'

The charcoal-burner's hut was half hidden beneath the hanging branches of a vast oak, the turf roof camouflaged by an enormous bank of sculpted snow. Billy Butcher spotted the frail lifeline of smoke which hung like a dried eelskin above the craftily hidden den. The beady eyed charcoal-burner hopped and hawed as Billy prodded him out on the barrel of his fowling-piece, sooty fingers clenched to his ragged sheepskin as he eyed the truculent intruders.

'We can't all pack in there, Will, there's not room to swing a rat, let alone a cat!' Butcher, their cockney sharpshooter, cried.

'We'll take turns,' Sparrow growled.

'Turn an old man aht 'is 'ome, wudger?' the woodsman wailed, tears sparkling his smoke-rimmed eyes. The swineherds meant to shoot him, that was for sure.

'Hold your water, gramfer,' Sparrow advised, peering around the snowy clearing trying to imagine what fantastical shapes lay beneath the virgin drifts. He cocked his head, pulled the raised collar of his coat down from his raw ears. He could have sworn he'd heard . . .

'Bleedin' 'ell, chickens!' Billy Butcher squawked, leaning his fowling-piece by the door to drop back inside the hut. The charcoal-burner seemed to shrink inside his greasy sheepskin, apparently resigned to his imminent execution. Butcher emerged from the confines of his home, clutching a brace of flapping fowls in each fist.

12

'Back you go, old 'un, and get those fowls roasting,' the heavyset warrior ordered. The charcoal-burner raised his sooty eyebrow in defiance.

'Breakfast for four score, is that it?' he sneered, defiant to the last. He had imagined he would have escaped the soldiers' attention, this far away from civilization. Damn him if they hadn't sought him out in the depths of the forest, in the middle of the worst winter he could remember.

'If you can run to it, we've coin to pay for it,' Sparrow replied, clapping his dirty palm to his bulky chest and silencing his jeering companions for a moment. The charcoal-burner could have sworn he'd heard the faintest, calico-cushioned tinkle of coins.

'Is it a fool ye take me for?'

'Get inside, you'll get your money.'

They had plenty of it, sure enough.

A smoke-blackened stick served as chalk and compass, and a few square feet of snow did for a map table. John Grey, the bullet-headed seaman, scraped this way and that, transferring the charts he kept between his red-raw ears to the snow-covered forest floor.

'We've gone twenty miles out of our way,' he reported. 'We must be somewhere north of Wareham, by my reckoning.'

'Wareham forest, the herdsman says,' Sparrow agreed. 'But at least we've thrown the King's men off our track. Nobody could have followed us through that lot,' he said, nodding over his shoulder at the silently packed trees. 'We've damn near lost ourselves, let alone any fool who cared to follow!'

Grey jabbed his stick into the empty space below his fanciful network of roads, ridges, and coastline. 'The coast road must run that way. Corfe, Wareham, Poole. We've got this far, aye, and glad we are of it. But we'll not walk straight into Poole without so much as a by-your-leave from the King's men, nor the garrison for that matter.'

'We daren't wait here, John,' Sparrow said quietly.

The old mate, his face burnt like bacon rinds, sucked the

stumps of his teeth, his battered frame racked by another fit of cold cramps.

'Poole's protected on three sides by its bays, look you,' he coughed. 'So the road's the only way in. You can rest assured it's more than adequately watched by both sides, which means the water's our only real hope. Me and Mr Rhodes here,' he gestured at one of the sullen seamen they had rescued from Penmethock's notorious quarry, 'might get down to the shore, to try and find a boat, fetch help.'

Sparrow blew a gust of air down his nose. Grey shrugged.

'We must find some way in, some way of warning the garrison who we are. It's freeze here or be shot down before the walls, else. Shot down by our own side after thirty miles marching? No thankee!'

The bone-weary mate glanced around at the approaching footfalls, frowned at the marvellously radiant features of Sir Gilbert Morrison, twice-turned turncoat, merchant, MP, and renegade officer of militia. The ruddy-faced gentleman was nodding and smiling at them, trying to appear as serene and untroubled as possible while hopping from one boot to the other as if he had an urgent appointment behind the nearest tree.

'Don't mind me, gentlemen. Good counsel doesn't grow from seed, as I've often remarked in the past,' the jocular intruder observed, his small white teeth chattering with cold. He had thrown a snow-mottled blanket about his ample bulk, which had been considerably increased by half a dozen variously coloured coats he had stripped from the dead along the way.

'Sir Gilbert,' William breathed, giving his former employer and mentor a sickly smile. The merchant tilted his head to study the fanciful map, ran his red tongue over his generous, cold cracked lips.

'Ah, we're not far from Poole, I couldn't help overhearing,' he said conversationally.

'And you've thought of a cracking way to get in there without getting us shot down like dogs, is that it?'

Sir Gilbert smirked at William's sour remark.

'Sadly, William, military stratagems have never been my strong suit. I was merely reflecting, if we *were* to get within the walls, it might be better for all concerned if certain members of our brave company were no longer present to muddy the waters; to subject other, not necessarily associated, elements of the said company to the unwelcome scrutiny of the authorities.'

John Grey snorted in disgust at Sir Gilbert's all too familiar blustering, and stalked off to brief his unwilling companion Lieutenant Rhodes about their foolhardy mission towards the shore. William gazed ruefully at the snowy map. Sir Gilbert waited until the mate was safely out of earshot before elaborating on his theme.

'God's bones, Will, do I need to draw you another damned diagram? If you take me back to Poole, they'll hang me as a traitor!'

William grinned at the prospect. Why, there wasn't a rope in Christendom which would fit Sir Gilbert's brass neck!

'Ah, you can laugh, lad, after all I've done for you. But if you had a shred of common decency left you'd set me and poor Jamie free, aye, and old Maynard and poor Starling besides. God's nails, I'd suffer, thinking I'd dragged me own son, brother and my loyal servant down with me, a poor confused old man baffled by an unfortunately uncontrollable turn of events.'

'Poor old man, bollocks!' William snapped. 'You knew what you were doing, tagging along with us! Now we've got you out of the frying pan, you're wondering about the fire!'

'Aye! Well, I can't jump one way or the other without one side stringing me up! I'll have to try and strike out on me own all over again, rebuild me fortune in some backwater.' He glanced slyly at the hulking captain, the cheeky boy he had once employed to run his errands and print his pamphlets. 'Of course, you could employ me on a mission of your own, Will lad,' he said enticingly.

William raised one frosty eyebrow.

'Oh, yes?'

'You could set me and mine free, to do a certain young lady a favour,' he suggested.

William snorted in derision. 'Ah, Bella back on the slate, is she? Set you free and you'll marry her off to me after all!'

'Not Bella, you fool!' Sir Gilbert snapped, running out of honey. 'It's that poor splinter Mary I'm thinking of, the poor girl who took a stone in the ear from you and got a big belly for her troubles!'

Mary? What in the name of hell did Mary have to do with anything? He had hardly thought of his poor pregnant sweetheart during the cruel march from Penmethock.

'If you set me and mine free, lad,' Sir Gilbert went on shrewdly, 'we can track her down for you, get her some of that precious money you're so keen on! God's nails, man, she'll be needing it now, with your babe on the way! I've gone wrong somewhere, if I haven't taught you to take the consequences of your actions!'

William's shout of laughter startled the rooks from the trees. They flapped off to find quieter roosts, cawing to raise the dead as they went.

Somehow, it wasn't the most encouraging omen.

'You're mad, Will. He'll burst his guts to the first damn dragoons he finds, point them straight after us!' Colston Muffet complained the moment William had outlined his ridiculous plan. 'I wouldn't trust that slack-bladdered old goat as far as I could throw him!'

Sparrow nodded glumly, eyed the curious survivors loafing about outside the charcoal-burner's hut picking chicken bones clean. 'I'm not happy about it, Col, I know the old bugger as well as any man here,' he explained awkwardly. 'But the old soak's got a point about Mary, you know.'

Colston sighed, pulled at the pepper and salt stubble beneath his nose.

'And how does he propose to find your sweetheart? She might be anywhere by now,' the veteran said gently, anxious not to crack his captain's brittle concentration.

'Well, Sir Gilbert'll stand more chance than most. You know

what a nosy bugger he is. I've got to get her some money, Col, she might be starving away, she might, you know, lose the babe.'

Muffet frowned. 'Aye, well. It's your share you're handing over, not mine.'

'I've promised him five pounds. That ought to do it.'

Muffet, whose own wife had managed for over a year on the odd shilling here and there, grunted with astonishment.

'By Heaven, Will, it's a babe she's havin', not a troop of bliddy horse!'

THE OLD RECTORY,

ST CLEMENT'S, WAINBRIDGE, BERKSHIRE

T he players had defied snow, slush, and steady sleet, hurry-ing through the blizzard to the Reverend Edmund Telling's door. Their clumsy instruments were awkward to carry at the best of times, and they had found them almost unmanageable when contesting against an indifferently swept path and a faceful of icy rain. The musicians held on to their flapping black hats as they proceeded by fits and starts down the rutted main street, and up the winding gravel path between a double rank of threadbare conifers. The mischievous winds accompanied them every step, pulling at their coats and tugging at their knotted scarves as they hurried beneath the ivy-strangled gatehouse. The windswept party made a despairing dash for the front door, hastily thrown open by one of the Reverend Telling's tousled domestics.

'Hurry on, sirs, do, there's warm broth and a dish of spiced eggs within,' Mrs Gamble urged them, standing back in the cheerily lit hall as the bedraggled players hurried in and shook themselves off one after the other.

The Reverend Edmund Telling had stationed himself at the bottom of the stairs, where he could welcome each musician with a rigorous handshake without exposing his person to the trying draughts which were worrying the woollen fortifications of Mrs Gamble's many-layered petticoats. The minister was a tall, rather careworn man, slightly stooped, with a thatch of unkempt grey hair about his ears but very little left on his domed head. His mouth was large and mobile, his eyes small and precise, darting this way and that as he recognized his well-wrapped guests.

'John, good of you to call. Filthy weather, for the time of year.'

'Good afternoon, your Reverence,' the leader replied, snatching off his hat while manhandling his rain-splattered leather viol case past the banisters. 'Take a sight more than a bit of a blow, stop us playin' for you, sir,' the gallant player observed, nostrils twitching as he sampled the succulent aromas sidling down the hall. Mrs Gamble's accomplished cookery would be more than adequate compensation for undertaking the treacherous journey from Wainbridge, and besides, the village ensemble had precious few appointments these days, what with the war and all.

Mrs Gamble hurried past to collect plates of sweetmeats for the new arrivals while the freshly scrubbed scullery maids bustled here and there filling glasses with hot punch.

'Warm yourselves up, everybody, there's plenty here. We can't have you delivering a recital with frozen fingers now, can we?'

'Very kind of you to invite us, your Reverence,' John Belcher said through a mouthful of melting pastry. His own wife's culinary efforts would have given a hog the bellyache, and he meant to have his fill while he could.

'I thought the study might suit, the hall being difficult to heat, what with the coal situation,' the Reverend called. 'We haven't seen a decent sack for weeks,' he went on hopefully. The players munched thoughtfully, avoiding the rector's inquisitive gaze for a moment. Reverend Telling coughed politely as if absolving them of any further responsibilities in that direction, resigning himself to the prospect of a good many more evenings beside a cold grate. 'There's just room for the family and our guests, and the staff of course.'

As well as his frequent attempts to persuade his grateful parishioners to part with the occasional bag of coals, the rector was well known in the village for his ceaseless efforts to educate his fellow man. He was determined to invigorate his flock through frequently administered doses of classical music, poetry and fine literature, in a well-meant crusade to convert the lowliest stable boy into an aficionado of the arts.

'Why, these pestilential Roundheads might take issue with me, with their blasted pamphlets and petitions, but you'd have to travel a good way before you found labouring men who could hum extracts from Thomas Tallis, eh, John?'

'Right you are, sir.'

'You can't play this and you can't play that,' Reverend Telling mimicked. 'Impudent rascals, to suggest my sermons lean toward Popery.'

'Scandalous, sir. As if decent folk would entertain such a notion.'

There was a sharp bump from the hall as if to echo the stout yeoman's sentiments. The philanthropic minister stood back in surprise as a ragamuffin boy in a scruffy sheepskin hurried through the door, colliding with the bustling Mrs Gamble and scattering sheet music from the leather portfolio he had been promised a penny to carry up from the village.

'Ah, steady on, lad! We'll save a place for you as well,' the rector called, misapprehending the boy's haste as he bent to lift the grubby parchments from the scullery floor.

'Good heavens, Simon, have a care with that music! We don't make it up as we go along, you know,' John Belcher called from the fierce heat beside the range.

The boy hopped from one sodden shoe to the other, pointing back the way he had come. 'There's soldiers come Mr Belcher sir,' the youngster said breathlessly, nodding over his shoulder toward the front door.

The roaring grate lost its warmth in a blink. The players glanced around the cramped kitchen as if they had been lured into some barbarous Turkish encampment by the fiendish clergyman. Reverend Telling frowned, his jovial mood soured.

'By the saints, haven't they had their assessment this month?' he asked miserably, wondering if the filthy war bands which roamed the region could have eaten through their winter food-stuffs already. The various garrisons round about took it in turns to send out foraging parties, collecting produce from the local countryside under variously questionable commissions. Collecting assessments, they called it – a grand title for an activity which was little short of banditry, if you asked the rector. But then again, giving up a good half of their wheat, bacon, beer, milk and eggs was a sight less problematical than billeting a company of the rogues in the village itself.

'Who is it this time,' John Belcher muttered, 'those serpents from Donington?'

Further discussion was interrupted by a hesitant knock on the door.

'That doesn't sound like Baggot!'

Reverend Telling pulled at his chin for a moment, then strode down the hall with all the authority he could muster. The fearful players crowded into the doorway to watch the terrible encounter.

'All right, all right, I'm coming as quick as I can,' the rector called in response to a second, rather more persistent knock. He lifted the catch and opened the door a crack, peering out at the miserable intruders. One of the rogues – wrapped up in a dirty woollen scarf against the wintry chills – was stamping his boots in the slush by the door, while two of his robber colleagues sat astride panting horses beside the gatehouse. Their vaporous breath seemed to wrap around the horses' bellies and legs, turning the steaming creatures into beasts of the underworld.

'Well?'

The soldier nodded familiarly, but his brief speech was obscured by the dew-drenched scarf he had tied about his mouth. The rider tugged the garment away.

'It's me, father,' he said shortly, as if irritated he had not been recognized in his outlandish soldier garb. 'Hugo,' the Cavalier reminded his parent with a flicker of annoyance.

'Hugo? Great God above, boy, what are you doing here?' Reverend Telling gaped at his youngest son, absent these twelve months at the war. Off and away with barely a by-your-leave from his university, and back out of the blue scaring folk with his mummery. The rider peered over his shoulder, waved at his misty companions.

'I've brought Bella with me,' the prodigal youth said hopefully.

'Bella?'

'My wife,' Hugo said thickly.

'Your WIFE?'

Bella Margueritte Morrison flicked her shoe in annoyance, wondering when the dismal screeching would end. Couldn't the fools play something cheerful? Their welcome had been chilly enough as it was, without having to listen to this monstrous dirge. The woman glanced at her alleged husband, sitting stiffly beside her in his parents' best room. A pokey, chill little chamber packed with a selection of local misfits who gaped and stared as if they had dropped in from the very heavens. The audience seemed far more interested in her than they were in the caterwauling din being produced by the ragged-arsed players, that was for sure. Bella leaned over towards Hugo, who was paying rapt attention to the musicians as if he had never heard such sweet and soulful music.

'What's this piece called again?' she whispered in his red ear. Hugo glanced around sharply, apparently annoyed by the interruption.

'*Lachrimae Antiquae* by John Dowland,' he hissed. 'The piece is called "Flow My Teares".'

Bella sniffed. 'Flow my tears is about right and all,' she whispered. 'What a dreary racket!'

'Shush!' Hugo scolded her, giving her leg a warning squeeze. He glanced up nervously, and noted with dismay the freezing frown his mother had adopted on being introduced to her new daughter-in-law had not yet thawed.

Aye, and never would, if Bella kept on like this, he thought darkly.

He had imagined his safe return from twelve months of war, bloodshed, pestilence, and famine might have sparked a little more enthusiasm from his beloved parents. They had stood back in astonishment, regarded him with awkward concern as if they were worried their son's arrival might somehow compromise the promised recital.

Bella's excitable entrance a moment later had struck the pair of them dumb. She had swept her hood away from her beautiful face with a theatrical flourish, and stood before them in all her terrible glory. An Ice Queen, a succubus, a semi-frozen Delilah come to steal away their menfolk. The cold had penetrated the old pistol-bullet wound towards her ear, obliging her to wrap a broad green band about her forehead, but the bright velvet had highlighted rather than hidden her features, drawn even more attention to her flashing hazel eyes.

'Mother, father. This is Bella. We were but lately married, away in Dorset.'

'Dorset? What on earth were you doing in Dorset? I thought the war was in the Midlands!' his astonished father replied, flabbergasted by his young son's ragged appearance, transparent skin and most of all, his bewitching minx of a wife. Bella smiled serenely, unclasped her cloak and passed it to the drop-jawed cook.

'I have heard so much about you both,' she purred, curtseying so deeply Reverend Telling felt obliged to offer her his hand to lift the creature upright once more.

'Why, you're chilled to the marrow!' he exclaimed, giving her hand a brisk rub with his warm fingers. 'You'd best come into the scullery!' Reverend Telling hurried the poor girl towards the crowded kitchen, patting her hand as he went. Hugo's mother opened and closed her mouth in distraction, but was unable to locate her tongue for the present. Hugo's elder brothers, Edward, John, and Michael, suffered no such disadvantage, piling out of the study to greet their long-lost sibling with bantering bonhomie and slaps to the back which loosened his teeth. But their boorish observations turned to ashes in their mouths when they came face to face with their new sister-in-law. The clumsy trio appeared pole-axed by the arresting vision their little brother had brought with him. Hugo smirked at their cross-eyed reaction, an all too familiar response when he introduced Bella in rude company. He opened the door, peered out into the grey-bearded blizzard.

'Thackray, see the horses are stabled,' he called to his faithful servant, waiting loyally, but forgotten as usual, beside the gatehouse.

'God's bones, he's only got himself a servant,' Michael shrieked, peering out of the fish-eyed window pane as the reluctant groom kicked his exhausted mount on around the corner of the rectory. Hugo pulled at his misshapen moustache in agitation.

'Well? What of it? Haven't you seen an officer of the King before now? Has Wainbridge been left to its own devices that long?' he called out, throwing off his snow-stained travel cloak and handing it to the comically gaping cook.

'Officer of the King, you look more like a Turk in that get-up,' Edward, the elder and by far the most persistent of his former tormentors, replied, dragging his piercing grey eyes from Bella for a moment. Reverend Telling's eldest son had inherited all his father's height, but had added his own girth and more. Hugo remembered him as a bully, and recognized all too well the hot flush of excitement which turned his thick, badly shaven neck a livid, lobsterish red. His plain black suit and soberly folded collar seemed strangely at odds with his rather thuggish appearance. The other two, always content to follow his brutal example, regarded Hugo as if he was some tinker come to sell them brushes.

'Come into the warm, my dear,' Reverend Telling insisted, clearing a path through to the fire with an annoyed flick of his wrist and escorting Bella into the kitchen. The players, cooks, and scullery maids backed away from the fantastical Sheba, who leaned over daintily and helped herself to a pastry, cramming the morsel into her mouth as if she hadn't eaten for a week.

'We've not eaten for a while,' Hugo called foolishly, watching his putative bride swallow the sweetmeat whole and cast about for a replacement. 'We have been on the road . . .'

'Reverend Telling,' Hugo's mother called from the forgotten

threshold. 'You forget yourself,' the austere woman warned, finding her tongue at last. 'We have guests and players about to perform. I suggest we leave Hugo and . . . his wife . . . to warm themselves while we retire to the study. They can join us presently,' she said primly.

Hugo tugged a hank of hair from his eyes, and smiled. 'I would have, you know, written before, mother. But the war,' he shrugged despairingly.

Mrs Telling ran her tongue over her teeth as if she was checking the fortifications along the orchard wall. 'The war, of course,' she said shortly. 'Nobody could be expected to put pen to paper in that time. Fifty-two weeks must have simply flown by.' She smiled weakly at her astonished guests, all of whom were itching to get home to tell family and friends the news: Young Telling back from the wars, cocky as you like with a strumpet in tow!

Mrs Telling, divining their mood in a moment, began shooing them towards the luxurious captivity of the study.

'Come along, everybody, places, please. Mr Belcher and his friends have come a long way this day, it would be impolite to refuse them the opportunity of entertaining us.'

Hugo frowned, nervously tugging at his threadbare moustache. A long way? They had only come up from the village! He and Bella had ridden through five feet of snow across half of Wiltshire and a fair portion of Berkshire besides. The roads had proved virtually impassable on the few occasions they had dared to use them. Hugo had felt safer away from prying eyes – up on the high downs where the winds blew straight through their chilled skins, or skirting the vast white robed woodlands which marched along the apparently endless snow-peaked ridges. They had been obliged to dismount and stamp a passage through immense drifts, pick their way across creaking sheets of ice as they worked their way north, towards the heart of the bitterly divided kingdom. Thankfully, the ferocious blizzards had kept the majority of the population indoors, and they had completed their desperate journey without interruption from the authorities: Royalist, Roundhead, or otherwise.

Despite their good fortune Hugo had not dared to lower his guard. He had barely slept, nodding off for a few moments in the saddle as his panting horse picked its own path over the deserted wastes. He wouldn't relax until he was back at camp, where please God Prince Rupert's enormous reputation would protect him and his wife from any unfortunate accusations which might be winging their way north after them.

It had been an evil winter, in which no quarter had been offered to man or beast. They had endured killing cold and fought murderous men, survived crippling frosts and desperate, eye-gouging blood bouts where King, Cause, or Parliament hadn't mattered.

A struggle for simple survival.

Bella, his dearest, beloved Bella, had been chased from pillar to post by murderous dragoons, bent on revenging themselves on the brave maiden who had thwarted their craven enterprises. Pursued into the hostile West Country by the despicable fiends, she had unwittingly wandered into the web of a fanatical judge, and been ensnared by his ruthless henchmen. Imprisoned in the vile dungeons of Penmethock Assizes, Bella had been put on trial for her life on a trumped-up charge, accused of conniving to kill the King's own well-appointed agents. Hugo, the student of law turned soldier, had defended her as best he could given his patchy grasp of Judge Dyle's jurisprudence, and in truth she had only been saved from the gallows when the reeking hornet's nest had been unexpectedly invaded by a desperate band of seaborne rebels led by his own sworn enemy: William Sparrow.

Hugo had managed to whisk Bella away from the furious bloodletting which had followed, and he would shield her from the angry accusations which were bound to come their way. Hugo had vowed on what was left of his honour that he would never again let the wayward girl out of his sight, so help him God.

*

Hugo felt Bella twitch beside him, a tiny spark in a blacked-out chamber, reminding him where he was all over again. Vital, elemental, and very much alive, she was enduring the recital as if she was back in the dock at Penmethock Assizes, grimly regarding the shadows thrown by the overworked gallows. The musicians played on, towering chord sequences which brought tears to Hugo's eyes just as the song had promised.

Bella huffed and hawed, tapped her slipper and examined her horribly chewed nails.

'I swear I'll harm myself, much more of this!' she hissed into his ear.

Hugo paled at the prospect. Harm herself? Never.

Shot and shackled, shorn of her best friend in that murderous firefight back in the village, Bella had nevertheless ploughed on alongside him, refusing to curl up in the snow and die. Many of the men he had known in twelve long months of war would have collapsed under the strain long since, unable to endure the excruciating ordeals they had been subjected to. Bella, though, was made of sterner stuff. Perhaps she had inherited some hidden strength from her conniving father, that never-say-die snake of a merchant. Bella's frenzied spirit seemed strengthened rather than shrivelled by their winter trial, and Hugo marvelled at her capacity to absorb stresses and grief which would have broken any other woman.

He could hardly help overhearing her heartfelt sigh as she twitched impatiently on the rigid wooden seat his father had set out for her.

'How much longer are they going to go on?' Bella whispered, flashing him another angry look. Hugo shrugged despairingly, torn between all-conquering awe of his lover and simple respect for his music-loving parents' feelings. Miraculously, the village players seemed to sense his dumbstruck dilemma. They energetically nodded their heads, fingers crabbed around the necks of their viols as they reached the final, awe-inspiring chord sequence, and dragged their bows across their instruments in one final, shuddering crescendo. Reverend Telling leapt to his feet in a rapture.

'Bravo! I swear I've never heard you play as finely, John!' he cried.

His elder sons, who had spent much of the recital casting sly glances at their young brother's new wife, led the applause with reckless enthusiasm. 'Bravo! Encore!'

Hugo crammed his palms into his eyes, horrified to find he had been so moved by the melancholic strain. 'Flow My Teares', a suitable anthem for war, he thought mournfully. Bella continued to fidget beside him, straightening her skirts and looking around the room, desperately relieved her ordeal by Dowland had come to an end at last.

Edward, his heavy features flushed by wine and warmth, couldn't drag his eyes away from her heaved cleavage. He swivelled about in his chair and showed his teeth, baited by her elemental presence.

'God's nails, she'd tempt the very devil himself,' Edward slurred, drunker than Hugo had imagined. He bristled up all over again before the vacuous bully who had tormented him down the years.

'What did you say?'

'You must tell us all about it, Hughie,' John drawled, placing an arm across his brother's back as if to restrain him from any further unholy utterances. 'Your adventures away at the war and all,' John encouraged.

Hugo shot to his feet, clasping Bella's hand in his.

'Aye. Fetch the glasses out, Mrs Gamble, Hughie's going to tell us all about the brave battles he's been in!' the younger Michael chimed in, ignoring his father's warning look.

'There's precious little to tell,' Hugo said thickly, avoiding his parents' gaze. His brothers, the musicians, guests, and domestics had surrounded him, cut off all his escape routes. He eyed them all through a shifting grey mist, especially his despised brother Edward, swaying back and forth in front of him.

'Come along, Hugo! Don't be bashful!' his brother Michael encouraged, jogging his arm with his goblet. 'You must let old Edward here know just what he's signed up for!' he guffawed.

Hugo blinked in confusion, ran his trembling hand across the bridge of his nose. Edward leered at him, thick lips wet with the wine he had drained from his tankard.

'Let himself in for?' Hugo asked dumbly.

John nodded his head like a donkey. 'Aye, let himself in for, my lad! You are looking at the latest recruit to the Earl of Manchester's regiment! The most upstanding chaplain in all Parliament's loyal forces,' his brother crowed, slapping Edward on his broad, black back.

Hugo glanced at his father, who was tugging his flushed chin in exasperation.

'Parliament's forces?'

'Aye, brother! Edward's going off to be a Roundhead!'

HOLTON FLATS,

T he sharpshooter closed one blue eye and squinted along the dull barrel of his fowling-piece. The blue-grey flute was misted with cold, subtle colours flaring and fading as his vaporous breath condensed on the finely turned steel. Rich bronzes swirled and shimmered, shadowed by coarser seams of whaleback grey. The minute fractures where the gunsmith had worked and polished, worked and polished the barrel were etched in vivid blackbird blacks. He opened his eye a fraction more – just enough to register the stumbling figure leading the horse out of the treeline without being blinded by the glaringly white snow which lay in luxurious drifts on the otherwise feature-less landscape.

'Can't miss 'im,' he said, his blue lips barely moving as he formed the half-frozen words.

'I told you we were being followed. Shoot the dog down,' Hereward Gillingfeather hissed, his frosted fingers closing about the sticky barrel of his own musket.

Across the white heath, the horseman seemed to register his peril, lifting his carefully rolled coat collar to squint across the windblown wilderness he would be obliged to cross if he was to remain in contact with the straggling column. The shambling wretches toiled on, almost out of sight now, a crawling slug in the virgin snowfield a bare mile or two from the shifting grey sea.

The apparently overlooked musketeers formed the rearguard, watching out behind as their comrades trudged on, clustered about their creaking wagon as if it was a pot-bellied stove glowing orange with life-saving warmth.

'Billy,' Gillingfeather repeated, his busy eyes glazed with murderous intent, 'shoot the bugger down, I tell you. It's one of their dragoons, scouting ahead.'

Well, if he's scouting ahead his mates can't be far behind, and they'd hear the shot ten miles away in this frozen silence, the sharpshooter thought angrily, raising his eye from the smoky barrel. 'We'd do better to knife him!'

'From here?'

'They'll hear the shot,' Billy Butcher argued, lowering the fowling-piece.

'Billy's right,' Colston Muffet said gruffly, shielding his eyes from the snowy glare to study the mysterious stranger waiting patiently by the trees. The ragged pony he'd been leading lowered its head, blowing great clouds of steam as if he intended to cloak his familiar in some witchbrew vapour.

'Has he seen us, Colston?' Gillingfeather enquired, blinking against the frightful white light reflected by the trampled snowfields.

'Well, if he hasn't, he's no damned scout.' The lean veteran climbed to his feet, musket cradled across his chest. 'If he runs, shoot him.' The sharpshooter ducked back over the long barrel, watched their mysterious tracker peer over the drifts, and wave his arm as if out on a Sunday afternoon stroll!

'He's signalling us! Who is it?'

'He's been sent on to parley,' Gillingfeather reasoned. 'There'll be more of them, aye, in that damn wood, and if they catch us on these flats we're done for!'

'Well, if they thought they had us we'd know it by now,' Muffet argued. He began to stalk towards the waiting rider, lifting his boots out of the foot-deep snow. 'I'm going to see what he wants. You two stay here. Billy, shoot him down if he as much as farts.'

'I will, Col,' Billy Butcher replied.

William Sparrow cursed at the delay, and wondered where his trusted musketeers had got to. Without Muffet, Gillingfeather, and Butcher he would be practically alone with boys and strangers, slinkers and sailors, the misbegotten company of thieves, deserters, and backsliding cut-throats he had led out of the silent forest on the final and most dangerous leg of their alarming anabasis about eastern Dorset.

The final details of their fanciful escape had been hammered out back in the woods, the snow-covered sanctuary they had been obliged to leave behind. It was that or freeze to death, William thought glumly.

John Grey, the vastly experienced mate, and his scabby faced lieutenant, Rhodes, had been the first to leave the confines of the forest, charged with reaching the coast and finding a boat, or failing that attracting the attention of one of the Parliamentarian sloops on permanent patrol in the bay. William hadn't quite worked out exactly how Grey was proposing to communicate with the vessels off shore, but the veteran seaman seemed sure he would succeed. With the stern mate out of the way, William had decided it was safe to order the release of the blustering merchant. Sir Gilbert, his wretched brother Maynard, inscrutable manservant and clerk Algernon Starling, and woebegone son Jamie had headed off towards the north, hoping to find the main road for Blandford. From there they intended to cut back across country towards Maynard Morrison's mill out on the Dorset moors, and from there ... well, that was Sir Gilbert's business. Sparrow had handed over a pair of pistols, a jug of wine, and a small fortune from their jealously guarded hoard, in return for the merry merchant's promise he would not rest until he had found poor Mary Keziah and ensured she was comfortable during her imminent confinement.

'Rest assured, William, that babe's as good as delivered,' the capering merchant had cried, ignoring the filthy looks from the famished scarecrows gathered about the charcoal-burner's hut. Muffet had snorted something to the equally disgusted Gillingfeather, but neither the veteran nor the gimlet-eyed agitator had offered any further objection to William's absurdly naive plans.

'The greasy turd won't get far whichever way he runs,' Gilling-feather had snarled. 'He's a marked man now, aye.'

William was terrified he would be denied the massively reassuring presence of his most experienced soldiers if the long-expected enemy appeared. He stamped along their trampled tracks, squinting back over the frozen landscape they had found that dawn. Nicodemus Burke, the baby-faced ensign, was standing up on the wagon shielding his eyes against the snowy glare.

'Well? What is it?' Sparrow called up to the ragged youth, dreading the youngster's excited reply.

'Three men . . . no, four. One on a horse.'

Four? The damned musketeers were multiplying like hob-goblins.

'Horse?' William croaked. If they were caught on this ground they would be done for, slashed to pieces before they could find any cover worth the name. Sparrow blew on his purple hands, tried to stimulate his stalled circulation. He fingered the reassuring lumps beneath his snowy coat – the butt of a pistol, the iron beak of his looted pole-axe, the twin hilts of the bloodstained swords he had lugged back from Penmethock. As well as his various sidearms William was carrying a good portion of Cruik-shank's gold, slung in bulging leather purses about his neck, as well as the flags they had torn from their Royalist owners during the fight back in the village. The shrivelled banners were wound about his waist, the trophies he would use to redeem his tarnished reputation. Wrapped up in his odd assortment of armour, Sparrow would be as well protected as any knight of old – a reassuring thought so long as they weren't obliged to leg it back to the woods. Weighed down as he was, the captain wouldn't get ten yards.

'I think . . . I'm sure,' Nicodemus called, 'I reckon it's Long Col and the others, and that feller from Penmethock.'

Sparrow swallowed.

'Which one? Not that cock-eyed runt Telling?'

Nicodemus shook his tangled red head. 'No. The lordling.'

Lordling?

Sparrow stood and stared, blinked against the bitter glare thrown up by the sun on the snowy wilderness of Holton flats. The white-capped forest they had just left stretched as far as he could see behind them, a luxurious mass of timber crowning every back-breaking ridge. He felt drawn to the trees, a twinge of panic as he realized just how horribly exposed they were. The trees had protected them from prying eyes, concealed them from the cavalry patrols which would have slashed them to bloody shreds in an instant. Out here, they were as plain as peas on a drum.

Burke's eyesight hadn't let him down: the well-wrapped rider turned out to be none other than John St John Dyle, Lord Clavincale, the Earl of Dartland's surviving son. The red-cheeked boy they had captured in the ruins of his Penmethock fiefdom. Sparrow hardly dared imagine how it was the lone lordling had followed them all that way. If this puppy could do it, so could Telling and a few hundred of his Cavalier horseboys, Sparrow reflected, casting another anxious glance at the silent trees.

'He says he's come alone,' Muffet called, following William's gaze as if he couldn't quite believe it either.

'The scum's been sent to parley, he's a troop of horse at his back or I'm a Froglander!' Gillingfeather cried, jabbing his musket into the boy's back.

Clavincale jumped in surprise, nervously shaking his fleshy head. Pale flecks of spittle clung to his cracked lips.

'I tell you I've come alone. I left them all back there.' He gestured with his red paw towards the woods.

'What, back in the forest?'

'Back in Penmethock,' Clavincale insisted, his eyes almost starting out of his head. He stared imploringly at Sparrow as if he had divined the captain was his only hope of survival.

'Come to offer us quarter, have you?' the captain snarled, recalling for a moment the piggeries they had witnessed in this young nobleman's back yard. His damned father, that wizened rogue of a judge. Black Bob Dyle, they called him, a notorious tyrant who ruled his corner of Dorset like some Turkish satrap, beyond the reach of his alleged liege lord King Charles. Dartland hadn't been the only knave to take his duty to his sovereign to extreme lengths.

The miserable boy had begun to blubber. 'There's no horse nor foot with me. I've come alone,' he stammered. 'I'm not here to hunt you down, I'm here to join you,' he cried.

Gillingfeather snorted with derision. Sparrow narrowed his eyes, glared at the obviously distressed youth.

'Join us, here?'

'I mean to change my allegiance, to the Parliament,' the boy said, cheering a little and running his nose over his borrowed coat.

'You've spent too much time with our friend Sir Gilbert,' Billy Butcher joked. 'He's turned his coat so many times the buttons have dropped off!'

Clavincale ignored the sharpshooter's laughter, looked up at Sparrow. The grim captain was grinding his jaw in deliberation, looking from the beseeching boy to the silent trees.

'He's here to slow us down or spy us out,' Gillingfeather snapped. 'A snot-nosed lordling come begging to us? We burned his own hall down to the foundations and he follows us here, through the blizzards, to join us?'

Sparrow studied the miserable object of Gillingfeather's scorn. A velvet-suited mascot, a valuable ambassador who might save their necks yet. Lord Clavincale would make an excellent intermediary, if their escape ran awry.

'Well, we can't stand here all day, that's one thing,' he concluded. 'We'll sort out this candle-waster's story when we get back to Poole,' he growled.

Clavincale smiled wanly, rubbed his palms into his red eyes.

'I knew that's where you were headed, no matter how much

you tried to throw me off,' he exclaimed. 'That's what I was trying to tell you. The road is covered by guns and a half-moon work, they put up chains across the gate, you'd be shot to pieces before you could tell them who you were!'

'And what do you care?'

'You seem mighty well informed, my lord,' Sparrow said ironically.

Clavincale nodded. 'We heard the Earl of Crawford had attempted the town by a stratagem, but the captain from the garrison with whom he had conspired had betrayed his plan to the governor. The earl lost fifty men and more, trapped between the half-moon and the gate!'

'I believe I read something about it in the news-sheets,' Muffet grumbled.

Clavincale nodded, childishly eager to please the bloody ruffians.

'Poole has been a thorn in the King's side since the summer. We – that is, my father's people – were intending to build up a base in eastern Dorset, but the garrison and fleet in Poole had been proving too much of a handful. That's why we were building up supplies in Penmethock, that's why Cruikshank was forced to use Crossbone Quay!'

Sparrow fidgeted, barely digesting the boy's eager explanations.

'Of course I intend to make a full report to your superiors, the moment I am delivered to safety,' Clavincale cried, playing his remaining trump card. 'I've information about the King's operations in Dorset which the Parliament might find significant,' he added.

Sparrow frowned, waving his hand in distraction. 'We've wasted enough time. On to the shore! Col, you'd best go ahead. Nicodemus can watch behind from the back of the wagon.' He clapped his red hands together as if he could reanimate his frozen command all over again. 'Come on, you lousy screws, one more mile and we'll be paddling in the Channel!'

Gillingfeather scowled, took a long look back at the sinister woods.

'Paddling? Have a care, William. If you ask me we'll be stuck between the Devil and the deep blue sea!'

Sparrow shoved the agitator forward. 'Why don't you keep your mouth closed and your eyes open, and leave the moaning to me?' Sparrow snarled.

STERTE BACKWATER,

POOLE HARBOUR, DORSET

The *Anne and Joyce* might not have been a First Rate – she wasn't anywhere near as well armed as some of the Parliamentarian men-o'-war lying at anchor out in Brownsea Roads – but she was the pride of Poole all the same. She had been fitted out in the port, provisioned from the town's slender resources and manned by volunteers from the bays roundabout. The stubbornly held town, safe and snug as a guillemot's egg on its jutting peninsula, might not have had the wherewithal to break the Royalist siege, but the determined inhabitants had certainly not been idle during their captivity. Breaking out overland might have been out of the question, but running rampage along the enemy held coastline certainly was not. The small but determined flotilla based in Poole harbour had roamed at will, the sleek, home-grown privateers faster and more manoeuvrable than the clumsy warships dispatched to their aid from London. Back in October the newly completed *Anne and Joyce* had intercepted two Royalist transports, and took them back in triumph to the cheering quays. The crews had shared the fat prizes between them: one ship had been crammed to the gunwales with linen, cloth, and merchandise, the other a rather more valuable cargo of gunpowder and arms. The brave sailors had even felt flush enough to present the town with a handsome bounty of £500, a massive boost for morale at a time when Parliamentary fortunes in the West were at their lowest ebb since the beginning of the war.

Now, though, a bare few weeks later, the pride of Poole was lying at anchor in a quiet, reed-ringed backwater, its triumphant raiding forgotten. Its brave exploits had been on everybody's lips that winter, only to be eclipsed by the arrival of the Earl of Warwick himself. The Lord High Admiral of the Parliamentary fleet had arrived in Poole to supervise a seaborne attack on nearby Wareham, and the stout-hearted crew of the *Anne and Joyce* were left behind to fret and fume and guard the western shore while the fleet got to work storming Poole's malignant sister town.

The demoralized volunteers remained at their posts all the same, the brave privateer riding at anchor in a quiet inlet called Sterte Backwater. The lonely ship was surrounded by grey seas and shifting sedge, by endless ranks of brittle reeds, bending and creaking this way and that in the stiff winds. The encircling marshes were scored by narrow reed-lined gullies, muddy ravines which snaked towards the higher ground, held for the Lords of Heaven by great wheeling flocks of plovers, hordes of neatly uniformed waders and invisible bitterns and corncrakes which boomed and screeched and set their teeth on edge. The dreadful winter weather had confined the surrounding Royalists to their quarters further inland; no doubt they were living it up in some fragrant farmhouse while the Poole men sat aboard their stuck ship, at the mercy of every wind in creation.

Henry Lock wished for hell – at least it would be warmer. He was colder than a kittywake on a cliff, his seaman's jacket and greasy shirt pricked and jabbed by the remorseless winds sliding over the flats. By God, how much longer would he be standing there? It wasn't as if there was anything to look out for, after all. The *Anne and Joyce* should have been detailed to assist the fleet's attack on Wareham, not left behind to guard the graveyard shore. The dispirited seaman blinked at the broken-down jetty which had been constructed beside the muddy creek across the water. The rickety structure was his only point of reference on the featureless shoreline. It wouldn't support a mouse now, left these six months to wither and rot by those blasted King's men. Colonel Griffin's bandits had been down with axes to carry off most of it as kindling, virtually destroying one of very few facilities the empty heath had boasted. Lock had used the jetty himself, landing catches of oysters, sand eels, crabs and magnificent silver bass for Poole market. They would have to rebuild the whole thing, if this blasted war ever ended, aye, and he would have to rebuild his livelihood and all, he thought ruefully. The former fisherman sighed, racked by another bone-sucking chill. Another half an hour and his watch would be over, he could get below for some broth and a warming bellyful of spiced wine.

Lock looked up sharply, startled from his hungry reverie by the sudden movement beside the jetty. A well-wrapped intruder had stepped out from the sheltering reeds, waving his arms above his head in furious greeting. Lock squinted, made out the tiny red maw of the man's mouth, and then heard his dim 'halloo' bound across the sullen water. The sailor straightened, shielding his eyes as he studied the intruder. If he jumped up and down much more he'd crash straight through the jetty, that was for certain. The furious stranger tore at his clothing as if he were on fire, discarding his outer coat to reveal a short, seaman's jacket rather like . . .

'Ahoy there!' The stranger's frantic bellow had the officer of the watch hurrying down the gunwale in moments. Curious crew members held the rails as they watched the fool's antics.

'Who the devil is it? Some madman leftover from the Earl's fleet?'

'He's tryin' to attract our attention, whoever he is!' Lock called back.

'I think I'd managed to work that out for myself,' young Lieutenant Hercules Brock snapped back. 'I'd put a boat out, but we don't know who's with him,' he called nervously.

'Mr Brock, sir!' one of the lookouts halfway up the frosted rigging yelled, gesturing towards the shore. 'There's more of them over yonder, a wagon and all!'

William Sparrow's company had reached the sea at last.

*

John Grey had done his best in Fey's place, assuming responsibility for finding a way off the dangerous shore. He had bawled himself hoarse trying to persuade the nervous privateers to risk sending a boat out towards the stricken jetty. The sudden arrival of the rest of the fugitives from the whispering reeds behind had prompted Grey to redouble his efforts, turning the water blue with his fury.

'Do we look like play-acting Cavaliers! We're for the Parliament, same as you!' Grey screamed, his red face contorted with the effort. 'Let me aboard to speak to your captain, it's a matter of life or death!'

'Lice or debt?' Lock translated, brows furrowed.

'What's the word of the day?' Brock roared back.

'Bugger the word of the day! Get us off before they cut us to ribbons, you candle-wasting whoreson . . .' The rest of the stranger's furious instruction was lost on a gust of wind. Brock wiped his mouth, turned to his brooding captain for instructions. The veteran commander had been taking a well-earned rest below when the alarm had been raised on the enemy held shore.

'What are we to do, sir?' Brock asked breathlessly.

'We'd best put a boat out, we can cover them with the swivel gun aft,' Captain Jones ordered, refusing to be carried along with his young lieutenant's all too evident excitement. 'Lighted match for the musketeers!'

Brock cursed under his breath, realizing in his haste he had forgotten his basic boarding drill. 'Permission to command the shore party!'

Captain Jones eyed the excited youth for a moment, nodded distractedly.

'Aye, and have a care for those reeds, it might be an ambuscade . . .'

Brock dashed off towards the ship's boat, tied up easily behind her. The vessel reared and dipped as the shore party scrambled over the gunwales. Brock took his place at the stern, urged the

41

men to hurry as they took their places on the thwarts, pushed themselves off with their oars. Away by the jetty, the mysterious strangers jostled and waved, crammed in on the narrow mudflat.

'Put your backs into it!' Brock roared.

The ship's boat had made three trips already, ferrying men from the threadbare jetty to the patient sloop lying just offshore. Lieutenant Brock and half a dozen well-armed sailors had helped speed the embarkation, harrying and carrying the wretched survivors aboard the bobbing longboat. Now their salvation was at hand, however, many of the fugitives seemed strangely reluctant to step aboard the rescue craft, returning to their battered wagon to retrieve various good-luck charms they had apparently left behind. Bulky plate and tableware, silver goblets, tarnished jewels. Bolts of scorched cloth and torn canvas hastily stripped from some deadweight frame – the creaking wain turned out to be a regular treasure trove, stuffed to the gunwales with their wondrous baggage.

'They'll have the boat under, much more of this,' the wide-eyed Brock complained to John Grey. The mate, who knew his rag-tag command would rather fight to the death than be parted from their hard-won loot, sighed in shamefaced agreement.

'Ah, cut 'em some slack, Mr Brock, sir, they've had it hard, truly they have. What you see 'em luggin' is all they've left in the world.'

'I don't doubt it, sir, but the fact remains they can't haul it all aboard!'

The miraculously regenerated survivors hurried to and fro as if bent on proving the youngster wrong. Brock, who had only recently joined the *Anne and Joyce*, hardly knew what to make of the famished fugitives. They were a mixed bag and no mistake, though the bulk of them were seafaring men. A dozen and more had been shipwrecked during the ill-fated siege of Exeter earlier in the summer when their brave battleship, the *Conqueror*, had fallen prey to the Royalist batteries massed along the bank of the

River Exe. Grey, their vastly experienced mate, told Brock about their various misadventures since that black day, concluding his account with a description of the vicious firefight back in Penmethock, the grim reckoning which had been the death of the *Conqueror*'s legendary captain, Gallen Fey.

Grey nodded with satisfaction as the volunteer sailors bent their backs to their oars, the pitiful survivors of their attack on Penmethock jammed on the thwarts next to them or squatting in the scummy water between their feet, clutching what remained of their loot.

'Another boatload should do it, Mr Brock,' he called. The young lieutenant smiled broadly, ridiculously eager to please the gruff old warrior. The mate bustled and prodded, shouted and kicked the scampering rogues into line, ordered them out onto the frail jetty one by one.

'Wait your turn, don't push! We'll get you off!'

John Ruell, a beady eyed raider, was casting furtive glances over his shoulder, trying to locate their absent captain.

'Where's Mr Sparrow?' he called suspiciously.

'Never mind your gold, you cock-eyed prickster,' Grey bawled back. 'He's bringing in the rearguard!'

'Gold?' Brock enquired with a nervous smile.

'As I said, Mr Brock, they've gone a pretty time with never a penny of money,' Grey explained.

'Ah!' Brock sighed, wondering at these rascally cut-throats who wanted their pick of the plate and full settlement of all monies owed before they went about their proper duty. When your town was surrounded by a horde of barbarian Cavaliers, bent on the destruction of your home and your creed, you didn't need coin to take up the service.

Brock looked up as the rattling reeds beside the jetty parted once more, disgorging a mob of wild-eyed musketeers who careered along the creaking jetty as if all the imps of hell were at their tails. The newcomers were too afraid to dawdle by the wagon to pick over what little their comrades had left behind. They threw themselves down behind the gutted wain, furiously cocking their ready weapons. A couple of the more agile fighters clambered up the six-foot wheel to take cover inside the looted hull. Mr Brock stared in appalled delight, his fingers twitching about his cutlass at the sudden excitement. Everybody was shouting at once: the crew in the longboat were bawling instructions at the crew on the sloop, while their comrades on the ship were urging them back.

'Get aboard now, William,' Grey called to the panting captain who had brought up the rear. The big officer looked more like a brigand from the hills. The bearded brute wore a bulky, ill-fitting coat and carried a small studded chest under his right arm. He steadied himself against the wagon's oaken ribs for a moment, his features contorted with effort as he fought to get his breath.

'Have a care!' the brigand yelled at the terrified men crowding about the muddy shore. 'Get off quick, the enemy are upon us!' He threw the chest to the terrified red-haired ensign who had scrambled down from the wagon to make room for the older musketeers.

'Get off lad, swim for your life!' Sparrow yelled, turning to face the screaming riders.

The enemy? Here? Brock wondered, wishing he knew what to do next.

'Don't just stand there gawping! Pull your pistol!'

Scipio Porthcurn tracked the lousy bastards halfway across Wiltshire before he realized they had given him the slip. The Cornish colonel had imagined the renegade Roundheads might march for Wardour Castle, and led a troop of dragoons and volunteers through hellish blizzards after them. They struggled to find the roads, let alone the Roundheads. Porthcurn led them in a hopeful sweep to the north of Dorchester, expecting to beat the renegades out of some snowy drift, busy pawing the goods and chattels they had carried off from Penmethock. Goods and chattels, aye, and Cruikshank's blasted gold, if the rumour-mongers had it right. Why else would a gang of cut-throats turn up at the lousy hole, if it hadn't been for that wretched pirate's ill-earned fortune?

The worried colonel ignored the complaints of his recently recruited dragoons and ordered the troop back towards the coast. They marched for three days, scouring the windswept hills above Lulworth Cove before heading north to find the main coast road. Captain Curry, the flabby butcher who commanded the newly raised men, pleaded with him to call off the search, beseeched him in the name of merciful God to give up.

'Let those bastards make sport anywhere they like along the King's coast? I won't have it!' Porthcurn growled. The renegades had razed Penmethock to the ground, slaughtered half of its inhabitants, and butchered a dozen and more of his own men into the bargain. He'd lie down and die before he gave up chasing the scoundrels.

Four days out of Dorchester, Porthcurn was tracking ahead when he spotted fresh tracks leading towards the east. A lone rider, tacking this way and that as if he too was searching the crisp snowfields. It might be a farmer after lost flocks, it might be a merchant riding home from market the worse for drink, or a Roundhead straggler, sent off from the main body to collect food from the outlying farmsteads. Porthcurn frowned, chewing the ends of his black beard in frustrated imaginings. Then again, it might be that traitor Clavincale, the swine he had watched cross the ridge bare days before. The witless rogue who had apparently deserted the cause at the hour of his family's greatest need.

Porthcurn decided to crack on regardless, urging the miserable dragoons to one last effort. Five miles further on the pony tracks were swallowed up, lost amongst a broader, though admittedly older trail. Parallel wagon tracks surrounded by the shuffling prints of a large body of men, heading north. That made sense at least: the rogues would have been risking a brush with the Royalist garrison of Corfe Castle if they had held fast to the coast road. The dispirited troop followed the snowbound ridges north, and under the creaking eaves of Wareham forest. The trail was fresher now, Porthcurn knew the dogs weren't that far ahead. He urged them on, across the chill River Piddle, along steep-sided gullies practically stuffed with snow. Another bizarre change of direction led the riders to a trampled clearing and an empty charcoal-burner's hut. Even the dullard dragoons could sense the proximity of their prey now, hurrying to climb back into their saddles and going without their usual morning break for once.

An hour later they broke out of the trees and Porthcurn ordered them into line, drawing his sword and pointing the way over the barren snowfields. The clumsy trail was clear to see, individual footprints wandering in and out of the deep wheel ruts. Somewhere between the broad white waste and the steel-grey sea were the traitor raiders, loaded with gold and loot and God knew what besides.

'There they are!' he roared, tugging his frosted scarf aside to urge the excited amateurs on. Thirty of them, God knew how many of the enemy, but they were on horseback and relatively fresh – the rebels were nearing the end of a fifty-mile march. A march they would only complete over his dead body.

'At a steady trot,' he bawled. 'Forward!'

The newly raised dragoons, many of them in action for the first time, fired their pistols and carbines the moment they breasted the low ridge. Their quarry, a flock of ill-armed desperadoes fleeing through a trampled breach in the reed-lined creek, threw themselves down beside a broken-down wagon.

'Hold your fire, you dogs! You'll not hit a man at that range!' Porthcurn's face turned black with fury as he cursed the incompetent marksmen. 'Draw your swords, we'll charge straight through them!' he called, bringing the flat of his blade down on his steaming stallion's sweat-roped rump. The black charger led the tumbling troop down the rough slope towards the narrow jetty, the screeching riders funnelled by rank upon rank of stiff reeds which hissed and swayed as he hurtled past. The big horse slipped, and Porthcurn grabbed its tangled mane as the first shots whistled through the chill air. One of the terrified dragoons cantering behind him slumped forward then abruptly leaned back, throwing his arms out like some buff-coated crucifix. Porthcurn glanced over his shoulder as the rider tipped backwards, horribly comic as he fell head over heels over the plunging hindquarters of his frantically kicking piebald, to be pummelled and crushed by its clumsy hoofs. The enemy musketeers hadn't dropped their weapons, as he had expected – they had crouched behind what little cover there was, ducked beneath the leaning wagon to face the thundering hoofs with dour resolve. Porthcurn yanked out his pistol and fired at the nearest man, catching the rebel dog in the middle of his bunched bandoliers. The musketeer fell sideways clutching the rattling pots, crashing through a worn rail and dropping into the swirling waters below the splintered jetty. Porthcurn brought the smoking pistol down on another man's head, braining the startled fool as he stumbled out of the sheltering reeds. His horse reared in fright, hoofs sliding on the loose scree which lay round about the broken-backed jetty.

William Sparrow was crouching down behind a wormholed post, feverishly tugging his pole-axe from the clanking ironmongery he had stuffed in his belt. The rider saw him, tugged the horse about with a vicious yank on the reins and leaned over in his saddle to jab at him with his sword. Sparrow flailed at the hopeful stroke, knocking the Cavalier's blade aside. The point of the pole-axe sparked on the stony path. Sparrow prised himself to his feet, galvanized by the crashing hoofs and flashing blade and the fearful braying of the terrified horse. He ducked this way and that, flattening his arms against the frightened animal and heaving it backwards with all his might. The rider lashed out with the smoking pistol, catching William a glancing blow on the side of his head. The beast's plunging momentum carried it straight into the astonished naval lieutenant, who clutched at its bridle like some ancient Greek acrobat. Hercules Brock clung on for dear life as Porthcurn slashed at his ducked head with his sword. The snorting stallion whinnied in terror as its hoofs clanked hollowly on the broken jetty. Sparrow kicked and writhed for all he was worth, clinging over the horse's heaving flank and its rider's desperately kicking leg.

'Leave off, you rebel scum!' Porthcurn growled, elbowing him in the face.

Sparrow yelled in pain and terror, his madly flailing boots catching the horse in the withers. The stallion plunged to its left, cracking a post and smashing through what was left of the broken-down rail. The four of them lost their balance, plunging at once into the astonishingly cold water.

Behind them, Captain Curry pulled his cob to a halt, fiddling with the tricky mechanism of his long horse-pistol. He looked up as a hairy, wizened little man jumped up from the belly of the huge wagon, swinging his musket like a club. The brass-bound butt collided with his forehead with a sickening crunch, and the Barnstaple butcher collapsed like a sack of giblets, trapped in his stirrups as his frantic horse reared and kicked. A dragoon lunged with his sword, speared the splintered panelling which protected the musketeer's chest. Gillingfeather scrambled out of the fortress wain, knocking the dragoon and his terrified grey to the ground.

'Retire!'

'Save yourselves!'

Porthcurn's dragoons turned their panting mounts as best they could, the dismounted riders leaping into the cover of the seven-foot reeds. In a moment, the triumphant charge had been broken.

Its furious author was coughing and choking on bubbling sea-water, his boots scraping the shallow bottom as the plunging stallion reared and lurched and found its feet at last. The taut harness snapped, freeing the drowning colonel trapped beneath its heaving belly. Porthcurn broke the surface, thrashing the churning water as he fought to get his breath. Sparrow hauled Brock from the waves, thrust the coughing officer away as he turned to face Porthcurn's murderous attack. By God, the rogue had spirit, Sparrow thought grimly, wrenching his dagger from his waterlogged boot. Porthcurn was a moment too quick for him, cramming his bunched fist into the captain's ducked head. Sparrow's brain seemed filled with dancing lights as if he had swallowed a lantern. He reeled back, dazed by the furious blow. Just then, a dripping paddle passed over his head, stark and splintered against the grey sky. A dozen iron hands grabbed at his bunched coat, hauled him through the churned water.

The skilful boatmen from the *Anne and Joyce* had brought their craft in beside the jetty and were jabbing their oars at the screaming Royalist, forcing him backwards. A seaman in a soiled jacket fired a pistol at the black-headed devil, but the ball plopped harmlessly into the swirling water. Porthcurn realized his peril and struck out clumsily, opening the gap between him and the Roundhead longboat.

'Shoot the bastard!' He saw a musketeer running along the jetty from the corner of his eye, ducked beneath the waves as the wretched man aimed the long gun at his bobbing head. Porthcurn ducked down under the water, saw the white passage of the bullet as it slowed, creasing his outstretched arm. He felt no pain, but kicked away for all he was worth. He came up again, heavy as lead in his saturated clothing, and gulped air as the enemy sailors hauled their wounded lieutenant and the big, cursing officer aboard their longboat. He felt the bottom beneath his boots, propelled himself towards the reeds which lapped the water's edge. With one final effort Porthcurn hauled himself from the freezing water and crawled into the cracking reeds. More shots tore through the shredded vegetation. He threw himself down, pulled himself along on his belly, his hands covered in watery blood.

'We'll be back for you, muckraker!' a West Country voice yelled over the rustling sedge. Porthcurn tasted freezing grit, his body racked with chills and cramps as he writhed in the frosted undergrowth. He'd been hit all right, but he couldn't feel any pain. After what seemed like an age the shots and shouting died away. He could hear the reeds rustle and bustle amongst themselves as the tiny creatures who had hidden themselves beneath the dripping forest scuttled from the man-made maelstrom. Presently, he could make out the satisfying lap of the wavelets on the trampled shoreline.

And then, in the distance, the angry croak of a corncrake, disturbed from its invisible den amongst the shifting sedge.

PART TWO

THAW AND ORDERS

'I put them all to the sword, which I find the best way to proceed with these people, for mercy to them is cruelty.'

Lord Byron, Royalist commander in Cheshire, after a detachment of Roundhead troops in Barthomly Church refused quarter

TWIZEL BRIDGE, ON THE RIVER TWEED,

19 JANUARY 1644

The biting wind and freezing snow which scoured all England hardly seemed to trouble the twenty thousand men marching into the bitterly divided kingdom from the North. The closely packed ranks seemed to relish the weather, welcoming the English winter like some long-lost friend. They had endured far worse that year, isolated in their sturdy crofts high in the snow-buckled glens, or shivering through an interminable sermon in some wind-racked church in one of the chill, grey towns along the coast. The bitter winds off the North Sea rattled their banners as they followed the road from Dunbar, striking inland to cross the Tweed with the eerie wail of their pipes ringing in their ears.

To the horrified Northumberland folk watching from the frail shelter of their listing hovels, however, the coming of the Scots was no time for good cheer. Centuries of border warfare and raiding had hardened them to adversity, prepared them for the trying ordeals to come. There was no last-minute panic, no mad dash over the moors to escape the probing Scots lancers, but a calm and orderly withdrawal to the high ground. They took up their quilts and blankets, herded their flocks up into the snowy hills out of the way of the marauding heathens from over the border.

But this was no mere mob of red-haired reivers, come for their stock and maybe an apple-cheeked English maiden. This was a large, well-disciplined, and highly motivated army: an army without an equal anywhere south of the border, whether it fought for the King or the Parliament.

A Scots army which by its appearance alone would tip the precariously balanced forces and fortunes of King and Commoner.

The northern shires reckoned from bitter – and recent – experience that the grandly marching Scots would not be long in their country. They expected the devils would be chased back over the border by the slowly assembling northern militias – however badly officered and equipped the Englishmen were in comparison to the duffel-coated Scots.

History had taught them that the Scots always went home – eventually. It was just five years since the heathens had last invaded the cold-hearthed North, driving through King Charles' useless army as if they were herding sheep from their ransacked farms along the way. The Scots were officered by expert soldiers, used to hard marching and bitter battles over on the Continent. They were well clothed, well armed, and well fortified against anything the puny pock-puddings might throw against them by their fierce and united belief in their God and their religion.

It was the stiff-necked Stuart's attempts to reform their religion which had set them marching in the first place.

King Charles, egged on by his egotistical Archbishop William Laud, had been persuaded to impose his control over the northern Church, re-establishing his hold over Scotland through a network of powerful bishoprics. The bishops came equipped with wagonloads of newly printed prayer books, and they used them as the basis for sermons which to the fiercely Protestant Scots sounded one step away from Popery – the despised dog-Latin of Rome.

The Book of Common Prayer sparked horrendous riots wherever it appeared. The pious Presbyterian elders were outraged by its questionable content and the majority of the Scots nobles, driven on by the fearful tumults from their towns and estates, did not dare to intervene on their Sovereign's behalf. The mighty lords of the North were dismayed by Charles' lack of foresight and shocked by his subsequent high-handed manner. King Charles refused to back down despite riot and reason, and practically all of Scotland united in resistance to him. The Scots responded to his chill ultimatums by drawing up a sacred oath of their own. The National Covenant bound Highlander and Lowlander alike, brought simple fisherman and mighty chieftain together beneath the same colour.

Charles sent two armies north to confront the fierce and well-organized Scots, but his hungry, ill-paid, and indifferently officered militia forces had been smashed in moments and scattered in all directions.

Worse even than that, King Charles was forced to recall Parliament for the first time since 1628 to raise money to fund his desperate ventures. But instead of diligently raising coin to pay his starving armies, Parliament bombarded the troubled King with a list of grievances of its own, demanding a full and forthright hand in all his policies at home and abroad.

The outraged King, convinced he ruled by Divine Right and not on the whim of some grimy cheesemonger, was hounded by fanatical and adept MPs on one side and by grimly defiant northern lairds on the other. His peculiarly stubborn nature prevented him from bending under the pressure, and instead of attempting to settle the various disputes threatening to engulf his realm, Charles was persuaded into spiteful defiance. His counsellors stoked the fires of his resistance. The squabbling cabal included Archbishop Laud, double-dealing Scots noblemen, and ambitious courtiers with stratagems and purposes of their own, as well as his Catholic Queen, Henrietta Maria. She used her own not inconsiderable charms to harden her husband's resolve against his teeming enemies.

Now, five years on, the House of Commons was in armed revolt and the Scots King Charles had tried to browbeat into obedience were on the march once more, crossing the Tweed with Parliament's gold clinking and clanking in their baggage.

The renegade MPs had finally managed to convince the northern nobles, presently organized by the cunning and capable

Archibald Campbell, Marquess of Argyll, to throw their might behind England's embattled Parliament. The brilliant courtier (and reformed rake) Sir Henry Vane had led the English delegation to the north, charged with bringing the Scots into the two-year-old struggle at whatever cost. The cost was indeed high: the English would sign the Covenant, binding the two nations with a single, sacred oath. Episcopacy would be abolished and the Church of England would be reformed on the Scots model – according to the word of God. The get-out clause was innocently inserted by Vane – a politician every bit as capable and cunning as the dour marquess. Argyll realized what the younger Vane intended, but imagined in his conceit the perfect example set by the Scots Church would persuade the English into grateful compliance.

But the tiny clause would prove the most damningly divisive in the entire document, in the bitter years to come.

Rory George Dunblane of Candlewood tugged on his reins, bringing the sure-footed highland garron to a steaming halt on a low ridge overlooking the river. Away over the frozen moors to the south-west was Flodden, scene of one of Scotland's bloodiest defeats at the hands of the perfidious Sassenach. Auld Rory hadn't been taken in by the damned English any more than his compatriot Argyll – they were too long in the tooth to believe the English Parliament would keep *all* its pious promises – but the first instalments of the monies they had agreed had been delivered at Leith, and so the Scots had kept their part of the bargain and marched south to their succour.

Rory's lands lay between Lochs Tay and Earn, a remote hill fastness bordered by the lords of Callander, Crief, and Breadalbane. His hearth lay at Candlewood, a fortified manor house above the small fisher-village of Tullymallock. His surviving sons, his cousins, crofters, and tenants obeyed his call to the wapenshaw, every man between the ages of sixteen and forty-five appearing as ordered with his bonnet, coat and arms. The gouty old chieftain, his matted hair hanging in rusty grey braids over his cloak, had stood by with the rather better-dressed officers, watching approvingly as the men drew lots for the service, one in every four standing beneath his blue and yellow banner.

'Ach, you again, Drew? Did I not give word the married men should remain?' he called to one of his red-bearded retainers, a leather-faced old hillman with a white eye. The old rascal glowered back, his unusual familiarity bred from years of companionship – hunting, fighting, and struggling to survive in the hard glens they had made home.

'Ye'd niver find ye way sooth, Rory George, wi'out a decent guidesman!'

'Aye, ye're right. Be sure and point one out if ye see one noo?' the chief had roared back to the delight of his rapidly expanding company.

The Tullymallock men had been placed in the Earl of Cassillis' blue-bonneted regiment, one of the carefully organized brigades in the powerful army presently crossing the Tweed below his windy eyrie on the ridge.

Auld Rory swung around in his saddle, his sore buttocks reminding him he had been out of the saddle far too long for comfort, and watched the long files of duffel-coated musketeers marking time on the stone bridge as the pikemen hurried to catch them up. He couldn't recognize faces from his position on the ridge, but he knew every man by name. The blue St Andrew's cross rippled and cracked on its saffron field as the wind found them out, teased their coats and reddened their faces. Their colonel couldn't help a warm flush of pride as he watched his men cross the border. By Heaven, the English would quake in their boots when they saw these northern avengers! His lieutenant colonel, Dougal Muir of Killybeg, from just down the loch, removed his plumed hat and nodded his slate-grey head, his large ears red as blood from the chill blasts whipping over the moors.

'I swear I've never seen a fitter set of men,' the vastly experienced officer called. 'Would I'd had the same men in Germany!'

Muir was among the thousands of Scots who had served in the

Swedish army during the long religious wars on the Continent, following the Lion of the North, Gustavus Adolphus, from one triumph to another before his untimely death at the appallingly destructive Battle of Lutzen.

Muir made a minute inspection of every musket, pistol, and sword, and snorted with annoyance as he checked the length of the crofters' pikes.

'Ah, ye've cut a few feet off for ease of marching, ye damned knaves! Fine and dandy till you're at push o' pike with men lugging longer!'

Auld Rory wiped his palm into his bright blue eye, watched the toiling company march off the bridge and mingle with the long grey files threading towards the South. Scotland's finest regiments were present with their legendary commanders: Douglas of Kilhead, the Master of Yester's, Gibsons, Gordons, Livingston, Cassilliss, Buccleugh, Lauderdale, and Loudon. The regimental colonels carried hereditary titles which had featured on rolls of honour from Bannockburn to Flodden, in a military tradition which stretched back before the coming of the Romans. Their commander was none other than the Earl of Leven, another veteran of Gustavus Adolphus's campaigns. They took with them sixty cannon, trained gunners, and as many ministers of the cloth, each cleric responsible for the spiritual well-being of his regiment. There were to be no whores, no dicing, no swearing, and no impertinent references to the King. The Scots were coming to persuade His Majesty to see sense, to lever him away from the vicious counsels which had hardened his hand.

Just like their colleagues at Westminster, the Covenanters were taking up arms against the King – but only for his own good.

Auld Rory's sentimental reverie was immediately soured by the thought that his younger son would not see such a march. Ross had been killed that summer, murdered in some cut-throat piece of treachery outside Gloucester. Ross had always been a head-strong lad, reluctant to follow his father's wishes. He had gone against the grain by seeking his fortune with the troubled King, travelling south to Oxford to offer his sword to the Stuart while his elders inclined to the opposite party. The fiercely independent youngster had been drawn into some private piece of mischief hatched in the trenches outside Gloucester. Auld Rory had never gotten to the bottom of it, and never expected to either. The letters he had received from the King's capital later that summer had been full of exasperating apology, but short on hard fact. A knife in the dark, an ambuscade in the woods near some godforsaken village called Brockworth. Ross should never have gone south, but he was as stubborn as his father, and Auld Rory hadn't managed to deflect his purpose however much he had tried.

It might not have hurt him so deep if Ross had fallen in battle fighting for the reputation of the Stuart. But to be cut down like a dog in some midnight knife-fight – the whole business stank like week-old herring.

The Master of Candlewood had been in the moderate party himself, reluctant to take up arms against the *Ard Righ* – his High King Charles. But the squalid and shameful death of his son had disgusted the old man, hardened his heart to the lacklustre King and his damned weathervane court. Young Ross's death had propelled him towards the all-powerful Argyll, head of the massive Campbell clan, who presently masterminded Scotland's political destiny. Personally speaking, the proud Master of Candlewood despised the cunning Argyll, but he could not let his son's death go unavenged. Somebody at King Charles's court had been to blame, King Charles, therefore, would take the consequences.

Auld Rory looked up, his reverie interrupted by a flurry of snow and clatter of hoofs. He watched a small party of horsemen canter back along the long grey ranks, then peel off up the hill towards the officers waiting on the ridge.

'Ah, see you, it's Patrick and the scouts!' Muir called, shielding his eyes against the glare thrown up by the patchy snow.

Dunblane's elder son Patrick spurred up through the scattered furze, beating his shaggy pony with the flat of his sword. Where Ross had been slight and quick, Patrick was large and clumsy. Too dull to bother overmuch with the chaotic and confused politics of the time, Patrick made a perfect soldier. He was strong, determined, and obedient. He never questioned his father, nor queried any order. Told to charge a regiment of English horse on his own, Patrick would have done so without further thought. Would he had his wiser brother alongside him, the old man thought glumly.

The heavily built officer reined in beside his father, and touched his hand to his steel bonnet.

'Three miles on, sir, a passel of their dragooners,' he called.

'Aye?'

'They ran like hares, the moment they saw us! I doubt they drew rein before Newcastle!'

The great Scots invasion had begun.

The handful of dragoons from the Northumberland militia Patrick Dunblane had chased from the bridge approaches drew rein rather earlier than the Scotsman had predicted. They belonged to the small Royalist army commanded by the fabulously rich Marquis of Newcastle, a charismatic Northern magnate and expert equestrian who had already spent hundreds of thousands of pounds in the King's cause.

He had been opposed in the North by his Parliamentary opposites, the Fairfax family – gouty Lord Ferdinando and his brilliantly gifted son Sir Thomas. Beaten half a dozen times in open battle and chased from town after town, the Fairfaxes had nevertheless refused to give up the bitter fight. As fast as Newcastle defeated father or son, the other would rise up, find another thousand or so misfits, and take the field all over again.

Finally defeated on Adwalton Moor with all their carefully assembled forces back in June, the Fairfaxes fled to Bradford. The town was bombarded and stormed, and all the remaining foot taken prisoner. Sir Thomas escaped, wounded, with a few troops of horse from the debacle, but his wife was captured in the chaotic flight. The elegantly mannered Marquis of Newcastle insisted she be returned to her rebel husband, and sent her on to Hull in his own carriage. Secure behind the walls of the great port and magazine of Hull, however, the ungrateful Fairfax family immediately set about raising yet another mushroom army for the Parliament. Despite the pre-eminence of the King's party and their own fluctuating fortunes the popular Fairfaxes had little difficulty finding recruits, much to the long-suffering Marquis of Newcastle's disgust.

Now, though, Newcastle had an even more pressing problem on his hands: the unwelcome appearance of twenty thousand Scots in what had until that winter been a secure rear area.

And the well-drilled Scots force presently crossing the border was no mushroom army.

THE OLD RECTORY,

WAINBRIDGE

B ella, allowed some time to collect her scattered thoughts in the haven which was the Old Rectory, had been sickened by her crowding memories. She had tried hard to forget Penmethock, to fortify her mind against the insidious images of the courthouse; the leering men and gossiping women who had come to watch her hang. She had attempted to blank the memory of the whole spirit-sapping ordeal but had instead found herself reminded time and time again of her miraculous deliverance from that terrible place.

Anneliese Ramsay, Bella's closest friend, had not been as fortunate. She had only gone along to nurse the injured Bella, to offer what help she could during her sham trial at the Assizes. But Anneliese had been shot down by trigger-happy looters during the swirling firefight around Penmethock's cramped streets – it hardly seemed to matter which side her murderers claimed to have served. Bella had imagined for a while she might be able to forget, to put the whole miserable experience behind her. But her charming smiles were undermined by exhausted nerves, her bright eyes betrayed by fiery images she could never have imagined in her worst nightmares.

The endless escape from Penmethock, the chill ride across the frozen wastes of Wiltshire and Berkshire and their subsequent arrival at the Rectory had given Bella opportunity to brood, and reflect on her grievous mistakes. The mindless ambition and girlish fancies which had driven her to the foot of Black Bob's gallows.

Why shouldn't she suffer? God's wounds, she deserved to.

The tyrannical judge's own son Anthony slaughtered outside Gloucester because he had uncovered his wayward fiancée's infatuation with Hugo. The Scots laird who had tagged along for the drunken fun of it done in like a lame dog by bandits. Her closest relations reduced to the level of mere fugitives because of their connection to her, and worst of all, her best friend shot dead on a dusty road and draped in a dog cart for all to see.

Bella remembered Anneliese as she found her, imagined every tiny, appalling detail of her lonely death. She was wearing a crumpled black gown with a grubby collar, contrasting horribly with her frail neck. The soldiers had tied a tawny sash about her bullet-ruptured waist, turning the frivolous decoration into a blood-soaked tourniquet. Anneliese was piled in a cart with the loot they had pulled from the Earl of Dartland's ransacked house, half-buried in trinkets and bolts of bloodstained cloth.

Bella rushed to the wagon, stood in the street with one frozen hand resting on the running-board as she stared in at the broken cargo. Anneliese's lifeblood had run along the cracks between the planks, formed dusty puddles around the badly hammered nails. The waxy grime encrusted on the filthy wagon floor was pitted and scratched, clawed by the desperate girl in her death agonies. She had died alone, on the slopes above the town, the sulphurous stink of the smoke hanging like a shroud over her funeral carriage. Bella tried to close her eyes tight shut, to extinguish the hatefully vivid image from her mind's eye. But she could not, nor did she think she would ever be able to.

She had tried to banish the hateful memories, concentrate instead on her own future, however uncertain. Bella hadn't been cheered by the chilly reception they had received at Hugo's parents' house in Wainbridge, it seemed to bode ill for their future together. Hugo's father had been civil to the point of being obsequious, fetching her titbits and scraping her chair a little nearer the roaring fire. But Mrs Telling had reminded her of so many of the scowling matrons she had met in the past, of poor Anneliese's stern mother in particular. She realized with a start the widow Ramsay had been left all alone in the world, robbed of her husband, son, and now (God forgive her) her precious daughter. Bella wondered whether Lady Ramsay had yet learned of Anneliese's death.

Hugo, with his pale face, cross looks, and suspicious stares, had fallen out with his red-necked bully of a brother, and stormed away from the dinner table with his fists clenched by his sides. Edward was a leery, sweat-steeped brute who reminded her of the slavering jailers back at Penmethock, forever licking their lips as they looked her over like a filly at a fair. He claimed to be a minister, a man of God responsible for the spiritual care of his fellow men. Back in Hugo's old bedroom she laughed sourly, shaking her bound head at the preposterous notion.

'A man of God? By Heaven, he'd never find an office in hell,' she cried spitefully. 'Did you see the way he was looking at me?' She turned, caught Hugo staring at her with languid uninterest. He hadn't been unaffected by his experiences in Penmethock either, despite the fact he had seen far worse bloodshed on half a dozen fields about the kingdom.

'Pardon? Oh yes, looking at you. Well, he would, wouldn't he?' Hugo asked, his hands crossed behind his head, shirt unbuttoned to his belly.

Bella eyed the dishevelled Cavalier, a mischievous urge warming her sorry heart. She wanted to talk, to discuss the vile chapter in their relationship, but Hugo seemed to prefer to bury his thoughts deep in his being, to nail planks over the windows of his conscience. Perhaps she should learn to do the same.

She took a brush to her auburn hair, squinting to catch her reflection in the pitifully small and rather pitted mirror she had borrowed from his mother.

'You sound as if you mean I'm to blame for tempting him. I've met men I haven't tempted.'

Hugo scratched his ruckled breeches, his bright eyes busy about the curves of her body, fetchingly revealed beneath her thin shift by the glowing candles on the sideboard behind her. He patted the piled bedclothes, licked his lips as she tiptoed across the cold flags and slipped over the covers to cuddle up beside him.

'I see you no longer fall into the latter category,' she observed tartly, running her palm over his worn clothing. He grinned, encircled her slim, warm waist. Penmethock couldn't erase her spirit, not for long at any rate, and not even jealous hypocrites like his brother could deny the awesome impact of her sexuality. Bella dug her fist into his ribs as he chuckled.

'What is it now?'

'It's this. Lying here with you in my old room. I was a beardless boy when I left for university, here I am returned, with my delightful wife by my side,' he chuckled throatily, nuzzling her fragrant neck.

'Do you realize, dear husband, this is the first time we've lain in a bed together, a proper bed? As man and wife?' she asked huskily, gently raking her fingers through his tangled hair. Hugo looked up for a moment, a small boy all over again. She was fascinated and thrilled by his dual personality – callow youth and cocksure Cavalier. Lovesick boy and lover in one spare frame. She sometimes wondered where he found his everlasting energies.

'Aye, and it's the first time I've lain in a proper bed since we left your uncle's mill,' he remarked. 'To be married,' he added in subdued afterthought. She tugged him playfully by the hair, concentrated his wandering thoughts all over again.

'Well, then, this must be our wedding night,' she giggled, then next moment found to her astonishment she was sobbing uncontrollably. Hugo was startled by her sudden tears. He'd hoped she'd done her crying.

'What on earth have I done now?' he asked, tugging away from her. Bella clung to him, closed her fingers in his shirt.

'You've done nothing. Hold me. Just hold me now,' she croaked. Hugo locked his arms about her, patted the back of her head as she cried freely into his chest.

And so they spent their wedding night.

*

The next morning Hugo awoke damn near boiled by the girl's heat. It was as if he had lain all night with his legs wrapped around a warming pan. His shirt was sticky with sweat and tears, her tangled hair caught up in his buttons.

'You snored like a bear all night,' she accused him, cuffing him about the arm as she disentangled herself from the sleepy soldier.

'Well, I had nothing better to do,' he said archly. 'Apart from mourn the uneventful passing of our nuptial night.'

Bella climbed off the bed and tiptoed to the window, haloed by the fierce sunshine streaming in through the shutters. She threw them back with a flourish and was swallowed up by the eye-watering golden glow. He propped himself up in the noisome linen, admired his would-be wife in all her stunning, sunning glory.

'Do you remember the morning at the mill? When we woke you up shouting? Anneliese, Mary and me?' Bella asked.

'I wonder what has become of your Mary? How long is it now before she calves down?' Hugo enquired, hoping to steer Bella away from any morbid memories.

Bella turned, illuminated by the lancing sunshine, fingers on her lips. 'I'd forgotten all about it!'

Not for the first time, Hugo thought sourly. His mistress had never been noted for her constant care and companionship.

'I wonder where she's got to? We left her on the way to the church, do you remember? She was upset by the carriage,' Bella fretted. Mary Keziah, her absent maid, was heavily pregnant when they set off on their ill-fated journey to the church where she and Hugo had been due to wed. Due to. The service had been interrupted by the arrival of Speedwell and his dragoons, armed with warrants for their immediate arrest.

'She's probably off to find that wretched Roundhead of hers. What was his name?'

Both Bella and Hugo knew full well what his name was. Bella had known William Sparrow since he had started working for her father. Hugo had only got to know the strapping pamphleteer in the middle of half a dozen bloody battles, when they had found each other – not for the first time – on opposing sides.

'She wouldn't get far in that condition! She could barely get to the church, let alone back to London!'

Always presuming William had managed to get back to London, that is. The damned braggart had marched his blasted rebels off into the blizzards, fled the horrors of Penmethock just as they had themselves. He could be anywhere by now.

Hugo climbed off the bed and lifted his breeches from the floor, his mood thoroughly spoiled by their talk.

'Well, wherever he is, it's time we were back in Oxford,' he concluded, crossly buttoning his breeches and tucking in his flapping shirt. 'We've got a mountain of explaining to do ourselves, before we're off the hook.'

Bella nodded wearily, and closed the shutters once again.

'Ah, there you are, lad,' Reverend Telling called gladly, waving the wary couple in from the hallway. 'Come in and take a bite, we were wondering if you'd join us.' Bella swore she saw Mrs Telling mouth 'indeed' under her breath. She smiled nervously, allowed Hugo to pull back her chair. His brothers were already tucking in to their meals, Edward slurping loudly from a bound beaker. He caught her sudden glance, lowered the tankard and ran his coat sleeve over his wet maw of a mouth. Bella shuddered. Trapped between the frigid matriarch to her right and that brute to her left.

'It's strange, having you back, Hughie,' Michael observed with a wink. 'So different and yet . . .'

'The same,' Edward concluded with a belch.

Reverend Telling frowned at his elder son's appalling manners.

'Not a bit of it. I think he has been transformed, wouldn't you say, Hannah?'

'Indeed.' Her lips had moved in precisely the same direction as they had before.

Bella bristled. She had endured similar treatment from Anneliese's mother. Perhaps Almighty God spied out such cruelties, and punished them by taking away their children. She immediately told herself off for even thinking such a thing.

'I cannot claim to understand why he has thought to offer his services to our troubled monarch in these dark times, but I can only say this: the service has done wonders, made a man of him!' Reverend Telling said with touching pride. The younger brothers grinned like tomcats, Edward lifted his beaker to hide his jealous sneer.

'Well, I'm as much of a man as I'll ever be,' he said thickly. 'Save round my waist,' he said, patting his round belly. 'I wonder what the service will do for me?'

Reverend Telling ran his tongue over his mouth, glancing at his elder son at the far end of the table. Hugo munched a piece of bread, avoided his brother's eye.

'Mind you,' Edward went on, warming to his theme now he had his runt of a brother back home to pick on once more, 'as I am to take service with a Godly army, rather than a rabble of cut-throat bandits and Cavaliers . . .'

'Edward, I instructed you both last eve on this matter,' the Reverend said sternly. 'It is bad enough either of you should go at all, let alone you choose opposing parties. But I will not have guttersnipe sloganeering at my table. Do I make myself clear?'

Bella glanced from the frowning clergyman to his brute of a son, wondered how it was two children could turn out so unalike. Edward reminded her more of the slobbering servants she had met on her travels about the land. Loud-mouthed boors who held forth in alehouses, but did precious little in the way of fighting for what they claimed to believe in with such passionate intensity. This was a man of God?

Well, Edward was as much a man of God as she was a wife.

'Bella and I will be leaving for Oxford this morning. My duties prevent me from remaining at home any longer,' Hugo said stiffly, but not unkindly.

Edward snorted. 'Aye, and I shall ride for my lord Manchester to rendezvous with my regiment,' he cried, pushing himself away from the table. 'And you can think on this while you go, brother,' he snarled. 'Our father has rightly ruled there should be no ill-feeling between us beneath his roof. But I tell you this here and now—'

'Edward!'

'No, let him speak out, father, he has bullied me in secret long enough, it would be fitting if he came out and said what he intended, aye, even on the field of battle!' Hugo barked, his colour draining from his features in marked contrast to Edward's flushed cheeks and watery eye.

'I intend this, little brother. I intend to join the army which will chase your hotchpotch of adventurers and Irishers from one end of the kingdom to another, and so help me God, if I have to give you another beating in the process, so be it!'

'I would like to see you try a fall with me now, brother,' Hugo snarled, jumping to his feet.

Reverend Telling rose slowly, alarmed to his bones by their undisguised menace. He stood behind his son with his hands clamped over Hugo's shoulders, as if he had divined the younger to be the more dangerous of the two.

'Am I overlooked at my own hearth? Am I in my dotage, that you bicker like knaves at my graveside?' he roared, thrusting Hugo back in his seat. 'I will not have you bringing the troubles of the kingdom to my table. If you are so set on this course of self-destruction, then you can go, aye, go now!'

'Edmund!' Mrs Telling moaned, tears springing into her eyes as the Reverend pointed to the door. His elder son clambered to his feet, adjusted his tired black suit.

'I'll not stop a moment longer, in the company of this precious popinjay!' he shouted, flinging his napkin to the table and storming off up the hallway past the astonished Mrs Gamble. Hugo got to his feet with all the dignity he could muster, held out his hand to the dumbstruck Bella.

'My dear. We must make ready to leave. Mother, father, I hope I shall see you again, in happier circumstances.'

Reverend Telling, glowing red as coal with fury, compressed his lips and said nothing.

And so they parted.

THE WINDMILL,

BAITER PENINSULA, POOLE HARBOUR, DORSET

Wᴵᴵᴵᴵᵃᵐ Sparrow despised the view. He despised the surrounding hills and the turf downs rolling away like ruckled carpets from the bay. He despised the emerald harbour and its quicksilver crop of aimlessly drifting sails, the squalling seabirds who had made it their business to bombard them every time they so much as stepped out of the shelter of the pest-house windmill.

But most of all, William Sparrow despised the waiting. A prison sentence of inactivity handed down by the nepotistic Skutts, the iron-jawed fanatics who seemed to rule Poole like the despised Dyles had run their fiefdom of Penmethock. The wretched family seemed to breed like hobgoblins; Sparrow was forever left wondering which high and mighty brother, uncle, or son he was supposed to be corresponding with. Corresponding was about all he could do, seeing as how the fugitives had been put ashore safely out of the way on this damned breakwater – a thin neck of featureless shoreland called the Baiter Peninsula. The windswept point was an ideal place to build a windmill – and to keep any unwanted guests at arm's length, Sparrow reflected sourly.

The wretched remains of the Penmethock company had been left pretty much to their own devices, while these damned Skutts decided what should be done with them. Sparrow had talked himself hoarse, explained in ever more detail how his men had come to be washed up on Holton Flats, trying to cadge a ride on a ferry which no longer operated. The fact they had apparently fought off a troop of Royalist dragoons while they awaited their rescue had tended to substantiate the greater part of Sparrow's unlikely story. John Grey, the vastly experienced mate, had played his part, convincing the doubting officers of the *Anne and Joyce* they were genuine refugees, victims of the frightening firefight down the coast. His detailed knowledge of the Parliamentarian fleet, its assorted captains, ships, and recent activities, tended to reinforce his credibility, at least.

But gaining the trust (and subsequently, the respect) of the crew of the brave privateer had turned out to be the least of their difficulties. The sloop had carried them off on the next tide, and sailed the short distance around the craggy headland into the main harbour. The dour Captain Jones and his principal officers had then gone ashore, hardly bothering to disguise their misgivings at leaving the famished and frozen survivors loose on deck instead of locked up safe in the hold.

'You'd think we were going to mutiny! By God, don't you reckon we're who we say we are?'

Sparrow's loud complaints were ignored, as were all his subsequent outbursts. His men seemed content to have survived. They had endured the hideous fights in Penmethock and lived to tell the tale of the cruel march across Dorset. Now they were keeping quiet, in the hope the windfall they had brought with them would be overlooked by the garrison authorities. They did not intend to part with their gold, and were becoming increasingly restive.

The ship's officers returned at nightfall with a delegation from the town's standing committee, to oversee another three hours of detailed questioning. Sparrow wondered for a moment if the damned screws planned to relieve them of their hard-won loot after all, charge them for their safe deliverance from the enemy-held shore into the bargain.

If they were any judge of men they would realize the rogues Sparrow had brought back from Penmethock would fight to the death to protect their prizes; that they would rather endanger the entire garrison than be parted from as much as a brass farthing.

The highly suspicious delegation, made up of leading town aldermen and a whole platoon of the busybody Skutts, finally turned their attention to Clavincale. They seemed especially unwilling to accept the identity of the youngster.

'Dartland's son? Black Bob's boy?' the elder, George Skutt, queried, narrowing his grey eyes on the nervous youth as if he thought he was the victim of some unpleasant trick.

Clavincale nodded.

'When did you last see your father?' the laconic soldier, Francis Sydenham, asked.

Clavincale shrugged. 'Back at home, I suppose.'

The suspicious counsellors exchanged a significant look, retired to deliberate for another half an hour.

'By Christ, you'd think we were Irishers straight off the boat, the way they're carrying on,' Sparrow complained.

Grey nodded his head, patient as ever and content to puff on a borrowed pipe.

'Hold your water, lad. We're safe, fed and rested. That'll do for me, for now.'

Well, it wouldn't do for Sparrow. The interrogation aboard the *Anne and Joyce* didn't succeed in convincing the pious Poole men for one moment. The fugitives expected a dry billet and some decent grub: instead they were put ashore across the other side of the harbour, out on a limb as it were. The authorities did not attempt to interfere with the goods the fugitives had so obviously hidden down their coats, or relieve Sparrow of the jangling purses he had hung about his neck – but they had precious little to do with their fortune, stuck out there.

The standing committee dispatched a cart every morning with what supplies they could spare from their own straitened resources. It wasn't much, but to the survivors of Penmethock it was a feast worthy of the King himself. Billy Butcher cut a fishing

pole from the windswept copse further down the exposed headland, and supplemented their diet with young pollack and the
occasional wrasse, pulled from the lapping waters of the bay.
He charged his comrades a penny a fillet, on the understanding
he would be paid in full once they had gotten off the damned
point.

'Sitting here, it's like we're hooked ourselves,' he moaned.

'Ah, it's no so bad now, Billy,' Muffet drawled, sucking on the
stem of his pipe. 'It's a sight better than being back in Penmethock, and that was a sight better than Newbury, if I'm not mistaken,'
the elder sergeant said, blowing an ironic smoke ring at the
webbed ceiling of their draughty hut beside the windmill.

'Well, that's all very well and good, but we're not going to
settle anything in this backwater,' Billy complained, bored out of
his wits by their enforced inactivity. 'The bloody war'll be finished
by the time we get home.'

Sparrow shook his head in sullen agreement. They were as
isolated on their windblown headland as the town itself; a Parliamentary jewel on the Royalist coast. Why wouldn't the damned
committee believe them?

'You're not wrong, Billy,' Muffet agreed, jabbing his pipe-stem
at the idle sharpshooter. 'The Thames valley and the Midlands,
that's the key to it. We're not going to affect the outcome one
way or the other sitting down here.'

Hereward Gillingfeather, fanatical bearer of the company conscience, shook his head in dismay at the desultory conversation.
He had enjoyed his fortnight's respite from the war, but he was
now looking forward to taking up the cudgels once again – and
he didn't particularly mind where.

'I'll tell you this,' he said, rolling his eyes, 'this war *will* go on.
And it will be fought in every hearth and courtyard, on every
village green. It's a people's crusade we've embarked upon, not a
game of murder ball! It is up to every man, aye, and woman, to
do their duty, to bring the King to heel!'

William, as irritated as any of them by the endless wait on the
point, turned to their agitator with a grunt of disbelief.

'Women and children and all, eh? I saw my fill of dead women back in Penmethock. Is that what you're proposing, for every village in England?' William barked, more than usually appalled by the deranged musketeer. He pulled his sword free in its scabbard. 'I ran a woman through on this back there, and I'm not exactly proud of it!'

The lazy company was shocked by his exasperated confession. There had been more than one woman done in back in Penmethock, true enough, but the raiders wouldn't care to admit as much now. Not stuck out on their windy peninsula, as far from the wretched war as it was from the moon.

Muffet climbed to his feet, patted the big captain's broad back.

'Easy, Will. He meant nothing by it,' he reasoned.

'He damn well did and all!'

'Aye, I did!' Gillingfeather shouted. 'I'd do the same, aye, and ask no questions of it either! She was a thrice-damned painted whore same as the rest of them, and deserved no better!'

'That could have been your sweetheart, your daughter, your sister. Would you cut them down and all?'

'Needs must when the devil drives!' Gillingfeather raged, his face contorted, swirling with unhealthy colours. 'The enemy must be cast out, sir, the King must be dragged down and defeated, dispatched like the craven fool he is, aye, if necessary.' Even the mad musketeer seemed to realize he had gone too far. Muffet shoved him out of the hut, none too gently, to get some air.

'He doesn't mean anything by it,' he explained over his shoulder.

William wasn't so sure. Gillingfeather knew exactly what he meant.

Dispatch the King? Execute him? Would Gillingfeather go that far, if it lay within his power? By God's bones, it was just such hare-brained resolutions which had carried the country into the wretched conflict in the first place.

'You'd turn your country into a wilderness, like the fools have done in Germany!' William shouted after the diminutive woman-hating musketeer, shoving the sergeant aside. The astonished soldiery scrambled back out of Sparrow's way, wondering if he was about to throttle the little turkeycock once and for all.

Gillingfeather, whose punishing standards and zealous moral code left most of them shaking their heads in contempt, was not a popular member of the party. Sparrow paused on the threshold, took a lungful of good, clean air. The inactivity had undermined the men, preyed on their already frayed nerves. It was those damned Skutts who were to blame. He'd skewer the bastards if they kept them cooped up much longer. He ducked his head under the greasy beam and strode out of doors. Muffet glanced at Butcher, and followed the captain out over the rabbit-cropped turf. The wind pulled at his greying hair, gnawed his sunken chest. He hawked noisily and spat the mess towards an inquisitive cat.

'Bloody weeks we've been stuck here,' William exaggerated, bracing himself against the low stone wall which surrounded the old windmill.

'You mustn't mind Gilly now, Will,' Muffet encouraged him, nodding over at the lone musketeer who had clambered up on a broken-down cart to roar hair-raising prayers at the tumbling clouds overhead. 'He's as sound a man as we have, though he goes on some.' He peered out over the deep green bay, a vast natural harbour which looked as if it had been gouged by God as a gift for all seamen. 'He just wants to get on, get it over with, same as the rest of us.'

William leaned over the wall, watched the heavy swell surge about the tree-capped mass of Brownsea Island and swarm up and around their lonely outpost. No matter how huge and menacing the waves, no matter how awesome the impact, the black limpet-lined walls remained firm. Parliament was clinging to its fragile toeholds in Dorset just as the shells clung to the rocks. He looked up, shielding his eyes to squint at the warships out in the bay. As far as William could tell, the sea was their only way out. If only they could wangle their way aboard one of those impassive leviathans, the floating fortifications which helped maintain the precarious stronghold ashore.

The only other route out was through the enemy siege lines. The Royalist forces were not exactly pressing their attacks, but even if his men penetrated the blockade lines they would then face another march over the blizzard-swept downs. God knew none of his command were up to such demanding exertions just yet.

In the meantime they sat in their hovels like so many lepers, squabbling amongst themselves waiting for official recognition, for orders which never came. Good Christ above, they weren't even supposed to be there, why on earth should they receive any orders? They were no more than bandits, washed up on the strand. As far as the distant Parliament was concerned, they hardly even existed. The entire operation had been a bloody farce from beginning to end, drawn up by haphazard fanatics like Gallen Fey without reference to the Parliamentary High Command.

William straightened up with a sigh, massaged his numbed backside with his large filth-encrusted hands. A writer, that's what he had been at the start of this bloody war, he thought miserably. A promising career as a pamphleteer, a key player in Parliament's propaganda war with the King.

Look at him now, a clumsy butcher with bloody paws, half a forefinger, and a weak right arm, a saw-toothed scar which ached like buggery in this damned cold. He had no means of existence without the wretched war.

William sighed, rubbed the raw wound on his forearm in a bid to stimulate his flagging circulation.

'Come on back, out of this damned wind,' Muffet suggested, tugging his coat about him and heading off towards the dank and dripping outbuilding which they had pressed into service as a draughty headquarters.

'Popped out for a swim, did yer, Will?' Billy Butcher called as they ducked back under the filthy doorway.

'Ah, he farted again and left us to sift it!' another wag called from the crowded corner. William ignored their ribald banter, felt the rancid, smoky air inflame his lungs all over again. The tearing wind had knifed through his clothing and inflamed his congested chest – they hadn't marched through fifty miles of snow and slush without collecting a chill or two – and the sudden change in temperature set him coughing. He slumped down in a straw-strewn corner and noisily cleared his throat. He'd live, which was more than could be said for a dozen or so of his lesser companions who had marched east with him. The weak willed and the wounded who had succumbed to the desperate weather had been rolled into the ditches along the way. Stripped and searched and thrust beneath the drifts – they hadn't dared spare time burying them. The choking snow had done the job for them, smothering the cold corpses before the rest of the bedraggled column had marched out of sight. William dreaded the spring thaw, the crop of frozen bodies which would be blossoming in the boggy roadside verges.

The heavily built soldier rubbed his jaw, reflected on the spiralling series of events which had brought him to the edge of the precipice – the sour flats surrounding Poole harbour. He hawked and coughed a wad of yellow mucus into the trampled snow. Damn this cold, he thought vindictively, turning his head to watch a party of officers hurry up the stony path towards their isolated refuge on the headland. Those damned Skutts again, with a whole posse of Poole aldermen. William straightened up by the door, tugged his threadbare coat about him. He watched his veteran musketeers escort the delegation into the cluttered yard, the suspicious townsmen shaking their heads as they looked about the refuse-strewn camp.

'What's this, an inspection party?' the morose captain enquired, giving the younger Skutt an insolent leer.

The officer took off his gauntlets, gave Sparrow a watery smile.

'The Earl of Dartland, is he within?'

'Who?'

Skutt raised his eyes towards the sky at Sparrow's ignorant enquiry. Unwashed soldiers peered out of the door or crowded at the window to steal a peek at their visitors from the town.

'Have they brought some decent grub?' Billy Butcher asked from the anonymity of the secluded corner.

'Seagull shite and fish piss,' another replied, blowing a loud raspberry at the twitching delegation.

'The Earl of Dartland, the young man you fetched back from Penmethock,' a black-suited gnome with a mad brush of red hair exclaimed, standing on tiptoe to peer over Sparrow's unwashed bulk.

'Oh, him.'

Skutt flashed the captain a warning look.

'This is Master Nathaniel Eagleton, commissioner of Parliament. He arrived this morning to settle the details of your transportation,' Skutt growled.

Sparrow gave the squinting commissioner a stiff salute, turned his head to shout at the crowding men to be quiet.

'Where's Clavincale?'

'Practising his sword strokes with old Gilly,' Nicodemus Burke called, pointing a half-chewed carrot over the yard.

'Sword strokes?' Eagleton repeated, glancing at his agitated escort as if they had led him into some evil-intentioned pirate's den.

'Do they make sport with an earl?' he asked, shocked to his Puritan core.

'Ah, he's safe enough. He's been pestering Gilly for days, him being our best swordsman,' young Nicodemus added helpfully.

'Earl, you say? He reckons he's a lord. Lord Clavincale,' Sparrow observed, puzzled.

Skutt gave the captain a withering look. 'You had best run and fetch him, Captain Sparrow,' he said maliciously. 'We have had word from this Penmethock place. It seems the boy's father did not survive your damned banditry.'

'Banditry?' Muffet called, shoving past the soldiers at the door to take his place beside the dumbstruck captain. Sparrow lifted his arm, held the defiant musketeer back. 'It was no more banditry than any other battle I've seen, and I've seen a damn few more than you, mate!' Skutt flared red, clamped his jaw at this outrage.

'So he's inherited the old bastard's title, is that it?' Sparrow enquired in a rather more pacific tone. No point in antagonizing them now, not if there was talk of a ship.

'Just so. He's inherited about a quarter of Dorset, much good it'll do him now,' Skutt breathed.

Eagleton bristled, clearly anxious to be about his business.

'Sparrow, is it? Have your men ready to move in half an hour. We sail for Portsmouth on the tide.'

The little commissioner's instructions were drowned by an immediate surge of cheers. Hats, papers, and half-gnawed food were flung into the air by the whooping troops.

'You're taking us off?' Sparrow spluttered, barely able to believe his ringing ears.

The commissioner nodded sourly.

'Your regiment is being relocated, assuredly,' the red-haired official sniffed, straightening his grubby collar.

'Regiment? What regiment?'

The Earl of Dartland's regiment of foot, that's what! William Sparrow had served in some fanciful formations during his eventful six months with the colours, but this was beyond doubt the most unlikely yet.

Regiment? If this damned shower was a regiment, one plank and three square wheels made a carriage.

Politics, that's what it was. The long arm of Whitehall, William thought ruefully. Parliament's fortunes were at their lowest ebb since the war had broken out; they had been held up in the centre, trounced in the North and routed in the South.

In the midst of their widespread misfortunes, with daily reports of lost battles and stormed towns, Parliament had to cling to every advantage, no matter how tenuous. The new Earl of Dartland, a resonant name throughout the malignant West, would be a valuable recruit to the cause. He might bring wavering noblemen over with him, he might persuade some of his troubled tenants to throw in their lot with the Parliament. Above all, Dartland was a figure-head, a top-ranking Western magnate. His lands might have been swallowed up by the enemy, but he was worth his weight in gold for the prestige his name alone would bring to the tottering cause.

Master Eagleton had spent ten minutes with the rather flushed Clavincale, hastily summoned from his sword practice to be told of the death of his father and his subsequent inheritance of the family title. He had then taken John Grey and William Sparrow aside, and informed them of the gist of the arrangements made on their behalf.

'Mr Grey and Mr Rhodes will remain in Poole, where they will be reassigned to one of Parliament's ships in Brownsea Roads. The rest of the survivors, including you, Mr Sparrow, will be taken to Portsmouth, where you will be re-equipped and readied to march.'

The Earl of Dartland's foot! Eagleton seemed to imagine you could click your fingers and turn a mob into a fighting formation. Give a bunch of farm boys a flag and call them soldiers. The commissioner waxed lyrical about Sir William Waller's spring campaign, a Heaven-sent opportunity to swing the fortunes of war in Parliament's favour.

The Earl of Dartland's arse! Sparrow thought grimly. Eagleton ignored his sour frown, worked himself up into a self-righteous frenzy over the awesome possibilities. Disenchanted West Country men would flock to the colours once more, doubtful troops might take heart, besieged towns might hold out an extra week or two knowing they were serving one of their own. Dartland's rapidly expanded force might one day be set marching down the coast, liberating their own lands from the King's yoke.

And pigs might fly, Sparrow thought gruffly.

Of course this legion of eager West Country volunteers would not be recruited overnight. The young earl would take the field with whatever resources were presently at hand. And Sparrow had a sneaking suspicion Parliament's resources amounted to little more than the eighty or so stragglers he had brought back from Penmethock.

Commissioner Eagleton shook his head in dismay at the captain's disparaging assessment of the strategic situation.

'We have assembled several companies from the Trained Bands and garrisons further along the coast.'

Swivel-eyed deserters, lousy thieves, and pox-diddled whore-mongers, Sparrow thought glumly. Scum-bellied slackers who had managed to avoid service in one of the regular regiments currently campaigning with Sir William Waller a few miles to the north.

'In addition, several dozens of volunteers have but lately come in to Sir William's camp.'

Even worse. Royalist prisoners who had re-enlisted with the Roundheads rather than starve in some castle in the rear. The wretched regiment would be stuffed out with leftovers and sweepings, they wouldn't make much more of a show than the renegades Sparrow had led into Penmethock.

'We will form companies in Portsmouth, you are needed in the field by the end of the month,' Eagleton went on.

Sparrow shook his head in disgust. 'These men might not be too keen on much more soldiering. They've had a bellyful already, I reckon.'

Eagleton had considered this possibility. He showed his teeth in a vague impersonation of a smile.

'So I have been given to understand. But I am relying on you to persuade them otherwise, Mr Sparrow.'

'How?'

Eagleton's shadow smile vanished altogether. 'Why come now, let us not mislead ourselves. You took part in the attack on Penmethock, an action unauthorized by the Parliament. You had no business there, it was an act of piracy, sir.'

Piracy?

'We sail on the next tide. Either your men agree to serve, or they will be detained here and hung at our convenience.'

Sparrow's blood ran cold, appalled by the commissioner's laconic summary. It was as if Eagleton had no real interest whether they served or died.

'I have discussed the matter in detail with the Poole standing committee. They are prepared to allow your men aboard ship on the understanding they will indeed continue to serve the Parliament, and in addition retain one half of the goods carried from Penmethock as their prize money.'

Sparrow's spluttered objections failed to move the insolent clerk.

'One half of all goods, and a promise of regular pay with Sir William Waller's army. I would have thought your course was clear, Mr Sparrow.'

Sparrow looked about him, the hushed company reckoning how much they might have left if such a penalty was imposed upon them. They had already hidden most of the more easily concealed treasure where only the most vigorous search would discover it. They could bribe the greedy committee and still be better off than they had ever been.

Clavincale, his cheeks still flushed from his sword practice, threw his shoulders back and eyed the commissioner.

'My men will require money for new arms and equipment at Portsmouth. I mean to command a regiment for the Parliament, not a pack of half-naked scoundrels,' he said stoutly.

Eagleton frowned, reluctant to gainsay the valued nobleman.

'There are monies for that purpose in Portsmouth . . .'

'Not enough, I'll warrant. These men recovered that damned pirate's hoard, and it is only right and proper they get their share of it. One half to be retained by the men, one quarter to the town of Poole towards the upkeep of the brave garrison, and one quarter towards equipping the men at Portsmouth. You have my mind on the matter, sir,' Clavincale sniffed.

Eagleton nodded his red head, the surrounding soldiery holding their breath as they tried to follow the complex negotiations.

Hand over half the rubbish they couldn't carry. It was that or die here on this damned rock.

'Aye, Will. Pay up and let's be off,' Muffet had advised, summing up the mood of the fickle company in an instant.

'Pay up? Hand over our gold?'

'Or hang as pirates,' Eagleton snarled, turning his anger on the captain.

Sparrow closed his eyes, cursed the entire rotten crew to hell.

*

William marched off with the rest of them, loaded down with his weapons, spare clothing, and his share of what remained of the loot. In truth, they still carried a fortune in coin, jewels, and trinkets, more than they could ever have earned in a regular regiment. The bulkier items, plate and ornaments, had been deposited in the cart, the earl's contribution to Poole's tireless war effort.

The survivors, delighted to have kept their lives, their liberty, and the lion's share of their loot, gave Clavincale three cheers, and voted him a capital fellow. Sparrow shook his head at the greedy traitors. He stood by the gate as they marched out, singing and humming as they went, shouting insults to the seabirds, stamping on the wild grasses growing in fractured beds beside the path. Muffet was grinning like an idiot, Butcher whistling a merry jig. Even Gillingfeather was smiling broadly as he thanked the Lord for their deliverance.

'Deliverance? We're no better than we were before,' Sparrow complained. 'Cannon fodder, that's all we are.'

Muffet frowned, shook his grey head. 'Yer wrong, Will. We're men again, soldiers. A proper regiment, not a band of bloody cut-throats. Huzzah for the Earl of Dartland, and huzzah for Captain Sparrow!'

Clavincale clapped his hands in delight at the tumultuous greeting, turned to the scowling soldier beside the gate.

'Captain Sparrow got them ... got us all home,' he said earnestly. 'He will be my second in command, if he will accept.'

Clavincale nodded, willing the captain to accept the unexpected promotion. Sparrow sighed, exasperated by the earl's well-meant offer. He didn't know whether to be angry or delighted.

'You will be my major, sir. The men need sound officers, aye, if we are to triumph.'

'Huzzah for Major Sparrow!' Muffet roared, making the big man's mind up for him.

He thought too much, that was his trouble.

THE QUEEN'S PRIVATE QUARTERS,

MERTON COLLEGE, OXFORD

Hugo Telling might have escaped with his life but he had brought precious little else back from Penmethock. He had been relieved of his personal papers, the signed pass and orders which would have proved his identity and gone some way towards guaranteeing his safe conduct about the Royalist-held West. Without documentation he was a nobody, no better than a bandit should he be apprehended on the road. He had no illusions what might happen to him if he was caught by probing enemy patrols, or if he stumbled into one of the King's trigger-happy sentinels, for that matter. The captain had no intention of breaking his journey overnight or dilly-dallying along the way – thereby increasing their chances of trouble. Bella, instead of insisting on some amusing diversion, would have to close her mouth and do as she was bid for once, he thought stiffly. Wainbridge was less than a day's ride from Oxford and Hugo expected to make good time on the lonely byroads. He knew he could not hope to ride all the way back to his headquarters without interference, but he hoped to penetrate close enough to convince any guard he was a friend rather than a foe.

He was unusually quiet during the journey, mulling over the various explanations he would offer for his unauthorized absence. He had originally been detailed to escort a party of Royalist officers – wounded during September's battle at Newbury – to take the waters at Bath. His unexpected anabasis about Dorset had added more than two months to that straightforward journey, two months in which his regiment would certainly not have been idle. Bella and Thackray rode close behind, conversing in desultory undertones while the heroic Cavalier rehearsed his feeble excuses.

'Mayhap he could say he's had a dry blow to the head, like what happened to your brother, miss,' Thackray suggested. 'Scrambling his brains bad and making him forgetful and sichlike.'

Bella glanced around at the impertinent groom riding hopefully beside her.

'I would prefer you didn't remind me of my brother's existence,' she said primly. It was Daft Jamie's fault Anneliese had been killed. Come to think of it, it was her idiot brother's antics which had forced them to flee in the first place. The trouble he'd caused, and he wasn't even aware poor Anneliese had gone, she thought ruefully. Jamie had never been the same since he'd been on Roundway with William.

'Ah, right you are, then, ma'am,' Thackray mumbled, dropping in behind the scowling maiden and wondering how much further they had to go.

In the event they had not got any further than Faringdon before they were intercepted by a heavily armed cavalry patrol – half a dozen well-wrapped riders led by a dishevelled corporal. The small market town was one of an extensive ring of satellite garrisons which guarded the approaches to the King's overcrowded capital. As well as breaking up any large-scale assault on Oxford, the fortress made an excellent base for roving patrols as well as bands of foragers. Their job was to collect the assessment from the farms and villages roundabout and dispatch the reluctantly donated foodstuffs to the hungry capital. Telling was relieved of his pistol and sword and marched into a filthy farm worker's hut while the cavalry corporal checked his unlikely credentials.

'Rupert's, eh? They don't usually sneak in the back way,' Corporal Rufus Barnes observed, giving the pale newcomer a suspicious sneer.

'I was assigned to escort wounded from Newbury to Bath. I was delayed.'

'Delayed? Newbury was last September! Took the pretty way, did you? By Christ you could have escorted them to the Americas, the time you've had,' the cheeky corporal observed.

'I hadn't realized I would be meeting one of His Majesty's cartographers along the way,' Hugo sneered.

Corporal Barnes narrowed his off-centre eyes.

'I was delayed by enemy activity,' Telling insisted. 'I shall be making a full report at headquarters, you can rely on that,' he said stiffly.

'Ah, no doubt. And who's this, then?' The inquisitive cavalryman gave the docile Bella a lingering look.

'My wife, who has been travelling with me from her home in the West.'

'No wonder you've been delayed,' the rider said archly, but under his breath.

Hugo and Bella were left in the evil-smelling hovel for hours while sweaty messengers came and went, exchanging their panting horses for fresh mounts in the busy yard. It was nightfall before a rider arrived with instructions for the alleged Cavalier to report post-haste to Prince Rupert's command. Telling scanned the brief note, looked up sharply at his overtired sweetheart. Bella's thighs were chafed as raw as if she had been born into that wretched saddle, her abdomen felt as if she had been lending a hand at an overworked whorehouse. She smiled sourly to herself, wondering what the precious Mrs Telling would have made of her crude imaginings. The unhappy break at Wainbridge had done little to repair Bella's strained constitution, or her frost-ravaged complexion.

'What is it now? Don't they believe you?' Bella asked wearily, alarmed by Hugo's perplexed frown. It could be any one of half a thousand misdemeanours they had committed during the past few weeks. God's wounds, they hadn't exactly kept to the straight and narrow that winter – the wretched authorities could pick and choose which of their widely assorted offences they would hang for.

'There's a note from the adjutant. You're wanted at Merton, urgent.'

'Me? Merton?'

'The Queen's private quarters.'

Bella paled, her grubby fingers straying to her lazily throbbing head wound as if it had been Henrietta Maria herself who had fired the scarring shot. What on earth did the Queen want with her? Bella had only met her, very briefly, the summer before. She had promised to keep Her Majesty informed of . . . what had it been now? Something to do with the shambles at Gloucester. Bella closed her eyes, tried to remember exactly what it was she had promised to keep Her Majesty informed about. It must be the wound, she thought, fleetingly, because she couldn't remember for the life of her what they had discussed. An entire interview with the Queen of England, and Bella could no more recall it than her last conversation with her laundress!

Henrietta Maria liked to style herself the She Generalissima.

She was also rather tickled by the nickname she had been given by the common folk as well. To them she was the Catholic Spitfire, the bustling heroine who had travelled the courts of Europe in her husband's name, selling her own crown jewels to buy much needed muskets, cannon, and powder. She had accompanied her haul back from the Continent, running the valuable cargo ashore under the noses of the patrolling Parliamentarian fleet as if she was some black-bearded blockade runner and not the Queen of England. Her excitable Majesty occupied a suite of rooms at Merton College, hastily evacuated the previous year by some bookish don and his redundant students. The shelves had been stripped of their books and retorts and astrolabes, stacked instead with ornaments from the Royal household. Family keepsakes passed for paperweights, holding down sheaves of dispatches, various reports from the scattered garrisons, and heavily inked maps of England. Rather more important correspondence was filed in the bound chests carefully arranged beneath the laden tables. The Queen's personal papers were collected here, detailing her highly confidential dealings with the royal courts of France and Spain, as well as her carefully compiled correspondence with the Vatican. Fluently rendered notes in five languages, gushing addresses to her favoured ambassadors, courtiers and toadying nobles from Muscovy to Munster, Stockholm to the Scillies. A paperchase of pleas and petitions, pained confessions and tittle-tattle, all grist to the energetic Queen's mill.

Bella hardly imagined the rather untidily kept quarters could house such an important store of paper. The place looked more like a kennel, grubby documents scattered here and there in case any of the yapping pack of spaniels and snivelling lapdogs mistook themselves.

Bella Morrison, at bay beside the door, wondered if a set of snapping terriers might not have been more in keeping with the bristling Queen's notorious temper. Henrietta Maria was busy riffling through a sheaf of beribboned reports which had been haphazardly jammed into a loosely bound chest. She was a good head shorter than her anxious guest. Small and deceptively daintily made, her hair was piled and teased into an elaborate pearl-inlaid headdress, which judging by her frequent and noisy adjustments had not been worn in the interests of comfort. The Queen waved her aides out of the room with an irritated flick of her wrist, motioned Bella to approach. There was a sudden, high-pitched shriek as Bella inadvertently trod on one of the squatting dogs. She paused, closed her eyes as if she had just signed her own death warrant – for hurting one of Her Majesty's pets if not her dutiful servants about the realm. Henrietta Maria jumped to her feet, clapping her hands at the yapping pack.

'Well, don't just stand there, girl, come closer,' she ordered, lifting a letter from the pile on her desk and absent-mindedly picking at the wax seal. She looked up curiously, watched the pale maiden tread softly across the room. Bella was glancing about nervously in case one of the growling lapdogs decided to dart beneath her feet. She curtsied deeply, head bowed before the inquisitive queen.

'Miss Bella Morrison, or is it Mrs Hugo Telling? I was wondering when you would have the decency to attend our court,' she said waspishly, studying the tall girl's shocked response. 'Be so good as to remove the headband,' the Queen instructed.

Bella quailed, wondered if she had broken some royal protocol by keeping her dark green velvet headband in place in the Queen's presence.

'Let me see what damage they did to you.'

Bella could hardly believe her ears, had difficulty in deciphering the Queen's simple instruction.

'Has the bullet robbed you of your wits?'

Henrietta Maria sprang to her feet as the dumbfounded girl pulled at the velvet band, dragged it from her auburn hair. She stood still, paying it through her fingers as the Queen examined the revealed scar.

'Has it spoiled your vision? Do you see double? Speak up, girl!'

Bella shook her head.

'Has it stolen your tongue? By the saints, you're no use to me dumb!'

'No, Your Majesty,' Bella quavered. 'The occasional headache, a dull throb in the cold weather, is all.'

The Queen snorted with satisfaction or irritation, Bella didn't dare imagine which.

'A handy enough reminder, the next time you take it into your head to interfere with the King's agents,' Henrietta Maria scolded.

Bella bowed her head, terrified at the appalling course of her unexpected interview. Neither she not Hugo had dared hope they would walk away scot-free from their recent disorders, but neither had they anticipated such a speedy response, such a rapidly activated indictment.

'An unsightly pucker, to be sure,' the Queen said, pushing

Bella's head to one side with her small, beringed fingers to examine the healing scar, 'but it hasn't entirely extinguished your fire.' The Queen withdrew her hand, motioned Bella to replace the band. She strode back behind her desk and snatched up the letters she had been studying when her visitor had been announced.

'Do feel free to correct me if I am wrong,' as if Bella would have dared, 'but I was under the impression, Miss Morrison, that I would be hearing *from* you, and not *about* you.'

Bella swallowed with difficulty, a ball of guilt tightening in her throat.

'You certainly have been busy, if not on my behalf. Did we not agree you were to send me regular accounts of your doings, and those of your – how shall we describe them – gentleman companions? Sure we are you undertook to keep us privately informed of the movements of His Highness Prince Rupert in particular, your lover being a captain in his Lifeguard?'

It was well known throughout the court, if not the land, that the Queen had little love for her husband's equally energetic nephew.

Not only was the triumphant Rupert the King's ablest commander in the field, he was also his principal adviser on military policy – when he was away from his troops, that was. He had encroached on the Queen's hard-won territory, replaced her as the principal prop of her husband's cause. She had spent the first years of her marriage being slighted and ignored by her cantankerous husband, and she had sworn never to be so sidelined ever again. The war had given her unexpected influence, and she didn't mean to share it with her Protestant warlock of a nephew-in-law.

The jealous Queen had even heard dark rumours that Rupert might be offered the crown himself one day, should King Charles prove unable to crush this dreadful rebellion. Rupert, darling of the cause and a fully fledged Protestant hero into the bargain, might be put forward as a pleasing alternative to the house of Stuart. His elder brother, the Elector Palatine, was already rumoured to be in league with the damned Parliament, set up ready and waiting in a London palace. Who knew what settlement might be made, over the King's dead body?

Even worse than that appalling scenario, the Catholic Spitfire was ever mindful of Rupert's potential impact on the wider stage: Europe. His father Frederick, Winter King of Bohemia, had sparked the German wars which had already dragged on the best part of thirty years. Frederick had been a fool, gullible and easily led. His Protestant cause had been initially routed by the powerful house of Habsburg, by the combined might of the Spanish and Austrian Empires allied to the Catholic princes in Germany. But the Protestant cause had not died, it had been taken up in the North by the Swedish King Gustavus Adolphus, and then by any number of his capable officers, in league with the French.

Henrietta Maria, French herself, dared not imagine what might happen to the Catholic cause if the handsome and formidable Rupert became the figurehead of resistance to the True Faith.

'Your Majesty, well . . .'

'Surely you recall the fellow, Miss Morrison,' the Queen snapped, 'even if it is unclear whether you have actually married him. Well, are you wed or not? Answer me, girl!'

Bella swayed backwards, frozen with terror at the gusting tornado whipping itself into a frenzy on the far side of the desk.

'I regret no, Your Majesty. The service was interrupted before—'

'It is as I was informed.'

Bella realized with an agonized cramp of alarm that there was little to be gained in attempting to withhold any intelligence from the well-informed Queen. How was it she could have known so much about her recent activities? And how much more did she know?

'Well, that can be remedied soon enough, perhaps,' Henrietta Maria observed in a somewhat gentler tone. 'Always presuming you are worth further cultivation, which I must say I presently doubt.'

Bella clamped her eyes against the bitter tears threatening to erupt over her trembling cheeks.

'I have several indictments before me,' the Queen went on with relish, 'from Bristol Castle and, where on earth is it, ah yes, Penmethock Assizes. A list of charges I confess I can scarce credit. The wilful murder of a number of dragoons in Chipping Marleward, escaping the King's custody, conspiring to betray the well-affected fisher-town of Penmethock to the rebels.' The Queen rustled the papers as if she could barely believe her own eyes. 'And from the Provost, Captain Malvern, a report which clearly implicates you and your lover in the murders of Anthony St John Dyle, Lord Clavincale no less, and Ross Dunblane, Laird of Tullymallock, in the woods outside Gloucester! Well my girl, you have certainly been busy this last six-month!' the Queen concluded.

Bella wiped her hand over her cheek, hanging her head in bewilderment. How could she ever explain such calamitous charges, make the Queen see she had not been entirely to blame for her assorted difficulties?

There would be no miraculous deliverance here, no knight in shining armour to whisk her from the very steps of the gallows. She could not believe the Queen had assembled such a damning catalogue in so short a time. Henrietta Maria must have been sent details of the appalling events in Penmethock by express courier – they had not exactly dallied on the journey themselves.

'It's no use blubbing now, girl. If it wasn't for the fact I had fondly imagined you might be of some use to me, you would presently be languishing in chains, awaiting your very well-deserved execution!'

Bella swayed, stung to her core by the Queen's brittle laugh, terrified she would faint away and miss some last opportunity to save herself. She concentrated on the Queen's livid features, her small mouth and darting eyes.

'I set you to watch on His Highness Prince Rupert.' She hissed the name. 'What good have you been to our cause, chasing about the country inflicting as many casualties on our armies as the Earl of Essex himself? By God's grace, girl, I fear I mistook your use to me!'

Bella had stopped crying. If the Queen meant to punish her, she had clearly assembled all the evidence she would ever need to obtain a conviction.

'I am truly sorry for the trouble I have caused, Your Majesty, but in truth I have been myself the victim . . .'

'Enough!' the Queen cried, clamping her lips on the small smile playing about the sides of her mouth. She guessed the girl had seen through her elaborate tirade and was no doubt wondering why she had been spared an immediate appointment with a firing squad.

'Understand this, Miss Morrison, I have full reports on all the hideous details, all of them.' She slapped the papers onto her desk. Bella swallowed, bewildered by the Queen's questions. What did she have in mind for her now?

'Perhaps I am at fault, for not making myself clear at our last meeting. You were at Gloucester, were you not? With the late lamented Lord Clavincale?' the Queen enquired. 'But no sooner has Clavincale announced that you two are to be wed than he is struck down during this squalid confrontation in the woods. Your lover Telling, instead of being hung up from the nearest tree as his likely murderer, is immediately promoted to a vacant captaincy in Prince Rupert's Lifeguard.' Henrietta Maria lowered her rasping voice as if she feared she was being overheard. 'How can you explain this conundrum?'

Bella's mouth had dried like a sack of oats. She knew she was on thin ice now, interrogated about her role in that bizarre and deadly night's work. And in protesting her own innocence she could only incriminate Hugo . . .

'Well, am I to remain in ignorance of my agent's doings? You were, directly or indirectly, responsible for the death of Lord Clavincale, one of His Majesty's most able agents in the West and as loyal a servant as ever lived. The Laird of Tullymallock done to death in the same ambuscade by parties unknown. He might not have made as useful a servant as Clavincale, but he had his uses nonetheless! His father writes day and night, demanding to know what we mean by concealing the details of his death. He believes we have conspired against him, and has therefore thrown his powers behind the Covenanting party! Am I making myself clear now, Miss Morrison? Do you begin to see the consequences of your foolhardy and short-sighted actions?'

The Queen had built herself up into another red-eyed rage but suddenly subsided, clutching her hands about her rounded abdomen. Bella realized with a start the Queen was heavily pregnant, in her sixth month, she would have thought. She had been so full of her own worries she had completely overlooked her condition! Her Majesty leaned against the desk, massaging her belly while she collected her breath and wits.

'I have heard this morning,' she went on slowly, 'that Clavincale's younger brother, with whom I believe you are also acquainted, has deserted our cause for that of the Parliament. He has fled with the very raiders who appeared in time to save your precious neck.'

It was all news to Bella. Somebody had been quick off the mark, keeping the Queen so minutely informed of events ninety miles off.

'In other words, three valuable noblemen lost to His Majesty's cause, not to mention half a hundred common soldiers.'

'If I may be permitted to explain . . .'

'I have waited long enough to hear from you, young lady. It is now time for you to make your full report. Pull up a chair, take up the pen and paper.'

She turned her back on the quaking girl, bent down slowly to lift one of the snapping lapdogs from the mess on the floor.

'I want a full confession, a precise account of the ambuscade outside Gloucester, how Clavincale came to be murdered, and why it was your lover Telling became so popular with Rupert all of a sudden. Is it not true Telling had already fallen foul of His Highness Prince Maurice? Relieved of his troop for abandoning his post? One would have thought the mighty Rupert might have been a trifle reluctant to take Telling on, in view of his less than magnificent service with his own brother!'

Bella realized the Queen would brook no omission, no pretence, no foolish forgery. If she was to keep her head she would have to tell all of it, every incriminating detail, no matter what it might mean for poor Hugo.

She would have to explain just why it was Prince Rupert had seen to it Telling had been whisked away from the scene of the crime, ensured that the provost's inquiry had been closed down before it had properly begun.

Why? Because she and Telling had not been the only star-crossed lovers keeping their tryst beneath the dripping conifers that night.

Rupert had been there as well, sitting on his horse across a frog-happy pond, head bent forward to whisper to an anonymous lady, her identity hidden beneath an all-enveloping travelling cloak.

Clavincale, Dunblane, and her own wretched father had intended to ensnare the pair of them, in the hope the subsequent scandal would break for ever Rupert's hold over the troubled King. The irresistible Prince was rumoured at court to be infatuated with the wife of his best friend and only ally, the Duke of Richmond. Head over heels in love with Mary Villiers, one of the Queen's own ladies-in-waiting.

'Well, girl? I am waiting. What happened that night, in those Godforsaken woods outside Gloucester?'

CHRIST CHURCH,

Hugo Telling anticipated an equally trying ordeal at the hands of his commander, the Queen's bitter rival Prince Rupert. But the scowling Prince had no time for absent captains or their futile excuses. Telling chewed his lower lip raw, waiting in the anteroom for permission to enter. His mind was in turmoil, frantically wondering what the Queen wanted with poor Bella, imagining all sorts of disasters. God's nails, Her Majesty could take her pick when it came to finding fault with his wayward mistress. He tried to tell himself he would hear all about it soon enough, but the moment he stopped thinking about Bella's troubles he remembered his own. Telling was eventually waved into his chief's personal quarters, and stood quietly by the door studying the vaulted ceiling as if he had become a keen student of classical architecture.

The Prince gave his nervous underling a sardonic glance, and immediately returned his attention to the maps spread on his dressing table before him. Telling held his breath and his hat, waiting stiffly beside the door while Rupert conferred with his few friends at court. Soldiers first and courtiers a poor second, they preferred to let their swords do the talking. Rupert, who had made as many enemies at Oxford as he had in London, straightened up, rolled the map, and handed it to his ever-present secretary.

'Where on earth have you been?' Rupert enquired at last, flinging off his doublet and accepting a new coat from his attendant.

'I beg permission to report, Your Highness, I was unavoidably detained whilst going about my business in the West,' Telling replied with all the dignity he could muster.

'Three months, sir, three months to take a party of our hurt gentlemen to Bath? You were to take the waters, you appear to have fallen in them,' Rupert snapped.

Telling stared straight ahead as Rupert completed his toilet, studying his grim reflection in a pitted glass. He straightened his sword, gave Telling a sour look.

'I have presented your secretary with a full report, I was—'

Rupert clapped his hat on, in no mood for Telling's stammered explanations.

'Well, I shouldn't bother unpacking, if I were you. I am to the King now, to discover whether His Majesty has made up his mind on our best course.' He frowned, anxious his uncle would insist on listening to the geriatric Jeremiahs who made up his Council of War. 'But we will be riding, north I shouldn't wonder, before dawn. Ensure you are present and fit to march.'

'Fit to march, of course, Your Highness. You may . . .'

Rupert strode past him without a further word. Telling frowned at his chief's rapidly retreating back, sighing with relief he hadn't been stripped of his command all over again.

'He's brought his whore with him, the turncoat's girl?' Rupert enquired over his shoulder. His secretary, hurrying along behind the foul-tempered Prince, tilted his head to ensure confidentiality. Oxford cloisters were notoriously keen of hearing.

'We had word from Her Majesty the Queen's quarters, she had ordered an immediate interview. The girl has already been ensconced with Her Majesty for almost an hour.'

'*An hour?*' The Prince paused, drumming his dark fingers on the hilt of his fabulously engraved sword. 'His Majesty himself seldom manages to share an hour with her,' he said sourly, completely astounded by this intelligence. 'Where have they been? What could they know?'

Not even his well-informed secretary could provide an answer.

'According to his report, a place on the Dorset coastline called—'

'Yes, yes, I know all about that. I mean, what could the *girl* know which might be of so much interest to the Queen?'

In truth Rupert knew exactly what she might know – the sorry details of his impetuous liaison in the woods outside Gloucester. God's wounds, he had imagined his remote rendezvous would have been safe enough from prying eyes. He had tried to forget her, told himself he could not afford dalliances with ladies at court. But she ... she ... He clamped his fingers to his long nose, closed his eyes in weary wonder.

'Well, whatever she knows, the Queen knows by now,' he snapped. 'It is of no matter.'

'Of course not, Your Highness.' His secretary coughed politely. 'And in any case, there are rather more pressing matters at hand, are there not? Might not the intelligence which troubles Your Highness be overlooked, in the general disorders of the realm?'

'Aye, they might at that,' Rupert growled, and stalked off down the cloister, his spurs and scabbard clanking to wake the dead.

He would deal with Master Telling and his troublesome sweetheart later.

Good news brought out the man in the King, bad news the King in the man. Rupert knew before any of the assembled grandees had opened their mouth that this time it was the latter.

Charles Stuart was standing beside his map table clutching a small wooden block, his own faithfully reproduced standard attached to its thin wire stem. Rupert swept off his hat and bowed, glanced at the large, garishly painted map.

Every river had been painted in fanciful blue, every town a black eye in a green field. Dolphins and sea monsters cavorted in the carefully painted waves which surrounded the troubled isle.

Rupert knew in a moment it was the North. It could only be the North.

'Good n–n–nephew, an express from Cheshire, but late–lately re–r–r–received.'

Sir Edward Walker, one of the frowning cabal who advised His Majesty on military affairs, passed the brief note to the towering German, who digested it in a moment.

'Lord Byron is defeated with all his forces, at N–Nan–Nantwich.' The King's stammer, as usual, became more marked as he frowned and fretted.

'Defeated?' Rupert snorted, turning the brief report over in his large hand. 'We had hoped to hear he had taken the place,' Rupert growled, glaring at the white-bearded earls and ambitious courtiers who attended the King. They had learned to keep their mouths shut, once Rupert was back at court. There would be plenty of time to dissect his arrogant advice and denounce the damned tyrant over their cups later that night.

'We had dispatched my lord Byron to meet reinforcements on the march in Ch–Ch–Cheshire,' the King said carefully.

'The Irish regiments, yes,' Rupert barked.

The King shot his nephew a warning glance, favoured his counsellors with a beatific smile. He had attempted to keep news of his long-expected aid from Ireland from becoming common gossip about the camps. He knew it was a double-edged blade – that for every man he shipped over from Ireland, two more might take up arms against him. The so-called Irish regiments were no such thing; they were Government troops dispatched several years previously to hold the rebellious Irish in check. A secretly negotiated treaty called the Cessation had succeeded in putting Irish affairs on hold for a while, enabling the King to bring selected regiments home to prop up his own creaking cause.

It was not a policy likely to win him much support from the fiercely Protestant English, however. Many of his best officers had already expressed their unwillingness to serve with the new troops – branding their own comrades in arms Papist butchers and idolatrous dogs. But Charles needed troops from somewhere – if the Parliament was to receive aid from the Covenanting Scots, he must have aid from Ireland.

It was as brutally simple as that.

'Lord Byron had been investing the place, yes, but there was a sudden thaw, his forces were divided by the River Weaver, and the enemy more numerous and well led,' a florid old gentleman in a fantastically engraved suit of Flemish armour reported. Rupert threw the report down in disgust.

'Fairfax again,' he breathed.

'Aye, Sir Thomas, at the head of a scratch force recruited from the towns and garrisons thereabouts.'

'This comes as no surprise, at least,' Rupert complained.

The King, radiating serene dignity in the charged atmosphere of his headquarters, tilted his head, his white hand pulling at his forked beard in earnest concentration.

'How so, nephew?'

'Byron's a fool. A murderous fool. His excesses have driven the local men to the enemy party. The business at that church, bloody and unnecessary. He kills thirty of them and recruits three hundred for Sir Thomas!'

'Traitors, let them rot in hell!' the florid old earl growled, irritated by the high-handed Prince's bitter accusations. 'They were offered quarter and refused it, and died like the dogs they were!'

'And their sons and brothers took their revenge on Byron's Irish!' Rupert snarled, deflecting the stares of all but the most stubborn of King Charles' counsellors.

'These men were wanted urgently in the North, to assist my lord the Marquis of Newcastle against the Scots! Now we will have to weaken in the Midlands to prop up the border!'

The angry Prince thrust the wooden blocks this way and that on the mighty map table, hurling the unwanted pieces into the corners where the feeble candles could not reach.

'We have w–w–w–word my lord Byron fought like a tiger, that he was significantly outnumbered by the en–ene–enemy forces,' the King argued.

Rupert was glaring at the table as if he could transform painted blocks and paste into pastures and towns, bridges and castles.

'This has cost us six months' effort,' he said, shaking his dark head. 'We ship three regiments across the Irish Sea and lose them in an afternoon. It is not to be borne,' he concluded, looking up at his troubled uncle.

Charles ran his tongue over his teeth, clearly agitated by his nephew's outburst. 'We must p–p–press home our advantages, while we may,' he said lamely, striding over to the table and studying the carefully positioned blocks which represented the armies presently in the field.

'We must shore up the North, and reinforce the South, reinforce our success,' he said to himself. Charles glanced up at his scowling nephew, nodded encouragingly. 'Your honoured brother, His Highness Prince Maurice, can move at will along the coast.'

Aye, Rupert thought quickly, he can move at will as long as he doesn't try a fall with the last few Parliamentary garrisons. Plymouth, still defying Maurice's heavy guns; Lyme and Poole, troublesome wasps' nests which packed a sting of their own.

'Could he not move eastward, supporting my lord Hopton in Hampshire?'

'Hopton's not the man he was,' Rupert snapped. 'This skirmish at Alton seems to have broken his will.'

There was a gasp of astonishment from the silenced officers. Lord Hopton was among the ablest generals presently serving King Charles. True, he had been caught out by his old adversary Sir William Waller, ejected from his widespread winter quarters by an unexpected thrust from Farnham, but he had brought his army back together with commendable speed and skill and seemed set to rectify the damage done at Alton and Arundel. This upstart Rupert appeared to dismiss his efforts and ability with a click of his fingers.

'He's had a couple of regiments ruined, and lost men to Waller. He'll need considerable reinforcement if he is to be of any further use,' Rupert concluded, staring demoniacally at the assembled officers as if daring them to gainsay him. 'We don't have enough men for Hopton, the Midlands, and the North,' he added unnecessarily.

Charles pondered this for a moment, stroking his beard as he studied the map.

'My lord Forth,' he said quietly. The florid earl limped to the table, bowed shortly. 'You will march as soon as you may, with all the forces we can spare, to join my lord Hopton in time for his campaign against Waller. This I perceive to be our soundest opportunity for inflicting a damaging defeat on the rebels.'

Even the mighty Rupert was moved to nod his dark head in subdued agreement with his uncle's decision.

'His Highness Prince Rupert will depart for the North, where he will assume command of our existing forces, gathering more recruits as he goes from our depots on the Welsh marches. He will then put the northern counties into a posture of defence against the Scots, until we can bring sufficient force to smash them once and for all.'

Rupert stared down at the map table, the King and Parliament's flags standing in neat pairs up and down the country. The experienced commander knew the reality was more than somewhat different from this idealized perspective. If truth were told, the rebels ought to count three battle flags for every two Royal standards. The Scots invasion had added twenty thousand men to the game, weighed the precariously balanced scales heavily in favour of the rebels.

He would have to right that wrong, balance those heavily weighted scales in the North, if his uncle was to hang on to his tarnished crown.

MERTON COLLEGE,

OXFORD, 6 FEBRUARY 1644

Hugo paced the rainswept cloister with his hat pulled down and his coat turned up, his bloodless fists clasping his blowing cloak beneath his grimly set chin. He looked like a footpad, lurking in the shadows like a common pickpocket, but he couldn't help that now. Half the population of Oxford appeared to be made up of lurkers, shifters, purse lifters, and sharpers. The once quiet cloister had always been used as a handy short cut between the various colleges, but instead of hurrying students and wistful dons the dank passage was now the haunt of a whole tribe of gaily painted whores, drunken soldiers, and bloodily bandaged beggars. Hugo though, resplendent in filthy travel cloak and greasy felt hat, was virtually ignored. He hardly looked worth bothering with. The one fool who had tried his luck had pulled up short, when Hugo had wrenched his cloak back to reveal a small arsenal of pistols, swords and dirks.

'Ah, no offence, sir, I thought you was someone else,' the drunk had murmured, hastily retracing his steps and shouldering his way into the mob.

Hugo listened to the college bells chime midnight, and wondered once more where Bella had got to. He'd already been given his marching orders, and he could hardly afford to let his commander down again.

Hugo would be riding out with Rupert that dawn, whatever thrice-damned mischief had befallen Bella.

*

Her entire world might have been turned upside down by war but Bella Morrison remained blissfully ignorant of its inner workings. Her personal fortunes had swung like a weathervane in a gale, driven by fickle winds of victory and defeat, but Bella had only the vaguest grasp of the finer points of military strategy, the flimsiest notion of why an apparent success might result in calamitous consequences for all concerned.

It seemed to her that the King's cause might prosper a good deal more than it had of late if the various factions which divided his court were united behind a common goal – if they concentrated on finding the best way to beat the rebels rather than score points off one another.

Sadly for His Majesty, the very people he seemed to rely on the most were gripped by the most bewildering jealousies, entirely possessed by their burning desire to vanquish their rivals at Oxford rather than the Roundhead serpents in London. Surely the Queen could see she would advance her husband's cause more effectively with Rupert as her trusted ally rather than as a sworn enemy? The formidable duo, equally devoted to the King, might have worked wonders by cooperating with one another, by aiding rather than hindering the other's efforts.

Ah well, Bella sighed to herself, Henrietta Maria clearly knew her own mind, and would not thank a woefully bedraggled country girl with a dirty dress and a grubby scarf for suggesting otherwise.

The vindictive Queen had left Bella in little doubt as to her coming role, spelling out exactly what she expected of her wayward agent during her interview.

'I want names, dates, and locations. I want to know what he gets up to, with whom and where,' Henrietta Maria rasped, busy writing the bewildered girl an equally specific commission. 'You say you have had no first-hand knowledge of Prince Rupert's affairs; well, now you must make it your business to find them out.'

Bella dabbed her eyes on her sodden sleeve, anxious not to annoy the energetic Queen with feminine frivolities like tears.

'I will leave the details to you, Miss Morrison, please ensure for your own sake you are worthy of my continued patronage.'

Bella nodded dumbly, her mind reeling with alarming possibilities. Rupert? She had only ever caught the briefest of glimpses of the taciturn German, how was she supposed to uncover details of his notorious (though unsubstantiated) love life?

Rupert's rumoured infatuation with the beautiful Duchess of Richmond was one of the most popular and enduring subjects being debated at Oxford that winter. Never mind his prowess on the field of battle, it was his bedwork which intrigued the gossiping toadies thronging Oxford's noisome cloisters.

The bewitching Duchess – known to King and courtier alike as the Butterfly because of her fragile good looks – had been brought up in the highly charged atmosphere of the King's household and was well used to gossip and intrigue. Almost everybody at court (apart from Henrietta Maria, of course) imagined they would make a superb couple: he the awe-inspiring son of one of the noblest houses in Europe, she one of the most irresistible women in England.

But the Butterfly was already married, and worse than that, she was married to one of Rupert's few friends at court.

The crucial question being debated in every gloomy garret and sawdust-strewn alehouse was whether Rupert's cast-iron code of honour would prevent him from surrendering to his ungovernable lusts. Everybody from the lowliest chambermaid to the goutiest earl had an opinion, one way or the other. Inevitably, their delicious gossip had reached the ever alert ears of the Queen, and she had been absolutely and utterly infuriated by their rumoured affair. The Duchess was one of her own ladies-in-waiting, privy to the secrets of a kingdom, a once-trusted confidante.

The Prince was the Protestant prodigal, an avenging angel who might turn this war, the German wars, and every other bloody war entirely on its head! Why, Rupert was as much a hero to the London mobs as he was on the overcrowded streets of Oxford. A masculine ideal, a born champion with infinitely more appeal than her own stuttering, stubborn Charles Stuart. Stuart, why in its original Scots the name represented nothing but the power *behind* the throne, an elder, an experienced guardian who would guide the true King through to manhood, nurturing and advising – placing the crown on his charge's worthier head!

In truth, Henrietta Maria feared Rupert more than she feared the rebels.

She feared what the rebels might make of the detested Prince. It was her sworn duty, as a devoted wife and as a Catholic, to keep this prodigal son away from the throne.

'Here, take this,' the Queen snapped, passing Bella the brief commission she had hastily penned. 'This is your pass, use it if anybody questions what you do. You are to report to the Duchess of Richmond's household quarters, where you will be taught to attend her as she in turn attends me. Is that clear?'

It wasn't clear at all, it was completely confusing, but Bella nodded her swimming head anyway, not daring to gainsay the energetic Frenchwoman.

'I have included instructions for my chief seamstress, we can't have you staggering about in those dreadful rags. You will report back here at a quarter past four this Friday morning, when I will complete your briefing. Now you may go. Well?'

Bella swallowed with difficulty, found her tongue in the hard-baked dough she seemed to have been chewing.

'Your Majesty, forgive me, I had imagined you meant me to accompany my hu— to accompany Captain Telling, to travel with His Highness Prince Rupert,' she corrected herself quickly.

Henrietta Maria flicked her wrist in agitation.

'Travel? He's not off on a Grand Tour! With the speed he moves you'd be lucky to last the day, hanging about his saddle bow like a spare set of shirts! No, no, no, you will be of more use to me here. Rupert's being sent to the North, he'll no doubt be taking your precious captain with him.' The Queen's busy brown eyes locked on Bella's flushed face. 'You will be keeping your eyes on a slower moving quarry, intercepting any messages she tries to pass on to him or he to her. She wouldn't dare meet him now, not with all the whole court buzzing with expectation. She's as clever as he's clumsy, it will take time and cunning to catch her out. But catch her out you will. I insist upon it.'

The Queen's voice dropped to a reptilian rasp.

'Take care you attend to it well, Miss Morrison, otherwise the indictments forwarded to me by my trusted and loyal agents about the kingdom will be sent forthwith to the Provost Marshal's headquarters.'

The Queen tapped the sheaf of indictments with her ringed finger.

'There is more than enough here to see you hung, drawn, and quartered a dozen times over, and your precious captain with you. Now, you have detained me overlong. You may go about my business,' the Queen ordered with a dismissive flick of her chin.

Bella tiptoed out of the Queen's personal quarters between curled-up heaps of sleeping spaniels, anxious not to cause any further injury, upset, or distress to her formidable mistress by inadvertently stepping on her snoring pets. She wandered the dim corridors as if in a trance, heard snatches of whispered conversations from behind partially closed doors, sudden shrieks of well-oiled laughter. Bella was convinced they were ridiculing her, whispering her secrets to one another like the spotted jackals they were. A gentleman of the bedchamber in immaculate Stuart livery finally showed mercy and led the crying girl out, closing the door in her bewildered face with a subdued click.

On the far side of the old oak, the royal court of the Queen of England. This side, the bustling, bawdy, and bloody world of her teeming subjects.

Bella stared at the worn, wormholed panelling as if it was a fantastic portcullis, a magical gateway to some faery kingdom barely noticed by the snarling, shouting, jostling inhabitants.

'Hello, darlin'! No use standin' there gawpin', my peach, they won't let the likes of you in there!'

A filthy soldier in a torn purple tunic belched and nodded, running his crusty sleeve over his wet mouth as he made dragon eyes at the distressed damsel. Bella recoiled from his revolting vinegar and incense breath, tugged up her skirts, and pushed her way through the noisy cloister, slick and dank in the midnight drizzle.

Hugo leapt out of the shadows after her, took her arm like a thief in the night.

'Good Lord, where have you been? Who was that clown?' he asked, giving the King's Guardsman a challenging look. The offending musketeer sneered, slouched off after a reeking caravan of rickety carts bringing food from the surrounding countryside into the city. Bella blinked in abject misery, opening and closing her mouth as if she was breathing the fine, drenching rain falling steadily from the night skies.

'I'm to march with Rupert this dawn and I couldn't find hide nor hair of you!' the pale Cavalier exclaimed, confused and concerned by his lover's stare. He shook her.

'Bella, what on earth is it? Didn't you hear me? What has she said?' he hissed, dragging the bewildered girl off through the milling crowds, away from the Queen's commandeered quarters.

Oxford, the capital of the Royalist hinterland, was as full of soldiers, carters, captains, earls, tinkers, and whores as ever – the narrow streets fouled and choked with wet and weary humanity. The crude drains had long since stopped functioning, and passers-by had to duck beneath any opened windows as they ran the gauntlet of the narrow lanes and refuse-strewn highways.

As well as the garrison, Oxford housed any number of reserve units, both horse and foot. Each regiment, every company, appeared to be on the march at once – in precisely the opposite direction to its nearest neighbour. The result was a shambles of clogged streets and shouting officers, angry men and stalled carts. The noise, even at this late hour of the night, was appalling, the stench of human and animal excrement almost overpowering. Bella thought she might faint as Hugo hurried her along the clogged arteries of the city. There was a great hullabaloo up ahead, as a party of Cavaliers vomited from some pigpen inn, sprawled about the street shouting insults at one another.

'Good Christ above, what a damned harlot's web this is,' Hugo cursed under his breath, guiding his flustered sweetheart through their log-jammed bodies.

As well as several thousand dirty troops and a proportionate number of fine officers to command them, the city had attracted a horde of lesser men – ensigns, lieutenants, and captains who had lost (or been lost by) their units. These enthusiastic but unemployed cadets went under the all-embracing title of refor-madoes, shiftless swells who had nobody left to order about but each other. They were the most dangerous, ill-disciplined, and argumentative set of men in the entire army, well versed in street brawls and drunken showdowns, less experienced when it came to dealing with the usually sober enemy. Hugo gave the drunken rascals as wide a berth as possible, slapping down several roving hands from Bella's carefully clenched skirts.

'Don't be a spoilsport, sir, share the wench! She looks lively enough to take the lot of us and the Earl of Essex's besides!' a cross-eyed drunk in a striped red suit called from the vomit-flecked gutter. Hugo kicked his grasping arm away from Bella's calves with more force than he had intended. The reformado squealed with pain, rolling over on his face and clutching his bruised wrist. Another drunk staggered out from the inn, bend-ing double as he attempted to wrest his sword from his scabbard.

'Sh . . . teady on, shir! You'll not lay handsh on . . .'

Telling thrust the brute back into the wall, strode on past with his arm around Bella's shoulder.

'Don't whisk her away!'

'Away with her whiskers!' another Cavalier guffawed, walking in ever decreasing circles before slumping on his behind.

'Come back, shir! We meant no harm!'

'Filthy bandits, the lot of them!' Hugo cursed when they had finally barged and kicked their way back to the bustling quadrangle which housed Prince Rupert's Lifeguard. 'What despicable swine, no wonder the King's armies are melting away!' he complained, settling Bella back against a wall while he regained his breath. The drenching rain had turned their clothes black, the saturated wool weighing them down like leaden shrouds. Damn the rain, it was all he needed now!

'Hugo, it was awful,' Bella croaked, finding her voice at last. 'She knows all about it . . . all of it, you know, all about us!'

Telling licked his lips nervously, glanced over his shoulder towards a pair of rogues standing their watch by the college gate.

'All of it?' he squealed.

'Gloucester, Chipping Marleward, Penmethock,' she hissed in agreement, fists clenched in his sodden coat. 'She wants me to spy, spy on Prince Rupert and his lady friends!'

'What? For God's sake keep your voice down,' he snarled. Hugo looked over his shoulder, nodded at the pair of officers in businesslike black cassocks who were warming themselves by the glowing brazier. They gave the young couple an inquisitive glance as they leaned by the wall, forehead to forehead, whispering endearments like lovelorn students.

'She let you go, though? Without charges?'

'For now,' Bella whispered. 'She knows everything. She knows everything about everything!' she wailed. The girl's distressed cry brought the officers away from the comforting glow of the brazier.

'Who goes there? This is Rupert's Lifeguard, not a damned knocking shop!'

Telling sighed with frustration, straightened up and took off his hat.

111

'Captain Telling, Rupert's Lifeguard,' he growled in greeting.

The bigger of the two raised his chin a notch, examined the wasted intruder with interest.

'Ah, Captain Telling has found his way home,' he chuckled to his wet colleague.

Hugo swallowed nervously, recognizing the rainswept officer as his troop commander, none other than Sir Richard Crane himself. On guard duty at this hour?

'Captain Telling, reporting for duty, sir,' he said as crisply as he could. The bearded veteran gave the tousled youngster an indulgent grin, nudged his nodding neighbour.

'Ah, you go on, lad. It'll be a week or two before you get your leg over a filly like her, eh, O'Neill?'

'Nice of you to remember us, Telling. Have you heard we're off this morning, to the North?'

The captain wiped the saturated strands of his hair from his eyes, grinned wearily at the two Cavaliers. 'I was just saying goodbye, to my wife,' Telling stammered.

O'Neill snorted with laughter, slapped his wet thigh in amusement.

'He's a regular Roundhead, this fellow,' he called. 'Says it's his wife!'

'I told the Queen we weren't properly married,' Bella whispered urgently.

Telling smiled broadly.

'Ah, call her what you want, lad. Give her one for me and all, eh?' O'Neill called, turning back to the spluttering brazier.

'She knows all about us, everything I've done, everything Father's done, everything you've done,' Bella went on, tugging at Hugo's dripping shirt in agitation. 'I'm to spy on her, catch her out if he ever comes to visit, open all her letters in case he's writing to her!'

'They wouldn't allow themselves to be caught like a couple of finches in a cage! He's for the North, anyway, how will he ever find time for her?'

'That didn't stop them before. We caught them both at Gloucester!'

112

Telling frowned, caught Bella by her elbows.

'You haven't gone telling her about that nonsense?' he asked urgently. 'I would have thought she had better things to do than collect latrine-line gossip like that,' he said loyally.

Bella glowered up at Hugo, his wet skin whiter than his grubby collar.

'I'm to live in her household, keep watch, and report back to the Queen at the end of the week,' she insisted wearily. 'She's given me a pass and all!'

Telling wiped his eyes, chronically tired and sick to his stomach. There would be no chance of a bed tonight, not anywhere in Oxford.

By Christ, he needed rest, he felt as if he could sleep for days.

'I march in the morning, for the North,' he repeated, swaying on his suddenly aching feet. Suddenly he felt a heavy gloved hand rest on his trembling shoulder. He peered around at his concerned commander, smiled nervously.

'You look all in, lad. I'm not going to sleep any more this night, you might as well take your . . . wife, back to my quarters.'

Telling grinned stupidly at this invitation.

'Go on, get yourself warmed up for an hour or two. It'll be cold enough, where we're going.'

PART THREE

ROTTEN APPLES

'Newark is not taken, Lincolnshire is lost,
Gloucester is unsupplied, and the last week
there was but a step between us and death,
and what is worse, slavery.'

The Earl of Essex berates the House,
spring 1644

FARNHAM PARK,

The host encamped in the rolling parkland around Farnham Castle was Waller's army right enough, but William Sparrow, footsore and famished after the long march from Portsmouth, hardly recognized any of the assembled regiments. Most of the flags and banners cracking and snapping above the scattered command posts were new to him, the devices they carried as alien as the enemy's. Stiff new colours borne by units from Kent and the Home Counties, colourful totems the men would flock to, and please God stand beneath, in the heat, horror, and confusion of the battlefield.

For the newly raised foot, simple red, green, or yellow flags fully six feet square. Some plain, some carrying a St George's cross in the top corner, others adding wavy white piles or combinations of dots to represent the various companies. The horse and dragoons carried smaller, more detailed devices, carrying heraldic symbols or overtly political slogans. Here, at last, were flags William recognized.

A cloud and descending anchor borne by Haselrig's armoured regiment – the Lobsters so beloved of the news-sheets. Waller's personal standard, a tree bearing a blue shield and his Latin motto, *Fructus Virtutis*, and there, at last, his old friend Archibald McNabb's troop cornet, a black fist on a yellow field. Good old Archie, William thought, cheerfully looking forward to their long-delayed reunion. He'd shown his worth in that pig-sticking shambles at Penmethock – now he would convince the Scot he'd been mistaken about his clumsy apprentice. William

117

would prove, once and for all, he was worth his hard-won commission.

Now where was the auld devil?

They toiled past the steaming horselines, the well-groomed but skittish chargers stretching their necks to crop the grass or lick the leftovers from the fodder buckets. The horses were picketed along the main track through the camp, an apparently endless line of black and tan backs, ragged halters tied off to reeking ropes. The cavalry had been with Waller since the beginning of the previous year, but most of the foot were new to the colours.

The South-eastern counties men had been raised the previous autumn and organized into hastily improvised units to replace the foot regiments Waller had lost on Roundway Down in the summer. The inner circle of counties around the capital had escaped the worst ravages of the war, but Hopton's invasion of Sussex changed all that. The previously peaceful shires found themselves in the front line, a bitterly contested buffer zone between the Royalist hinterland and the bedrock of the rebellion – London and the South-east.

The terrifying prospect of a new Royalist thrust at London galvanized the Parliament into urgent action, finding weapons and recruits and more importantly, the money to pay them. London itself furnished whole brigades of eager (and not so eager) volunteers, multicoloured regiments from the London Trained Bands complete with auxiliaries. The London volunteers served on a rota basis, one brigade taking the field with Waller or the Earl of Essex while the others rested. Despite their frequent complaints and heartfelt pleas to be allowed home, the London regiments had already done sterling work at Newbury and bled beneath the formidable walls of Basing House.

The bloody veterans thought they had done their fair share of the fighting, and the new troops sent to replace them found the reality of field service at variance with the lurid impression created by the cunning recruiting sergeants. The newly raised men had been promised a romp in the country, as much food as they could eat, all the beer they could drink, and the chance to have a crack at a cowardly and degenerate enemy. Their morale had not been improved by the presence of an increasing number of substitutes. These men were little more than guttersnipes and vagrants, paid replacements who would take the place of some of the capital's more cautious (and well-to-do) soldier-citizens. The stout yeomen had been expecting to help guard London's walls, not march about the countryside during the worst winter in living memory.

The wide-eyed recruits found life at camp brutally miserable and bone-grindingly boring, the uncomfortable tedium interspersed with bouts of frightening action in which friend and foe alike were blown to atoms or beheaded by roundshot before their shocked eyes.

They went cold, they went hungry. They lacked for decent food and clean water, kit, clothes, and tents. They went without bed and bawd, grog and grub. They were marched in all directions to no apparent purpose other than to drain any energy they had left, leaving the wretched starvelings too exhausted to run off into the woods.

Ah, it was a grand old life, in Waller's army.

The Earl of Dartland's newly raised corps marched into the heart of Waller's camp just as the old sweats were busy about their ablutions. William peered into the various tents and pavilions, studied their staring faces but failed to recognize his friend and mentor.

Instead, he found abuse and ridicule from the old hands, the pikemen, musketeers, and veteran horsemen who had remained with Waller throughout the hard winter.

'Who's this lot, then?' one wag called, looking up from his greasy saddlery as the earl's fanciful formation traipsed into camp, staring about the packed tents and overcrowded wagon lines as if they had arrived on hell's doorstep.

'Cheer up, boys, we're not Turks!'

'Cah! I can smell 'em from 'ere! More fish fingers from along the bliddy coast!'

'Fishermen? No better than Froglanders for fighting!'

'They look like a proper set of candle-wasters either way!'

'Nah, it's choirboys they've sent us!'

William glared back at the noisy rogues, more than familiar with their genial though highly ill-informed banter. You could hardly call this damned crew choirboys, that was for sure. William knew better and so would the army – before very much longer.

The scowling major had heard the same ribald commentaries in half a dozen encampments and knew the inter-regimental rivalry would serve to sharpen the men's appetites when it came to facing up to the rather more damaging insults the enemy might throw at them.

'You've found your nags, then, boys?' he enquired, lifting his plumed hat in an ironic greeting. 'Last time I saw your lot you were chasing them off Roundway!' William called. 'If you'd gone half as quick towards the King's men you would have shat all over them,' he barked.

The cavalrymen were taken aback by the big officer's angry accusation, stepping out from between their panting mounts as the newcomers bristled and stared.

'And who might you be, done up in yer finery? It's not Prince Rupert as changed sides, is it?'

'Would for you lot of fornicating whore-shites he had, you might stay with us longer than twenty minutes, next time we face him!'

The hard-bitten cavalrymen could hardly believe their ears. One of their own officers able to out-curse the lot of them – but they weren't about to allow the heavyset intruder to get away with such hideous slurs on their martial reputation.

'Ah, another wide-mouth straw-head from down country, come to tell us how to fight!'

'It's time somebody did, you scrofulous prickster!' William retorted.

The leading company of the earl's regiment had come to a ragged halt about their champion, as eager to prove themselves as some wet-behind-the-ears lieutenant on his first day at court. They were delighted with their major's aggressive stance, by his willingness to get in amongst them – even in a fist fight with their own damned cavalry.

The two sets of soldiers squared up to one another, insults forgotten. In another moment the camp would have erupted, the angry exchange sparking all their pent-up aggression. But then, over the clank and clatter of loosened weapons, came a hoarse Scots shout, an iron-edged rasp of command which dissolved the dangerous mood in an instant.

'Usher, Mason! You damned runts, clear back there!'

A bow-legged colonel with cropped red hair and flashing fox eyes hurried down the horselines, barging his own men and Sparrow's out of the trampled highway.

'Step back there! Put that pike down, laddie, unless ye want a crack at me!'

William Sparrow recognized that bark! He shoved the argumentative cavalrymen aside, peered down the angry files as Archibald McNabb stalked through the mob towards him. The vastly experienced Scot tilted his red head, narrowed his eyes as he spied out the reckless troublemakers who had dared disturb his breakfast of oatcakes and ale.

'William! It's yourself! Ye got my letter, then?'

The opposing troops parted as the fiery Scot barged through the press and flung his arms about the equally delighted Sparrow.

'You couldn't do without me, is that it?' Sparrow cried, clapping his arms about the Scot's narrow shoulders. 'And any rate, I didn't know you could write!'

'Well, I wrote for you, lad, but not this lot,' McNabb observed, peering at William's command and picking out a few familiar faces.

'You wrote to me? I've not heard from a living soul for six months!' William cried, falling in beside the Scot as the opposing

121

troops parted muttering – McNabb's back to their greasy tack, Sparrow's to the churned track through the camp.

'Look at ye! And this lot! Somebody's spent a pretty penny on 'em,' McNabb commented, standing back out of the way as the earl's cocksure command strode down the main track which bisected the mushroom city of stained canvas and stalled carts.

They carried newly sewn colours, freshly turned pikes, new-forged swords. They were well shod and most of them were wearing smart blue coats with grey breeches. Even their snap sacks were crisp and clean with the straps still properly attached and not knotted up with lengths of old leather.

'Don't tell me they're yours, man? They've never given ye your own regiment?' McNabb laughed. Sparrow shook his head, nodded to Colston Muffet.

'Keep going and turn left at the field kitchens,' he told the reliable elder sergeant. 'Better keep a lookout for the earl and all, he'll never find us in all this lot.'

Their fresh-faced colonel had ridden on ahead with his newly commissioned and equally eager to please captains, anxious to report to the army headquarters and present his credentials to Sir William. The excited youngster had detailed Sparrow to remain with the slow-moving men. Muffet nodded, clamped his pipe between his sooty teeth and sloped off with his musket upended against the weather, leading the regiment towards their assigned quarter of the bustling camp.

'You're looking on the Earl of Dartland's foot, Archie, the bravest set of rogues ever to march out of Portsmouth,' Sparrow replied, easing his aching body on to the running-board of one of the many wagons which stood about the camp, up to their axles in mud and slush.

'Portsmouth? The last I saw of you was at that tavern, back in Lambeth. It's where I sent you word of our need.'

'Need?'

'A cornet. Mine's gone off to join your old friend Cromwell, and as our well-beloved old colonel has finally popped his clogs, I'm free to appoint who I want in his place!'

McNabb frowned at Sparrow's brand-new grey suit, inlaid with black and silver ribbons, expensive leather boots and the ornate Walloon sword hanging from his splendidly engraved baldric.

'Christ's bones, man, you seem to have landed on your feet this time! Ye'll not afford such finery in my troop, laddie!'

Sparrow smiled broadly for the first time in months, showed off his expensive and well-fitting suit.

'I had it made up in Portsmouth, before we marched.'

'Ye've not gone bad, followed yon Morrison's example and run off with the payroll?'

William raised his eyebrows, shook his tangled head.

'Morrison's off with the most of my share,' he sighed, wondering for a moment where the devious merchant had got to, and whether he had succeeded – or even attempted – to see poor Mary had received the hard-earned cash. 'Let's just say I came into some money.'

'Share? Share in what money? You could hardly afford a jug of ale the last time I set eyes on ye!'

'We took a Royalist ship, that damned privateer I told you about, shared the prize money between us.'

'Who did? Where?' McNabb folded his arms across his chest, eyed the major and his fine new sword. 'And that's a sight grander than the ironmongery you're used to,' he commented. 'You picked that off the captain fellow, I suppose?'

Sparrow's good humour was undermined by a ripple of remorse. He shook his head.

'It's old Toby's, he wanted me to have it, you know.'

The Scot's merrily flushed face was immediately masked with concern.

'Auld Toby? He's never deed?'

William nodded soberly. 'He never made it to Penmethock, died aboard the ship.'

'Penmethock? Where on God's good green earth is that? You'd best come aside and tell me all about it, aye.'

*

123

McNabb sat back in his fetid tent, shaking his closely cropped red head in disbelief as Sparrow wound up his astonishing tale. His solid Presbyterian features had undergone an alarming metamorphosis as the younger man described the hair-raising voyage down the coast, the fight on the quay, the gleeful looting of the *Messalina's Purse,* and the subsequent retreat from Penmethock. The Scot alternately squinted in disbelief, growled with rage, and purred with delight as Sparrow shared the bare bones of his dreadful adventures.

'You wouldna try and fool me now, laddie,' the colonel rasped, impaling Sparrow on his ferocious, stone-eyed gaze. 'Sakes man, I thought I'd a tale or two, but our fun here pales, aye, compared with yours doon there!'

'I wouldna try and fool ye,' Sparrow agreed, mirthlessly impersonating the colonel's robust Scots brogue. 'And I can prove it and all,' he said.

William had already dispatched Nicodemus Burke, his underaged but enthusiastic ensign, to the baggage carts, charging the red-haired tyke with recovering particular items they had carried away from the town. A moment later Nicodemus ducked under the filthy canvas flap, grinned at the officers crouched within, and handed William an awkwardly folded bundle of filthy, scorched cloth.

'And ye've brought me your laundry, is that it?' McNabb enquired, taking a swig from the stone jar they had shared. He watched William unpick the dirty bundles, fold the torn flags over his lap.

'You'll recall, Archie, I was carrying the cornet on Roundway, the one I lost.'

'I told you before, laddie, the troop lost it, not you.'

'Unusually civil of you to say so, Archie, but the troop's not been permitted to carry a colour since. I know the rules,' he went on over the colonel's objections. 'The troop won't be permitted to carry another until we take one from the enemy.'

'Aye, I ken that well enough, but—'

'We took these colours in Penmethock. This one's Major

Brinks' of Porthcurn's foot. And this one . . .' William unpicked the second flag, a torn and scorched ship's ensign, the skull motif just discernible in the rapidly decomposing black cotton. 'This one's Cruikshank's, the bastard whoreson of a pirate I told you about. This is the *Messalina*'s colours,' William announced proudly. 'We brought them back, to redeem the troop's honour.' William gazed expectantly at the rugged colonel, the Scot's dour features in rather unfamiliar disarray.

'Ye've done well laddie, aye. More than well. But did ye not mark the cornet by the gate? Did ye not see my flag?'

William realized with a start he had. Blowing proudly beside Haselrig's cloud and anchor standard. He closed his eyes, realizing at once what had happened.

'It was on yon braeside at the Alton place, we had the better of them that day. Their horse didna stand more than ten minutes, man, scattering in all directions. I took the colour mysen,' the Scot said, his stony-faced confession barely escaping his rat trap of a mouth. 'The damned rogue had me by the bridle, so I took him with my dirk,' McNabb mumbled, subdued by William's all too evident disappointment. William sat like a straw statue, absorbed the information with a quiet sigh. He had damn near killed himself and half his men, bringing the cursed rags back from that hell-hole.

'You can keep the credit, lad, you and this fine new regiment of yours,' McNabb encouraged. 'This is of no matter, they are but tatty old cloths, after all's said and done. We've our flag and ye've got yours, aye. And please God we'll keep 'em, come what may.'

SIR WILLIAM WALLER'S HEADQUARTERS,

FARNHAM PARK

The senior field officers looked on the Earl of Dartland's fanciful new formation with barely more approval than their scornful and suspicious troopers. They knew this widely advertised new Western regiment was little more than a propaganda exercise, a crude demonstration intended to disguise Parliament's perilously weakened hold along the coast. The new regiment might not have been worth much militarily, but its very existence suggested the rebel Parliament could still exert some influence on swaths of country the opposing party had hitherto considered its own. The earl himself was worth his weight in gold – a real-life lord whose family's dogged devotion to King Charles had until recently been beyond question.

The youngster's tyrant of a father might have been too set in his ways to waver one inch from the Royalist line, but his notorious extremism only served to emphasize the importance of the son's defection. Dartland's change of heart had undermined the Royalist position in western Dorset, left a bloody vacuum in a region which had up until then been as strong for the King as any other in England.

In short, Sir William Waller's field officers had been left in no doubt as to their new colleague's importance. The boy might be a liability on a field of battle and probably couldn't be trusted with a length of burnt-out match, but he and his men were to be treated with the utmost courtesy and respect all the same.

Sir William, a tall and heavily built officer with thin sandy hair and a rather threadbare beard, looked up from his scattered maps and smiled broadly as the young nobleman was shown in to his cramped headquarters in the castle. Waller had used Farnham as a secure base throughout the long hard winter, planning his variously successful strategies from the cold comfort of the great hall.

His old adversary Sir Ralph Hopton had been searching in vain for such a valuable base, a foothold from which he could threaten the western approaches to the capital. Hopton had tried to take Farnham by main force earlier that winter, driving his worn out forces at the heart of Waller's domain. But his crafty compatriot had drawn up his entire army in battle order beneath the castle walls, and the exhausted Royalists had not dared to risk a bloody showdown before Waller's bristling guns. Since then the castle had been Sir William's undisputed strongpoint, supply depot, and training ground. Immense stores of powder, arms, and foodstuffs had flowed to Farnham from all over the South-east. The garrison troops belonging to Samuel Jones' regiment of foot had provided the manpower for half a dozen successful raids and skirmishes. The castle itself would serve as a promising starting point for Waller's long-awaited spring offensive – wherever that might be directed.

'My lord,' Sir William greeted the nervous newcomer, 'you are right welcome to our headquarters, aye, and your men with you.'

The Earl of Dartland, familiar enough with any number of knights, baronets, lords, and ladies, blushed to his bones as if he had never ventured any further than his notorious father's bleak hall outside Penmethock – the blackened foundations he had turned his back on.

'May I introduce you, sir, to my principal field officers. You will have heard of Sir Arthur Haselrig, commander of my heavy cavalry.'

'The Lobsters we have heard so much about,' Dartland stammered, bowing his head to greet the fleshy faced, round-eyed cavalryman Waller had indicated.

'Ah, not all of it bad, I would have hoped,' Haselrig replied, not altogether in jest. His famous regiment of fully armoured cuirassiers had reminded the London pamphleteers of impregnable crustaceans when they began their long march from the capital the previous summer. Sadly, the heavy cavalry proved less effective than the breathless news-sheets had predicted. The Lobsters were broken and crushed on Roundway Down, dozens of them driven off a sheer cliff by the lighter armed but more manoeuvrable Royalist horse. The remainder retired with Waller via Evesham, and formed the core of the army hastily raised to replace the one 'William the Conqueror' had so unexpectedly lost.

'And here, sir, my principal commanders, Colonel Carr, Lieutenant Colonel Birch, Sergeant Major General Potley, and Sir Richard Grenville.'

The Earl of Dartland saluted the battle-hardened veterans, who bowed back, stiffly formal in their rusting armour and mud-caked boots. 'Gentlemen, I am delighted to make your acquaintance,' Dartland said, trying to avoid their intent glares.

Waller turned to the final member of his impromptu council of war, none other than Master Eagleton, the fiery commissioner who had organized the regiment's deliverance from Poole and its subsequent mustering at Portsmouth. Eagleton bowed graciously, hands clasped to his sober black coat. He was an experienced enough courtier, well suited to the tricky business of encouraging a beardless boy to imagine himself at home in the company of so many distinguished warriors.

'My lord, may I take the liberty of seconding Sir William's most cordial greeting, and adding my own personal invitation to regard both myself and I am sure the gentlemen presently assembled as your most trusted and obedient servants. Please do not hesitate to send for me, if you find yourself in need of assistance or advice in the days to come,' he said piously.

Dartland smiled at the wily commissioner, anxious now to be among the soldiers – not serpents like Eagleton. His father's household had been riddled with reptiles like him, self-serving rogues who lined their own pockets in the most disreputable fashion. His father, twisted by his own hatreds and blinded by fanatical bigotry, had seemed unaware he was served by such base knaves. They, in turn, seemed to flock to the Dartland colours like crows around a dead ewe. The thoughtful youngster had sworn to evade the clutches of cunning counsellors, to rid himself of these leeches and spotted toads once and for all.

'You are to be congratulated on your recent inheritance, sir,' the curly haired officer in the lacquered armour commented, giving the youngster an enquiring look. 'So much responsibility, unexpectedly thrust on one so young,' he added with a peculiar sneer.

Sir William glanced at the hard-bitten cavalryman, stroked his bedraggled beard.

'Sir Richard's elder brother, Sir Bevil Grenville, was killed upon Lansdown field,' he reported, his heavily lidded eyes reflecting his heartfelt sorrow.

Bevil Grenville had died leading his Cornish pikemen against Waller's gunline on top of the hill. The apparent contradiction – the younger son willingly serving the army his elder brother had perished fighting – might have been remarked upon in an army other than Waller's. But for Sir William the country's bitter internecine struggle was a peculiarly brotherly, though none the less bloody, affair.

Sir William, his adversary Sir Ralph Hopton, and the deeply mourned Sir Bevil had all served together in Sir Horace Vere's regiment in the German wars years before. Brothers in arms in the Palatinate, they had found themselves on opposing sides in England, their divided loyalties turning friend against friend, brother against brother. Waller's personal regard both for Hopton and the late, lamented Sir Bevil had remained undiminished, despite the fact his old comrades had chosen the King's side, Waller the Parliament's.

'My lord Earl's elder brother perished outside Gloucester, during the late siege,' Waller told the frosty Grenville.

The latter raised his eyebrows, modified his expression somewhat. 'You have my deepest sympathies, my lord,' he said with a short bow.

Dartland smiled weakly. The truth of it was he had never gotten on with his bullying elder brother, and he had thought even less of him since he had discovered how Anthony had been busy about the country – scheming and dealing and selling good men into virtual slavery in the name of an unknowing King. He had not gotten to the bottom of the murky business at Gloucester, although he knew his brother's fiancée, that bewitching minx Bella Morrison, had had something to do with the squalid affair. It was this sense of misplaced guilt which had driven him to change sides in the first place, prompted his shocking about-face. The melancholic youth had imagined he might be setting matters to rights, by serving with those very men his elder brother had so dishonourably betrayed.

It would be up to him to remove the stain from his family name. The name Lord Clavincale had so foully besmirched.

'My lord, I fear we detain you overmuch,' Waller said, bringing the awkward conversation to an end. 'My officers have much to discuss regarding the coming campaign, trifling matters of logistics and support you need not yet trouble yourself with,' the commander said smoothly.

Dartland nodded dumbly. He was being dismissed, like the shaveling he was. He felt the colour rise under his collar, his eyes prickle with embarrassment. Waller, sensing the boy's discomfiture, glanced about at Grenville.

'Sir Richard, perhaps you would like to take my lord the Earl of Dartland on a brief tour of our encampment. Your shared misfortunes bring you together in adversity, God give you both the strength to persevere,' he said, oddly sincere in his rusty black armour.

Grenville looked pained at being given so menial a task – escorting the snot-nosed boy about the horselines, indeed – but he disguised his contempt behind a genial smile.

'Of course. I will bid you a good evening, gentlemen.'

The subdued officers watched Grenville follow the mortified youth out of doors. Colonel Birch looked up from the maps, his hazel eyes glinting alarmingly.

'I wouldn't trust him as far as I could throw him,' he rasped.

Haselrig, his superior, frowned, reluctant to pass judgement.

Eagleton, the commissioner, glared at the impudent officer. 'How can it be sir, you have formed such a dislike to the boy? He may yet be of great service to the Parliament,' the commissioner corrected him sharply.

Birch shook his head. 'Not Dartland. That rogue Grenville, I mean.'

'You mistake yourself, sir,' Waller said stiffly. 'I knew his brother well, an excellent man, despite his misplaced allegiance. I have every confidence in Sir Richard.'

Birch pursed his lips, his sandy moustache twitching with agitation.

'Straight off the boat from Ireland? He only serves in order to redeem his back pay,' Birch growled. 'I have heard he intends to desert the moment he has an opportunity. The moment we've filled his purse.'

Waller seemed shaken by his officer's doubt. Eagleton, to whom such questions were meat and drink, shook his bristling red head in dismay.

'Then you are ill informed, sir. Do you imagine the Parliament commissioned Sir Richard without examination of his character and record?'

'Well, he's been butchering Papists by the hundred over in Ireland,' Birch snapped, before remembering to guard his tongue. It would not be considered prudent to accuse his superiors of employing the rogue on the basis of his apparent willingness to slaughter Catholics, no matter how the news-sheets clamoured for such brutal solutions.

'He is said to be a wild, dissolute fellow,' Birch added, reddening. 'That business with his wife and the Earl of Suffolk. Divorce, slander, endless scandals . . .'

'You speak your mind on matters of which you can have no understanding, sir,' Eagleton replied shortly. 'Your purpose is to obey your orders and see to your men, ours is to examine the whole picture, subtleties you could not be aware of,' he said scornfully.

'Subtleties? Oh, this fellow's subtle, I'll give him that,' Birch retorted, hot under the collar himself now.

'Do you imagine Parliament has enlisted Grenville, and Dartland besides, for their martial abilities alone? They are powerful men in their own right, noblemen with vast estates in the West, sir! Where they lead, hundreds, if not thousands, might follow. Surely you remember when young Chudleigh took himself off? He took half the West Country over to the King with him!' Eagleton bristled in self-righteous fury. 'Our superiors in Whitehall are ever mindful they must use every means at their disposal – there are effective enough weapons besides swords and muskets and clubs,' Eagleton scolded.

Sir William Waller looked pained by the outburst. He did not care overmuch for Eagleton or his damnable subtleties either, but he knew Sir Richard's brother, and that was enough for him.

'Gentlemen, please. I am sure we have no need to fear any such subtlety, on either part.'

For once, the usually shrewd commander had made an appalling misjudgement.

'Your men are out of Portsmouth, for the most part, I understand?' Sir Richard enquired, leading the youngster out of the heavily guarded main gate and out into the chill evening air. Dartland nodded eagerly, desperate to impress the veteran warrior.

Sir Richard had been fighting the rebels in Ireland, achieving notable successes in the vicious civil war around Dublin and Wexford. Now he was back in England, serving the Parliament – after much tortured heart-searching.

'We have Londoners too, a core of veterans from the Earl of Essex's army, as well as several dozen . . . unfortunates, who had fallen foul of my father's court.'

'The sweepings of Penmethock Assizes, eh?' Sir Richard asked, leading the way around a gaggle of noisy artillerymen, busily hauling one of Waller's famous leather guns down the rutted track leading away from the castle. The light guns were said to be Waller's secret weapon, the fiendish surprise with which he would greet his old adversary Hopton, the next time he came to call. Dartland examined the small gun with interest, smiled faintly at the elder man.

'They have remained with the colours, since the raid on the village,' he said uneasily, annoyed at the elder man's disdainful tone.

'No offence meant, my lord,' Sir Richard said easily. 'They've commissioned me to raise a regiment of horse, but I've barely found a decent troop. Good men are devilish hard to come by, these days.'

Dartland licked his chapped lips, slightly reassured by the veteran's good-natured confession.

'And I hear you took on some of those West Countrymen, the ones as mutinied marching up to join Hopton?'

Dartland nodded. They had filled out several companies with the belligerent levies, the men content enough for now with a few shillings in their purses and some decent food in their bellies.

Royalist recruiting in the West had gone well, but the men's initial enthusiasm had rapidly worn thin without regular pay and decent provision. It was a common enough complaint all around the King's hard-won territories – the men were willing enough to serve their liege lord, but not on an empty stomach.

'And another few dozen turncoats Sir William picked up at Alton and Arundel?'

Dartland halted, gave the bigger man the stoniest stare he could manage.

'Indeed, sir, you are remarkably well informed of the make-up of my regiment,' he said hotly. 'I had not realized my men were the subject of such detailed study.'

'Ah, well, you'll forgive me for being blunt,' Sir Richard said, apparently unconcerned whether he was forgiven or not, 'but we're rather in the same boat, so to speak. We have both come but lately to Parliament's cause, and our backgrounds suggest – how shall I say – suggest we ought rather to incline towards the opposing party.'

'Serve the King, you mean.'

'Aye, in a nutshell, my lord. They're a stuffy lot on this side, as I imagine you'll find.'

'On the contrary, sir,' Dartland replied. 'I am encouraged by Sir William's single-minded purpose, and his sober consideration of the nation's plight. I confess, sir, I could no longer stomach the company my elder brother and father kept. Rogues, sir, pirates and cut-purses all.'

Sir Richard seemed to stand back a little, astounded by the plump youngster's self-righteous attitude. He smiled broadly.

'Ah, how can we lose, when we attract such high-minded fellows to our camp? Sir, you see the main track through the camp before you. I am afraid I must be about my duty elsewhere.' Sir Richard bowed low, and strode off into the gathering night.

The young Earl of Dartland watched him go, listened to the merry jingle of his spurs. He had met his sort many times before. Aye, clinging like lampreys to his father's coat-tails. Off about his duties? It would be a bottle and a whore for that one, the earl thought hotly.

FARNHAM PARK

Monday was drill.

And so was Tuesday, Wednesday, Thursday, Friday, and Saturday for that matter. Sir William refused to allow his men manual exercise on the Sabbath, so the vindictive sergeants gave the raw recruits a double dose at the beginning of the week – week in week out, rain or shine.

'You're going to face the toughest foot in the King's army! Do you know why we haven't beaten them yet? Because they'll march all over turds like you, you candle-wasting whoresons!'

And so it went on. Marching and counter-marching. Wheeling left and wheeling right. Advance pikes, porte pikes, charge pikes. The men moaned and cursed, wondering aloud how such idiot manoeuvres were going to win them anything. All they had succeeded in doing so far was to blister their feet and wear out their new shoes!

'Stand at your ease! Assume a lazy posture!' The tired pikemen rammed their butts into the bruised grass a yard in front of them, gripped their weapons in their raw fists, and leaned gratefully on their splintered props. The musketeers alongside, unable to copy their colleagues' posture, leaned on their heavy matchlocks as best they could, wiped the sweat from their faces, and blew on their fuming match cords.

Colston Muffet, the exasperatingly demanding elder sergeant, stalked through the panting ranks, straightening clinking bandoliers and checking each man's match was lit, his eyes alert for the most insignificant misdemeanour.

'I'll tell you why we're marching, you miserable Egyptians!

Because proper drill will save your lives!' the Londoner rasped, his normally narrow mouth pulled in all directions. 'You heard what happened to those pox-ridden coxcombs in the Westminster band outside Basing! Two ranks fired point-blank into the backs of their comrades! They killed more of their own men than the enemy did! That's why we're training you, so you can kill the King's men, not your shag-daft mates!'

Muffet, the veteran musketeer who had served half a dozen different regiments since he had first rushed to join Merrick's foot back in the summer of 1642, had refused the Earl of Dartland's offer of a commission, claiming he couldn't bear such a hateful responsibility. He was content enough to be the elder sergeant, the senior non-commissioned rank he had held as long as anybody else could remember.

'He's been in longer than Essex 'isself,' Billy Butcher commented to one of the new men, a keen-eyed poacher with rather indistinct antecedents called Richard Luke. 'By rights he ought to be a marquis or somefin'. 'E'll be catchin' up with old Will isself, one day,' the sharpshooter added, nodding at the grandly turned-out major picking his way along the rutted track beside their well-trampled parade ground. The snow had blown out at last, but the sudden thaw had turned the rolling parklands around the great keep into a lagoon of oozing mud which seemed able to penetrate every tent, bed, stocking, and boot.

William Sparrow, touring the refuse-strewn camp with the company clerk and an armful of ink-smeared ledger rolls, stopped to watch the exhausted companies put through their paces.

'Morning, Major!' Sparrow returned Butcher's cheerful wave with an irritated flick of his wrist. 'Unless you've made lieutenant colonel already! It's been a week or two since your last promotion, high time you were going up again, ain't it?'

William strode over, gave the insolent musketeer a stern stare.

'Do you have to cock your beaver in front of the men? I'm supposed to be the officer, not some strolling player!'

Billy Butcher raised his colourless eyebrows, feigning surprise.

'Course you are, sir, God bless you, sir! You're an example to us all!' he called cheekily, as Sparrow trudged off down the rank towards Muffet, his clerk splashing along behind him.

Muffet tipped his tatty felt hat in salute as William frowned down at his muddied boots, the elegant lace carefully folded over the tops splattered with thick gobs of red soil.

'Get whoever's in the guardhouse to lay some straw, can't you?' Sparrow ordered, scraping his new footwear with a stick. 'This place is worse than a hog wallow!'

'Sorry about that, Major Sparrow, sir,' Muffet replied with a carefully vacant expression.

Sparrow snorted in agitation, nodded over his shoulder. 'All here, are they? No more snowbirds flown home for the winter?'

As widely predicted, the Earl of Dartland's rapidly recruited regiment had shed men almost as quickly as it had found them. Most of the survivors of the shambles in Penmethock had drifted away, glad to have escaped with their lives and what remained of their loot. The feckless knaves from Hopton's army had made off in ones and twos as if doomed to wander in the twilight zone between the various forces, while the Portsmouth men as were left yearned for their homes by the sea, singing mournful shanties around their miserable fires. Some of the London soldiers had simply tagged along at the back when an auxiliary regiment of the Trained Band had departed for its monthly furlough in the capital.

A few short weeks after its widely advertised mustering, the Earl of Dartland's grand regiment was little more than a reinforced company.

'One of Captain Pye's musketeers was caught on the London road, he's locked up in the castle with the rest of the buggers. Apart from that, they're all present and correct,' Muffet reported.

'Well, that's a relief. If we'd lost many more I'd be back to captain, sharp as you like.'

Muffet sucked thoughtfully on his cold clay pipe as the big officer finished scraping his boots on a patch of woebegone dock leaves. 'Terrible shame, that'd be,' he reflected quietly. 'You with all this finery to keep and all.'

Sparrow eyed the veteran with suspicion. 'Don't you start rolling your eyes! You'd best tell Butcher to button his lip and all, we can't have 'em swapping jokes in the middle of a firefight!' he scolded, irked by his non-commissioned officer's irreverence.

'Right you are, sir,' Muffet allowed, nodding his slate grey head. 'I'll be sure to pass it on.'

'Aye, make sure you do,' Sparrow growled.

William knew Muffet, Butcher, and the rest of the old sweats were worth a whole brigade when it came to a fight. Long Col seemed to possess a supernatural instinct for survival, knowing in his bones when it was time to turn and run, but never running away. He would simply find another scrap of cover, call the men together, and reload like the excellent soldier he was. Muffet and his deputies, the cantankerous sergeants Goodrich and Jameson, could boast a dozen and more years of service between them, invaluable experience in an army still largely made up of amateurs. Whereas Muffet was as lean as well-gnawed bacon rind, his fellow Londoners were larger than life – great fleshy trolls in straining buff coats with gin-blossomed noses and slack mouths which seemed to open up before the new recruits like the very pits of hellfire. While Muffet took charge of the musketeers, Goodrich and Jameson stalked between the ranks of pikemen, straightening weapons and slapping shoulders, roaring spittle-flecked abuse at their hapless charges.

'You've sawn a length from your stick, you chicken-livered scut! What good's a damned toothpick when you're fightin' the King's Cavaliers?'

Sparrow waited while John Ruell, the undernourished company clerk, scribbled numbers into the heavy ledger. He hadn't imagined there would be so much paperwork keeping the fanciful regiment together.

'Two hundred and forty-three, Major Sparrow, sir,' Ruell reported.

William nodded sourly. They had left Portsmouth with going on four hundred men! There would be more officers than pikes, if this went on much longer. Muffet lifted his hat to rub his raw scalp, nodded encouragingly at the dwindling ranks.

'We're better off without 'em, slackers and deserters and thieves,' he said. 'I'd rather have two 'undred I could trust as a thousand scoundrels ready to run at the first whiff of powder!'

William wiped his eye, accepted the sergeant's assessment with a noncommittal grunt. 'How are they doing, Col?'

He had asked the veteran a thousand times, constantly reckoning their worth, wondering whether the cowed ranks would stand when it came to push of pike with the enemy. He had been in the wars for seven months now, ample time to learn one lesson by heart. It was no use standing in the front rank if you couldn't rely on the men in the second and third. Muffet took his pipe-stem from his mouth, raised his bony chin a notch.

'They'll do, as well as any have done before,' he said curtly.

'Well, they'd better. As soon as the thaw's finished, we'll be off.'

'Aye. And as soon as we get stuck in with Hopton, we'll see what this lot are made of,' Muffet said glumly.

William Sparrow had spent fifteen pounds – fifteen precious pounds – on this damned outfit! It was without a doubt the finest set of clothes he had ever possessed in his life. The doublet was cunningly tailored to fit trimly about his bulky frame, the sleeves roomy enough to swing his sword without hindrance, the waist carefully cut to flatter his figure. The matching breeches, rather than rub his thighs raw as a piece of beef, felt as if they had been stitched together from a Turkish maiden's drawers. They hadn't chafed a bit – despite the fact he had been forced to ride a horse for the first time in three months. Bouncing about the country on a swaybacked mare usually left him bow-legged for days.

William had topped off the expensive grey suit with a fine set of black leather boots and a wide-brimmed hat which Prince Rupert himself might have taken a shine to. He had decided to pay the grateful tailor in cash, finally overcoming his natural reluctance to part with such a vast sum. The Earl of Dartland, equally resplendent in his light blue velvet and lace, encouraged the former printer's apprentice to splash out, make a good show for the men.

'They'll never respect you in those old rags, Will,' the youngster cried, digging into his own purse to find silver for urgently needed linen, cassock, and spare hose. 'Why, we were no better than bandits, coming back from Penmethock,' he said with a peculiar half-smile. Sparrow allowed himself to be persuaded to extend his wardrobe, but refused to part with more cash for the handsome chestnut charger the earl picked out for him at the stables next door.

'I'd rather walk,' he argued, remembering his less than happy experiences with his old piebald cob Jasper. The wretched wind-bag had carried him into trouble a damn sight faster than he had ever carried him out of it.

'Very well, then, the grey. I'll advance you a guinea or three against your next pay, it's no use expecting them to look up to you if you're standing slap bang in front of them!'

Despite his misgivings, Sparrow agreed he needed a good mount, and decided to buy the sixteen-hand dapple-grey hunter Dartland had suggested.

A big horse for a big man carrying a good deal of ironmongery – nine pounds. Saddle and tack another three. He'd gone through the best part of thirty pounds in one day – more money than he had ever earned as a ragged-arsed printer's mate, or ever would have done, come to that!

Dartland, on the other hand, had been brought up in a different world.

He was used to fine suits and good swords, the best horseflesh money could buy. He had ridden away from the ruins of his fine family home on a stolen pony carrying little but his name. The young earl was an important West Country magnate and colonel of a regiment of foot, however, and couldn't expect to live on a few shillings. He received an emergency advance from the grateful Parliament to enable him to reassume some of the trappings of high command. He quickly replaced the stolen pony with a coal-black stallion, a high-stepping charger complete with intricately inlaid equestrian saddle and a brace of elegantly engraved Dutch horse-pistols. He ordered several new suits, a fine Polish helmet, and a good Walloon sword.

Sparrow was forced to admit a rather ungodly surge of pride when the pair of them returned from their shopping expedition in crisp new uniforms astride powerful cavalry mounts. He only wished Bella ... not Bella, Mary Keziah, he corrected himself carefully, he only wished poor Mary was there to see him in it.

Well, I'm in it well enough now, he thought crossly, looking down at the fierce brown splashes on his carefully folded lace and elegantly cut breeches. He hadn't remembered having to take care of his appearance before now – perhaps this was some subtle punishment for his ill-gotten fortune. Muffet glanced down at the Major's caked breeches, raised his eyebrows in mock concern.

'Ah, I'd take myself over to see the laundress. She'll put yer right,' Muffet had suggested, stony faced.

'Well, I've got this damned banquet, I've got to look my best,' Sparrow moaned. 'Sir William wants to greet all his senior officers personally, explain the plan for the spring campaign.'

Muffet tilted his head, anxious as any of them to pick up details of the coming offensive against the old enemy: Sir Ralph Hopton's West Country Royalists.

'It's no good asking, they haven't told the earl, let alone me.'

'Where is the lad? I haven't seen hide or hair of him all week.'

'Off with that red haired cu— coxcomb, what's his name, Grenville.' Sparrow had already been warned about his bad language. Sir William Waller did not tolerate foul-mouthed officers. 'I hear he's some kind of Irish wifebeater or something, God only knows what those two have got in common, as far as I know the boy's not dipped his wick yet, let alone bedded a lady!'

Muffet squawked with laughter, shook his narrow grey head in agreement.

'I've heard tales which would turn milk sour! Divorced, they say. No more than a Papist himself, if the quartermaster's clerk's got it right.'

'I can't imagine what he's doing with us, he sticks out like a sore thumb with that lot,' Sparrow observed with a fruity chuckle. 'I would have thought he would have had more sport and better company the other side of the hill!'

'Ah,' Muffet sighed, stroking his long chin. 'Other side of the hill all right. Where do you reckon we'll be headed then? Winchester? Oxford?'

Sparrow shrugged. His faulty geography didn't give him any clues as to the direction of their long-awaited march.

'It's going to be Basing again, I can feel it in me water,' Muffet predicted.

THE SARACEN'S HEAD,

NEAR WINDSOR

The wine had gone straight to Dartland's head, but he was damned if he was going to show it with his new friend Sir Richard looking on. He blinked and sighed and took deep breaths when he could, covering his embarrassingly frequent belches behind his bunched fist. The smoky beams seemed to bend and swell above his head like the creaking bows of some great ship. He jammed his eyes shut to clear the watery visions.

'Are you all right there, Dartland? You look a bit peaky!'

'Right as rain, sir!' Dartland slurred, desperate to conceal his condition. It wouldn't do, giving Grenville the impression he couldn't hold his drink with the best of them!

'Ah, it's a strong drop of stuff, and there's no damned air in here at all,' the older man complained, making a great fuss of getting up and opening the webbed window. His flushed features were immediately jewelled with rain as the weather intruded into the noisome interior of the roadside inn. Dartland watched him take an enormous draft of clean air and clap the window shut again.

'That's better. Nothing clears the old brainbox like a good lungful of air, I always say.'

Grenville seemed to have taken to Dartland like a long-lost son – regarding the tipsy youngster with fond and fatherly concern. Dartland had responded in kind, quite carried away with all the attention – the attention he had been denied during his grinding childhood back in Penmethock. He was enjoying himself immensely at Sir Richard's temporary headquarters at the Saracen's Head, one of the half-dozen or so locations the busy colonel seemed to visit during the course of his present recruiting campaign. The fellow seemed to relish his widespread commission, positively thriving on the wandering regime which prevented him laying his head on the same pillow more than two nights in a row. The jolly host seemed to know him well enough, though, bringing fresh bottles over to their table with disturbing regularity.

'Ah now, where were we?' Grenville wondered, drawing up his chair next to the blinking youngster and leaning over to ensure confidentiality.

'You were just mentioning Sir William's plans for the spring,' Dartland replied.

Grenville raised his broad hands in agitation, shushed the eager youngster with an exaggerated nod.

'Be on your guard, sir, not so loud,' he advised, waiting for the potman he had indicated to retire before continuing his nerve-tingling narrative.

Dartland wished to God he would go on. He had been teasing him with rumour and half truth since they had arrived, dangling little pieces of intelligence before him as if he was fishing for perch. It was as if Grenville couldn't quite make up his mind whether to confide in him.

'You can rely on me, sir,' Dartland swore, hands spread on the wet table.

'I know lad, I know,' Grenville said sincerely, 'But if we're not careful every man jack between here and the Tower will be discussing Sir William's business in as much detail as the enemy. This place is almost as bad as the camp, full of damned agents, you know.'

Dartland looked about the quiet inn, wondering which of the half-dozen slouching scoundrels present was an eavesdropping spy.

'Well, you're a bright enough lad, you've guessed his intention already, I'll warrant. It's to be Basing,' Grenville whispered. Dartland nodded smugly. He'd thought as much! 'And I can tell you this: Sir William plans to use brains rather than brawn, this time around.'

'Brains?'

'Aye. Brawn's got him nowhere, three sieges and nothing to show but a pit full of casualties. It'll be different, this time.'

'How so?'

Grenville paused once more, apparently unwilling to confide in him any further and yet anxious not to hurt the boy's feelings.

'It's not that I don't trust you, lad. It's just . . . it is a matter of the most extreme delicacy, involving gentlemen of the opposing persuasion – on the other side of the wall, if you see what I mean,' Grenville went on.

Dartland frowned. 'Other side? You mean we are to undermine their defences, open a shaft beneath the wall?' he asked.

Grenville closed his eyes, shook his wild red head.

'No, no, no. Mining is as much brawn-work as a full frontal assault,' he pointed out, losing his temper a little. 'What I mean to say, there are certain gentlemen already in place who might help our enterprise, from the other side of the wall,' he explained.

A spy within the house! Dartland swallowed with difficulty, half-choked on his own excitement. A spy in Basing House, a traitor in a traitor's nest!

'There I go, running off at the mouth again,' the older man worried, clapping his hand to his immodestly curled red hair. 'Now promise me here and now, sir, you'll not go blathering about it.'

'I assure you, sir, Parliament can rely on me,' Dartland exclaimed.

Grenville smiled wearily. 'That is what I had heard,' he said slowly. 'Which is why I am confiding in you now.'

'Are you to be the go-between, then? Is that why you have been sent ahead?'

Grenville nodded. 'In a nutshell, yes. We are to attempt the place by ruse rather than brute force.'

'What a fiendish plan! Who would have imagined a traitor in that pit of Popery?' Dartland had overheard Gillingfeather use the term to describe the place. The hairy little musketeer – who had been all for shooting him during their dreadful flight from Wareham forest – seemed amazingly well informed about these things.

Grenville nodded his head wisely, running his calloused thumb this way and that through the flickering flame of the candle which lay melting in a dish on the table between them.

'Well, as I said, it's not all my plan,' Grenville had sighed, 'I'm not one for grand designs, as well you know. All credit to Sir William, he's the canny fellow.'

The Earl of Dartland nodded soberly, acknowledging this was true indeed.

'But you see, John,' Grenville explained, leaning forward conspiratorially, 'Sir William has as many rotten apples in his command as the enemy has at Basing. He can't trust half his men together, most have friends on the other side, if they've not turned their coats themselves.'

'Swine.'

'Swine indeed. Which is why I was sent on ahead. I have been assigned the forlorn hope, in short, I'm to lead the attack!'

Dartland was doubled up with excitement, gripping the table in a frenzy of alcoholic anticipation.

'A flying column of horse and dragoons, and a battery of leather guns. We are to attempt by speed and surprise what we have failed to do through cautious assaults.'

'Ah! Sir William's just the man to think of such a thing! I swear there's no better shifter of ground in the whole of England!'

'So they say,' Sir Richard agreed. 'So you recognize the need for complete secrecy? I can trust you, can't I?'

'Of course,' the youngster cried, irritated his loyalty to his new cause appeared to be being called in question once more.

'As I thought, a damn forward fellow, a man after my own heart! Sitting outside castles up to our breeches in shit, it's not for you or me, eh? Not for a moment!'

'Nor me! A flying column,' Dartland wondered aloud, devilishly excited by this innovation. 'Will you want for foot at all?'

'Ah, I see your game, volunteer your men to be first through the breach after us, is that it?' Grenville smiled indulgently. 'Ah, more's the pity we can't wait for footsloggers, your men are just the fellows, I hear.'

'Could we not march through the night? Rendezvous nearby?'

'You've a sound grasp of tactics, my friend, for your age,' the veteran allowed, nodding fondly. 'But we can't wait about for your mob. I suppose . . . no, it's far too hazardous.'

'What? You've thought of a way?' Dartland cried.

'Well, not exactly . . . not for your men, at any rate. Perhaps I could make room for one or two junior officers, give them a taste of the glory too, eh?'

'You'd take me?'

It took Dartland the best part of an hour and more to persuade the doubting veteran to allow him to join the ambitious venture, but in the end, the weary Grenville relented.

'Aye, God's wounds, that braggart Rupert was fighting at the age of thirteen! It won't do you any harm to get your hands bloody, eh!'

Dartland clapped the table in excitement, knocking the guttering candle to the floor. He swore on his life he would not mention the highly confidential details to a living soul.

Well, possibly Sparrow. He couldn't simply ride off without a by your leave, could he? Waller would think his absence most odd, he might even suspect Dartland had ridden off to rejoin the King's party, and that wouldn't do at all!

FARNHAM CASTLE AND ELSEWHERE,

2 MARCH 1644

The sudden loud rap on the door brought the earl up sharp. He folded the letter he had been avidly digesting and jammed it under his shirt, turned on his heels as Sparrow marched in with the company ledgers under one arm and his assorted dirty linen in the other.

'Captain Pye's musketeers have turned up,' Sparrow reported with his customary gruffness. 'They're in the guardhouse, cooling their heels a while. Other than that, they're all present and correct.' He placed the company ledgers on the dresser. Who knows, Dartland might get around to studying them some time that afternoon. The earl nodded crisply, and patted the worn leather books as if they were holy relics.

'Very good, Major Sparrow. And how goes the training?'

Sparrow shrugged, watched his fresh-faced commander cross the room to his rather overloaded bed. He was still in his stockings and shirt, as if he had been caught in the middle of a sweaty liaison with a servant girl.

Hah, Sparrow thought. Chance would be a fine thing. The young puppy would have blushed to his boots at the sight of a pair of tits, despite all the lessons he was getting from that damned rogue Grenville. The pair of them had been as thick as thieves lately.

'We've got good sergeants and sound corporals, but not enough of them. They'll do, as long as they stick close and pay attention,' the major reported, watching the half-dressed youngster pick through the haphazardly scattered clothing piled on the bed. The young nobleman's allowance had proved generous enough to employ a servant or two, but the rogues didn't seem to be earning their money.

'Ah, we should promote some of the promising men from the ranks. Have you anybody in mind?'

Sparrow rubbed his chin, reminding himself he needed to shave before attending the banquet that evening.

'There's a couple of likely lads, we'll see how they get on, first time out,' he advised.

The earl seemed completely satisfied to leave the day-to-day running of the regiment to Sparrow. At the moment, he seemed more concerned with what to wear to Sir William's sober-minded celebration. The all too easily excitable earl seemed fit to burst, his plump features flushed as he rummaged through the pile of rich clothing he had arranged over the bed. He snatched up one of his new doublets, held the well-tailored red coat to his chest, and stood on tiptoes to study his reflection in the pitted glass he had found at the bottom of the wardrobe. Sparrow stood by the door, wondering if he would ever hold the youngster's wandering attention.

'What do you think, Will, this or the grey?' the young nobleman enquired, unable to maintain proper military protocol for more than a few moments at a stretch. He muttered to himself, flinging the doublet down and snatching up a richly embroidered dress suit.

Sparrow shrugged. 'This is Waller's headquarters, not your father's house,' he said carefully. 'I would stick with the grey.'

The Earl of Dartland frowned at his meagre reflection. 'The red's a better fit, warmer too.'

'You'll roast! Thirty officers plus all the servants, a banked-up fire and good . . .'

The earl flung the grey suit back down and returned his attention to the red. 'This one, I think,' he said, ignoring the older man's sound advice. 'It'll look better with my breastplate.'

'Breastplate? It's a banquet, not a battle! I don't imagine Sir William will be wearing all his ironmongery, not at table!'

The earl turned on his heel, gave William a sly wink. 'Ah! We shall have to see,' he said with a peculiarly secretive smile.

The damned fool is up to something, Sparrow thought, perplexed. He had only arrived back in camp that noon, having spent most of the previous week up in London with that red-haired rake Grenville. They were an odd pair, the innocent boy apparently infatuated with the notorious hellraiser. Perhaps it was something to do with their Royalist antecedents.

'Is Sir Richard coming down for the banquet?' Sparrow wondered aloud.

Dartland gave him another lopsided smile. 'He might be, and then again, he might not,' he said archly. 'Now I thought you said you were off to the laundress?'

William held up his grubby linen, nodded wearily.

'Aye. It's no good hanging around here,' he said, making way for one of Dartland's servants, struggling manfully beneath a carefully stacked load of armour and accoutrements. 'If I want my stuff done, I'd best do it myself.'

The youngster didn't hear him. He was busy relieving the panting servant of his weapons. Sword, baldric, and ornate Polish helmet along with a brand-new back and breast. That little lot had cost a pretty penny, but William doubted it would do much to impress the dour Roundhead commanders they would be dining with that night.

'I'm off to the camp, I'll see you this evening, sir,' Sparrow said.

Dartland pulled his sword from its scabbard and waved it about the room. The poor servant ducked past Sparrow and scuttled off down the corridor. Sparrow left him to it.

The camp laundry operated from a vast blue wagon, the peeling galleon up to its red wheels in oozing mud. It wasn't a promising place to get cleaned up, slap bang in the middle of a swamp, but then again, it was only a stone's throw from seven and a half thousand dirty soldiers, every one of whom (give or take a few particularly filthy fellows) could be looked upon as potential customers.

Sparrow picked his way up to the unlikely laundry, its brood of bubbling cauldrons belching soap-flavoured steam into the fetid air above the camp. The laundress was a vast bag of a woman with frizzy red hair. He watched for a moment as she thrust her fleshy pink arms into a large tub, straightened up with a bundle of saturated shirts.

'Any chance of putting this lot through in time for this evening?' Sparrow called out as the laundress began to bind and beat the lifeless linen, wringing the dirty water from the strangled garments.

'I could run 'em through for you, sir, but how do you imagine they're going to . . .' The woman looked up from her washing, studied the Major with drop-jawed disbelief. Sparrow twitched before her red-eyed stare, wondered if he recognized her. The flushed laundress wiped a strand of red hair from her small round eyes, and raised her fleshy chin a few notches.

'Well, well, well. Look what the cat's dragged in.'

Yes, Sparrow thought, alarmed by her murderously intense glare, he knew her right enough.

'Mrs Pitt, Gwen, it is you, isn't it?' he asked with a sickly smile.

Gwen Pitt picked up the enormous well-worn ladle she had left leaning by the wagon, tapped on the peeling blue wain.

'Mordy! Jerry! Look who's come calling,' she called, loud enough to bring half the camp trotting up through the thick red mire.

A couple of dishevelled peasants rose from the back of the wagon, gripped the gunwales as they peered out to see what the trouble was. The younger one, a gangly boy of sixteen or so, grinned with delight.

'It's Will! Will from home!' he cried, nudging his rather more soberly staring elder brother and pointing out their visitor with a dirty finger.

'Look, Mordy, Captain Sparrow's here!'

Mordecai Pitt needed no such introductions. He had served with William in their village militia, and up on Bristol's walls – and he had stopped a ball for his trouble. The wound had left his thigh puckered and leg crooked, and he hadn't fought since. Sparrow nodded up at his former comrade in arms, glanced back nervously

151

as Mrs Pitt emerged from her tubs and cauldrons, ladle gripped in her hamlike fists.

'Fancy seeing you here,' she said with spine-rasping relish. 'Then again, it is going on three hunnerd mile from our Mary,' she added. 'So maybe it's no surprise at all?'

Mrs Pitt's geography might not have been of the first order, but Sparrow knew precisely what she was getting at. He swallowed nervously, nodded with all the humble sincerity he could muster.

'She's not here with you? I wish to God she was, Mrs Pitt, truly I do. I never meant things to turn out . . .'

'You nivver meant things?' Mrs Pitt snorted, as a whole battalion of camp women materialized from the steam spewing out of the bubbling cauldrons. 'I don't imagine you did, young man, but she took heavy anyway! Left her in the middle of a bliddy field wi'out so much as a goodbye kiss to call her own!'

Sparrow licked his lips, tried to ignore the delighted spectators who seemed to have risen out of the mud to watch his humiliation.

Mrs Pitt was Mary Keziah's recently widowed mother. As well as having lost her husband Gregory in one of the very first skirmishes of the summer campaign, Mrs Pitt had been obliged to endure the ignominy of an unmarried daughter in the family way. She had one son lame and two others off fighting with the Royalists, and the youngest, Jeremiah, was straining at the leash to join up with Waller.

She had been chased out of her home village of Chipping Marleward after some trouble with a party of drunken dragoons, and had been hunted halfway around the country for her troubles. She had fetched up that autumn at Sir William Waller's filthy camp, reduced to the level of common washerwoman by her diverse misfortunes, but glad enough to have gotten off as lightly as she had.

The war had brought her nothing but bloody misery and cruel grief, ruining her prospects and those of her children. And here was young Will Sparrow, the printer's boy, cocking his beaver in his gladrags, stomping about the camp like the town bull.

'I would have ridden straight back and married her, Mrs Pitt, straight I would,' Sparrow vowed, hand on heart. 'It was only the battle that prevented it. Why, if Mary was here now, I'd get the chaplain to marry us on the spot!'

'Ah, I wager you would,' Mrs Pitt allowed, taking another threatening step forward. 'Funny as how young men remember their duty, when their cocks are limp and balls are empty,' she said crudely.

'I know my duty to her,' Sparrow snapped back, stung by her inaccurate observations and the various off-colour comments offered by the delighted spectators. 'You don't need to remind me of it. But I've been dragged from one end of the country to the other, same as she has. I haven't seen her since the night before Roundway,' he said.

Mrs Pitt glared at the overgrown printer's boy, the cheeky apprentice who had run errands for Sir Gilbert back in the good days before the war.

'Have you had word from her at all?' he asked flatly.

The curious onlookers drifted off, disappointed with the direction of the acrimonious debate. A cocky officer beaten to a pulp by a washerwoman with a ladle would have been something to see.

Gwen lowered the offending weapon to the mud, leaned some of her enormous pink bulk on it.

'She's never been quick with her letters, our Mary. We haven't had word of her since the business at Morrison's mill.'

William, who had bumped into some of her fellow adventurers down on the coast that winter, had heard the gist of their eventful escape.

Gwen, Bella, Mary, Mordecai, and poor Jamie Morrison had been forced to take to the roads after a skirmish with a party of dragoons in their home village of Chipping Marleward. They had taken refuge down on the north Dorset moors with Sir Gilbert's brother Maynard. And that's where they might have stayed if it hadn't been for that runt Telling sticking his beak in. He had arrived and insisted his planned marriage to Bella Morrison went ahead without further delay. The frosty party set out to the church at Horn's Cross, but Mary Keziah, unable to bear the bumpy roads, was let out of the wagon a few miles short of her mistress's destination. She missed the beginning of the wedding service, when Bella and Telling came within an ace of becoming man and wife. Sparrow felt a twist of jealous rage flicker behind his eyes, his swollen heart stung by the thought of Bella lying in that vile serpent's coiling embrace. The pursuing dragoons put paid to Telling's little scheme, arriving in the nick of time to stop the ceremony and cart them all off to the Assizes at Penmethock. Which was where he had bumped into the wedding party all over again.

'All we know,' Gwen went on tearfully, 'is that she got off safe, back to Maynard's mill and off with that housekeeper.'

William digested this intelligence carefully, relieved she had at least been spared the ordeal of Penmethock.

That would have killed her and the babe for sure.

'I would have written, but I didn't know where she was, any more than you do,' William mumbled, dropping his linen on the running-board as the two remaining Pitt brothers clambered down to join the impromptu reunion. 'As God's my witness, I never meant to leave her like it,' he said earnestly. 'As soon as I am able, I'll marry her, you have my word on that. Sir Gilbert is searching for her even now, I've given him money for her.'

'Given money for her?' Gwen squawked.

Sparrow closed his eyes. 'So she doesn't want for anything,' he explained patiently. 'Her or the babe. Sir Gilbert swore on his life he'd find her, bring her to me.'

The laundress shook her head at that, but otherwise seemed satisfied for now with William's heartfelt vow, impressed by his new-found maturity.

'Ah, that's as maybe,' she said in a gentler tone. The last time she had seen him, Will was a spotty, overweight apprentice without a care in the world, happy to chase about with her own idiot sons. The war had altered him almost beyond recognition, just as it had poor Mordecai with his lame leg. His face seemed to have turned half to stone, the previously fluid, merry features more used to frowns and sober reflection. His heavy body was thicker now, but more formidable somehow. Nine months with the colours had made a man of him, she thought. Gwen wiped her forearm across her flushed features, nodded heavily.

'The moment he finds her, he'll explain everything, how the war has torn us all apart, not just me and your Mary.'

'Aye, well. I dare say that's true enough. I've not heard from Eli and Zach since they went off,' she complained, wondering for a moment if her elder sons were still with Hopton's army. The army about to find itself on the receiving end of Sir William Waller's carefully planned spring offensive.

FARNHAM PARK

The Earl of Dartland wasn't cut out for conspiracy. He lacked his notorious father's capacity for careful consideration, and was as transparent as a piece of best glass in comparison with his double-dealing serpent of a brother. Anxious to be about his long-awaited adventure, he was beside himself all afternoon, willing the dreary hours away as he paced his chilled quarters in the castle. He had been instructed to leave under cover of darkness making sure not to tell his fellow officers where he was going, but he wasn't able to resist the temptation of leaving stuffy old Sparrow a juicy note, giving his glum deputy a tantalizing clue to his supposedly secret destination.

William Sparrow, My Major of Foot, Sir,
I have been called away on matters of the most pressing urgency towards B, of which you will find out all details in good time. Be so good as to offer my humblest apologies to Sir William for my absence at the feast this eve, and assure him I remain, sir, his most loyal and obedient servant meantimes. I will see you before you are aware I am gone, wish me Godspeed William,
John Dyle, Colonel (Earl of Dartland his regiment of foot)

William Sparrow crushed the hastily penned note in his fist and growled with rage. 'B?' he roared, eyeing the twitching servant he had just hoicked from his supper. 'B what?'
The earl had been immediately missed as Sir William Waller's

officers had assembled for their banquet, and William had volunteered to run to his quarters and fetch his colonel down. But instead of locating the preening youth, William had found his carefully folded note, propped up on his dresser.

'B, what's that, Basing? Bristol?' He gave the miserable wretch a vigorous shake.

'God save us, zor, 'e niver said! Off he went without a word, zor, 'im and the other gennlemunns,' the nervous servant squawked.

'He knew damn fine we were at table tonight, where's he got to? How many of them were there?' William bawled, alarmed at the unexplained absence of his youthful commander.

'A fair troop, zor, the men as Sir Richard left 'ere with us, zor, while he were away up in Windsor!'

Grenville! He might have known. The two of them were up to something, that was for sure.

William felt an all too familiar surge of nervous dread – as if he was about to ride into battle rather than merely search for a missing boy. He felt distinctly uneasy, knowing in his bones there was more than met the eye to the earl's perplexing disappearance. Where had the damned fool got to? B? It had to be Basing. What was the candle-wasting prick doing at that damned pit? He'd get himself killed for nothing, egged on by that scoundrel Grenville to prove some vague point of honour.

Honour? There was no place for it on a battlefield. It was kill and be killed and to hell with the consequences for every poor wretch who couldn't hide himself away.

This was war, not a steeplechase.

The idle grooms William turned out of their slumbers in the stables weren't able to provide many answers. The earl had ridden out ('In all 'is finery, mind') with the party of horse from Grenville's regiment which had apparently been sent down from Windsor as an escort. Alarmed, William hurried down from the castle, out of the gate, and into the bustling camp beneath the walls, making further enquiries from the troops still lounging about their cooking fires. Many of them had seen the cavalry ride out, but the mysterious party had taken the Camberley road to the north-east rather than the dreaded main road towards Winchester and Basing – the road which had already carried Waller's veterans to three signal defeats. William cursed his faulty geography, wondering if the earl might have been taken on some circuitous route to approach the enemy-held house from the east. Damn it all, he wasn't even sure Basing was their destination, and the gnawing uncertainty only added to his keen sense of imminent disaster.

There was a splatter of muddy boots behind him as Muffet and his sharpshooters hurried up from their bivouac. The experienced musketeers had quickly responded to William's alarm, grabbing their weapons and throwing their bandoliers over their shoulders.

'What's up, then, Will? Taken off, has he?' Muffet asked, familiar as ever despite his friend's exalted rank.

William was far too concerned with their commander's absence to remember to correct him. 'Clavincale's buggered off somewhere,' he growled, handing the elder sergeant the note he had taken from the youngster's deserted headquarters.

Muffet squinted at it in the feeble light given off by Caleb Cruikshank's torch.

'B? Basing?'

'It's not B for baa, is it, he's not out after a ewe, is he?' Butcher giggled.

'Basing's what I thought, but this lot reckon they took the Camberley road, towards London,' Sparrow explained, ignoring the grinning cockney.

'Well, if not a ewe, he's off dipping his wick with old Carrot-Tops,' Butcher went on, annoyed nobody had responded to his off-colour jest.

'With a troop of Grenville's horse? What are they going to do, hold on to his arse hairs and lift him up and down?' Sparrow barked, irritated by the sharpshooter's mindless contribution.

'The buggers are up to something, that's clear enough. He's talked the candle-wasting clod into some piece of mischief, you can rely on that.'

'B,' Muffet wondered, stroking his bony chin. Born and bred in the capital, the elder sergeant had a rough idea of the surrounding countryside. 'Bracknell, Basingstoke, Bagshot, could be anywhere,' he shrugged.

Sparrow shook his head, strode back towards the dimly lit castle.

'On the Camberley road, though?' he asked over his shoulder. 'We'd best get after him before he gets himself in too deep. Try and rustle up some horses from McNabb's boys and meet me by the east gate.'

None of the staff officers William had spoken to knew anything about any troop movements that night – this was something Grenville had cooked up himself. Grenville's deputy, a squint-eyed fellow named Thorpe, claimed he hadn't been informed of any last-minute change of plan.

'He's always off somewhere, Windsor, London, you name it. He sends us what men he's managed to raise, but we've not exactly been overburdened with them.'

'Do you know where he is at present?'

'Difficult man to pin down,' the lieutenant colonel admitted, perplexed by this red-faced intruder's rather rude line of questioning. 'Owes you money, does he?'

Sparrow didn't like the look of it, and the intelligence from the guardhouse failed to ease his anxieties. The guards had proved to be unusually attentive to their duties, noting the departure of the rogue troop of horse some two and a half hours earlier.

'Two dozen horse in full kit, with a dog cart and all,' the young ensign in command of the post had reported, glad to demonstrate his efficiency before the scowling officer on the big grey. Sparrow leaned over his saddle, puzzling this new twist.

'Full kit?'

'Loaded down like Egyptians! We thought the lucky buggers were off to London for a few weeks!'

'They might be at that,' Sparrow said doubtfully, tugging the grey's head up and glancing over his shoulder at his uncertain followers. As well as Muffet, Butcher, Gillingfeather, and the giant Caleb, McNabb had reluctantly lent him a brace of his best men, Virgil Usher and Roger Mason, the two troublemakers who had almost brought their respective regiments to blows a few weeks before. Both of them looked happy to demonstrate their superior horsemanship to the flat-footed sharpshooters from the absent earl's rag-tag unit.

Full kit? Sparrow racked his brains for an explanation. He had assumed the earl's mysterious night ride must have been prompted by some secret assignment, some piece of mischief hatched by the far more experienced Grenville. A surprise assault, a late-night descent on some enemy encampment perhaps. A fast-moving column of horse riding by deserted highways through the dead hours of the night. Both Sir William and his old adversary Hopton regarded such enterprises as meat and drink, and had employed similar tactics on dozens of occasions since the beginning of the war.

But midnight raiders seldom carried anything more than a water bottle and a pair of pistols. This lot sounded more like a supply convoy than a flying column.

B. Which B?

Luckily for the perplexed pursuit, the heavily laden cavalry had left a clear trail along the muddy road, most of the day's traffic between Farnham and the capital having long since come or gone. They could clearly make out the tracks left behind by the fugitives' dog cart, despite the hoof prints which criss-crossed the deeply dug ruts.

'Well, they're a couple of hours ahead, but they can't move too fast with all their luggage,' Sparrow said gruffly.

Muffet looked doubtful. 'Have you thought why they might want their luggage?' he enquired.

Sparrow frowned. 'Aye, they might need it if they were going somewhere,' he said guardedly.

'The other side, you mean?' Muffet replied.

Sparrow shrugged his shoulders. It might be at that, he thought darkly. Dartland might have found his regiment a little too mean for his taste, his new officers a mite too Puritan for his liking. It was no secret he'd spent an age with old Grenville, and that rogue was a regular fish out of water, washed up on the arid shores of Waller's Roundhead camp.

'We'll catch 'em quick enough, if we ride hard.'

Muffet's grey features crumpled into an unfamiliar frown. 'Ride hard? I haven't ridden one of these windbags since I was courting,' he complained.

Butcher, anxious not to appear too flat-footed in the presence of their bitter rivals from McNabb's regiment, raised his chin in defiance.

'Get on, Col, there's nothin' to bein' an 'orse boy,' he drawled, trying to keep the apprehension out of his voice.

Sparrow was in no mood for their grumbling. Dartland had either turned traitor or gotten himself entangled in some devilry, and there were precious few back at that damned banquet who cared what the silly boy got up to.

Well, Sparrow cared, he couldn't afford not to. He wasn't going to pass muster as major in any other regiment, that was for sure.

'We're moving out,' he growled, nodding down at young Ensign Oldfield. 'Keep a watch for us coming back,' he warned.

'We will, sir! The word of the day is Jehovah!'

'Jehovah it is,' Sparrow muttered, tugging the eager grey's head up once again. The small patrol kicked their mounts on, and clattered off down the dark track into the gloomy night.

161

BAGSHOT, SURREY,

The earl was having a cracking night. The troop of horse to which he had attached himself had left camp earlier that evening, swallowed up by banks of cold drizzle which had turned the well-used road to a hog wallow. Their progress was slowed by the treacherous tracks and by the small cart they had brought with them, mired to its axles by the sticky red earth. Dartland followed Sir Richard's instructions to the letter, sticking closely to the burly sergeant who commanded the escort. The rugged rider was one of Grenville's own retainers, a sour-faced Devonian with sea-bleached grey hair and a rusty beard. He seemed to have been stuck to his saddle with horse glue, his bow legs wrapped tightly about his chestnut's sweat-lathered belly. The unsmiling oaf seemed to know where he was going though, which was more than Dartland did. The few times he attempted to ask a question, Sergeant Hendy lowered his chin and growled something into his whiskers, urged his tired gelding on without replying.

The young nobleman was enjoying himself despite his apparently monastic company. He had done as he was told and wrapped up warm, brought his sword and pistols with him. He had been rather surprised to see that his companions, on the other hand, had burdened themselves with all manner of luggage as if they were off on a trip to the outer isles of Scotland – but no doubt Grenville knew what he was up to. He could barely wait to rendezvous with Sir Richard, ride at the older man's side into the captured fortress. That would make his stuffy superiors sit up and take notice, he thought with satisfaction.

The silent party reached a secluded crossroads on the main Guildford to Winchester road, pausing to allow the toiling driver to whip up his muddy dog cart. The outriders held up spluttering torches, hardly more than will-o'-the-wisps in the gloom, but enough to allow Hendy to make a quick reconnaissance. The surly devil pointed on over the crossroads, stood to one side as his troop clattered over the ruts, and followed a side road towards the north. Dartland blinked through the driving rain, refusing to allow his fatigue to overtake him. All he could hear was the harsh panting of man and beast, the dull clank of armour and weapons.

It must have been half an hour past midnight when Hendy led the troop down a steep slope into an isolated dell, half choked with bramble and elder bushes. He left the troop where it was, the horses shivering and steaming with the long night ride, while he spurred to the end of the steep-sided gulley and up the slope opposite. Dartland blinked and stifled a yawn, watched Hendy pick his way back down the gulley.

'Gunter and Furlong, get up to the top of this 'ill, and keep your eyes open, too, you poxy dogs.'

Dartland raised his eyebrows at Hendy's impudent order, but remembered to do as he was told and sat patiently on the prancing black charger. He was pleased to see his horse was considerably fresher than the rest of them. Hendy glanced at the wide-eyed nobleman and favoured him with a sour grin.

'Not long now, sir, just waiting for Sir Richard.'

'We've come a long way round about, they'll never know what hit them,' Dartland exclaimed.

Hendy gave him another weary smile, and tugged his horse aside.

'Bagshot, it has to be Bagshot now,' Muffet panted, bouncing uncomfortably in his borrowed saddle as he tried to keep up with Sparrow's surprisingly leggy grey. The Major, rather preoccupied with staying on the beast's powerfully muscled back, nodded grimly.

'And what's he going to find at Bagshot, wherever in hell that is?' he asked, hunching his shoulders against another squall of rain.

The small patrol had made surprisingly good time considering the fact most of them hadn't been in the saddle for months – if ever at all. Butcher and the rest had been determined to stay on, dreading they might lose face in front of their rivals from the cavalry.

'I'd like to see those bow-legged bleeders hit an apple at a 'undred yards,' Butcher had complained, easing a hand under his raw behind to pick his breeches from his backside. Usher and Mason, for their part, had scouted ahead, waited for the rest to catch up and then spurred on once more, finding the best way for the less experienced equestrians.

'Taken it on his toes, has he, your colonel?' Virgil Usher asked insolently.

Sparrow glared back at the bristling rider, remembering the men from Cromwell's regiment who had come to arrest him the previous autumn. Tough, wiry veterans in well-fitting buffs, they were as difficult to kill as lice and about as numerous in this damned army.

'He's been put up to it by that bastard Grenville, mark my words,' he growled, urging the big grey past the grinning cavalryman.

'And what are we going to do if we catch up with 'em, Major Sparrow?' Usher called archly.

'Bring the bugger back.'

The night seemed to have conspired against him, time standing still as he hunched over his shivering horse, willing the drowsy hours away. The furtive nightlife which had twitched and squeaked in the dripping undergrowth had long since hidden itself away again, leaving the lonely gulley to the ghosts of air and darkness. The saturated troopers stood in sullen groups about their patient mounts, conversing in hushed undertones as the night wore on.

None of them spoke to Dartland. They left the nervous noble-man to his own devices, refusing to acknowledge his presence. The boy shivered in his drenched cloak and glanced up at the moon, drawn and quartered by scudding clouds and squalling rain. He tried to cheer himself by imagining the signal success they would achieve when the attack went in, the complete surprise they would enjoy over Basing's dozing defenders. Not even the most alert sentinel would guess such an assault was afoot, not in this killing hour of the morning. Nobody would believe soldiers could endure such hardship, Dartland thought, thanking God he possessed the determination to see the venture through.

He closed his eyes in private anguish, cursing his own ambitious conceit. His role was to be a minor one – little more than an observer – he reminded himself, full of self-righteous ardour.

And in truth there would be little honour for any of them, if the great fortress was to fall through treachery and deceit rather than force of arms.

At last, after what seemed like an age of agonized inactivity, Sergeant Hendy appeared out of the driving sleet, his peculiar rolling gait unmistakable despite the blinking rushlights. The gruff veteran waved the men into the saddle, hissing orders from the side of his mouth.

'Mount up, we're moving out.'

At last! Dartland gripped his sodden saddle and hauled himself up, tugged the wet charger's head about and followed Hendy back up the stony slope. The grey riders picked their way out of the gulley and spurred their horses into a ragged trot down the other side. Dartland peered about, but could pick nothing from the gloomy curtains of rain besides the occasional stunted rowan or coiling bramble outcrop. Hendy seemed to suffer no such disadvantage, leading them at an ungainly canter across a deserted common and on into a tangled maze of market gardens and vegetable plots. A dozen torches spluttered and winked up ahead, illuminating the squat stone shapes of half a dozen houses. Dartland could see dim shapes moving between the blacked-out buildings, and a moment later horses and carts drawn up outside a large inn. The advance party must have been running late for the rendezvous, rider and mount alike black with rain and sweat, cloaks and hats slick with moisture.

Hendy drew his sword and rode up a steep track and into the crowded courtyard at the rear of the inn. Soldiers appeared on all sides, grasping his reins and peering up at his rain-washed features.

'This all of 'em?' the footman asked, stretching his neck to look down the saturated column.

'Aye. Where's Grenville?'

Dartland waited patiently for an opportunity of reminding the strangers of his presence, but the men at the inn didn't seem overly interested in his identity. He was about to say something to Hendy when the unsmiling brute leaned over and took his left rein in his scarred fist – as if he was concerned the nobleman's fretful stallion might gallop off with its exhausted rider.

'There's no need for that,' Dartland snapped, mortified the sergeant seemed to be watching out for him as if he was a six-year-old child on some milksop mare.

'Keep quiet, my lord,' Hendy said, leading Dartland's horse out of the gate and into the busy main street. The puddled thoroughfare was crowded with men despite the unholy hour. Musketeers with arms sloped against the filthy weather, cavalry-men stamping through the slush pulling reluctant horses, carters in their inevitable smocks grey with rain. The brightest lights had been thrust into the mud around a stalled convoy; a fine coach complete with carefully matched team, a large hay wain and any number of smaller carts. A whole host of hurrying servants were going to and fro beneath dripping burdens, loudly directed by a set of anxious officers in saturated finery.

Dartland stared, completely bewildered by this unexpected development.

There must have been fifty or more of the commonest sort of rogues out and about, ready to run off and report Sir Richard's all too evident preparations to anybody who might care to listen! Why the dimmest serving wench could have carried word to the threatened fortress.

He would mention it to Sir Richard the moment he set eyes on him.

BAGSHOT, SURREY

The snarled caravan resembled a band of travelling players, with men, women, and even a few children kicking up enough noise to wake the dead. It didn't look much like a military operation to Dartland, stuck on his horse behind the belligerent sergeant like a snot-nosed boy at riding school.

'Ah, there you are, my lord.'

The bewildered youngster swivelled in the saddle, grinned with weary relief at the grandly turned-out colonel.

Despite the deadly nature of their midnight mission, Sir Richard Grenville had inexplicably plumped to mount the attack wearing a sumptuous suit of red Spanish cloth, finely inlaid with black and gold lace. Instead of a workmanlike helmet and back and breast, the flamboyant commander had chosen a wide-brimmed black hat sporting a clutch of eagle feathers and an elegantly trimmed riding cloak. He didn't exactly inspire confidence – turned out for a ball rather than a battle.

'You decided to come along after all. I've just been having a little chat with the men, rather a winning speech, if I say so myself.'

The young earl blinked in bewilderment, puzzled by his boisterous tone. Had he inspired the men like some latter-day Caesar, quoted from Livy or Virgil to fill their hearts with martial ardour?

'Half of a dozen of them didn't take to my theme, though, and have just taken themselves back off towards Windsor, but I think we've enough to make a good show, what?'

Dartland glanced over the colonel's beribboned shoulder,

studied the disorderly convoy which had apparently accompanied him from his base in London.

'I would have thought so many carriages and carts would delay our march,' Dartland stammered, ill at ease. 'Or are you planning to employ them in some sort of ruse?'

'A ruse? Ah, excellently put, my dear Lord Dartland.' Grenville tilted his head, gave the boy a teasing look. 'But surely you jest?' he asked flatly, his grey eyes – dead as roadstones – returning the youngster's anxious gaze. 'You know full well why we are come, I think.'

In a blink Dartland realized the horrible extent of his innocent misapprehension. Grenville had not planned an early morning assault on Basing House, a sudden descent on a treacherously betrayed fortress.

He planned to desert the cause he had so recently taken up, take himself and his noisy household over to the King. The boy swallowed nervously, glanced about. Hendy and his troopers leered back at him, grimly contemptuous of the gullible boy. He had been led by the nose like a young bullock, teased and tickled and played like a set of aces. Dartland curled up in shame, wishing his saddle would swallow him whole.

'No use dropping your jaw like that, young fellow,' Grenville said coldly. 'You knew damn fine I was intent on returning to the King. I knew you had your doubts about Waller's damned pious crew same as I did, and I guessed you had regretted your earlier mistake. Now is your chance to put the record straight, return to your natural allegiance and beg His Majesty's pardon,' Grenville went on in his usual bantering tone.

Dartland's mouth was as dry as a chalk pit. He straightened his shoulders, eyed the grinning colonel with all the dignity he could muster.

'You mistake me, sir,' he said gravely. 'I have no doubts as to the righteousness of *my* cause. I serve Sir William, I serve the Parliament,' he announced.

His youthful declaration brought a shout of well-oiled laughter from Sir Richard.

'Hah! They filled your head with their Puritan nonsense! Those blasted pirates you followed back from the coast have quite stolen your wits, sir! I would be failing in my duty if I left you to wither under their influence.'

'I shall not go with you,' Dartland cried petulantly. 'You cannot make me change my mind any more than my father!'

Sir Richard frowned at the outburst, resting his gloved hand on the boy's twitching rein.

'I know my duty, sir, and I know yours better than you seem to. You will return with me to Oxford, and plead your case before the King. If you will not fulfil your proper duty as an earl, mayhap the King will find someone who will,' Grenville threatened.

Hendy drew Dartland's horse-pistol from beneath the owner's trembling knee, and rested the barrel along his thigh to point at the youth's churning stomach.

'This is an outrage. It ill becomes you, sir, resorting to common banditry. Do you mean to kidnap me in addition to your own treachery?'

'Don't bleat to me about treachery, boy, those dogs at White-hall would have clapped me in irons the moment I stepped off the boat if I hadn't agreed to sign on for their damned cause,' Sir Richard rasped. He flicked his lacy wrist in annoyance. 'Take the impudent pup away and have an eye on him. If he tries to run, shoot him.'

William Sparrow's weary hunters had hidden themselves in the very same gulley where Dartland had spent half the night, armed and alert while Muffet and Butcher went ahead on foot to scour the spoiled ground. The musketeers weren't gone long, weaving their way back up the slope through outcrops of furze bushes. Muffet took off his felt hat and patiently wrung it out, nodded over his shoulder.

'They're holed up away over the common. Bagshot it was, not Basing. Half a hundred of 'em,' he reported gloomily.

Sparrow frowned down at the veteran scout, wondering what

was going on. More than they had guessed, that was for sure. 'That many? And Grenville with them?'

Muffet hawked and spat in the grass.

'Aye, done up like a Flanders tart. A carriage and six, carts, whores, tinkers, and God knows who else besides. He's taken half of London with him, wherever it is he's off.'

'Did you see Dartland?' the major asked, perplexed by Grenville's strategy. If he meant to desert, why not simply ride off into the night with a few companions? Carriages would slow them down, reduce their escape to a ponderous trot.

Unless Grenville intended to make some grand demonstration, a publicity stunt to turn the heads of those pox-sorry dogs at Oxford, Sparrow thought, picturing the scene for a moment. As a former pamphleteer himself, he knew just how newsworthy such a coup would be to the damned rogue. And he knew all he needed to know about Grenville's character and all: Sir Richard was a boastful coxcomb, a strutting rake who had pulled the wool over Parliament's eyes. He could well imagine him riding into the King's court, the Prodigal Son returned.

'He looked like he was under guard, four men close up around him, pistols out,' the sharp-eyed Butcher reported. 'They were getting set to move, and all.'

So at least the boy hadn't intended to desert. Sparrow rubbed his chin, trying to work out some kind of plan. Dartland must have been hoodwinked into joining Grenville's little enterprise. Tricked by the cunning candle-waster just as Sir William Waller had been. He was mightily relieved to hear the dolt hadn't been there by choice.

'Maybe they'll let him go?' he wondered. Muffet shook his head. Sparrow sighed. No, he hadn't really thought so either. He might not be a formidable soldier, but he could be expected to raise the alarm about Grenville's intended flight, alert the sleeping Roundhead outposts about the traitor in their midst.

'We can't take on fifty of them,' Sparrow said angrily, cursing the daft youngster's woeful inexperience. The idiot boy would get them all killed, if he didn't learn some common sense damn soon. He had followed Fulke through hairier adventures, but the old man had always known exactly what he was doing – and what to do next.

What a contrast between the desperately missed old hero and this beardless wonder of a boy!

'We can't just leave him, roped up like some slave,' Muffet protested. 'We'll look the jobberknols, losing our own colonel before the regiment's fired a shot.'

Sparrow was stung by the elder sergeant's shrewd assessment. Their own chief tricked out of his command by a serpent-tongued traitor. Jobberknols indeed.

Usher looked as smug as a dairy cat.

'You'd never live it down,' he smirked, slouched over his saddle bow like some Tartar from the steppes, his outlandish moustache waxed with rain. 'You might just as well pack up and get after him,' he suggested mischievously.

Sparrow glared at the armoured cavalryman, knowing in his bones Usher had it about right. They would never endure the scorn of the camp.

'We'll tag along behind them, see if we can spot an opportunity to snatch him back,' Sparrow decided miserably. 'If Grenville's really deserting, he won't dare waste time chasing after us,' he theorized.

The grim riders nodded wearily, unable for the moment to come up with any viable alternatives to the major's unlikely proposal. They mounted up in the continual drizzle, glanced up at the slowly lightening sky. Damn it all, it would be dawn soon.

Sir Richard Grenville was well satisfied with the night's work. He had led the merry procession out of London, making a magnificent show despite the late hour. Footmen had held torches to light the way, marching along in neat files alongside his creaking carriages. He had piled all sorts of goods onto the handsome coach and its brood of carts; his entire household plus a flock of servants and a sack of Parliamentary gold into the bargain. He had been given the fortune to equip his new regiment for Waller – instead it would go on a troop of volunteers for the King.

He grinned to himself, picturing his grateful Majesty welcoming him back to the fold before a delighted court. Lords and ladies bowing and scraping, congratulating him on his fearful exploits. Those cynical whoremongers would be fawning all over him, marvelling at his audacity. Marching out of London like some prince of the blood on a summer holiday! How those Roundhead dogs would howl about it when they heard.

Grenville looked back along the slow-moving column, momentarily disconcerted by the poor progress they seemed to be making, these few hours later. He wanted to be safe at Reading – one of Oxford's outer ring of fortresses – by mid-morning. Loaded down as they were, they wouldn't stand much of a chance of breaking through should the alarm be raised by some outlying Roundhead patrol.

He turned his horse and trotted back down the drenched column. The downpour had dampened their spirits, reduced the merry band to a funeral procession of soaked mourners.

Dartland, bound and gagged, glowered at him, his wet eyes bright above the soggy cloth tight about his mouth. The grubby rag had cut into his plump features, making his cheeks appear fatter than ever.

Grenville couldn't resist leaning over and pinching the red flesh, giving the boy a contemptuous grin.

'Not far now, my lord, I wager you've been busy rehearsing what you are going to say to the King to explain your treachery,' he said easily. The youngster averted his eyes. 'Keep an eye on him, Hendy, I don't want him harmed,' he instructed, spurring off towards the lumbering coaches.

'There you are, lad, see how fond he is of yer?' Hendy asked with a leer, clicking his tongue in the vile tarpit he called a mouth.

*

The madly creaking carriages had fallen badly behind, opening up a hundred-yard gap between the drooping escort and the rest of the convoy. Sparrow pulled his hat down over his eyes, urged the grey out of the closely packed trees and out into their muddy tracks. Usher and Mason followed him, their carbines slung over their laps, cocked mechanisms hidden beneath their riding cloaks to keep out the weather.

The small group of riders up ahead were hunched over their steaming mounts keeping a lazy eye on the slouched earl. They failed to notice the intruders creeping out behind them. Sparrow felt his cold limbs vibrate with tension, his fingers flexing about the cold stock of his petronel – a clumsy pistol which could be tucked into the shoulder leaving a hand free for the reins. He opened his cracked lips and snickered, urged the big grey on to close up on the leading riders. He knew Muffet, Butcher, and Gillingfeather were in the trees, shadowing the slow-moving column as it wound its way through the dripping woods. Their sharp-eyed intervention might save him from being gutted by one of these treacherous horse guards.

Even as he reassured himself with this useful intelligence a squinting cavalryman at the back must have overheard their jangling progress. He turned his head sharply to study the newcomers.

Sparrow gave the rider a long look. The man's eyes flicked over his unfamiliar face as if he was trying to place the heavily built stranger. Sparrow rode closer, yawning like a culverin.

'Grenville says to watch out for the brat,' he said, mastering his nerves as his horse took another precious step closer to the suspicious guard.

'You one of the lads from Windsor?' Hendy snorted, peering at him from beneath his dripping hat.

'Windsor?'

Dartland, gagged and miserable and dreading the end of the dismal journey, swivelled in his saddle at the sound of Sparrow's voice. Hendy, instantly alerted by the lordling's excited reaction, raised his pistol from his lap. Sparrow snatched up the petronel and pulled the trigger. The shattering bang startled his horse, which shied away in alarm, tipping the inexperienced equestrian back in the saddle. The bullet went high, clipping Hendy's hat from his head. The sergeant regained his startled wits in a blink, brought the pistol up as Sparrow's horse plunged and reared through the puddle behind him, its terrified rider clutching at its mane and cursing through clenched teeth.

There was a second shot from the woods to the left, and a carefully aimed musket ball buried itself in Hendy's cheek, smashing his jaw and shattering a row of blackened molars before exiting through his open mouth. The wounded sergeant fired his pistol – missing his rearing target by several feet – and slumped over his saddle clutching at his ruined face. A second and third shot hit his companion, a wide-eyed youth in a outsize coat, as he bent over to reach for Dartland's swinging reins. The panic-stricken rider threw back his head and grabbed at his coat as his piebald pony took off along the path, knocking one of the surviving guards aside. The startled cavalryman groped for his pistol while the other drew his sword, wrenched his own bucking horse's head about.

Usher was on him in a moment, bent over his saddle with his head lowered to the horse's wet mane, carbine levelled at his desperate target. The turncoat took the ball square in the belly, closed his fingers over the searing wound. Dartland's black stallion took off like a hare, leaping along the track dragging the slower beast with it. Dartland lifted his boot and kicked at the wounded rider, knocking the terrified youth out of his saddle. He shrieked like a goose girl, grasping at the trailing reins as he slipped further down the horse's wet withers. The last guard fired wild, hit Mason's scuffed breastplate. The ball whined off into the trees, leaving the veteran winded but unhurt.

Sparrow had by then recovered control of his terrified mare, dragged her head about with a series of hair-raising curses. The grey's careering progress had carried him alongside the wide-eyed marksman, who was bending over to pull his second pistol. Sparrow crammed the curved butt of the smoking petronel into the traitor's contorted face, knocking him back into the saddle. The powerful grey knocked the wounded man's horse aside, opening a gap in the crowded path.

'Run for it!' Usher screamed, the expert horseman spurring after the struggling colonel who was in danger of being dashed into the dripping trees by his own frantically galloping mount. He guided his horse alongside with an expert flick of his wrist and bent to lift the boy's dangling reins.

'Ride!'

There was a flurry of angry shouts behind them as the lucky intruders kicked their horses on, forcing a passage through the confused tangle on the path. A ball whined over Sparrow's head as he copied the skilful Usher, ducking down over the grey's stretched neck. The mare accelerated away beneath him, and he felt a reassuring surge of power lift him from the blood splattered mud and carry him on down the track.

Usher led the madly bouncing boy, eyes popping above his gag, while Mason fired both his pistols at the milling shadows behind them.

'Don't stop,' Usher yelled furiously. 'Get out of it!' he screamed.

They were away into the woods before Grenville was fully aware what had occurred, their grateful chief crying freely as he was tugged along between them.

PART FOUR

'YOUR HAPPY SUCCESS'

*'If your Highness do not please come hither,
and that very soon too, the great game of
your uncle's will be endangered, if not lost.'*

The Marquis of Newcastle appeals to
Rupert, late spring 1644

OXFORD AND ELSEWHERE,

MARCH 1644

Away from the smouldering flashpoints of the struggle, the *civil* war went on as usual. A war of intrigue and accus-ation, of blind ambition and personal greed every bit as dangerous as the armed conflict which had engulfed the land.

The cruel war of words was waged by agents and spies, by courtiers and clerks in dimly lit chambers and quiet cloisters. A vast network of non-combatants stretched over the kingdom like a web, each spiderlike individual at the centre of his or her private universe, busy pulling and tweaking the coiling tendrils which held the bloody war together.

The cause they served was often subsidiary to their own agen-das, secondary to their prime objectives: wealth, power, position.

Their weapons were whispers, a ceaseless barrage of dislocated intelligence, lying letters, dubious commissions, and fanciful reports.

It was into this shadow world of smooth lie and effortless exaggeration that Bella Morrison found herself thrust against her will by the calculating Queen. The teeming underbelly of Oxford, the slime-clogged sinews of the King's War. Bella might not have made a master spy – she was far too impulsive to make a plausible agent – but even she realized the hopelessness of her current assignment.

Queen Henrietta Maria had intended to use her as her eyes and ears, eavesdropping on her own lady-in-waiting, the Duchess of Richmond. The Queen had set Bella up, hoping the naive girl might uncover some damning evidence of the Duchess's breath-lessly rumoured association with the despised Rupert.

But although the fabulously attractive noblewoman treated Bella with perfect courtesy, the Butterfly's icy blue eyes saw straight through the flimsy pretence. The Duchess was about as likely to confide in Bella as the King was in Cromwell.

The Duchess of Richmond kept the bewildered girl at arm's length, lowering her voice whenever Bella entered the room, and her sideways smiles were daggers to the lonely girl's heart. The distressed maiden endured a week or so of this torture before slipping back to the Queen's quarters at Merton College to report her failure. Bella was terrified she and Hugo – and her poor father and brother and everybody else who had ever known her – would be punished for her singular lack of success.

The Queen listened to Bella's tearful report in angry silence, her fingers drumming on her rounded belly. She was nearly eight months pregnant now, breathless and heavy and running very short of patience.

'Not one word, not one mention of His Highness Prince Rupert?' Henrietta Maria enquired, her notorious Latin temper barely restrained by her matronly gown and silver shawl.

'I did as you bid me, Your Majesty, fretting over Hugo going off to war as you told me – but she never even blinked. I sang Rupert's praises all morning when we were sewing – ' if only the Queen knew how much Bella hated sewing – 'and she just nodded her head. She never even dropped a stitch!'

Henrietta Maria winced as the infant in her belly gave her a sharp kick under the ribs. 'You must have overdone it, girl,' she rasped distractedly.

'I played her for all I was worth, Your Majesty, I swear on the Book,' Bella cried, eyes brimming with the tears the Queen despised. 'She was well aware who I was before we ever met,' she blurted.

The Queen looked up sharply, her dark eyes gleaming with mischievous wonder.

'Ah, she might at that, Rupert could have warned her of your identity after that business at Gloucester.'

'If Your Majesty was to honour me with a different . . .'

'There will be plenty of opportunity for different assignments,' Henrietta Maria snapped. 'Do not presume to tell me what you will and will not do, my girl.'

Bella lowered her eyes, tears falling freely now onto the sterile grey flags beneath her feet.

'Now, then. You are clearly wasting my time dallying with the Duchess of Richmond, perhaps we should try another tack. Have you met the brute's boor of a brother, Maurice?'

Bella admitted she hadn't.

'My hus— Captain Telling served in his regiment of horse for a while.'

'Before he was cashiered outside Bristol,' the well-informed Queen added snidely. 'But he has never met you in Telling's company?'

'I do not believe so, Majesty.'

'You do not believe so,' Henrietta Maria breathed dangerously. 'Think, girl. I am not going to send you to Plymouth on a whim. Have you met the man or not?'

'No, Your Majesty, never.' Bella closed her eyes, dredging her reeling brain to confirm her terrified claim. She had met so many soldiers, they tended to blur into one buff-coated form.

'Well, then, Prince Maurice has been away at the wars for months. It is high time he had some decent-looking company.' The Queen paused for a moment, wondering if the dangerous rumours which had come to her ears about Maurice's sexual orientation might be true. Well, there was one way to find out.

'Pack your bags, you will accompany me into the West.'

'Yes, Your Majesty.'

The Queen had seriously overestimated Bella Morrison's usefulness. The jewel she thought she had unearthed in Gloucester had turned out to be paste – fluttering petals in an empty vase. But the silly girl's stories of mayhem and mutilation on the south coast had intrigued her – and she decided to waste no time exploiting the possibilities. After all, she might well be able to extend her own influence in the West, already chosen as the safest location for her coming confinement, and recruit some rather more useful disciples while she was about it.

The death of the notoriously stubborn Earl of Dartland and subsequent defection of his feeble-minded son had clearly created something of a vacuum, opening up a new opportunity of extending her network of servants and spies, creatures sworn to serve her first and her husband's troubled cause second.

Having heard all about the debacle at Penmethock from Bella, the Queen wasted no time in contacting the only man she knew of with any authority left down there.

Abraham Bacon, the old earl's clerk and counsellor, might well prove a willing servant.

In return, the fortunate Bacon might find himself promoted to the highest post in the district: High Sheriff and Chief Justice at Penmethock Assizes, almost certainly. A knighthood, perhaps. Clear proof, if any was needed, of the benefits of such all-powerful patronage. In return for his power and titles Bacon would act as the Queen's personal representative on the west coast, keeping her informed of all important personalities and developments.

Within two days of the Queen's unsatisfactory interview with Bella Morrison, Bacon had received an urgent dispatch from his new patron, ordering him to surrender all evidence, warrants and affidavits regarding the recent prosecution of the Morrison clan. Under no circumstances were Bella's co-conspirators to be arrested, tried or otherwise held without the express permission of the Queen.

Bacon certainly had enough on his plate without chasing about the country after Sir Gilbert Morrison and his cronies, and was only too glad to dispatch the documents in question to Oxford.

Let the Queen sort the sorry matter out. The troublesome family had brought nothing but ruin down on the entire village. The shrewd clerk had always found it deeply suspicious that the Round-head pirates who had caused such terrible destruction had arrived in the harbour – thirty miles from the nearest friendly garrison – on practically the same tide as the dangerously beautiful Bella and her rascally crew. He had wondered whether the whole incident had been set up by the enemy to destabilize the Royalist-held West. Whether his late and unlamented master the Earl of Dartland had been inadvertently drawn into some fiendish Whitehall plot. Well, it didn't seem important now, Bacon mused, idly watching the busy workmen clear the worst of the debris from his former master's ravaged courthouse. He had barely rested since the battle, a thousand and one pressing matters requiring his urgent attention.

One thing was certain: if it hadn't been for the bloody massacre he would still be sharpening quills for Black Bob instead of supervising the lives of half the population of Dorset. He was judge and jury now, aye, and could no doubt appoint himself colonel of the militia and all. Somebody had to take charge after the carnage those damn rebels had left behind.

The Queen prided herself on her cunning, and drew immense satisfaction from outwitting her most feared opponent: Prince Rupert. On this particular occasion, her creatures were crucial hours ahead of Rupert's own agents. Penmethock would soon be back under control: her control. The appalling devastation this Bacon fellow reported in his letter hardly troubled her – what were the sufferings of a few fishwives compared to the triumph of her husband's cause?

But she cried and wailed over every slaughtered soul as she read the bloody letter to the troubled King, stressing Bacon's brave role in the squalid affair and recommending he authorize the adequate reward she had already promised him – small recompense for his efficient and resourceful efforts on His Majesty's behalf.

'See here, he warned the old Earl of Dartland this son of his was not to be trusted, he says he suspected the boy was wavering,' she cried excitedly.

The King turned his sorrowful eyes on his tireless wife, thanking God for her devoted and selfless assistance.

'I am told Sir Richard Grenville attempted to l–l–lead the boy back to Oxford during his recent escape, but the young man re– re–refused,' the mystified monarch said sadly.

Henrietta Maria paused for a moment, wondering at the truth of that particular piece of nonsense. Sir Richard was the biggest rogue ever to have ridden into Oxford, no matter what her poor misled husband imagined. Her quick eyes darted back over Bacon's familiar dispatch.

'Riding off like a thief in the night, think of it, an earl, old blood. We ought to issue a proclamation forthwith stripping him of all land, titles, and assets,' the Queen suggested.

The King closed his eyes at this distressing development. The highest in the land abandoning his cause like rats fleeing a sinking ship. The Queen glanced sideways at her husband and decided to strike while the iron was hot, piling on the misery and scoring valuable points off the hated Princes while they were safely away at the war. No wonder they had taken themselves off, leaving the King with so many troubles.

She nagged and cried, hooted with laughter and purred with hatred, indignantly questioning Prince Maurice's ability to successfully hold the coast he had been sent to conquer.

'He's bogged down outside Plymouth, this illness of his is a sham, a feeble excuse for all these mistakes. Fancy allowing himself to be surprised by a mere boatload of rebels,' she complained. Surely the King's honest and loyal West Country citizens should be able to sleep safe in their beds – Maurice had ten thousand men in arms, after all.

'Luckily for us, this man Bacon of yours seems a reliable and sensible sort, we ought to appoint him colonel of the militia as well as everything else. Let him begin rebuilding before it is too late,' she warned. King Charles nodded his head, dismayed by the shocking account of slaughter and mayhem in that far-flung corner of his troubled realm. His own subjects butchered like pigs in their own homes, it was too appalling to contemplate. He cast his hands over his face, pinching his long nose between his fingers.

'As you wish, my dear,' he murmured.

News of Sir Abraham Bacon's new-found pre-eminence in Dorset was quickly communicated to the watchful staff at Prince Rupert's headquarters – where it caused some consternation among his few trusted officers and aides. Rupert sent an urgent dispatch to his brother before he had left for the North, but by the time it had reached Maurice outside Plymouth, the vacuum had been filled by Sir Abraham. A hitherto unknown justice's clerk promoted so rapidly? Rupert's shrewd staff knew it could only be the work of the interfering Queen.

By the time Maurice had sent one of his own colonels back to Penmethock to pick up the pieces, Bacon had been busy putting himself about – organizing repairs to the harbour and defences and recruiting new men into the bargain. Bacon had barely been able to restrain himself from laughing out loud as he apologized to Colonel Porthcurn, loudly lamenting his wasted journey.

'They caught the garrison with its breeches down, that's true enough, but I wager they will never do so again,' Bacon had told the scowling soldier, chuckling into his sleeve as Porthcurn stared grimly out to sea. There was little more to say.

His mistress the Queen had trumped the damned Princes at every turn!

Two weeks later, Prince Rupert had received word of the apparently unimportant slip at his camp in Shrewsbury. Immediately aware he had been outmanoeuvred over the command at

Penmethock, the Prince wasn't about to allow the Queen the satisfaction of a bloodless victory! The damned harridan might have succeeded in installing one of her repulsive toadies in place of one of Maurice's trusted officers, but there were many such commands about the country, and countless commanders ready to take the responsibility for them.

Maurice had sent his brother a copy of Colonel Porthcurn's preliminary report over the massacre at Penmethock, a report in which Rupert was intrigued to discover the names of Hugo Telling and Bella Morrison.

Names which the allegedly thick-skinned Prince knew only too well!

Rather than being completely impervious to the idle gossip of the camp (as both Royalist and Roundhead news-sheets solemnly maintained), Rupert was in fact alive to every shade of rumour and fancy, keenly aware of the importance of maintaining an intelligence operation to balance the Queen's. He knew his own tenure at his uncle's court depended primarily on his skill on the field of battle, but he was not the uninformed oaf the Queen and her cronies made him out to be.

Prince Rupert was as capable in a corner as he was in a cavalry charge, well aware of the risk Captain Telling and his damned sweetheart posed to his spotless reputation. They had witnessed some (if not all) of his own dealings in the woods outside Gloucester that night, and by God he didn't mean to leave them lying around – ready to go off like a dragoon's pistol if they weren't properly watched.

While he had been busy recruiting at Shrewsbury, the surprisingly subtle warlord had also received a short, coded note from a certain lady at the court, a brief entreaty warning him that the wretched Morrison girl had recently been placed in her own household – without any reasonable explanation. It wasn't as if the girl was good company – she could neither sew, play, nor entertain in any other way. It appeared she had been placed in her household solely to watch out for any interplay between her and the absent Prince.

Interplay which might be reported back to the jealous Queen, with dire consequences for Rupert and his highly cherished honour.

He still harboured ambitions to high command in the West. It was no secret around the court he had deeply resented the fact he had not received the governorship of Bristol the previous summer. He had taken the place from the Roundheads, after all! Instead of awarding Rupert's unquestioned bravery, the King had intended to present the keys of Bristol to the Marquis of Hertford.

The squabbling parties had finally agreed a compromise, and chosen Sir Ralph Hopton as Governor, but not before everybody's feathers had been more than usually ruffled.

Perhaps the girl's rogue of a father might be useful after all – especially if, as he suspected, the turncoat's daughter had been enlisted by the Queen. She wouldn't do Her Majesty much service, if she was being spied on by her own father. They might even be able to feed Morrison with false information to be passed on (in the strictest confidence) to his daughter, knowing it would eventually be reported to the Queen. Rupert had allowed himself a small smile as he contemplated such a ploy. Playing the Queen as she played so many foolish fish about the land. He had immediately ordered a new commission be drawn up for the turncoat merchant, appointing him colonel in chief of a regiment of foot to be raised in the King's name. That should keep Gilbert Morrison busy for a while – busy about Rupert's work.

And so it was that the terrified fugitives from the massacre at Penmethock found their whole lives turned upside down by strangers, their miserable destinies decided by the most powerful in the land.

BLIND MAN'S MOOR,

DORSET

Sir Gilbert Morrison could hardly bear to look at his son any more. Jamie, his own poor daft-headed lad, had landed his family in more scrapes than the merchant cared to remember. The boy had come back from Roundway without a scratch, but he had left his wits on the battlefield with the dead and the dying. He had been quite cracked up ever since, coming within an ace of getting them all shot back at Chipping Marleward. His haphazard behaviour during their subsequent exile in Dorset had cost poor Anneliese her life. Sir Gilbert liked to think of himself as a hard-hearted sort of fellow who put business first and friends afterwards, but the girl's squalid death in the dusty road overlooking Penmethock had seared his vitals, robbed the jolly gentleman of his extravagant good humour. What had those rogues been thinking of, taking pot-shots at the poor maid as she rushed to rescue his mindless dolt of a son? Terrified the renegades would harm the lad, she had flung herself under their muskets, an act of selfless devotion for which she had paid with her young life.

It was enough to make a fellow weep.

It was especially galling to Sir Gilbert, silently watching the boy she had saved frolic about the courtyard like a carefree five-year-old, as blissfully unaware as ever. Jamie had not registered the fact that his devoted nurse had gone for good, and would often look up from his soup and enquire where she had got to.

The merchant sighed and glanced guiltily at his brother Maynard, slouching on the step beside him with a stone jar between his bony red knees.

The miller had also paid the price for aiding and abetting their escape from Chipping Marleward, hiding the family away from the angry Royalist authorities. Sir Gilbert had needed a hideout, well away from prying eyes, and Maynard's isolated mill on Blind Man's Moor had seemed the obvious destination. Miller Morrison hadn't exactly relished the unexpected reunion. By Christ, he hadn't seen Gilbert since his poor wife had died going on fifteen years previously, and they had never been what you might call close.

Well, they were close enough now, by God. Brothers in exile if not in arms. Maynard was in it up to his wrinkled neck, as guilty as Gilbert of God knew what. Murdering dragoons, fleeing the King's justice, sparking the appalling bloodbath down the road at Penmethock ... Miller Morrison would hang, the same as his brother, if His Majesty's men ever caught up with them again.

And they couldn't throw themselves on the mercy of the rebels in London – Sir Gilbert was as much a wanted man at Whitehall as he was at Oxford. The civil war had split the country down the middle, leaving fugitives like the Morrisons to tread a precarious knife-edge between the embattled forces. One slip and ... it was all too terrible to contemplate.

Miller Morrison stirred beside him, took another long pull at the chipped stone jar, and handed the cider over to his brooding brother.

'They'll not be expecting us back in this neighbourhood,' Sir Gilbert thought aloud, taking the jar on his little finger and swinging it towards his moist mouth. The miller shook his head, watching young Jamie gambol about the yard on his long be-ribboned legs.

'You don't sound too convinced, Gilbert,' his brother observed, as his daft nephew began to dance a merry Springle Ring around the courtyard, delighting the flock of urchins who had turned out to watch him play the fool.

Jamie played the part only too well.

*

It was Sir Gilbert's idea, of course. Dressing Jamie up like a travelling jester in a bid to give the authorities the slip. The cunning costume the merchant had improvised for his delighted son had given endless amusement to the village children, and brought the curious workmen in from the surrounding fields to see what the commotion was about. Jamie's threadbare disguise consisted of a tired old sheet with a hole in the middle for his head. The grubby calico was torn into a hundred knotted strips and wound about with lengths of coloured wool and twine, creating a gaudy skirt which whirled and whipped around his thin shanks as he danced and played. As well as his coat of many colours Jamie wore a country crown of old leaves and twined twigs. They braided his unkempt hair into two stiff horns and hung a necklace of chiming bells (bought from a passing tinker for threepence) around his bare throat.

Jamie was as daft as a mummer, why not dress him up as one?

Sir Gilbert shook his head as his son cavorted in front of the screaming children, glumly congratulating himself that his cunning strategy seemed to work so well. Nobody would notice poor Jamie, dressed up amongst a band of strolling players. It was an exquisite ruse, one of the best ideas the resourceful merchant had come up with in a twelvemonth, but the very fact Jamie was so suited to the role robbed Sir Gilbert of the pleasure of its invention. Still, these were trying times for everybody. He couldn't afford to let sentimentality get in the way of survival.

Instead of trying to sneak between the counties like overweight foxes, they would march into every village along their way to the brazen fanfare of a cheap brass trumpet (also acquired from the well-equipped tinker). Rather than slink about at midnight – stealing scraps from the refuse heaps – he would march into a town at dawn, his greasepaint make-up serving as his cloak of disguise, aye, and passing the hat round to collect a few pennies for their stay.

Well, it wouldn't do to perform for nothing, Sir Gilbert had reasoned. Players had to live, same as merchants and soldiers!

Nobody would recognize the turncoat merchant, dressed up as

an errant knight. Sir Gilbert made a first-rate Falstaff and a superlative Saucy Friar. His cadaverous clerk Algernon Starling made an all too convincing rat-catcher's apprentice and a creditable Richard III, while the morose miller played assorted fathers, thieves, and henchmen – the bumbling straight man to his brother's larger than life characterizations.

All Sir Gilbert's company lacked was a leading lady – a nice-looking wench to giggle and squirm in all the right places, to wriggle her bum in their spotty faces! There – all this role-playing had brought out the poet in him!

The merchant allowed himself a small grunt of satisfaction. They had made it this far, at least. Less than five miles from the Heaven-sent sanctuary of Maynard's Mill, but less than twenty from the wasp's nest of Penmethock. If Sir Gilbert's strolling players were going to be caught out anywhere, it would be here, where their faces were only too well known. He ran his finger over his face, examined the thick smear of make-up. It was running like slurry over his flushed features, turning the brave knight into a frightful corpse.

'Ah, we've got this far, Maynard. It's been a good forty miles from Poole.'

Maynard Morrison couldn't argue with that.

They had parted company with William Sparrow's depleted battalion in Wareham Forest, and quickly put as much territory as possible between themselves and the rebel fugitives. It wouldn't have done to get caught with Sparrow's renegades, not after the business at Penmethock. The four of them hid themselves away in a lonely inn near Stokeford for a few days, waiting for the weather to break and any pursuit to pass. When they had finally ventured out of doors, the roads had seemed deserted – the inclement weather keeping most decent folk at home – and so Sir Gilbert led them on, taking the byroads towards the coast. They decided to head for the nearest friendly hearth – Maynard Morrison's mill – to collect clothes and money and plan what to do next. Sir Gilbert, shocked and stunned by his narrow escapes, needed time to rest, to think of the best course. Surely the angry Royalists would have searched the mill by now? They would in all probability have sent riders up to Bristol to check the merchant's abandoned home and his temporarily idle warehouses. Perhaps their long march *towards* Poole had thrown the vengeful dragoons off their tracks, convinced them the fugitives had taken refuge in the Parliamentary outpost?

There was one other major advantage returning to Maynard's Mill rather than Bristol. It was only a short step from the coast, a friendly port where they might (if necessary) take ship away from the bitterly divided kingdom, spend a few months in France until the wretched war was over. Sir Gilbert had more than enough money for such a scheme. After all, there was no point in burying a hoard of gold beneath the nearest elm if you ended up swinging from one of the branches!

'It's been getting on a fortnight, brother. They'll have other fish to fry by now,' Sir Gilbert encouraged doubtfully. 'And besides, I'm beginning to warm to this travelling theatre lark,' the merchant went on, looking on the bright side once more. 'Why, if we can only persuade young Mary to throw in her lot with us, we'll have a regular touring company! She's always been a looker, that one,' the avuncular merchant remembered fondly.

'Aye, she's a comely lass and no mistake. But she's about to calve down, brother, in case you've forgotten. That's why her major friend gave you all that money, to see her right,' the miller reminded him. 'I can't imagine she'll be ready for too many roles besides motherhood, not just yet.'

Sir Gilbert glanced at his shrewd brother, gave the worried miller an encouraging smile.

'Ah, you always were a sharp lad, Maynard. But you needn't trouble yourself, I mean to give Mary that money, aye, every penny.'

'I should think so too. He saved your bacon for you, that Sparrow fellow, the least you can do is get the money to his, er, wife.'

Sir Gilbert closed his eyes and silently reckoned how much he could lay his hands on at that moment. Cash, you see. It didn't grow from seed.

'I'll follow that girl to the ends of the earth if necessary,' the merchant lied. 'She won't go without, nor the babe.'

Mary Keziah staggered to the shutter and held herself upright while she swallowed a good lungful of fresh air. Mrs Pride was a caring midwife – she had been an absolute angel during Mary's long confinement – but she didn't hold with mothers-to-be hanging out of the windows.

'You'll catch your death, girl, with all the windies open to the elements!' the loyal goodwife scolded, hurrying round the little house to close the shutters all over again. 'It's bitter outdoors, and that cloak's no thicker than my shift!'

Mary Keziah felt the babe in her belly react to the cold air by turning a slow somersault, held her hand over her bulging abdomen while the little horror made itself comfortable.

'That's it, you bugger, don't mind me,' she whispered. Where was the bloody father, that's what she wanted to know. Off gallivanting somewhere, no doubt. She hadn't seen William bloody Sparrow since the conception, and had saved a store of spicy advice in case the hulking soldier ever decided to put in an appearance.

Mary turned and waddled back to the roughly hewn table and chairs – poor old cast-offs which passed as Mrs Pride's best furniture. The goodwife had kept house for Miller Morrison for years, but had clearly not prospered from the service. Just like his niggardly brother, Mary Keziah imagined. Happy enough to see you break your back over his flags, but more than reluctant to part with a penny for it. She dragged the chair back, held the table, and lowered herself into the splintered seat. If she got any fatter the wretched thing would collapse on her, and then where would she be? Flat on her back in a tumbledown cottage, miles out on the lonely moor. She felt a momentary twinge of concern, so far away from any help. What if something happened to Mrs Pride? She couldn't find her way back to the village in this condition! She had nearly killed herself walking here in the first place.

Still, freedom on the moor was a sight better than sharing Miss Bella's ordeal down at Penmethock. Mary thanked God she hadn't been caught with the rest of them, marched off to Black Bob's rat-infested prison.

If she'd been thrown in that hellish hole the babe would be dead by now, and so, in all probability, would she.

Mary Keziah massaged her belly, thought back to that bitterly cold day the previous autumn when her mistress Bella had left the mill to marry her sweetheart, Mr No Account Telling. Miss Bella hadn't been well pleased by the rather hastily laid wedding arrangements, and had been unusually short with her heavily pregnant maid as they took Miller Morrison's dog cart to the church.

'Oh, Mary, I swear you're taking up as much room as my father! Can't you squeeze yourself over a little?'

Mary, cold and uncomfortable herself, was in no mood for Bella's wisecracks or her furiously jabbing elbow, and demanded to be let down from the cramped coach that instant.

The angry descent certainly saved her baby's life.

Her haughty mistress continued the journey, arrived at the church, and was promptly captured by a party of Royalist dragoons who must have somehow tracked them down from Bristol. Mary and Mrs Pride hid themselves behind a wall as the hooting dragoons rode out with their ashen-faced prisoners, shouting and catcalling to wake the dead lying in the narrow, stony churchyard behind them.

Mrs Pride, terrified out of her wits by the unexpected turn of events, took the girl back to the mill, and thence to her own cottage two miles further out on the desolate moor. There was little else to do other than sit there and wait, with Mrs Pride making occasional forays over to the mill to see if the prisoners had been released (or otherwise disposed of).

She eventually bumped into one of the millhands, and listened in horror to the man's fantastical story of pirates, massacres, and bloody revenge. The millhand described (in particularly vivid detail) Miss Bella's trial and the subsequent slaughter at Penmethock Assizes. The Royalist authorities were left hopping mad at the bloody massacre, but their quarry apparently fled to the east, and were believed to have flung themselves into Poole.

Mrs Pride's informant was not specific as to the identity of these fortunate survivors, and unable to hazard a guess whether Bella, Hugo, Miller Morrison, or old Sir Gilbert escaped the massacre in the village.

And so they waited. And waited. And waited.

Mary must have dozed off at the table – laying her tired head on her warm forearm – because the next thing she knew the cottage door had swung open, filling the noisome hovel with blinding white sunlight. She threw her arm across her eyes, squinted at the large shadow in the doorway. Her heart leapt, jogging the dozing babe into a series of agonizing backflips.

'Mary, girl? Is it you?'

Mary Keziah pushed the chair back, clutching her belly as a nightmare vision loomed out of the light. A great troll in scaly armour, its fierce face distorted in rage, eyes dripping black gore.

'Mary, don't you recognize me?'

If she'd been the other way inclined, the poor pregnant maid would have crossed herself. Instead she staggered back from the table, an incoherent moan escaping from her constricted throat. What fiend of hell was this? What wild man of the moor had come to grab her? Drag her down to hellfire for all her sins!

'It's me, you daft cow. Gilbert Morrison!'

*

195

Mrs Pride dropped her packages and barged past the dumbstruck merchant, fell to her knees beside the groaning girl. She had completely fainted away, folding her bulky belly about Mrs Pride's threadbare chair like an overweight acrobat. The fall alone might have killed the baby – and the shock of coming face to face with Sir Gilbert Morrison wearing half an inch of stage make-up would no doubt be more than enough to account for its poor mother. The flabbergasted knight stepped back from the table, glaring down at the muttering serving woman and her unconscious charge, looking from one to the other in red-faced consternation.

'Well, it wasn't my fault!' he declared. 'What's up with her? Fainting away like a virgin in a cathouse! It's only me,' the heavily made up merchant complained, alarmed by Mary's deathly pallor, the thin blue lines of her lips. Mary groaned like an old horse at the knackers, a deep, resonant noise you wouldn't have expected to hear from a mere slip of a girl – pregnant or not!

'What d'you think's up with her?' Mrs Pride called, shrill with worry. 'You damn near frightened *me* out of me wits, and I'm not eight months gone! Scaring folk with your mummery!' Mrs Pride scolded.

Miller Morrison poked his head around the door, studied the agitated tableau in bewilderment. Suddenly, Mary opened her eyes, her white hands flying to her bulging abdomen.

'The babe ... it's coming!' she hissed, grasping Mrs Pride's hand as she made a fearful reconnaissance of the girl's great belly. Mrs Pride held her back as she tried to sit up.

'Whoa, girl, don't you dare!'

Mary closed her eyes and ground her teeth, doubling up on her side as another contraction gripped her abdomen. She panted like a dog and then let out a low whistle, lying sideways on the cold floor, her hot breath misting the stone flags.

'By Heaven, Mr Morrison, sir, don't just stand there catching flies! Fetch hot water, fetch needle and clean linen! Lord help us, she's going to calve down in my parlour!'

'What?' Morrison roared, gazing imploringly at his open-mouthed brother. Calve down? Here?

OXFORD

The Royalist press made Sir Richard Grenville a cause célè-bre, gleefully fastening on to his sensational story to encourage the war-weary masses in Oxford and elsewhere. The Roundhead news-sheets were equally vigorous, holding up the treacherous colonel as the most notorious scoundrel to infest the earth since Herod.

They pilloried the red-haired traitor, inventing half a dozen choice names for the dastardly rogue: Skellum was favourite, followed by Turk, Infidel, and Judas. The London mob, ready as ever to get its claws on somebody at a safe distance, burnt effigies of Grenville in the street and energetically looted what was left at his deserted headquarters.

Away at Oxford, His Majesty King Charles was delighted to welcome the cunning fox to his capital, and to add an experienced troop of horse to his army at the same time.

His rather more sober-minded staff officers, however, knew it was a drop in the ocean, an insignificant fraction of the numbers the King needed to maintain his war on Parliament. The rebels could count on the services of no less than five full-strength field armies – those of Essex, Manchester, Fairfax, Waller, and the Covenanting Scots. As well as these well-established and comparatively well-paid formations, Parliament had recruited numerous regional forces varying in size from a few hundred to several thousand. They might not always be equipped with the latest arms or officered by experts, but they were useful enough when it came to taking control of their own particular neighbourhoods.

Although the King had cleared the West Country and maintained a tolerable advantage in Wales and the North, he simply could not keep pace with the fearful progress of the rebellion which had eaten up his realm for going on two years. Not even his nephew – the great Rupert himself – could be in a dozen places at once, and the moment his weary fire brigade marched away to some distant conflagration, fresh fires broke out in their rear.

Twenty thousand Scots entering the war for the Parliament had tipped what little balance had existed that winter, given the rebels a distinct advantage in numbers as well as the undoubted domination of commerce and trade. Parliament had always been economically more capable of waging war than the King; now it seemed to possess the manpower it required to turn its financial dominance into military pre-eminence.

Nowhere was the King's chronic shortage of men more evident than in the brutal cockpit of the Midlands. Here rival towns and garrisons just a few miles apart jostled for control of the surrounding countryside, each battling colony at another's throat. Garrisons changed hands with monotonous regularity, but to the struggling farmers and hungry villagers roundabout every soldier seemed identical: filthy, back-stabbing robbers come to devour their foodstuffs, drink their beer, interfere with their women, and make sport with their goods.

It was into this hellish landscape of burning valleys and sacked townships that the King dispatched Rupert, charging the irresistible Prince with securing the Midlands and saving the North. But every foot soldier he possessed had already been dispatched to the South-east as reinforcement for Lord Hopton, and there were precious few cavalry left in Oxford. It was for this reason Rupert departed with a flying column of horse, dragoons, and foot – little more than a reinforced bodyguard, rather than an all-conquering army. To raise such a force he would need to rob Peter to pay Paul, weakening half a hundred garrisons in order to give himself an effective army. Rupert took men from manor house wall and earth fort, from prison, church, and backwater encampment and set them marching behind his dreaded black and blue banner.

Sir Richard Grenville's famous defection sent shock waves throughout the land, news of his insolent coup quickly reaching Hugo Telling's lonely outpost up in dank and dreary Worcestershire. The morose captain had been kicking his heels for weeks, he and a tribe of fellow reformadoes searching for men they might command once more.

Without common soldiers the unemployed officers were little better than a pack of snarling hounds, forever yapping and snapping at one another in their wine-stained finery. Rupert's plan was to use them as the kernel of a new army, building a troop of recruits around each superannuated officer. It was high time they earned their wages – God knew they cost enough to keep. Every beardless lieutenant, dandified cornet, and boorish captain drew full pay whether or not he had a company to call his own. The maintenance of such a large number of reformadoes was yet another ruinous drain on the King's finances, already desperately stretched by the bitter demands of his warlords.

Rupert, warlord in chief of all the King's forces, had planned his spring campaign with considerable care, dispatching a whole flock of messengers ahead of his flying column to warn the local commanders to assemble every spare man and musket for his new Midlands army. He then marched to Worcester and on to Shrewsbury, where he set up his headquarters, drilled the new recruits and waited for his roving officers to bring in new men.

Hugo was exhilarated to be marching behind the Prince once more, another careless Cavalier in his colourful cavalcade. The peacock officers were decked out in the finest velvet and lace, brilliant taffeta and silks, which seemed to overawe the suspicious country folk. The noisy, boisterous column seemed to dazzle its rather more sober opponents and they had been allowed to roam at will by the lurking Roundhead patrols. No enemy squadron dared bar the Prince's path, that was for sure.

Hugo eagerly expected to be in action within days of their arrival, but instead of the bloody battle he had anticipated, Telling's troop was sent away from the main column, ordered out into the lush green Vale of Evesham to collect supplies and bring in the outlying garrisons of several insignificant strongholds: Flood Fort, Crippletree Castle, and Bernham Manor. The restless captain bitterly resented his tedious commission, surely a straightforward enough job for one of the fat-bellied staff officers who seemed to swarm about the camps. Hugo craved another chance to prove himself before the imperious Prince, yearned for the opportunity of riding into battle with Rupert's fantastically splendid Lifeguard. The Sacred Band of blue-blooded Cavaliers would have gladly lain down their lives for their chief, followed him into the pits of hell with a smile on their faces and a jest for the devil himself.

But the thoughtful chevalier was bitterly aware he hadn't earned his place – yet. He had been promoted into the elite troop in order that Rupert might keep an eye on a potential troublemaker, not because the dreaded Prince valued his fighting capabilities. Hugo knew he was only there on sufferance – because he had been in the right place at the wrong time.

The entire camp was talking about Grenville's shocking defection, praising the veteran cavalryman's martial skill. Rumour had swollen the size of his small troop and trebled its achievement. He hadn't brought forty men over, it was nearer four hundred! He hadn't escaped with £600 in Roundhead gold, he had snatched the entire exchequer and loaded it about the Lord Mayor of London's best coach into the bargain! Hugo shook his head, refusing to be carried away by the foolish reports. He knew full well the type of scoundrels who wrote these news-sheets, the lying, impious worms who earned their bread scribbling the vicious doggerel. Aye, and he had met Grenville's type before and all.

Rakes and whoremasters like that fat baggage Clavincale back at Gloucester!

His fellow officers looked around in surprise as Hugo screwed the journal into a ball and threw it out of the wet tent flap with a fearsome scowl.

'What's afoot, Telling? Not jealous of a little competition, are you? Sir Richard's said to be one of the finest cavalry commanders in the country, we're damned lucky to get him back!'

Hugo rolled his eyes at the tipsy cornet.

'Nonsense. He's deserted once and will in all probability do so again. I've met his sort before,' he said grimly. 'Whoremongers and rogues the lot of them,' he exclaimed hotly. 'If I was the King I should send him as far away as possible, I would want nothing to do with scoundrels like that!'

'He's just back from Ireland, is that far enough?' Cornet Frederick Bent laughed, taking another swig from a looted stone jar of strong cider. The merry cornet's comrades giggled, casting wary glances at their melancholic companion. He was an odd fish, that Telling – more a Puritan than a piss-head. Perhaps it was the influence of that bewitching wife of his, that fiendish little honeyblob Bella they had all heard so much about. Fancy leaving a little flirt-gill like her back in Oxford!

'Ah, cut him some slack, Telling, he's just spent a month or two with those privy-sneaking turds at Whitehall! I would have thought he deserved a few weeks' grace, aye, and as many whores as he likes!'

BERNHAM MANOR, EVESHAM,

10 MARCH 1644

The muddy River Skew seemed to flow by fits and starts, running like treacle between steep red banks one moment, and then abruptly changing tack to chatter around mossy boulders in some willow-enclosed gulley. The not-quite river was one of the few recognizable features of the valley, the coiling tributary of the Avon leading into a range of round-backed hills. Somewhere at the far end of the deserted valley was the last of Telling's destinations, Bernham Manor, home of Sir George Winter, presently serving in Lord Gerard's army up on the Welsh marches.

Telling surveyed the bare grey heights, the clay slopes drenched by successive curtains of fine rain.

What a worthless outpost! Hugo didn't imagine the hills would support a squad of half-starved sheep, let alone a garrison of roving horsemen. A garrison he had been instructed to reduce by half to provide manpower for his commander's slowly forming army. Rupert had lent him half a dozen of the least likely-looking reformadoes and a squad of ill-mounted misfits to complete his thankless assignment – a questionable core on which to build a regiment, but orders were orders.

The common men were for the most part sour-faced northerners who conversed in a local dialect so broad as to defy understanding. They looked as if they had spent rather too long in the rear, panting as hard as their horses as the recruiting party followed the Skew into the deserted valley. As far as Telling could make out, they were no more impressed by their commission than he was, cursing the road, the weather, and the arrogant Prince himself.

'Comes oop 'ere like Christ come t' cleanse temple,' Cairnth-waite complained, the gloomy Yorkshireman urging his shaggy cob along the rough track they were following. 'Wa gen'uls a plenny, wi'out Jee'mens like 'im as puttin' 'is 'ook in.'

Telling scowled at the crop-haired recruit, a candle maker by trade who seemed to have lost his way and joined the Royalists by mistake. He seemed better cut out for the army on the other side of the hill.

'There's no officer in the country to stand comparison with His Highness,' Hugo said haughtily. 'On their side or ours.'

The glum troop rode on in silence, raising their eyebrows behind this foppish southern whippersnapper they had been saddled with. They had been in arms longer than he had, and played their part in half a dozen bitter actions. This posturing candle-waster went on as if he was the only man present to have drawn a sword in anger!

'Prince Rupert is the only general the King commands who stands the slightest chance of holding the North,' Telling went on, echoing his master's arrogant indifference – totally unaware of the effect he was having on his followers. 'He is presently collecting his strength, when he has enough, he'll show who is cock o' the north!'

His unruly troop bridled at this typical London arrogance. They might not be dandified Cavaliers in fancy hats and feathers, but they had fought long and hard, following the loyal Northern lords into battles every bit as grim as their southern counterparts'. They cast knowing glances at one another, shaking their unwashed heads at Telling's ill-informed assumptions.

The rain finally gave in, or at least stopped long enough for them to get their bearings, standing in their stirrups at the top of the next ridge. The steep-sided valley below them was studded with small farms surrounded by busy patchwork fields. There were a few sheep grazing the steeper hillsides, but not a single cow or horse in sight. Telling studied the dismal scene through his glass, bringing the borrowed instrument about to rest on a starkly built mansion house. The grey pile was every bit as uninviting as its surroundings, a square-built barn surrounded by deep red roadways. Hugo swung the glass back, realized the gouged workings were trenches, partially flooded zigzags radiating from the great house like the spokes of a broken wheel.

'Bernham Hall,' Corporal Cairnthwaite informed him, nodding his inexpertly razored head at the lonely outpost. 'T'other mob booggered off, like, when t'rains came. Filled 'em's 'oles all in agin,' he reported in his barely comprehensible dialect.

Telling licked his lips. The fortified house reminded him sharply of Kilmersden Hall, the once wealthy country seat in Somerset where he had first met Bella. He wondered for a moment how she was, stuck back at Oxford like a pullet in a fox den, pretty prey to the terrifying Queen.

The fretful captain suppressed a sigh and led the patrol on down the hill, into the narrow silver-green valley. The road ran away from the river now, straight across the deserted fields: a deep duckweed ditch to either side, dotted here and there with the decaying detritus of war. A smashed robinet, its narrow black barrel split and sooty. Disembowelled barrels with rusty hoops, broken-spined carts and slashed belts. Telling gazed at the miserable evidence of the weary war, brought his horse to a halt beneath a lone oak. Half the branches had been shot away and burnt as if it had been struck by successive blasts of lightning. The last sound bough was swaying and creaking under the weight of a brace of purple-shanked corpses. Their mud-splattered legs were scored white where their own hot urine had cut channels through the grime, their filthy feet turning and twisting in the moist breeze. They had been hung in their shirts, rough saffron sacks to which their assassins had pinned a scrawled warning Telling had to squint to make out.

'They be Tillier's Irish boys, straight off t'boat up Chesser way,' Cairnthwaite commented, wiping his nose along his sleeve as he contemplated his murdered comrades. Telling blinked up at the ghastly puppets, suspended from the oak by filthy scraps of hemp as if they hadn't even warranted a decent length of rope.

'Who did this? Whose men were they?'

'They must 'ave got snagged t'other week outside 'ouse. Arbright's work.'

Telling had been told Major Simon Arbright was the principal Roundhead commander in the area, a minor squire from the far side of the valley who had taken to war – or this brand of war at least – like a duck to water.

'Surely they must have been thieves, looters or suchlike? To warrant such summary barbarity?' Telling was no stranger to casual atrocity, but the sight of the hanged men had quite unnerved him. It was such a miserable place to die, a lone oak in a wheatfield.

'It's nowt to get fagged over, Cap' Telling, sir,' Cairnthwaite shrugged. 'We gave 'em worse, when we burned down 'is 'ouse and all.'

Telling peered at the morose northerner as if he had just wormed his way out of the tree trunk.

His first taste of warfare in the Midlands left a bitter afterburn in his mouth, a brassy tang he could taste all the way up to the house. The house presently held for the King by Caroline, Lady Winter.

'Henrietta Maria!' Telling bawled the word of the day across the wasteland outside the house, waited a moment while the defenders satisfied themselves as to the patrol's allegiance. After a quick conference the musketeers at the barricade warily waved them forward. Hugo was uncomfortably aware he was being watched as he led the wet patrol into the network of refuse-strewn trenches outside the once proud house. Half a dozen musket barrels protruded above the woolsack defences Lady Winter had installed before her bullet-pocked doorway. The alert sentinels peered out at their soggy saviours, watching out for any last-minute trickery, some ruse concocted by that bastard Arbright. The bedraggled Cavaliers dismounted and led their beasts through the filthy siege lines. Telling studied the ransacked works, full of every description of military and domestic trash. Hunks of mouldy bread, discarded shoes and clothing, and even bloody dressings had been scattered about, evidence of the rather abrupt departure of the Roundhead owners. The red earth had been scored by deep wheel ruts where the small besieging party had dragged up a culverin. Fortunately for the defenders the piece had only fired one or two shots – enough to remove a fluted pillar and most of a curtain wall and smash one of the ground-floor rooms behind but not sufficient to undermine the bravely held defences.

Heads began to appear above the apparently unscathed barricade, and a gaggle of sooty faced defenders appeared, waving the strangers forward over the abandoned obstacles.

'Thank God you're here,' a wounded youngster called, hurrying out of a woolsack-packed sally-port to help Telling drag his horse into the eyesore courtyard. 'Another six shots and we would have been at their mercy!'

The bandaged boy turned out to be Thomas Winter, thirteen-year-old son of the owner, Sir George Winter. The youngster bustled about fetching wine and refreshments out to the newcomers, eager to show off his youthful authority and the deep gash across his forehead where he had been clipped by a piece of debris. His wealthy father had already poured blood and money into the King's cause, fortifying his house and setting about his rebellious neighbours – old Arbright the mill owner in particular. Sir George had raised a troop of horse earlier in the war, and had recently taken them off to join Lord Gerard's army operating in the Welsh marches.

Their absence had not gone unnoticed, however.

Arbright – the local Roundhead commander – bore grudges against the Winters from before the war, and wasted no time in putting previous wrongs to right. The experienced brawler collected a few companies of foot and recruited a mob of ill-armed hill-folk, promising them the pick of the Winters' estate – once they had taken it. He marched his improvised army directly to Bernham Manor and set about digging trenches for his single heavy gun – borrowed for that express purpose from Warwick Castle. Sadly for the determined major, his men proved less than able engineers, and what little progress they made was undone by foul weather and determined resistance from the hall. Instead of the quick victory he had anticipated, Arbright was left stranded ten miles from his base with a force of surly infantry – at the mercy of roving columns of Royalist horsemen. His scouts warned of just such a force approaching up the valley – loudly estimating Telling's puny troop as being several hundred strong. Arbright wasted no time in packing up and going home, taking his spent force home by old sheep tracks through the hills.

Thomas, satisfied their welcome guests had been looked after for the present, made a quick reconnaissance of his ruined garden, peering out over the miserable waste his father's sworn rival had left behind. His eyes widened in horror and alarm as he spotted the dangling corpses Arbright left behind, pathetic scraps swinging from the mighty oak.

'Thomas, come away indoors at once.'

Telling looked up, startled by the woman's voice.

The lady of the house was a handsome if rather careworn Amazon, her naturally elegant bearing hardly troubled by her filthy gown and dishevelled hair. The resolute commander had rolled up her sleeves over her bloodstained arms, scored here and there with bloody thumbprints where some desperate musketeer had laid hold of his mistress in his extremity. Young Thomas retreated indoors as he had been instructed, leaving the awkward captain on the step.

'I thought you were Arbright, come to trick us out of our home,' the lady said huskily, wiping her hands on her equally splashed apron.

Hugo snatched off his hat and bowed at the soiled but dignified heroine, the brave housewife who had held the hall six nerve-racking days, losing half a dozen of her hard-pressed garrison in the bargain. The rest of the wounded had been laid out in the great hall, to groan and moan beneath Sir George's grand old dining table.

'Lady Winter, Captain Hugo Telling at your service. I bring you greetings and new orders from His Highness Prince Rupert,' Telling said formally, taking a rolled scroll from his doublet and brushing the worst of the damp creases from the smeared note. He handed it to the exhausted mistress of the house, noting her fingernails were chewed and broken, webbed with grime and congealed blood. Her sea-green eyes were misted, the whites heavily bloodshot and the sunken skin around them red and raw. She held his gaze for a moment as if she could read his mind, see herself reflected in his pitying gaze. Caroline Winter, the glory of the vale, reduced to rags and ashes by this blasted war.

Hugo blinked back at her. By Christ, she must have been a beauty, once, he thought.

'You have brought us reinforcements, of course,' she said, fingers straying to her cheek as if she was suddenly aware of the smeared powder and stray smuts.

'We are gathering an army for operations in the North, ma'am,' Telling said as kindly as he could. He watched her bloody fingers tear at the letter, her broken nails picking at the brittle wax seal. Lady Winter tore the order open, held it up to read the smeared script. Hugo watched her pale lips move silently, a flush of colour darken her dirty cheek.

'What foolishness is this?' she cried, turning her gaze back on the damp Cavalier. 'Fifty men? Where am I to find fifty men in this? I have not thirty left to hold the house,' she exclaimed, wiping her wrist across her mouth in agitation. The horrible anxieties of the previous week had stretched her nerves to breaking point and beyond – the gleeful enemy had swarmed and spoiled her husband's property, destroying anything they had been unable to carry off. Her home had been bombarded, her child terrified and hurt by the cruel detonations. The lands and gardens and outbuildings had been ransacked, livestock driven off and dead horses rolled in the pond. Her poor husband would not recognize the place he had entrusted her to keep! Lady Winter, who had maintained an iron hold over the men since the beginning of the siege, was reduced to tears, her weary body wracked by bitter sobs. Telling held his hand out, steadied her as she swooned towards the scuffed wall.

'There is no danger now, the enemy are away,' he encouraged, as poor Thomas began to show symptoms of a similarly severe breakdown.

'Aye, and they'll be back, back to finish the job and hang us all before we're done! My husband burned Arbright's lands and his mills before he left, burned him to the bone! I warned him this would happen,' she cried hoarsely, grabbing her son by his shoulders and wrenching him into the protection of her soiled skirts. Thomas pulled away, his wet eyes smoking with boyish fury.

'His Highness is in chronic need of manpower, if he is to carry out the commission he has been given by the King,' Hugo said apologetically.

'He can't have any men from us! We haven't enough to stop that braggart Arbright, let alone spare any for him!' Thomas cried, his beardless chin trembling with defiance.

Telling smiled weakly at the demoralized couple, standing forlorn in their wrecked hall, sooty musketeers gazing at them in apprehension. His orders were explicit and he dared not disobey. He was to gather as many men as possible from the three strongholds listed, and march them back to Evesham to await Rupert's pleasure. The Prince would decide where the new force would be directed.

'I am afraid His Highness was quite specific, ma'am. I am to collect every able-bodied man and march at once to Evesham.'

The bright-eyed matron tore the note in two and thrust the scraps into Hugo's chest.

'I shall refuse! He simply cannot have them! You see yourself the state of our affairs,' she declared hotly.

Telling tugged at his moustache. 'I am sorry, Lady Winter, the King himself has given His Highness supreme powers to override any existing commission. He has sent similar instructions to every garrison, large and small,' he replied, despising his unworthy instructions. What was the point in weakening every friendly garrison within a fifty-mile radius? Brave houses like this which had withstood the rebels for so long? They were handing the whole of Worcestershire to Parliament on a plate. Pitiful survivors like Lady Winter and her crying son were simply leftovers – to be scraped away as and when convenient. Telling shook his head, tortured by doubts.

But Rupert had to find a marching army from somewhere.

'But what about the house? We can't leave it to that rogue Arbright!' Lady Winter wailed.

Telling closed his eyes. Once again, Rupert's orders had been specific.

'Any house which cannot be left in an adequate posture of defence must be slighted to deny it to the enemy,' he recited dumbly.

It was a scorched earth tactic typical of the Prince. He had learnt war the hard way – in the endless struggles on the Continent his own father had helped ignite. He had no pity, he could not afford it.

'I am truly sorry ma'am, I have my orders, no matter how bitter they may be.'

The stub of candle he had been given by one of the tired old serving men had long since flickered down into its waxy pewter dish. A tiny glimmering flame which seemed about to extinguish itself at any moment, drown in the slick white ocean of itself. The pulsing illumination flickered and went out. Hugo stared at the glowing wick, the tiny point dying in a wisp of fragrant smoke. The room was silent save for Thomas's irregular breathing. The boy had volunteered to take the settle beside the boarded window, allowing the fantastic Cavalier the luxury of a decent bed. Hugo hadn't slept. It had been saddlecloth and cold floor since he had left Oxford, since he had torn himself away from that enormous feather bed and its decadently sprawled occupant. He remembered how Bella propped herself against the pillow with her knees under her chin, watching him dress as if she had never set eyes on a man before, her languid gaze both innocent and

erotic, knowing and knowing him. He suffered the same nauseat-
ing ache he had felt in his belly as he had looked back into the
room as he had finally closed the door on his silent sweetheart.

Hugo rubbed his tired eyes at the distressing memory.

Only the threat of dire punishment had drawn him away from
her side. He knew His Highness would not stand any more
unexplained absences on his part. He had been disgraced while
serving Maurice, and he had sworn to regain his reputation with
the taciturn German's even fiercer elder brother. Not even Bella
– luxuriantly warm and breathtakingly naked – had kept him
from his duty this time.

The old house creaked and rumbled to itself like an old ship
in dry dock. Hugo didn't know whether the night noises were the
cause of ancient foundations or rather more recent cannonballs.
He drew up his legs on the crumpled counterpane and rested his
tired head on the pillow, knowing he wouldn't sleep a wink that
night. A busy day tomorrow; a ten-mile ride back to the local
rendezvous at Evesham and a brief interview with the exacting
Rupert – if His Highness hadn't already taken himself off elsewhere, that was.

The sudden snicker from the other side of the room jolted the
dozing soldier from his slumbers in a blink. Hugo reached out to
the dresser and lifted the heavy horse-pistol from his tumbled
belongings, raised the loaded weapon in one fluid, well-practised
movement. He held his breath, tilting his head to sort the creaks
he had imagined from those he hadn't. Who in hell was it,
creeping about at this time of night? One of the garrison, sworn
to kill the insolent invader? One of Cairnthwaite's rebellious
riders out after his meagre purse? Hugo's eyes slowly adjusted to
the darkness, picked out a ghostly white shape beside the black
rectangle of the doorway. The phantasm swept across the room
towards him, towards the trembling pistol he had levelled in his
fist.

'Captain Telling!' Hugo closed his eyes, exhaled as quietly as
he could as he recognized the housewife's determined whisper.
Lady Winter floated into focus, her eyes as wide as an owl's in the

211

unfamiliar gloom of her son's chamber. She was dressed in nightgown and shawl, her auburn hair flowing loose over her trembling shoulders. Her freshly scrubbed skin looked almost translucent, the pearly sheen of an oyster cracked on a probing knife blade. Hugo sat up in alarm, wondering what on earth the woman could want at this time of night. Her pale face loomed out of the night above his bed, her generous mouth gathered into an unnatural smile.

'It is me, Caroline Winter,' she whispered unnecessarily, her white hands clutching the shawl beneath her extended neck, a cool marble statue come to life before his eyes.

Hugo nodded, laid the pistol back down on the dresser as quietly as he could.

'Lady Winter, whatever is the matter?' he croaked, his voice a forlorn whisper in the dead hush. Hugo couldn't hear any alarm bells or ragged shots in the night. He couldn't hear frightened horses or shouting sentinels or clanging bells or clattering pikes. He knew why she was here and he was glad, every inch of his thin frame tensely expectant.

Caroline Winter lifted his hand from the counterpane and sat down on the bed beside the captain, a doting nurse come to soothe away his frightful nightmares.

'I couldn't sleep . . . for thinking of my home, what you mean to do to us,' she said hoarsely.

Hugo swallowed, his throat as dry and cracked as his father's best tobacco.

'I know it's not your doing, I do not blame you, Captain,' she went on, leaning closer, peering into his staring eyes. 'But what are we to do, cast out onto the road, at the mercy of all our enemies?'

Hugo opened his mouth but nothing came out. He tried to sit up, but that only brought his hot mouth closer to her marble cheek and moist lips, and so he sat back again in anguished uncertainty. Was she pleading with him or seducing him or both? He hadn't felt such a fool since he had lost his virginity the previous summer, shagged daft by a red-haired doxy from the

camp. Matilda, her name was. He'd given her a shilling afterwards, but she had taken his hand and closed his fingers around
it. 'You can have that on the house, my dove.' Hugo squirmed on
the bed, wondered about clearing his throat but thought better
of it. He might wake Thomas, and God only knew what he would
think of this pretty picture. Caroline sighed in the darkness,
jabbed her palm at her eyes. He caught the tiny starburst glitter
of a tear in her eyes before she looked away from his reclining
figure. Hugo lifted his hand, touched her arm tenderly. She leapt
at the soft pressure of his fingers, but did not draw her arm away.
He heard her sob wretchedly.

'What are we to do?' she cried, huskily distressed by her
bewildering predicament. 'Where are we to go?'

'To Evesham and Worcester with the Prince. You won't be left
at Arbright's mercy,' Hugo reassured her, tracing the cold ridge
of her forearm with his index finger. He reached the bunched
material at her wrist, heard the minute rustle as she turned her
hand over, opened her palm. It was as hot and moist as if she had
brought a pan of coals to warm him.

'Damn you,' she said, closing her fist on his fingers.

PRINCE RUPERT'S HEADQUARTERS

OUTSIDE BRIDGNORTH, 15 MARCH 1644

H ugo couldn't tell whether he was suffering from saddle-
sores or bedsores – he'd hardly had a chance to get his
bearings let alone discover the cause of the angry rash
which had eaten up his groin and made every mile a wincing
nightmare. He could have sworn his privates were aflame, rubbed
raw by his cramped saddle all day, scratched and salted by the
alarmingly energetic Lady Winter at every available opportunity.
He had tried to examine himself while hidden behind a drooping dog rose a few miles back along the ridge, but his fearful
investigations were interrupted by the noisy arrival of a couple of
his swollen-bladdered troopers. The rogues spouted over the
brambles for what seemed like hours, obliging the distressed
cavalier to tuck himself away and limp back to his horse. Now he
was riding with his calico shirt tucked between his legs, in the
feeble hope he might spare himself further agonies as his wandering band approached Bridgnorth.

Bridgnorth! he thought sourly. He'd never been as far north
in his life.

He was on a journey into the unknown, right enough, cut loose
from his family and friends – thrust into the arms of a stranger
by conniving circumstance.

Hugo felt himself redden at the very thought of the wanton
stranger who had exploded into his world, turned his tumbling
fortunes upside down all over again. The fair-faced matron who
would blush and turn away at the very sound of his voice by day
and yet preyed on him like some gloating night beast through
the small hours of the morning.

It was as much as he could do to climb on his horse by the time Lady Winter had finished with him.

Hugo was no longer the blushing virgin who had ridden off to war the year before. He was as experienced as any of the dour old hands presently riding behind him, and could lay claim to a sweetheart whose bewitching charms had been discussed in detail around a thousand campfires. He knew all too well the grubby troopers would have given their right arms for a night with his Bella, for a chance to unpick her carelessly fastened bodice. Ah, he'd walloped the filthy rogues for even thinking such a thing, before now.

He had sampled her secrets, lost his mind between her fragrant thighs. They had steeplechased over the sheets, unlocking and releasing one another's passions until they had swooned in a dead faint.

He had never imagined there might be women on this earth more demanding than his Bella. Older, wiser, plainer women at that.

The thought he had betrayed his absent lover burned his heart just as the cramped saddle grated his raw groin. He closed his eyes, searched his aching brain for some explanation for his lamentable betrayal.

It wasn't as if he had been unable to resist Lady Winter's advances – he had simply felt sorry for her. She had been subjected to a hideous, possibly even deadly ordeal, with her husband away at the war which flowed to and fro over his own doorstep in his absence. If Sir George had been at home with Lady Winter instead of swanning about on the Welsh marches then nothing untoward would have occurred, Hugo reasoned. He was a man, a flesh and blood Cavalier, not some muttering Puritanical stinkfinger!

And besides all that, it would have been ungallant in the extreme to throw the wretched woman from his borrowed bed – to send the shamefaced creature back to her cold and lonely chambers with his indignant rejections ringing in her ears. What manner of man would have been capable of such cruelties? Giving

215

the poor woman a good rogering had been the least he could do, in her temporarily distressed circumstances. He had given her a shoulder to cry on, a comforting embrace when all her world had seemed about to collapse. By God, who on earth would have behaved differently? Where was the man who could have left an attractive housewife in such evident misery?

The well-used road led his motley band along the ridge overlooking the Severn valley, a patchwork plain of grassy meadows and clumped trees. The local farmers had dug numerous ditches and dykes in an effort to divert and restrain the rushing waters, but Hugo could still see large pools of flood water lapping beneath the lonely willow stands which marked the corner of each field.

The half-drowned meadows had been scoured by war, every town along the river garrisoned, every house held for one side or the other. The presence of such large numbers of opposing troops meant the local populace was more than usually at risk from bands of roving horsemen – hungry for their corn, their bread, their beer. They had been squeezed dry by callous collectors, particularly by the penniless Royalists who swarmed about their Midlands conquests despite the direst threats of court martial and summary execution for anybody caught looting.

As well as assembling an army from the splintered forces in the region, Prince Rupert had been charged with reorganizing the collection of the taxes and provisions which maintained the famished men, overhauling the entire Royalist war machine from Cheshire to Gloucestershire.

As the war entered its second summer, the King's counsellors had finally realized the frightful damage being caused by their headstrong local commanders. Hundreds of lords, generals, and colonels had encouraged wholesale looting to feed their forces, and their widespread depredations had sparked a vicious backlash against the King's cause, a backlash which threatened to undermine the success his ravenous armies were enjoying in battle. Parliament might not have had a general to match Rupert, but its

216

administrators were far more efficient, the collection and distribution of its apparently endless resources well organized and
effective. If at all possible, Parliament's troops paid cash for the
foodstuffs taken from the suffering country folk; if not, they used
chits which could be redeemed from the Roundhead war chest.

The villagers knew full well the papers they were given by the
King's men weren't worth a damn.

Stabilizing this dangerous situation would require massive will-
power and a properly organized exchequer. Troops would have
to be fed and clothed from properly collected funds – not
through free quarter on the hard-pressed populace. It was an
assignment which would have killed any mere mortal, reduced
the strongest to tears of frustrated rage. Rupert, however, seemed
to relish the challenge, taking the mind-numbing exercise in his
stride.

Hugo marvelled at the man's capacity – it was as if the Prince
believed he could win the war through his titanic efforts alone,
that he could bend the will of the entire country by his iron
example.

Less than a week earlier Prince Rupert had instructed Hugo
(and half a hundred young pups like him) to collect troops from
the outlying vales to join a general muster at Evesham. Now it
seemed the fiery Prince needed the weary soldiers fifty miles
away!

Hugo was already hanging with exhaustion, and he had only
covered a fraction of the ground his commander had. Hugo's
four-day march from Bernham Hall to the new rendezvous outside Bridgnorth was a mere detour in comparison to the epic
expeditions undertaken by the Prince. As far as Hugo could
gather from the hurrying messengers they met along the way, the
energetic Rupert had already ridden to Shrewsbury and then on
to Chester. He had hurtled through the north Midlands like a
flaming comet, sparking support for his uncle's cause in every
town and village, inspiring every garrison to greater efforts.

But now it appeared he had received an imperative order from
King Charles himself.

According to the breathless scouts, Newark – an important Royalist outpost on the River Trent – was under rigorous attack from a large and well-equipped Parliamentarian force.

Rupert's wide-ranging commission had been set aside at once, his urgent attention required in the East.

At last his mission was clear: to save Newark from the Roundheads.

'And where in God's name is Newark?' Hugo wanted to know, climbing down from his sweat-caked horse and handing the reins to his wraithlike groom. Joseph Thackray shrugged his shoulders. He hadn't got a clue where they had been, where they were, or where they were going for that matter. The pale-faced scarecrow stared at the bustling camp which had grown up overnight on the slopes below them, a sluggish sea of many-coloured coats shuffling between the occasional mouldy tent and broken-down cart. The noise was terrible: shouted orders and hoarse laughter, whinnying horses and creaking wheels. Officers were barging their way through the crowds, trying to sort their men from the tangle of regiments and squadrons which had been so hastily assembled for Rupert's relief army.

Bridgnorth was a busy little town, divided down the middle by the swiftly flowing Severn. Grandly gabled houses had been built in a series of terraces up the steep slopes on either bank, and the horrified owners were gaping out of their leaded windows as more and more soldiers arrived from every point of the compass. The unexpected horde had already spilled out of the town and taken over the steep slopes above the river, and squadrons of cavalry had invaded the leaning wreck of the old Norman castle on the hill. Hundreds of musketeers could be seen clambering out of a fleet of riverboats of all shapes and sizes, hurrying up through the dumbstruck town to swell the noisy throng on the ridge.

'Newark? No ideer, Cap'n Telling, sir,' Thackray replied miserably. He had never seen such a concentration of men before, but he had been with the ragged Cavalier long enough to know such an assembly could only mean one thing: a bloody gurt battle.

Corporal Cairnthwaite slid down from his horse and stretched his legs, wrinkling his nose as he sampled the foul breeze blowing across the crammed camp.

'By 'eck, they smell like a pack o' fookin' fishwives!' he exclaimed, clutching his hat to his offended face. ''Appen they'll know we're coomin'!'

Hugo frowned at his sour-faced corporal, wondering if his observation wasn't a classic example of the pot calling the kettle black. He watched the rest of his newly acquired troop dismount on the sandy ridge above the crowded town, their horses bending their sweat-roped necks to tug at the sweet grass while their riders flopped down exhausted beside them. Behind the ragged cavalry came the sixty-odd foot soldiers he had enlisted along the way, a shambling mob of ruffians and stragglers in patched coats and holed boots carrying a bizarre assortment of agricultural tools, ancient billhooks and badly turned pikes. Bringing up the rear were a couple of ancient carts and Lady Winter's battered coach. Hugo could see her excited son standing amongst their hastily packed belongings stowed on the roof, shielding his eyes to survey the grand assembly. Hugo wandered down the track towards his new lover, making a pretence of inspecting the famished troops as he went. He looked up, caught Caroline's eye for a moment. She looked blankly back at him, and then climbed down from the overloaded coach and began brushing the worst of the ruckles from her travel-stained gown. Her tireless son swung himself down the muddy wheel and dashed through the stragglers for a better view of the noisy camp. He grinned excitedly at Hugo as he scampered past, anxious not to miss anything. His mother followed at a rather more sedate pace, casting a discreet glance over her shoulder before coming to a halt beside her twitching lover.

'So this is where they've hidden themselves. Why, if we had a fraction of these men at Bernham Hall there would have been no need of burning it to the ground,' she rasped, her moist eyes fixed on the busy hillside opposite their windy ridge.

Telling ran his tongue over his teeth, glancing behind him to make sure Cairnthwaite and the rest had moved safely out of earshot.

'Prince Rupert needs all these men and more, if he is to fulfil his mission from the King,' he said wearily. 'We've been through all this, I told you I had my orders . . .'

Lady Winter glanced sideways at the scowling youth.

'You forget yourself!' she exclaimed. 'You are the ravager and spoiler of my home, you turned me and my family out of doors, sir! Don't you think these people might find it a little unusual for us to be engaged in pleasant conversation at a time like this?' She lowered her voice. 'I have my reputation to think of, sir, if you haven't. You had best steer clear of me, until we're away from them,' she decreed.

Telling understood her first point, but was confused by the qualification. Away from them? What did she mean by that? Was she planning on riding behind his saddle all the way to Newark? He opened his mouth to enquire but she had already gathered up her skirts and stalked off after her son. Hugo turned about in time to see Cairnthwaite raise his eyebrows at one of his grinning cronies. They imagined she had given him a piece of her mind, cut the strutting turkey-cock short.

Exactly as the calculating Lady Winter had intended.

Hugo felt like a naughty schoolboy who had been caught scrumping, trailing behind the frowning matron as she picked her way down the muddy track toward the crowded town, losing herself in the great mob of men Rupert had brought together.

They were mostly musketeers, Hugo noted, with bulging snap sacks and swinging bandoliers, but precious little baggage to encumber them. The captain knew by their faces they were veterans all, hardbitten rogues who returned his inquisitive stares with interest. He stopped before one gang of green-coated bandits, annoyed by their impudent manner.

'Where's your commanding officer?' Hugo snorted, casting his furious eye over the grinning mob.

A curly headed devil in a fading green jacket looked blankly at him.

'He don't have the English, zor, fresh off the boat like the rest of his muckers,' his older comrade replied, lifting his greasy leather hat in mock courtesy. 'You'll get no zense from 'is lips, zor, unless you 'ev the Gaelic, and then, God knows, not much.' The wrinkled musketeer gave Telling a broad wink.

'Are you saying these men don't speak English?' It was bad enough ordering infantry about as it was! The jovial veteran nodded, his quick brown eyes twinkling merrily. 'That's why thems brought me over with 'em, zor, to pass yer orders on to 'em, bog-trotting scum they are, zor!'

'Translate orders in the middle of a battle?' Telling bleated, alarmed at this horrifying possibility. It was as much as he could do to penetrate the northern troopers' frightful dialects, let alone bloody Gaelic!

'Whose regiment is this?'

''Enry Tillier's, zor. Fresh off the boat from across the water, zor!'

Telling narrowed his eyes. 'But you're no Irisher!'

'Great 'eavens, no, zor! Zumzet born and bred, me.'

'Well, then. Perhaps you can direct me to the headquarters?'

'Ah, that I can, zor. You see that leanin' tower yonder?'

Ten minutes later Telling realized the rogue had been pulling his leg. For one thing, where had that damned strawhead learned Gaelic? Telling had heard it took years learning the basics of the old tongue, let alone mastering enough to order men in battle. For another, the outrageous directions he had been given by the winking rogue would have surely brought Telling straight back to Bernham Hall! The young captain tugged his hat back on and stalked off into the shambolic camp.

The grinning sergeant watched the young fool go, turned to his chuckling comrades.

'Gaelic! You'd best babble like a bog-trotter, next time you see that sorry fucker.'

'Cocky little bugger,' the dumb musketeer replied. 'What asparagus patch did they dig 'im up from?' One of the musketeers shook his head gloomily, peered up at his laughing colleagues.

'Ye shouldn't go makin' sport about us being Gaels,' he warned. 'Mayhap there'll be no comeback from a young buck like yer man there, but if t'other side as catches 'old of us, you'd as best forget ye ever set foot on that bastard isle!'

Sergeant Hobbs tilted his weather-ravaged head back to regard his fellow veteran with contempt.

'Catch 'old of us? They 'asn't got the ballocks to stand agin us, boy! Old pot-wallopers and bare-chinned boys? We'll shite all over 'em!'

The miserable musketeer shook his long head mournfully.

'It don't matter ye and I were Yeovil bred, Peter Hobbs. I tell ye this. If they catches up with us, ye'd best forget ye'r 'Enry Tillier's men. Say as ye'r King's Guard or Rupert's, mayhap, but not Tillier's. All we'll get from them buggers yonder is a length of rope, ye mark me well, boys.'

The younger men looked away, studied the bustling hillsides for a moment. And the chuckling stopped, for a while.

It was perhaps fortunate for Hugo he had been given directions by the pseudo-Irishmen of Henry Tillier's regiment, otherwise he might have arrived at Rupert's temporary headquarters five minutes earlier – in the middle of a rather unexpected and awkward reunion.

By the time he had barged and shoved his way through the seething mass of musketeers and dismounted cavalry, Lady Winter had already reached the collection of tents, carts, and coaches which made up Rupert's highly mobile base camp. Telling straightened his hat and coat and strode into the bustling nerve centre, recognizing Lady Winter's sky-blue gown amongst the press of buff coats and breastplates. The hitherto formidable matron was swooning in the arms of some bullfrog-throated brute of an officer. Clearly embarrassed, he was holding her at arm's length like a sack of salt fish. Telling closed his eyes, dreading the headstrong matron's intentions. Clearly she was on her way to press some complaint about his behaviour on the Prince, and had only been prevented from doing so by this over-zealous guard. Telling bristled up all over again, his quick temper rubbed as raw as his privates. Expose him as a wretch and adventurer, no doubt. The double-dealing whore!

He strode forward, elbowing his way past captains and colonels, corporals and cooks. Young Thomas Winter was clawing at the guard's breeches, trying to cleave his way between his swooning mother and the angry officer.

'Caroline, what on earth is it? What brings you here? Thomas, leave my leg alone, boy!'

Telling clenched his fists, glared at the sentinel, who peered back at him in bewilderment.

'They had to burn the house down! Miller Arbright would have got it else!' Thomas reported, tugging excitedly at his father's sword belt. Sir George Winter lifted his swooning wife in his arms, glanced about for some assistance. His eyes fell on the quaking Telling, who had come to a fragile halt a few yards short of the reunited family.

'Well, don't just stand there, man, lend us a hand!' Winter growled in a sibilant Midlands accent, raising his bristling white eyebrows at the shocked youth. Telling staggered forward and rested his hands on Lady Winter's arms.

'Get hold of her, sir, she's no featherweight, you know!' the red-faced colonel ordered, easing a formidable forearm under his wife's armpit and boosting her upright. Telling leaned in for all he was worth, averting his face from the cuckolded husband.

'By heck, Caroline, what ails tha? What's our Thomas bumpin' his gums about the house for?'

'They had to burn it down so as Arbright wouldn't get it, tell him, Captain,' Thomas called brightly, looking up at the distressed Cavalier for affirmation.

'Well? What's oop with house? Ye've never burned it down?' Colonel Winter enquired, peering over his wife's shoulder.

'Prince Rupert's orders were clear, sir,' Telling stammered. 'The garrison was needed here, and the house could not be left in a posture of defence,' he went on, straining to hold the muttering housewife between himself and the furious husband. Sir George narrowed his moist blue eyes, his generous lips pursed in concentration.

'Ye've burnt down Bernham Hall? Is that what you're sayin'?' he exclaimed, his florid features paling by the second. 'Ye've turned me and mine out on t'road?' he roared, beginning to realize the full extent of the disaster his wife had so miserably failed to report. Lady Winter groaned. Telling swallowed.

'I am sure there are arrangements, to be made, in this trying situation,' Telling whined. 'Prince Rupert's orders were clear.'

'Indeed they were!' Telling looked up sharply from behind the perfumed battlements of Lady Winter's shoulder, and saw to his everlasting relief that the champion in question had strode out of his tent to see what the commotion was about. Rupert's angry face was masked with soap, his opened shirt hanging damply from his partly-washed body.

'Your Highness. I am afraid . . .'

'YOU'RE AFRAID?' Sir George roared, shoving his forgotten wife out of his way to get at the scrawny Cavalier. Lady Winter sprawled in the mud with a startling curse.

'Gentlemen!' Rupert stepped neatly between the antagonists, holding nothing more than his bare-backed razor. Winter growled and panted, but didn't dare lay a finger on his commanding officer. 'Sir George, I am afraid my orders were precise. All garrisons which could not be maintained in an adequate state of defence were to be slighted. I regret your argument is with me, sir, not my messenger.'

Telling sighed with relief, glanced about the crowding ring of officers who had come to watch the fun. Lady Winter hauled herself to her feet, looked down at her ruined gown. Sir George tore his gaze from the Prince and stared at his miserable wife, the colour seeping back in to his drawn cheeks.

'Do not fret about your losses for a moment, sir,' Rupert went on in a strikingly unfamiliar tone. 'I will personally ensure you receive full recompense for your grievous losses suffered in my uncle's cause. Indeed, sir, the first decent house we take from the rebels will be yours, lock, stock and barrel. You have my personal word on it, sir.'

Sir George bowed his head and nodded stiffly. Rupert turned to the shabby Captain, gave Telling a sardonic grin. 'Captain Telling was obeying my order, sir, to the letter.' Hugo swallowed nervously. He could hardly believe his ears! Approval from Rupert? It was practically unheard of. 'It is I who must assume the responsibility for such instructions, however much we all regret them.' The Prince wiped his face on a cloth and tossed it to one of his orderlies.

'Perhaps I can offer you a glass, sir, in part payment of His Majesty's debt to you and your family.'

Sir George nodded dumbly, his hand resting on his young son's shoulder. Rupert smiled at the boy and then bowed to his muddy mother.

'Allow me to offer you the use of my personal quarters, ma'am, to refresh yourself after your trying journey. My officers and I are at your service, please do not hesitate to obtain any essentials you might presently be wanting.'

A new gown, for a start, Hugo thought smugly, highly pleased with the morning's work.

ROUGHTON VILLAGE, EAST
OF BRIDGNORTH,

16 MARCH 1644

Much to the relief of the good citizens of Bridgnorth, Rupert's unwelcome invaders didn't stay long enough to do more than ruffle a few civic feathers. No sooner had the last of his hastily summoned musketeers disembarked from their boats than the Prince was off again, force-marching his growing army towards Wolverhampton, and another rendezvous with his Midlands levies. All the weary soldiers left to mark their short stay was rubbish and refuse – trampled pastures and broken-down gates. Their steaming latrine pits were soon loud with swarming flies, a hazard which provoked an immediate storm of protest from offended landowners and prompted the Bridgnorth burghers to dispatch a dozen common labourers up the hill with shovel and lime to back-fill the stinking trenches. Apart from that, the good citizens counted themselves lucky to have hosted such a gathering without further distress.

Rupert's army went by the east gate, leaving a trail of debris behind them as they negotiated the long sandy ridge which led out of the town. Shoes and boots, worn out by long marches on poor roads, were cast off by the hundred along with torn clothing and broken weapons. Dead horses and broken-backed carts were rolled into the ditches along the way, the debris concentrated in filthy rings about the few rest camps Rupert allowed.

The Prince greeted further reinforcements on the march, fast-moving musketeers hurrying behind hastily raised squadrons of Northern horsemen. The Prince's personal Lifeguard, although somewhat depleted by the necessity of detaching so many experienced officers to stiffen the new troops, rode in a colourful but compact body about their chief, their horses devouring the miles as if they were riding to hounds on Aldbourne Chase and not negotiating a passage through the bitterly divided Midland shires.

Hugo, however, refused to be carried away by the all-pervading excitement generated by Rupert's lightning march – his earlier optimism had been soured by the careless flick of some pen-pushing staff officer. Much to his apprehension and disgust, Telling had not been allowed to rejoin the Prince's elite body-guard. He had instead been placed in temporary command of the very same horsemen he had helped raise back in the Vale of Evesham – forty-odd Midlanders who he struggled to compre-hend, let alone inspire for the coming battle.

To add insult to injury, the motley band had been brigaded in turn under the command of a noted and experienced cavalry commander from the Welsh marches – none other than Sir George Winter, cuckolded husband of Hugo's illicit lover Caroline.

The apparently arbitrary piece of administration left Telling fuming and fretting, worrying if the appointment was part of some sinister conspiracy against him. Perhaps somebody had gotten wind of his impetuous dalliances with Lady Winter, and had determined to place him in the older man's firing line. Maybe it had been Rupert's work all along – stirring trouble in a deliberate bid to rid himself of the troublesome captain.

Hugo couldn't believe the Prince would have allowed himself to employ such mean devices. For one thing he had expressly forbidden any such dangerous divisions among his officers. Their foolish dispute might spark an outright challenge which could backfire on the cuckolded husband and expose him to the ridicule of the camp. But a pistol ball in the back in the heat of battle was another matter, Hugo thought darkly. Who was to know who had fired the fatal shot?

The brooding Cavalier frowned, peered over his shoulder at the troop he had been appointed to command. Hugo squinted at every dusty, sweat-streaked face, wondering which one of the blathering jackdaws might have caught him out.

Corporal Cairnthwaite perhaps, grinning like the cat who had gotten the cream. Maybe his crow-faced crony George Sheedy. And then there was the sardonic youngster carrying the troop cornet – Frederick Bent, arrogantly assuming he might usurp Telling's captaincy.

Ah, it was no use fretting now, Hugo thought sourly. He had imagined he and Lady Winter had been the model of discretion during the march from Bernham Hall – restricting their liaisons to frenzied couplings well away in the surrounding woodlands, passionate clinches in a draughty shed beside a broad and fragrant bean field. They had whispered and planned every move, hidden themselves away from prying eyes before falling upon one another like half-starved leeches. Telling blinked at the all too vivid memory, irrationally irritated the urgent march had rather cut short their lovemaking.

Cornet Bent, who had urged his panting bay alongside Hugo's gelding, lifted his hat to swat the flies from his features, cursing the endless ride.

'He'll blow these horses beneath us, forcing the pace like this,' the former reformado complained. 'We won't be fit to charge flour sacks, not without a decent remount.'

Telling shrugged. 'But they won't be expecting us. Speed and surprise will count for a sight more than fresh horses,' he pointed out.

The anxious cornet was not about to be deflected by Telling's stern confidence.

'Fresh horses? What about the men? He sent those Irish down from Chester. You might as well plough with dogs as expect 'em to fight by the time we get to Newark! They reckon the great Gustavus himself only managed ten miles a day, Rupert seems bent on doubling it,' Bent complained, apparently anxious to demonstrate his knowledge of Continental warfare and its most noteworthy warlord.

'Gustavus had to wait for his foot and all those guns,' Telling argued. 'Rupert won't wait for anybody,' he theorized.

'Ah, he'll come unstuck one day with his mad gallops, you

mark my words,' Bent concluded, straightening the newly sewn troop cornet with an irritated flick of his wrist.

Hugo glanced at the morose rider, wondered if he might be the privy-sneaking rogue who had betrayed him. If he had been betrayed at all, that was. Bent didn't seem to be paying Hugo any particular attention, but then again you could never . . .

Telling looked up sharply as a messenger on a lathered black stallion galloped down the fast-moving column, his horse's hoofs putting up a cloud of choking dust and flying chips. The rider snatched off his hat, waved it at the apprehensive captain as if Hugo would divine his intelligence from hand signals alone.

'All troop commanders to report to Colonel Winter! He's up the road at the Live and Let Live, the inn at the crossroads there,' the panting messenger cried, struggling to check his charger's pace.

'What's up now?' Telling enquired. The rider tugged his horse about, settled his hat back on his head for a moment.

'We're being pushed out ahead of the main body to scout the road. This damn county's lousy with rebels, and the Jovial Tinker's never far.' The dusty lieutenant hawked and spat into the road.

Jovial Tinker? What was the fool rattling on about? Hugo tugged at his sparse moustache.

'Of course, you've never made his acquaintance, have you, not seein' as you're up from Oxford,' the young officer went on breezily. 'Major Fox, a damned braggart of a Roundhead, sir, and a vagabond to boot!' The lively lieutenant sighed heavily. 'But he's put down his pots and picked up a sword, and damn me if hasn't given us a few bangs in his time. That's why Sir George wants you to push out, in case he's lurking somewhere.'

Pushing ahead? Flushing out ambushes more like, Hugo thought angrily. Damn it all, *somebody* knew *something* about him and Caroline! He swallowed nervously, alarmed by an even deadlier possibility – what if Bella got to hear about his midnight excursions? The first week away from his own true love and he hadn't been able to resist Lady Winter's breathlessly paraded temptations. What would his mistress make of such repellent behaviour?

God's wounds, he'd rather face a regiment of Jovial bloody Tinkers than Bella when her blood was up!

'Ah, there you are. Telling, isn't it?' Sir George Winter was buckling himself into his armour, a red-faced manservant struggling to tug the leather belt which held it together around his bulging girth. Sir George was a heavily built but vigorously active man, his coppery cheeks flushed with the effort of confining his large, awkward body into a tightly fitted back and breast. The servant tugged the belt as tight as it would go and gave his master a familiar pat on the back.

'Safe as 'ouses, sir.'

'Good man, Porter.' Sir George held his arms out as the busy squire began to wind Sir George's bright blue sash about his waist, tugging the rich silk into a huge knot. The grand knight studied the nervous youth, stepping from one boot to the other in the doorway. In contrast to Sir George's coarse-complexioned finery, Telling had ridden out in a well-travelled grey suit edged with grim black borders. His once proud sash had faded to a deep russet to match his whiskers. He must have looked more like a Puritan than a Cavalier. Sir George seemed to think so anyway, giving the newcomer a sardonic smile.

'It seems I owe you an apology, sir,' he said gravely, allowing Porter to slip his leather baldric over his gleaming breastplate. 'You were acting under the strictest instructions of His Highness Prince Rupert when you burnt my house down, and of course no blame for my loss,' he said with peculiar emphasis, 'can possibly be attached to you. Do you accept my apology, Captain Telling?'

Hugo smiled weakly, nodded his head while trying to decide whether Sir George was aware of his deception. My loss? He meant the house, of course. His house or his honour.

'Good. I am anxious there should be no misunderstandings

between us, as such unseemly behaviour only serves to undermine the King's cause.'

Telling stared blankly at the older man, formidable enough in his burnished breastplate and bright silk. His buff coat was an inch thick, scarred and burnt about the arms and shoulders, a greasy epaulette where the thick leather had rubbed against his shoulder straps. He looked every inch what he was: an experienced, loyal, and hard-fighting cavalryman. And a dangerous adversary, if push came to shove.

Telling was still pondering his apology, trying to pick the meat of his meaning from the bare bones he had offered. Misunderstandings? A shabby shaveling of a captain rogering the colonel's lady? Is that what he meant by 'unseemly'? Surely Sir George wouldn't have let such a dangerous transgression lie?

'Prince Rupert will press ahead to the relief of Newark, marching through country which remains largely loyal to our Sovereign. There are, however, several towns and garrisons within a day's ride of our route.'

'This Jovial Tinker I have heard so much about,' Telling observed, anxious not to appear too overawed in the colonel's company.

Sir George seemed to wince at the very mention of the unlikely nickname.

'Aye, him and a few others have yet to be brought to heel,' the older man rasped. 'We have been given the honour of providing the flanking force, watching the roads to the north and south. A hard ride, in other words. Are you up for it, lad?'

Now he sounded almost fatherly. Telling blinked in bewildered agitation. He'd been in his prospective father-in-law's company long enough to know full well what a man said and what he meant could be two dangerously different things. Sir Gilbert used honey on his hooks, and from what he had heard along the way this red-faced squire wasn't the kindly uncle he was pretending to be.

'I look forward to being in action once again,' Telling replied flatly.

Sir George's expression soured for a moment before he remembered himself and restored his inscrutable stare.

He knew, all right. He knew everything, Telling thought with a fresh surge of anxiety.

'I am sure you do,' the knight replied, lifting his sword from its scabbard and sliding it back with a businesslike clang.

The regiment had only remained at the crossroads long enough to pick up stragglers before pressing on once more. Rupert had not allowed them a moment's respite from the brutal march, forcing ten, twelve, even fourteen miles a day out of his weary troops. They had picked up another contingent at Wolverhampton and marched on again, pressing deeper and deeper into the disputed Midland counties.

Sir George Winter's regiment had been pushed out on the right flank, uncomfortably exposed to the enemy and the elements as they crossed a miserable wasteland a few miles out of Tamworth.

No Man's Heath was about right and all, Hugo thought grimly.

A grey wilderness of scrub and bramble, bisected by the muddy main road towards Ashby. The lonely plain suited Hugo's mood, throwing his gloomy imaginings into stark relief. Why, he might be stabbed or pistolled out here by some cheaply bought assassin, his young life not worth more than a few shillings to one of those pike-eyed musketeers he had bumped into back at Bridgnorth. The very speed of their march, however, seemed to have impeded any such design, prevented the leering troopers from fulfilling their deadly mission.

They had only been allowed the briefest rests, a bare hour here and there to give the horses a breather. By the time the creaking provision carts had caught up with them the men had barely had time to eat, drink, and relieve themselves before they were off again. God only knew where the poor musketeers had got to.

Telling rode alone at the head of the troop of strangers, Bent and Cairnthwaite maintaining their posts a few lengths behind him. Telling kept one eye on the dim horizon and the other on them. He had a pair of loaded pistols at his fingertips, ready to blast any bugger who broke ranks.

But nobody did.

They were swaying in their saddles like sacks of chaff, heads drooping with fatigue, backs and thighs screaming with cramps. The moment he called a halt they flopped into the tangled grass and lay there like dead men until he urged them up again. Mile after mile, crossroad after windy crossroad, and Telling began to relax. Perhaps he had imagined the whole thing, maybe his and Lady Winter's elaborate precautions had worked after all?

His reverie was interrupted once more by a brisk clatter of hoofs behind him. Telling swivelled around in his saddle, fingers straying for his pistol. Corporal Cairnthwaite spurred his tired mount alongside the suspicious captain, nodded in what he fondly imagined to be courtesy.

'Beggin' your pardon, sir, but the lads were wonderin' if we're goin' the whole way t'Ashby, like. It's a fair ride yet, sir, for them as don't know these parts.'

'We'll stop when Rupert says so,' Telling said curtly, keeping a beady eye on the unshaven wretch. Cairnthwaite sighed.

'Aye, it's all right for 'im, like, lying back in his coach wi' some wench, suppin' wine.'

Telling chuckled. 'Then you don't know the Prince,' he said smugly. 'Rupert never spares himself. He makes a point to share every trial along the way. He'll eat what you eat, drink what you drink, sleep when . . .'

'Give over,' Cairnthwaite protested. ''E's not flesh and blood, 'im. 'Is arse must be made from pig-iron,' the corporal complained.

They rode in silence for a while, the deserted road curving around a long bare ridge crowned with a small but abundant clump of trees. Telling was about to suggest riding up to investigate the lofty outpost when the indomitable corporal resumed his one-sided discourse.

'An' I've niver seen old Georgey boy move s'quick neither. 'E were at Edg'ull, tha knows. Slow Georgey they called 'un then. It were best 'e could do keepin' oop wi' King, let alone your precious Prince. Course, this were back in '42 now. Ah, happen we all know what kept 'im back in his coach, eh?'

Telling narrowed his eyes at the grinning cavalryman, slouched in his creaking saddle like some Mongol from the plains of Muscovy.

'No, what?'

'Ee, yer 'avin' me on,' Cairnthwaite leered. 'Tha knows as well as I who I'm ta'kin' about. Lady Splinter! The lass as gave thee a piece of 'er mind t'other day! By 'eck, Captain, tha's not the first who's laid 'tween her legs!'

Telling flared red, his buttocks clamped to his saddle by the corporal's carefree accusation. He dared not look around at the insolent northern trooper, staring instead at the grim slope stretching away from the high road.

'Come 'ead, Captain,' Cairnthwaite drawled. 'Tha didn't think we'd notice the two of ye scamperin' off into t'woods like that? She's taken a stone or two in 'er ear in 'er time, mark me words,' he chuckled.

Telling glanced sideways at the monstrous oracle.

'First off 'twere one of Sir George's bailiffs, so I 'eard. Then some lieutenant out of Warwick, then that fat staff bloater from Oxford. Course, them were all five-minute flings for her ladyship. 'Tweren't owt serious, till t'miller lad showed his face.'

Telling gazed at the cheerful corporal, bemused by his innocent tittle-tattle.

'Miller?'

'Aye,' Cairnthwaite nodded eagerly. 'Miller Arbright. What did tha reckon all trouble was twixt 'im and Sir George? She's 'ad it away wi' 'im more times than I've shat, man. 'Fore t'war they were ready to go gallivantin' over ter France, so I 'eard, t'avoid all trouble, like.'

'Trouble?' Telling repeated, concentrating hard to translate the trooper's slanderous babble.

'Divorce! Don't they 'ave that down Oxford, then? Slow

Georgey 'ad to get weavin' right smartish! They do say 'e bought 'er back off'n, that he paid Arbright ter sling 'is ook, like.'

'He paid him to renounce any claim on his wife, you mean?'

'Ee, Captain, tha's a reet pretty way with words!' the merry corporal shook his unshaven head. 'Aye. Set 'im up, like. Did she not mention any of this, then?' Cairnthwaite enquired with an innocent smile.

Telling swallowed, concentrated on the road ahead.

'Of course she didn't. I mean . . . I don't have the faintest idea what you're babbling about. There is nothing between Lady Winter and me which would have encouraged such intimacy.'

The corporal guffawed. 'Nothin' 'tween tha? Did yer not shag 'er daft, then?'

Telling glared at the cheerful corporal, all too aware of the fierce colour rising from his constricting collar.

'I did no such thing, and I forbid you to suggest otherwise,' Telling mumbled, his mind in turmoil. She had sworn she loved him and none other, that Sir George, away at the wars all that time, had lost interest in his forgotten wife!

He didn't know who to trust, but he couldn't see any particular reason why Cairnthwaite should want to lie to him. If the corporal was right then Arbright – this miller turned Roundhead – had in all probability attacked Bernham Hall in a fit of jealous passion rather than through military necessity. The long siege his lady-love had endured might have had nothing to do with the war at all! Hugo rode on, distressed and bewildered by the corporal's lurid intelligence.

ROPE WOOD,

The Roundhead cavalry had hidden themselves in a small wood a good furlong from the main road. They were local men and knew every track and gulley in the rolling hills roundabout. God knew they had followed the old fox up and down most of them in the last few months, hacking and stabbing at patrolling Royalist horsemen or falling on the King's slow-moving supply columns. Now, though, the Jovial Tinker had given them another assignment: to watch the high road for the coming of the Robber Prince himself – Rupert.

Over the last few weeks Parliament's busy spies had reported the Prince's tireless preparations, dispatched dire warnings about the large force he had assembled in the Welsh marches. The anxious Parliamentarian warlords had worried where the brute might strike next: a bold march towards the invading Scots, perhaps? A sudden descent on their vulnerable outposts in the Midlands? Or maybe a determined thrust across the country towards Newark – to lift the siege and save the threatened town for the King?

The Roundhead forces had come within an ace of taking the Royalist outpost on the River Trent at the beginning of the previous year, Colonel Thomas Ballard driving the garrison back inside Newark's hastily repaired defences. Since then the town had become an important staging post between the King's head-quarters in Oxford and the North, a vital link in his tenuous chain of command.

The Parliamentarian commanders had decided to break that chain, assembling a large and well-equipped army under the experienced Scots professional Sir John Meldrum. Meldrum had already distinguished himself at Edgehill and elsewhere, and his locally raised militias had settled down around the town to force its surrender. They had already captured Muskham bridge on the northern outskirts, scattering a Royalist regiment in the process, and were busy tightening their grip on the desperately held town.

Food was short, the walls were collapsing, and the dwindling garrison was seriously outgunned. Newark would fall within a week or two at the most – so long as the Roundheads could keep the dreaded Rupert at arm's length.

The young cornet in charge of the patrol ran his glass to and fro along the enemy column while his troopers kept a sharp lookout for the scouting dragoons they generally sent out ahead.

If his patrol got into trouble they were to ride off double quick – escape down one of the many gullies which scored the war-shorn hills. Cornet Timothy Locke had taken careful precautions, choosing his ground well. The wood stood at the end of a long, bare ridge, affording him a good view of the open down while denying the approaching enemy any realistic opportunity of getting behind him. Locke had satisfied himself the ridge was clear, and returned his attention to the main road.

So this was Rupert's grand army? The long-rumoured relief force which had thrown the quarrelling Roundhead commanders into such a panic?

Locke shook his head, studied the contemptible cavalry making their way along the muddy track. Two or three hundred horsemen riding beneath bright but rather crude colours. He could see no sign of the ornate flags some of the King's men carried, tasselled silks bearing some hateful slogan or dire Papist promise. The riders wore an odd assortment of topcoats and well-weathered hats, and only a very few of them seemed to carry pistols.

Cornet Locke, in comparison, was armed to the teeth and as well protected as comfort and convenience allowed. In addition to his lobster-tailed helmet and back and breastplate, the young cornet carried a pair of good pistols, a new carbine, and a long sword. The rogues away down the slope were clearly newly raised and poorly equipped – disappointingly unlike Rupert's legendary Cavaliers he had heard so much about.

The alert officer noted the number of colours and took a long look at the gaggle of better dressed men riding at the head of the column.

'Recognize that big bastard in the blue, John?' he called to one of his companions, a bearded veteran slumped over his horse behind a swath of leafy branches.

John Dando tipped his wide-brimmed hat back, nodded slowly.

'Aye. We've had a few run-ins with him. Colonel Winter, one of Gerard's horse colonels.'

'Winter's, eh? A pack of scrofulous starvers if ever I saw. So where's the mighty Rupert, then?' Cornet Locke asked, trying to keep the disappointment out of his voice.

Like most of the armed men roving about the bitterly divided Midlands that Saturday afternoon, Cornet Locke's local knowledge only extended a few miles from his home town of Tamworth. But the typically conscientious youngster had been determined to take his mission seriously, and had memorized every map he had been able to lay his hands on in order to be prepared for any eventuality.

Now, it seemed his unusual attention to detail had been unnecessary. It was obvious from the direction and urgency of their march that these ragged Royalists were marching for Newark.

Locke watched the poorly turned out regiment trot along the muddy road at the foot of the slope. It was the nearest he had ever come to the enemy, and he felt a peculiar urge to make some demonstration, to leap out of the undergrowth and defy the rogues to do their worst. One glance at the patiently set features of his companion was enough to dissuade him. Dando held a dirty finger to his lips, winked encouragingly. A hundred yards down the hill, the Royalist riders clicked their tongues and cursed the road, scratched and farted and stared into the middle distance. Locke could hear the insolent jangle of their harness, the soft plop of the hoofs as their horses struggled through the muddier stretches of the ill-made road. A few minutes behind the cavalry came a mob of road-weary musketeers, bandoliers clinking as they picked their way though the puddles and cursed the steaming manure their mounted brethren had left behind. Locke squinted, made out their smudged features – red as berries beneath their bobbing hats. A few carts and a handsome but rather mired carriage completed the uninspiring column. Locke bent over his horse's ears, nodded at his companion. Dando had stuck his tongue out while he concentrated on jotting down a rough estimate of their numbers onto a scrap of paper. He finished his sums and tugged his horse's head away from an outcrop of juicy dandelions.

'I don't recognize the foot colours, but Winter's are all local levies,' Dando summarized. 'Rupert's main body must be further back.'

'We were told to watch for Rupert,' Locke said uncertainly. The gutter-scrapings disappearing around the hill didn't look much like the fearsome Cavaliers he had read about in the news-books. They had looked, sounded, and smelled like the local Trained Bandsmen. All too ordinary mortals.

'We can't be sure Rupert means to come this way,' he fretted, torn between galloping off towards the threatened town and waiting for the monstrous German in person.

'Hartop's men are out on the high road, they'll slow the buggers down as likely as not,' the older man argued. 'We were told to watch the flanks.'

Cornet Locke chewed his lip as he pondered the distinction. 'Ah well, let's get back,' he decided at last.

Dando was already halfway down the rough slope, lying back on his saddle roll as his equally experienced horse picked its way down the steep and stony gulley. Locke took one last look over the empty down and wondered when he would ever be granted his most precious wish: to see the mighty Rupert ride by in all his glory.

Sir Edward Hartop – whose horsemen were supposed to be scouring the moors for the approaching Prince – was just one of the quarrelling cabal of Parliamentarian officers who had been ordered to report to the general rendezvous outside the closely besieged town of Newark. Like many of his fellow field officers, Sir Edward had resented the curt instructions he had received from Whitehall, and had been further annoyed to find himself under the command of a complete newcomer to the area – Sir John Meldrum. Up until that spring Hartop had been enjoying a roving commission about the Midlands, and he hadn't taken kindly to being treated like some naive beginner by the brusque Scots professional.

The stunning news that Rupert was marching to lift their bad-tempered siege had put the entire camp in a turmoil, and turned Meldrum's headquarters in the Spittal into a madhouse.

The hastily assembled officer corps had gathered in what was left of the draughty command post – a burnt-out mansion a musket shot from the River Trent – and listened in shocked silence as Meldrum read out the dog-eared dispatch. According to Major Fox's scouts, Rupert was less than three days' march away, having conjured an army of more than six thousand men from the garrisons along the Welsh marches.

'Impossible!' Hartop cried, thumping the map table. 'They couldn't have raised more than a few companies in that time. Old Tinker's been at the bottle again,' he scoffed.

Major Arbright scowled over the table at the agitated colonel.

'I'd trust Major Fox a main sight further than I would you,' he barked back. 'He's given the King's men a few run-ins in his time, which is more than we could say for you!'

Hartop straightened up, his gaunt features white with fury.

Meldrum held up his broad soldier's hands in horror.

'Gentlemen, please. This does our cause no service whatsoever,' he growled, his dark eyes fixed on the crudely painted map spread before them.

'We can't face Rupert in the field,' Sir Miles Hobart exclaimed, mentally calculating the distance between his own ill-equipped brigade and the notorious Prince. His ragged levies wouldn't last five minutes, charged by Rupert's damned fanatics. 'We'd best raise the siege at once, retire on Lincoln, and appeal to the Earl of Manchester to join us,' he argued.

Meldrum, vastly experienced and made of rather sterner stuff, raised his eyebrow at such a craven counsel.

'We'll not gae running back to his Lordship wi'out a fight,' he growled. 'We've seven thousand men in arms, and more horse than His Highness can possibly have collected in such time! I'd not shift if he had ten thousand!' the general declared.

His officers didn't seem to share his enthusiasm. Hartop was still bristling over Arbright's slanderous accusation. Hobart had taken umbrage at Meldrum's contemptuous refusal to retire on Lincoln. They glared at one another above the cursed map.

'We've more men than that scoundrel, and locals too. They'll fight all the better, knowing they are defending their own homes,' Major Arbright argued.

Meldrum nodded, convinced by the former miller's spirited prediction.

'Aye, that settles it! I want all the guns and foot brought up into the Spittal and put into a posture of defence.' He jabbed a broad finger at the map, followed the twisting course of the Trent back towards the empty west. 'In the meantime, Sir Edward's men will guard the approaches, the Fosseway here, see you. We'll reinforce the garrison at Muskham bridge to the north here, and draw the rest of the horse up on this bank here, ready to march out to meet him.' Meldrum eyed his dubious commanders. 'Let the damned rogue try it, we'll be ready for him,' he vowed.

BINGHAM,

Hugo felt like a sack of turnips, his leaden limbs bruised black, his poor callused buttocks an angry, inflamed red. His arms hung by his sides, the reins barely registering between his numbed fingertips. Thankfully, though, the smelly infection he had picked up between his legs seemed to have left what remained of his genitals intact. They finally called a halt shortly before midnight, sliding out of their saddles like dead men. They didn't possess the energy to untack their equally exhausted beasts, but simply lay between their trembling hoofs, snoring like so many old pot-wallopers outside an alehouse. A sudden stampede would have trampled two-thirds of Telling's troop into the rich Nottinghamshire loam – if they had possessed one animal capable of raising a trot, that was.

Telling flopped into the trampled grass, blinking against the swarming fatigue which threatened to engulf his body. Lying there like that, without as much as a blanket to protect himself, he felt as vulnerable as a sparrow chick freshly fallen from the nest. He might be stabbed or bludgeoned to death while his ravaged command lay about like logs. Nobody would wonder as to the identity of the culprit – other than to marvel at his superhuman capacity to go without sleep.

Hugo propped himself up on his elbow and peered through the tired charger's mud-caked legs, but the men's snoring coupled with the rhythmic champing of the tired horses was like a mother's lullaby, robbing him of what was left of his wits. He lay back on the dewy grass and felt sleep flood the forlorn hopes of his consciousness.

'Mount up! Have a care, you sacks! We're moving!'

The irate messenger blew another rasping blast on his trumpet, stretching their shattered nerves to breaking point. Telling rolled sideways as his bay hoofed the sod, coming within an inch of braining the comatose Cavalier.

'On your feet! Mount up!' Hugo prised himself up as far as his knees, peering around their improvised bivouac. Sleepy troopers rubbed their eyes or cursed the noisy intruder, jamming their hats over their ringing ears.

'The whole army will parade in ten minutes. On your bloody feet, you miserable vermin!'

'It's two o'clock in the morning, you prickster!'

'Parade? Who's bleedin' idea's that, then?' one irate lounger snarled, throwing a stone at the messenger's prancing piebald.

'Rupert's! Meldrum's making a dash for Lincoln and we're to catch him on the march!'

Telling grabbed his horse's girth and hauled himself to his feet, blinking like an owl as the messenger rode off to another corner of the drowsy camp. Two o'clock? He'd only been asleep a matter of minutes!

'On your feet, you heard the man,' he yawned, rubbing his fingers into his moist eye sockets to try and clear his sleepy vision.

'Parade? At this hour? The bastard's cracked up, I tell 'ee!'

'Look lively,' Telling called, clenching his fists as another wave of fatigue climbed out of his boots to drag him back down to the narcotically comfortable verge – the rocky ground which had been his bed.

A quarter of an hour later Prince Rupert himself rode by the yawning ranks, his black stallion lifting its hoofs as if it were competing at the Marquis of Newcastle's famous equestrian

243

school. The Prince, his hat pulled down over his demonic features, didn't take his eyes from the road ahead. Cairnthwaite chuckled mirthlessly.

'Didn't even look around,' he said, shaking his head in weary disgust. 'Some fookin' parade!' Before his equally emotional captain could comment, Rupert's principal officers trotted by in a compact body, casting the odd glance at the long line of reserve cavalry. Telling swayed in his saddle, dumbly aware the Lifeguard he had so longed to join were leaving without him. Were they made of iron? Didn't they need to sleep now and again? The bodyguard looked as fresh as daisies in comparison to Telling's men, but they must have covered at least twice the distance the Evesham men had tackled.

He closed his eyes, wondering whether he would ever be worthy to join those exalted ranks. He could barely sit straight in his saddle, let alone cut a dash with the best of the King's army! Rupert's elite cavalry regiment followed behind, five hundred strong, with Porter's bringing up the rear. Hugo blinked into the gloomy light cast by the spluttering torches, recognized the bulky figure of Sir George Winter approach at the head of his own troop of horse. The colonel gave Telling a sidelong glance as he trotted by, his gleaming armour concealed by a billowing grey cloak.

'Don't just sit there, Captain, get your levies in line behind us,' the colonel rasped, giving his horse a sharp taste of his spurs. Telling opened his mouth but his glowering commander was quickly swallowed up by the fractured night. Telling clamped his thighs about the tired bay, felt the animal's muscles slowly respond to his equally half-hearted urging. How much longer were they supposed to keep this up? You wouldn't treat a neighbour's ox like this, let alone your own men and horses!

He thought for one agonizing moment he might burst into tears of sheer exhaustion, and clamped his teeth on his trembling lip to settle himself for the ordeal ahead. Cairnthwaite and Cornet Bent muttered and cursed as they followed the captain out onto the churned Fosseway, the tired colour hanging listlessly from its stout pole.

'Keep up at the back! The musketeers are right behind you!'

Shouts and orders in the darkness, jingling harness and panting horses.

Telling looked around him, but his tired eyes couldn't penetrate the night for more than a few feet in any direction. He wrinkled his nose as the troop trotted past the hastily abandoned latrines, and followed the Prince's hurrying army towards its appointment with the dawn.

Rupert's gallopers had misunderstood Meldrum's frantic manoeuvrings outside the defiant town. They had watched his regiments march off towards the northern end of the line, and had concluded the Scots rogue was making a run for it while he could. They had raced back to report to Rupert, unaware the Roundhead general was merely digging his foot and guns in behind the burnt-out but still formidable walls of the Spittal, the derelict mansion on the Lincoln road. Meldrum hadn't trusted his grievously argumentative army to stand their ground in the open fields against Rupert's screaming imps. He had ordered his hastily reassembled cavalry up onto a commanding height above the town called Beacon Hill. Here they were to stand ready to make a sudden descent on Rupert's legions as they hurried along the Fosseway from the west. Meldrum, electrified by the news of the Prince's unexpectedly rapid approach, hoped to turn Rupert's very impetuosity against him. The rogue made war like lightning, striking here and there faster than a man could blink. He turned heavy cavalry into greyhounds and plodding infantry into hawks! He turned the drill books and military manuals the Scot had learnt by heart on their heads, and still came out triumphant, Meldrum had reflected with grudging admiration.

But he was also young and impatient, and had been known to take needless risks.

Let Rupert ride into the valley with his blasted shagpolls, let him ride like thunder on the poor Roundhead foot cowering in the Spittal!

He'd come down the hill behind him, kick him up the arse with his cavalry, and bowl the insolent puppy into the Trent!

The equally impetuous Cornet Locke had galloped all the way to Newark to report Rupert's meteoric progress across Nottingham-shire. He had expected to be sent back down the Fosseway to fetch his commander's cavalry for the coming battle. But Rupert's brilliant approach had caught the Roundhead warlords on the hop – there was no time to call in all the outlying forces, they needs must fight the Prince with the regiments already assembled. Much to the young cornet's delight, he and his men had been assigned to Major Marmaduke Jelly's troop in Sir Edward Rossi-ter's regiment. The prospect of taking part in an actual battle fired the youngster's imagination, and his nervous excitement kept his fatigue at bay. The little patrol tagged on to Jelly's men, returning their suspicious stares with nods and smiles.

'God's wounds, what a set of crows,' Dando whispered, falling in beside his officer as they followed the Nottinghamshire men up the steep hill to the south of the besieged town. 'You'd think we wore the King's colours, the looks these bleeders are givin' uz!'

Cornet Locke nodded distractedly, gazing out over the breath-taking panorama which had opened up below them.

Newark seemed to have been lit up for the occasion, hundreds of watchfires burning brightly around the troubled perimeter. Bright towers stood proud in the darkness, set out like a row of candles along a passageway. Away in the distance, Cornet Locke could see a cluster of orange lights flickering about the sheer black ruins of the Spittal – the busy headquarters where he had made his report bare hours earlier. Behind the teeming ruins where Meldrum had left his infantry the mighty Trent curved like a Turk's sabre, enveloping the eerily lit town in its spreading silver arms. The black isle stood forlorn but defiant, ringed by a double embrace of river and enemies.

Men and water to the north, water and men to the south.

And rolling, roaring, ripping towards them – a comet of fire and deadly destruction called Rupert, sworn to save the town for his uncle's cause.

'Pardon?' The youngster started as John Dando nudged his arm, disturbing his glad-eyed reverie.

'I said, it's a pretty sight, sir. All them lights a-flickerin', like. Pretty enough up here, anyway.'

'Where d'you think he is? Down on the Fosseway? It's the quickest way, if he means to relieve the town.'

Dando shrugged in the darkness. 'Who knows that bastard's mind? I wouldn't be surprised if he didn't up and fly in!'

'Stow that chatter, you apes! D'you mean to alert all his bliddy scouts?' The rasping whisper came from the bushes to their right.

Cornet Locke squinted, made out a gaggle of senior officers astride their chargers, backed into what had once been some-body's vegetable garden. Sir Edward Rossiter, he presumed. The colonel waved them on, returned his attention to the valley below.

The chastized troopers rode on in silence, through a deserted village on the summit of the windy hill. The sign above the village inn creaked and sighed as it swung in the gathering breeze, the shutters closed and bolted against all invaders.

'They seem to have scarpered quick enough,' the veteran commented quietly, peering down the deserted alleys between the squatting hovels. They rode on, leaving the expectant village behind. A horse snorted up ahead. And then a pistol shot, nearer at hand this time, a dry, rattling cough as though the ball . . .

'Have a care!' Locke stood up in his stirrups, the hair on his head bristling beneath his loosely fitting helmet at the sudden shout. He could hear the dull rumble of the guns from the town below, hoarse cursing up ahead, a sudden, brazen trumpet.

'Where are they?'

'It's 'im!'

And then all hell broke loose over them, around them, beneath them. The rumbling guns weren't guns at all but hoofs, thousands and thousands of galloping bloody hoofs. Cornet Locke twisted about in his saddle, petrified with uncertainty, shrivelling like a worm in his armour. Out of the darkness, a tumbling ball of brilliant colours and a silent plume of beautiful white smoke. And a pistol ball which chipped the tips from his clenched fingers and passed through the flapping sleeve of his shirt. He dropped the cornet as if it was a red-hot poker, held his numbed hand up to his face. The ball had shaved an inch from his middle finger and torn the nails from the two beside. White bone shone in amongst the welling ruby blood.

'Get back out of it!' John Dando screeched, bent over his horse like a Mongol, his carbine smoking in the super-heated air.

The next instant he was bowled aside, six, seven, a dozen riders hurtling past in a flash of blurred faces and bloody blades. Dando flopped over his saddle bow, the carbine dropping from his fingers. Locke felt an almighty crack on his head and dived into the grass as more Cavaliers flashed past him, swords rising and falling, glinting in the evil glimmer of dropped torches. Shouts and screams, a trumpet blowing hard enough to wake the dead. Pulverized with terror, Locke curled up like a baby in the rubble beneath a drystone wall, his screaming horse plunging off towards the steep hillside to his left. More riders galloped past, yelling and hooting like imps from the underworld.

And then a horse reared above him, its rider cursing as he brushed the leaning stonework. Locke prised himself to his knees and scrambled away, hardly daring to breathe as he clawed the mossy stones. Another horse pulled up in front of him, a big sweaty grey, a Royalist trooper already leaping down from his saddle, swinging his great boots in his face. Cornet Locke turned and leapt at the wall as the brute grabbed for his collar and yanked him back off his feet. Locke choked, grasped at his throat.

'Take it easy, yer daft sprat! Leave off bawlin' or I'll fockin' skin yer!'

The rider gave the terrified cornet a fearful shove, forcing the boy to his knees.

'Now keep still, lad, till they're past.' The Royalist reeked of horse sweat and excrement. He stood there panting, sword in his fist, a velvet-coated rock as his friends barrelled past after the scattered Roundhead vanguard.

'Yer dozy bastards, ain't yer 'eard of scouts?' he enquired, shaking his prisoner like an old mat. 'Came up on yer easy as pissin'!' the devil growled, hauling the bewildered boy to his feet.

Locke raised his arms as the Royalist removed his baldric. ''Ere, is that yer colour? Yer dropped it, ye great ninny!'

Cornet Locke, perplexed and bewildered by his first brush with the mighty Rupert's demon horsemen, had forgotten the rusty banner. The broken pole was lying in the churned track, its rusty emblem trampled by a hundred sets of hoofs. The bewildered youngster burst into tears.

Prince Rupert's cavalry had left the Fosseway six miles back, at a place called Balderton. They swung off to their right, made their way through a belt of trees and furze bushes and out onto the open hillside. The vanguard rested for a while in steaming silence, allowing the rest of the strung-out army to catch up before moving off again. On up the steep hillside, terrace after terrace of closely chewed turf and rabbit droppings. They drove in the sleepy Roundhead outposts and flowed around the deserted village of Codlington, herding the stragglers before them.

By dawn, Rupert's leading regiments were safe on the summit, Meldrum's awed cavalry abandoning the windy hill to the dread enemy.

By God, how did mortal men move so damnably quick?

BEACON HILL,

S ir John Meldrum had hoped to stop Rupert on the Fosse-way, but his insubordinate cavalry commanders had failed to act with the necessary vigour. He had then planned to entice the impudent German into a headlong dash towards the hastily abandoned siege lines around Newark, trapping his cavalry against the Trent with a sudden descent from Beacon Hill. But Rupert had refused to be drawn into a frontal assault. His brilliant gallop for the high ground had sprung Meldrum's trap and forced the Roundhead cavalry down into the plain, securing the tactical initiative for the Royalist forces.

And no commander in his right mind gave the Prince such a handsome advantage.

The day dawned as slowly as any other, thin grey light seeping over the bare slopes and illuminating the smouldering pits and battered towers which encircled the dreary streets of the sleeping town.

But Rupert had no time to watch the sun come up. He paced the gloomy summit, watching the enemy horse manoeuvre on the slopes below. Four great blocks of russet-coated horsemen, out-numbering his own force by many hundreds. He trained his spyglass on the burnt-out ruin behind them, the formidable bastion they called the Spittal. It was teeming with men and guns and windblown colours, an obvious strongpoint to be avoided at all costs. The enemy had built a bridge of boats behind the improvised fortress, linking the southern bank with the dimly discerned island beyond. He could just make out men and wagons hurrying over the rickety structure, taking refuge on the far bank.

The bulk of Meldrum's force was still on this side of the Trent, but how long did they intend to stay there, exposed as they were to a sudden sortie from the hill? He had neither the men nor guns to force a crossing, should the normally cautious Meldrum decide to withdraw the rest of his army over the river.

Rupert closed his glass with a flourish, his quick mind already made up. There was no time for elaborate planning and carefully coordinated strategies – the whole operation had depended upon speed and surprise, and the *coup de grâce* would be no exception.

The turbulent Prince called his colonels and captains together for the quickest of briefings, pointed out the enemy dispositions and outlined the simplest of solutions: a sudden swoop down the hill, driving the solid Roundhead horse back into the river! They would leave the Spittal isolated, worry about the well-armed garrison later. First, they had to clip Meldrum's claws, remove his precious cavalry from the board.

'To horse! Prepare to advance!'

Trumpets blared along the horselines, tired chargers pricked up their ears as their weary riders relieved their aching bladders over the trampled grass. Rupert's bodyguard closed about their impatient chief, their flapping cornets worried by the stiff breeze, an insolent challenge to the enemy waiting below. They moved off at a slow trot, five hundred cavalry in a double line behind their general. Sir George Porter's regiment followed at fifty paces. There was no sign of the rest of the army.

Hugo Telling's cursing troop arrived on the bare summit in time to see them go, a double line of dark smudges on the grey and green hillside, picking up speed as they rolled down the slope. Here and there individual riders pulled away from the ranks, ambitious Cavaliers eager to make a name for themselves in the desperate charge towards the town. The famished captain closed his eyes in dismay as the colourful squadrons launched their attack, finished the back-breaking campaign in one mad moment of horror and glory.

Without him.

The disciplined ranks began to fall apart with every yard they rode, the double regiment disintegrating into a horde of screaming infidels, colours and streamers and silk scarves cracking in their slipstream. The diabolical charge was in stark contrast to the measured advance of the Roundhead horse, awaiting their onset with nervous anticipation. Colonel Edward Rossiter commanded the left, Francis Thornaugh the right. The grim-faced commanders waved their men out to meet the screaming charge, the Midlands levies aghast as the colourful cavalcade tumbled down the hillside towards them. They clamped their thighs about their mounts, hunched under their helmets like fighting crabs, hands tugging at their reins.

And then the avalanche broke about them, flowing between troop formations or skewing to a halt before their iron-bound front. Horses shied and reared, hurling the inexperienced men on both sides to the juddering turf. The Royalist charge broke upon the Roundhead wall, carefully marshalled squadrons breaking up into a thousand individual struggles. Swords rose and fell, glinting in the meagre morning light. Pistols coughed and men screamed, barging and kicking and gouging a path through their pressing enemy. Dour Parliamentarians hacked and stabbed their way through the tangled squadrons on the Royalist right, while flamboyant King's men cut their way through the wavering ranks to their left. The charging horsemen seemed to swallow one another up like giant snakes, each army gorged upon the still-kicking corpse of the other.

Rupert aimed his charger at the biggest block of enemy horse, leading his Lifeguard into the heart of Thornaugh's squadrons. The quailing enemy parted about him, turning to try and jab him in the back as he barged his way through the roaring mob.

'Religion!' A beetroot-faced rider who had lost his helmet in the first charge locked his fists about Rupert's collar, dragging the Prince back over his charger's lathered hindquarters. Rupert lost a stirrup, clinging on to his saddle as his horse veered. Captain O'Neill saw the danger, urging his own horse into the gap between them and bringing his sword down in a whistling arc. The Prince's assailant fell away into the crush, his severed hand spouting over the turf. Rupert dragged himself upright as his horse clattered into a great press of white-faced riders, slashing them away with his notched sword while his bodyguards struggled through to his aid. Horses went down, kicking the crouching wounded. A young Royalist cornet had been cut off by a surge from the back, swords and daggers jabbing at his hunched back. A brace of bullets hit him in the arm and he slumped over his saddle, still clinging to his precious colour. A dismounted Roundhead launched himself at the brave youngster, clinging on to his breeches like a tiger and cursing as he tried to snatch the broken lance. Rupert wheeled round and spurred his horse straight at the screaming devil, pinning him between his own horse and the wounded cornet's. The rebel lost his footing and was crushed between the terrified beasts, his dirty hands clawing at their flanks before he was dragged beneath the hoofs.

The noise built in a terrible ear-splitting crescendo, a thousand smiths pounding out terrible tattoos on their human anvils. Skulls burst and arms split, fingers flew and eyes popped. Here and there isolated pockets of Parliamentarian horse held their ground and even drove the lighter Royalists back onto their reserves, but the left flank – made up of Thornaugh's Lincolnshire men – had already begun to break under the pressure, individual riders peeling away from the wavering blocks followed by troops, squadrons, and then entire regiments. Riderless horses plunged and kicked as they escaped the man-made storm. The Lincolnshire horse didn't wait to see the outcome of the fierce clash in the centre, but turned their horses and spurred off after the fugitives. The whooping Royalists drove through the dissolving mass, pressing home their attack on the defiant centre and turning the retreat into a rout. The hard-fighting Nottinghamshire men glanced over their shoulders and watched them go. With notched swords and empty pistols there was little more they could do to hold the swirling mass of Rupert's horse. Their grinding advance halted as fresh Royalist squadrons doubled into the attack, crowding into the knots of Roundhead horsemen, surrounding the toughest fighters in deadly nets of silk and steel.

In another moment Rossiter's brigade gave way, the bawling officers leading the flight from the carnage, frightened cornets tucking their flags beneath their knees as they raced off towards the Trent. The stampeding horsemen wheeled away from the town, a stream of tangled regiments pouring across the chewed meadows towards the bastion on the northern point of the abandoned siege line.

Here and there some overenthusiastic Royalist found himself set upon by snarling enemies – furious veterans who had been caught up against their will in the dismal rout. Elsewhere on the swirling field, teenaged Cavaliers pursued whole troops before them, screaming like banshees as they drove the Roundhead cattle towards the river.

Rupert, battered and bloody in the middle of the deadly mêlée, was too busy hacking at the diehards on the ridge to pay any attention to their craven colleagues' panicked defections, their headlong dash towards the rickety bridge of boats behind the Spittal. Had he stayed up on the summit to direct his rapidly arriving army, he might have spied the first enemy fugitives pound across the primitive bridge as if every fiend of hell was on their heels. He might have ordered his cavalry reserves to wheel around to the north, and launch a surprise attack on the crossing. If he could have inserted his men between the bravely held Spittal and the river, he would have trapped Meldrum's cavalry between a rock and a hard place, cutting them to pieces at his leisure.

But Rupert was away down the hill, trading blows with a punch-drunk, black-eyed brute in a bullet-pocked buff coat. He couldn't even see the damned river.

*

Hugo watched the battle unfold in the pearly morning light, sickened with fatigue and a punishing (and all too familiar) sense of failure. All that effort getting to this windy hill, only to sit out the battle as a bloody spectator!

Rupert's vanguard seemed determined on winning the day by themselves, the leading regiments pursuing the fragmenting Roundhead horse off the field before the bulk of his army had even arrived! Telling slumped in his saddle as his panting horse half-heartedly hoofed the stony ground, watching the weak morning light illuminate the ghastly flotsam of casualties and dead horses which had been left behind by Rupert's mad charge. Wounded men were staggering off as best they could, taking cover in one of the many pits and trenches which disfigured the plain. Some, knocked off their horses at the first onset, had worked their way down to the river on foot and were stripping off their buff coats to swim to the safety of the far bank – the broad island formed by the outflung arms of the Trent, where the fugitive cavalry had taken temporary refuge.

Telling looked up as a column of shabby prisoners was herded off towards Codlington, the deserted village they had ridden through that dawn. The brooding Roundheads looked almost comical, stripped of their arms and armour, shambling along in their shirts. Hugo knew exactly how they felt, paraded before the soldiers which had humbled their own army. He prickled at the memory, but added his own sneers to those of his troopers.

'Ah, where's your Lord Jesus now, boys?' Cairnthwaite enquired, spittle flying over their bowed heads. 'All you good Christian soldiers, he didn't do you much good, did he?' the delighted corporal taunted, turning his horse in and out of the shuffling column and forcing the downcast Roundheads to step out of his path.

The arrival of the regimental commander put a stop to his antics. Telling glanced to his right, watched the red-faced colonel trot down the stalled rank. The sour-faced Midlander took a long look at his adversary, his thick lips pulled back from his teeth in the rictus of a smile. How could Caroline have abided this oaf?

'Leave your fooling and fall in,' the colonel snarled. Cairnthwaite ducked back into line, casting an inquisitive look at the cheesy-faced captain. Sir George Winter ignored his underling, grinned instead at his nervous men.

'Don't worry, lads, there's plenty of the buggers left for us,' he encouraged, misunderstanding their all too evident apprehension. 'We'll chase them into the sea, once we've winkled them out of that damned fort!'

The disgruntled troopers leaned over to murmur to their colleagues, wondering aloud whether they were to be put to that formidable obstacle. Storming earthworks wasn't cavalry work, it was a job for the musketeers.

Only trouble was, Rupert's musketeers were still three miles back down the road.

Mid-morning, and the bulk of Meldrum's beaten cavalry had pulled back over the river, saving themselves from the swirling Royalist horsemen. Rupert's vanguard had scoured them from the southern meadows but hadn't dared attack the defiantly held Spittal. The Norfolk militia – already riven by half a hundred internal disputes and grievances – had deserted their posts, but Meldrum still had plenty of men to hold the derelict fortress, and had wheeled up a dozen well-served guns to support them. The first squadron to ride too close to the crude works had received a sharp volley of shot and had taken themselves off out of range, cheering the nervous garrison for a moment. After that first devastating charge the opposing forces had drawn off to lick their wounds, the fragile peace only disturbed by the occasional tormented scream of a dying horse, and the inevitable pistol shot which followed.

The gut-souring lull lasted another hour or so, and the Roundheads in the Spittal began to cheer up. Major Simon Arbright paced up and down his section of the hastily repaired walls, quietly encouraging his men. They had marched up here with more pikemen than musketeers, and Arbright knew they wouldn't be much use defending the earthworks which ran like powdery brown gums between the black stumps of the ruined house. His sector ran along the derelict northern wall, overlooking the kitchen gardens, orchard, and water-meadow beyond. They looked out over a churned track – the very route the Roundhead horse had used to escape the Royalists. Arbright shielded his eyes to study the tempting prize at the end of it – the haphazardly lashed bridge of boats swinging lazily in the strong current. A long queue of wounded and non-combatants was already forming beside the sorry structure, waiting while a drover in a dirty smock whipped up his oxen, struggling to drag a clattering ammunition wagon over the improvised pontoon. Arbright knew every man along the walls was itching to run off and join them, put the broad Trent between himself and Rupert's boisterous legions.

But the triumphant Prince had been forced to leave his foot and guns behind, and it would take more than a few cavalry to prise Meldrum's army out of the sooty ruins of the Spittal.

'He's shot his bolt, lads,' he called, striding down the muttering ranks to take their minds from the debilitating uncertainty of their position. 'He can't come on in with a few hundred horse-boys!' Arbright spat in the mud, scratched his broad backside as if he was back at the mill, supervising the workers as they attended the great grinding stones which had made his fortune.

'Just stick to it, you don't want to get caught on the flat,' he bawled.

The grim-faced company gazed at the miserably scored meadows over the wall, oblivious to his good-natured banter. Arbright sighed to himself, glanced up at the watery sun beginning to poke through the smoke. About ten of the clock, and God only knew what they were going to do next.

'Have a care! Here they come!' The alarm was raised by a dozing musketeer overlooking the orchard. Arbright hauled himself to

257

his feet and hurried to the threatened sector. He peered out over the trampled meadows, still littered with broken-backed carts and heaped soil. Arbright closed his fingers in the crumbling red earth wall, squinted through the streaming smoke which coiled about the cluttered approaches. The musketeers seemed to hold their breath as they gazed out into the mist.

There they were! A shambling band of ghost-men, turned grey by the smoke and their own fear. They wore multicoloured coats and pulled-down hats, as if the greasy felt could deflect a bullet. They had bunched together beneath a bobbing grey banner rather than form their usual extended skirmish line, backs bent as they crept forward over the broken ground. Arbright looked to their right, made out a body of equally unimpressive cavalry swinging out to guard their flank, swords drawn, heads bent. Arbright growled with laughter at their piss-poor showing – such a contrast to the juddering charge Rupert had unleashed bare hours before. This lot were mincing over the heaped refuse and sprawled corpses like little lost children, jumping out of their coats at every shot!

'What a bunch of pricksters! Look at them!' Arbright cried, drawing his sword as his musketeers clinked and clanked about him, preparing themselves for the sorry charge.

'If they want the bridge, they've going to have to fight us for it!' he yelled, shaking his fist at the legion of the lost, slowly emerging from the coiling cover of the battle smoke.

Hugo Telling felt cold, chilled to the bone. He knew now he had been set up for this. That the cowardly cuckold Sir George Winter, rather than call him out for his impudence, meant to feed him to the lions for his insolent liaison with his feckless wife. He meant to punish him, here, in front of the entire army. God knew everybody in the regiment must have been talking about it, if Corporal Cairnthwaite's jocular reminiscences were anything to go by. Telling turned and peered over his shoulder, saw the bloated knight bringing up the rear with three more troops of his blasted regiment. He didn't seem overly excited by his predicament, too concerned over his own safety to enjoy Telling's bloody end.

Sir George's regiment had been detailed to escort the locally levied infantry up to the walls of the Spittal, acting as flank guards in case the enemy launched a sortie from the far bank.

But every man jack of them knew they were merely a diversionary thrust – the real assault would be directed against the crucial bridge of boats further to their right.

They were to be thrown at the walls like the bloody cannon fodder they were, and Hugo Telling was going to lead them.

Telling's troop would bear the brunt of any sudden attack from the river, and absorb the sharpest volleys from the bravely held walls.

He had held his commander's gaze as Winter outlined his mission, daring the younger man to refuse his dangerous assignment. Telling was damned if he would give the craven colonel the satisfaction by refusing the grim task.

'Right flank, aye, sir,' he said, as crisply as he could given his chronic lack of sleep.

'Drive them all before you, Captain,' Sir George had invited, a ghost of a smile playing about his mouth.

Telling wondered for the thousandth time who could have told him.

The Roundhead cavalry lurking on the far bank had clearly had enough. Telling could see them trotting to and fro – reluctant to take up the challenge and cross the swaying bridge. He glanced over his right shoulder and saw the green-coated musketeers from Tillier's regiment making their way towards the main objective, ducking and diving behind every scrap of cover they could find.

There was an enormous bang in front of him and a sudden

spew of red earth. The dull clods thrown up by the roundshot clanged and banged over his ducked head as his trembling horse shied away from the defiant Spittal.

'Close up! Support the foot!' he yelled at the owl-eyed troopers crowded behind him. They were in the old orchard now, a bare fifty yards from the defences. He spat a mouthful of hot soil onto the turf and looked up, squinting at the rolling smoke.

Suddenly the drifting murk was horribly illuminated by a hundred bright orange flashes, young dragons spewing sparks over the heaped bank. He flinched at the sudden volley from the walls, ducking down even lower over his horse's neck. A mossy apple tree seemed to stagger in the sudden storm, the unfortunates hiding behind it hurled backwards, coats erupting with shocking gobbets of blood. The ragged survivors bunched closer, trusting their survival on the panic-stricken men in front.

Support the foot? It was more like herding sheep to slaughter! The bewildered Royalist musketeers returned their fire, their wildly aimed shots singing high into the boiling smoke.

'Second rank, make ready!'

Telling heard the awful command from the walls, gripped his reins in sheer terror as the Royalist attack wavered before the wall. He closed his eyes, sure he would be hit this time.

'Run! Save yourselves!'

His horse leapt up on its hind legs, hurling the captain into its dirty mane. Hugo grabbed at his reins, legs flailing as the terrified horse bucked and plunged. He saw the levied musketeers turn and run, felt the bay spring away beneath him. His hat flew off, his dropped sword dangled from its leather strap. He was still grasping for it when the Roundheads came down the wall in an avalanche of red earth, halberds and musket butts swinging and jabbing at the fools who hadn't run. The biggest of them seemed to bound across the obstacle, his tawny sash snagged by a broken-down apple tree. Telling could see his huge mouth move but couldn't hear anything. He wrenched the horse sideways and kicked out at the big officer, catching the man in the chest. The brute staggered, but held on to his boot, dragging the Cavalier from the saddle with a snarl of hatred. Telling felt a sudden splash of pain beneath him and rolled sideways, grasping at the broken sword protruding from his torn coat. The Roundhead brought his boot back and gave him an enormous kick in the stomach, the wounded captain doubling up in breathless agony. He curled into a ball, sucking air through scummed lips, face crushed into the churned soil. The Roundhead grabbed him by the collar and hauled him to his feet, tossed the wretch behind him as he searched for more victims.

The Royalist levies had run like rabbits, scuttled for the cover of the cavalry squadrons drawn up behind them. Tillier's men on the river flank had drawn off in good order, unable to make any headway against disciplined musket fire and wildly aimed pot-shots from the far bank of the Trent.

Hugo, lying face down beneath a bloody, bullet-tattered apple tree, didn't see them go. He could feel hot liquid running over his back and between his skinny buttocks. His searching fingers came back sticky with blood. His chest ached as if he had swallowed a cannonball, every breath a dagger between his ribs. He could see their mired boots stamp about the wrecked orchard as they turned bodies and rifled purses.

'Here's a likely lookin' feller!'

Telling felt himself lifted out of the dirt, turned over and dropped on his back. He shouted with pain, sat up so straight the Roundhead looter took an astonished step back.

'Not dead then, boy? Ah well!'

Telling scrambled back against the tree, ignoring the flaming agony in his back, as the sooty devil lifted the brass-bound butt of his musket.

'Edwards! Get that bleedin' horseboy back over the wall! You don't want to go murdering prisoners with that lot sitting on the doorstep, do you?'

Telling glanced at his saviour – none other than the belligerent officer who had dragged him down in the first place. The panting brute was tucking his knotted sash back over his buff coat, his broad face flushed with exertion.

261

'I thought he were one of them Oirish buggers,' the musketeer leered, cocking his curly head towards the river.

'Ne' mind Oirish,' the officer rasped, straightening his gauntlets and peering through the battered orchard. 'We'll need a few cards to play our way out of this one!'

THE SPITTAL,

NEWARK

Major Simon Arbright watched the barber-surgeon rummage under the wounded Cavalier's coat, his bald head dipping as he inspected the deep slash across the youngster's lower back.

'Not the first cut you've had there either, son,' the surgeon noted, running a grubby finger along a puckered scar – the thick keloid tissue dissected by the new wound. 'So it'll take a little longer to heal. You'll live though, as long as it's kept clean.'

Arbright nodded, fished a coin from his purse, and handed it to the blood-spotted gnome, his red and white sash proclaiming his alleged profession. The grubby band was splattered in blood and flakes of drying flesh now, a suitable totem to his occupation.

'Thanks for your time, Giles. This little house dove might prove useful, if we have to bargain our way out of here.' He grinned down at the wincing Cavalier, his teeth the colour of old cheese. 'You scratch my back, I'll scratch yours, eh? You for me, if it comes to an exchange, how's that sound?' Arbright enquired hopefully.

Telling fell back in a stupor at the major's coarse good humour, in no mind to bargain for anything.

'What's the matter with him? I thought you said he'd be all right?'

The surgeon narrowed his eyes at his patient–victim, thinking for a moment the youth had taken a fever or something. Wouldn't be the first trooper to fall foul of his treatment, that was for sure. He wiped a bloody hand across his cheek and peered up at the grey summit of Beacon Hill away over to the

263

south. The King's men had moved a sight closer now, he thought ruefully, running his fingers over his domed head. Like all barber-surgeons, Giles Hale was a free agent, theoretically allowed to move from one army to the other, depending on who paid most. Hale had already served both Royalist and Roundhead paymasters, and had last been employed by the hard-pressed garrison of Newark itself. He had left their service three weeks earlier – when the money had run out – and taken up with the rather more forthcoming Parliamentarians. It occurred to him he might not be too popular with the newly relieved citizens of the town. Barber-surgeons had occasionally been known to earn an extra shilling or two spying, their freedom of movement allowing them close observation of various camps, defences, and garrisons. It would be all too easy for some jaundiced Royalist to point the finger now, accuse him of selling more than just his medical services to the enemy.

Arbright misunderstood his apprehension, imagining Hale was more concerned with the future of the cause than his own neck. 'Aye, they're parleying over at headquarters,' he said sourly. 'Meldrum'll try and keep our arms – Rupert'll have a job parting us from 'em, that's for sure.' Arbright cursed under his breath. 'That damned rogue, sending out a trumpet. We could stand here a week and more, whether we've food or not!'

Sir John Meldrum had not shared his gallant major's optimism. His men had held the Spittal easily enough, but his position had been seriously undermined by the loss of Muskham bridge, his last remaining link to the outside world. The bridge was his back door to the North, his only way off the broad island behind the Spittal and the only possible route for fresh supplies to be brought in. The vital link had been captured by a sudden sortie from the town – the guards he had left chased off by the gleeful Royalists. Without the bridge he was isolated between the broad, outflung arms of the river and the newly united Royalist armies. Meldrum had as many men as Rupert, but some regiments had

already proved worryingly mutinous. They were running dangerously short of ammunition and now they had no opportunity of
collecting any further victuals. The wily Scot had decided to send
out a trumpet while his army was still fit enough to fight,
negotiate a conditional surrender before the critical situation
deteriorated any further.

'We should stick the horse up front and cut our way out,' the fire-
eating major told the dispirited captain. Hugo was lying on his
side beneath the sooty remains of an old fireplace, recovering
from the surgeon's brusque attention. He had been lucky to get
that, though, his captor apparently regretting the fact he had
kicked Hugo in the ribs while he was down. The blow had
apparently run contrary to Major Arbright's personal code of
honour. That's what the gruff, mastiff-jawed Midlander claimed,
at any rate.

The neat brick chimney which formed his windy infirmary had
once been the centrepiece of the grand hall, the proud feature
of a richly furnished mansion house. But the old house had been
destroyed the year before, its walls cast down by the elemental
forces of war. All that remained was a stark red and grey obelisk,
a poignant enough monument in the corpse-cluttered battlefield.
Hugo propped himself on his elbow, wincing at the searing pain
around his lower back. Arbright gave him a sardonic glance.

'It'll hurt a bit, aye,' he said awkwardly. 'But if you'd fallen on
your belly that blade would have ripped you open like a fat carp.
Look on the bright side, lad.'

Telling glanced up at the heavily built major, a clay-faced troll
in a battered buff coat, his closely clipped hair as stiff as a handful
of iron filings. His pockmarked jaw seemed set on his chest,
giving Arbright a permanently pugnacious expression completely
in tune with the brute's thrusting personality.

So this was the famous Major – the Miller Arbright so beloved
of the campfire gossips! Telling couldn't imagine him out courting – playing the sly lover to Caroline Winter's faithless wife. He

pictured the bullish Major halfway up a ladder, ordering the handsome Caroline down to his waiting coach.

'Something amusing you, lad?' the unevenly tempered Arbright snarled, turning his stern gaze on the wounded Royalist lying beneath the soaring chimney breast. 'Meldrum might have sent for a parley, but it doesn't mean we're finished yet!' he rasped.

Telling modified his expression, somewhat cheered by the prospect of an imminent Roundhead surrender. He would be released and returned to the Prince's triumphant ranks – the proud owner of a serious (but not life-threatening) wound. The attack on the Spittal might have been a dismal failure, but he could hardly be blamed for that. In the meantime, the boot would be on the other foot, this Arbright character might find himself on the receiving end of a damned good kicking – if nothing worse. Hugo's ribs still hurt like buggery from the terrific blow the mad major had given him, doubling him up in the filthy red earth. But he had gotten off lightly compared to those musketeers who had fallen into his hands back in the Vale of Evesham. He remembered the Irishmen Arbright had left hanging outside Bernham Park – a bizarre love token to the feckless housewife barricaded indoors. Telling frowned up at him, his keen sense of outrage overwhelming his sadly depleted store of common sense.

'If Byron's men have retaken the bridge like the surgeon says, then you've no way out of here. D'you think all these pikes of yours are going to charge through Rupert's cavalry?'

Arbright licked his lips, gave Telling a withering smile.

'Those were Tillier's men on the river there,' the clumsy Cavalier went on, 'they'll be pleased, catching up with the likes of you after that business . . .' Telling blundered on, turning his face away in sudden agitation as he finally sensed his danger. The brute hadn't thought twice about executing his prisoners – why should he treat Hugo any differently now?

Arbright seemed taken aback for a moment, his brutal face pinched by sudden doubt. Tillier's men? What business?

'What do I care which bloody rabble's out there?' he growled, pondering his own question for a moment.

Telling swallowed, wished he'd kept his mouth shut. This officer was a dangerous cut-throat who hadn't hesitated to string up those musketeers back at Bernham Manor. Here he was lying at his feet like a trussed goose, reminding the bloated devil of his past crimes. Arbright's grey eyes seemed to crackle with malice as he turned his wondering gaze on the helpless captain.

'You know something, or think you do, eh? Tillier's? I've bumped into a few of 'em in the last weeks. A couple of deserters straight off the boat, I seem to remember, aye.' He bent down, brought his beaten-up face close to the suddenly pale Telling's twitching moustache.

Telling scrambled away from the mad brute, realizing the so-called major possessed about as much honour as a slaughterman. He was a butcher in a tawny sash, a rogue from the ranks made good. Just the sort of trash one would expect to find commanding rebel bandits like these!

'You were there, were you? Bernham Hall?'

Telling clamped his lips together. Arbright lunged, grabbed him by the shoulder, and turned him on his back like a kicking fish. He grabbed a handful of sooty dirt from beneath the burnt out chimney, propped his knees on Telling's back, and tore the captain's ripped coat away from his flesh. Hugo kicked and squirmed, but the bastard must have weighed a ton.

'You start cockin' your beaver with me, lad, and I'll cut your balls off with a blunt knife!' he rasped. 'Your precious friends over the wall don't know how bad you were taken, they don't know whether you lived or died. Maybe your wound went manky on you, all this shit lying about, eh? Ever seen a man die of a gangrenous wound, have you?'

Telling lay still, his breath coming in agonized gasps as the fiend held his filthy paw above the seeping wound across his back. One handful of that and the clean cut would turn gangrenous within a few hours, it didn't take a barber-surgeon to work that out.

'So if you want to see the sunset, you'd best tell me exactly what you know, or think you know.'

Telling swallowed. 'Bernham Hall,' he gasped, half choked by the major's rearing strength, crushing the life-force out of him just like the snot running down his face.

'Bernham Hall?' Arbright leaned closer. 'What d'you know about it?'

'Lady Winter.'

Hugo felt the tremendous weight on his back shift a little.

'Never heard of her.'

'I heard you had.'

Arbright ground the wretched Cavalier into the dirt. 'You heard wrong, boy!' But the savage growl had lost its edge, turned into a knowing croak.

Telling blurted the rest. 'I heard about you and Lady Winter, how you were going to run away to France!'

Arbright seemed to shudder above him, Hugo saw him run his broad sleeve across his lantern jaw.

'You saw her, did you?'

Telling nodded.

'She and the boy . . . they were all right, I suppose?'

'They came with us. We had to burn the house down before we left, Rupert's orders.'

Arbright shouted with laughter, pulled himself off the terrified captain, and knelt down beside him.

'Came with you where? Here?' Arbright's excited features had been transformed, his eyes metamorphosing from gravel to gem-stones in an instant. 'She's not at your camp?'

Telling picked himself out of the filth, shook his head, and felt alarm bells jangle all down his sore spine.

'We haven't got a camp,' he groaned. 'We left her at Wolver-hampton, with her sister.'

Arbright muttered something Telling didn't catch.

'Burnt down, eh?' Arbright asked, almost apologetic now. 'I would have burnt it down, and that bastard in it.'

Telling realized at once he had a new card to play in the dangerous hand he had inadvertently dealt himself.

'Sir George, you mean? My commanding officer. He sent me to lead the attack,' Telling said, struggling to sit up in something approaching comfort. He gave up, reclined against the chimney wall. Arbright's chin dropped back on his chest.

'The droopy cunt, sending a boy in his place! Did he know I was here, eh?' Arbright enquired.

Telling shook his head. 'We were told to attack the Spittal, that's all. He didn't know you were here.'

Arbright gave the Cavalier a suspicious look.

'You seem mighty well informed, my lad, about my business!' Telling went white. 'He told you all this, did he? That close-mouthed shit wouldn't have washed his dirty linen in public! Who told you all about it, eh?' Arbright's moods seemed to change with every alternate breath.

'Lady Winter . . .'

'What?'

'Was deeply unhappy to be—'

Arbright grabbed the Cavalier's filthy shirt, dragged the howling youth to his feet. 'He chucked you in first, you slim-shanked shite! Why'd he do that?' the alert officer demanded, spittle flying from his open maw. Telling had blundered badly, underestimating the raw-boned major. He was sharper than he looked.

'Lady Winter was upset . . . she was furious at losing her home! Prince Rupert had ordered all houses which could not be put into a suitable posture of defence to be slighted . . .'

'And Slow Georgey blamed you, eh? He wouldn't have dared cross Rupert!'

'That's it!' Telling agreed, nodding his trapped head as vigorously as he could. 'He blamed me for burning down his hall!'

Arbright seemed to accept the logic of this. He set the battered Cavalier down on the ground, opening and closing his fists as he stamped about in turmoil.

'So Bernham Hall's burnt down, and Georgey's lost the best of

269

his lands. I should know, it was me as burned 'em! The privy-sneaking bastard . . . did you know I was there first? Ah, I didn't think so. Me and Caroline were to be wed, until that grasping bastard stuck his hooter in! He fetched her off to Bernham, all I had was the mill, see, not good enough for her, or so she thought! But she soon changed her mind when she had to bed that bell-wether turd! She soon saw she'd made a mistake, turning her back on Simon Arbright!'

Telling sat back against the chimney, listening to the major's fascinating confession.

'When George buggered off to Wales, I thought: Me luck's in. I took my men down there and tried to reason with her, but she wouldn't have it. Come out, Caroline, I said. You needn't stick with the tight-fisted bastard an hour longer! But she wouldn't see me, sends young Thomas . . . young Thomas, mind you – out to tell me she'd hold the hall in the name of the King if not her man! The goddamned bitch wouldn't listen! She knew she'd spite me, see, sending Thomas out! Well, you don't think that gut-bucket could have fathered a strapping lad like that, do you? He's mine, always was!'

Telling gawped at the remarkable revelation, oblivious to the growing sounds of tumult in the defiantly held Spittal. Trumpets were blowing, drums were beating. The stink of lighted match drifted across the ruined mansion.

Arbright looked around the bustling camp. Clumps of tired pikemen were leaning on their weapons, anxious files of musket-eers chatting amongst themselves while the officers shouted and gesticulated in the avenues between the worried ranks.

'Something's up. Bastard,' Arbright snarled.

In another moment the scattered drumming resolved itself into one electrifying pulse, a deadly clatter which vibrated through the battered foundations of the old mansion.

Meldrum was about to surrender the Spittal.

THE SPITTAL,

NEWARK

The negotiations went on for hours, the precise details of Meldrum's surrender taking longer to settle than the battle itself. The senior officers – including the volatile Arbright – took themselves off to join the mortified Scot at his hastily arranged council of war. They knew full well when they were beaten, but still had a few cards to play. That devil incarnate Rupert had performed miracles which bordered on the supernatural (his black arts aided, no doubt, by his familiar – the large white poodle named Boy), but he couldn't storm the Spittal without suffering fearful casualties, even if the isolated defenders were reduced to fighting with pike and sword, sticks and stones. He could not afford to starve the Roundheads out as this would leave his army perilously exposed to a counter-attack by the formidable enemy forces to the east.

The Royalists were determined to finish the business they had started so well – the dour Parliamentarians equally keen to rescue something from the wreckage.

In the meantime Telling was in a limbo. A prisoner stuck in the awkward no man's land between the two forces, his status yet to be decided by the squabbling generals. Surely the Roundheads would not be permitted to march off before they had returned all their prisoners to Rupert's triumphant command? One of their number, Colonel Charles Gerard, had already been sent out under a drum to begin the complex negotiations. He was probably back at Rupert's camp by now, surrounded by his cronies and enjoying a goblet or two of fine wine for his troubles. Nobody had thought to give Hugo as much as a mug of dirty water! He

271

lay on his side, propping himself up on his elbow to watch the subdued enemy soldiers moping behind their earth rampart – at bay behind their largely intact defences. The throbbing wound in his lower back hurt so much he was forced to roll over on his stomach again, the jagged cut leaking watery blood into the rough dressing Hale had applied hours before. He felt more foolish than ever, lying in the dirt like a beaten cur, peering at every pair of boots as if he was a child playing dead. He was in serious danger of being stepped on – if not deliberately kicked – by the anxious Roundhead troops wandering about in angry bewilderment while their chiefs decided their fate. Hugo kept his head down and his mouth shut. He was dimly aware the creeping fatigue in his lower limbs was working its way up his torso, shutting off the various parts of his body as if to conserve what was left of his miserable existence.

'How is it, then?' Giles Hale bent down beside the sleeping Cavalier, lifted the back of his coat to check Telling's grubby dressing. Hugo blinked up over his shoulder in bewilderment as the blood-splattered surgeon inspected the deep cut on his back, his pale lips pursed in concentration.

'You've been rolling around in this trash, filling it with smuts,' Hale complained, bending closer to pick at the wound with his razor-sharp knife.

Telling held his breath in agony as Hale probed the cut, working pieces of dirt out of the flesh.

'Now listen to me, lad,' he breathed in the fainting Cavalier's raw ear. 'Your pals over the wall aren't going to be best pleased with me, leaving them in the lurch as it were. Meldrum'll march out, but I can't afford to be taken with them, do you understand?' Telling frowned over the pain, narrowing his eyes as he struggled to follow the surgeon's whispers. 'I need to put a few miles between me and your mates – and you're my ticket out of here.'

'Damn you, Hale, you play-acting spy!'

Telling opened his eyes wider, cricked his neck to the left, and came nose to knee with Arbright – or the top of his filthy roll-top boots to be exact. The slightly unhinged major emerged from behind the sooty chimney breast, pistol in his hamlike fist. Telling squinted up at the towering figure, the brute's liverish lips pulled back from his dirty teeth in a rictus of angry delight. 'Run out on us, would you, is that it?' he rasped.

Telling winced as Hale lost his balance, propped himself up on the Cavalier's injured back. The barber-surgeon scrambled away from the mad officer, holding his bloody knife up in a feeble defence.

'Back off, Arbright, you damned fool! You know as well as I do they'll string me up the moment they set eyes on me! You know where I served before this!' he snarled, cornered against the ruined wall.

'We're all marching out according to the treaty, you and all, matey!' Arbright exclaimed.

'They won't honour any damned treaty once we've laid down our arms!' Hale argued, prising himself to his feet before the leering officer. 'I served 'em not a month since, and left 'em when they couldn't pay me. They'll drag me out, aye, and you and all if I've heard right!'

'Oh, this codfish been spilling the beans about those damned scumbellies back at Bernham, eh?'

'You've hung more than a few of 'em, Arbright,' Hale said fiercely. 'They'll have your card marked same as mine!'

Arbright considered this for a moment. He looked over his shoulder, his bored soldiers too caught up in their own sorry affairs to worry about an altercation between the Major and the bloody sawbones. They had divided up what was left of their food, drunk the little ale they had carried into the Spittal with them, and prepared to endure the ordeal beyond the wall. There was very little panic, most of the men apparently accepting their lot with equanimity. Here and there diehards vowed they would rather swim for it, but nobody had taken off his coat just yet.

Lincoln suddenly seemed a very long way off indeed.

'Ah, that's what you reckon, is it? Officers are to take swords, and I'll cut any man through who lays a finger on me!' the cracked-up major threatened, raising the barrel of his pistol in line with his swelling temple. Telling thought he must burst, the livid veins across his forehead throbbing with excess blood.

'You can't fight all Rupert's army! Don't be such a damned fool! Your only chance is to get across the Trent, same as me!' Hale insisted.

The angry officer closed his fingers about the walnut stock as if he meant to crack the pistol in two. He licked his lips, grimly surveying the nearby earth rampart as he digested the surgeon's stubborn advice.

'Cut and run? Never.'

'They know who you are. Once we've given up our arms we'll be helpless, they'll take whoever they want. Meldrum and the rest might get off, but they've got long memories, they'll know who to look out for.'

Arbright took a deep breath, his waxy features mottled red and blue as his temper cooled a few degrees.

'And what do you suggest, swimming for it?'

Hale pulled at his bloody paw-printed sack, tucked his knife away with the rest of his tools of the trade.

'We'll disguise ourselves as best we can, carry this bugger out the back way. Over the bridge, across the island, and over Muskham bridge.'

The plotters glanced down at Telling, lying in the dirt, teeth clenched against the pain in his back.

'He'll holler as soon as we try and get past,' Arbright theorized.

'No, he won't. I'll hold a shite-rag an inch from his bloody cut. If he so much as farts I'll poison the bastard. And in any case, he's starting to burn up, look, he'll be in a raging fever in another hour.'

Telling slumped at the rogue's feet, chest racked by great dry sobs he tried to disguise as coughs.

The bastards would do it and all, rub him with soil and sentence him to a long, lingering death. The fact they might be put up against the nearest wall for their past crimes would hardly compensate for such a vile end.

'Ah, you've got something there, Hale. Slip out the back way while they're watching the gate, eh? We carry this limp fish over to the bridge, give 'em some blather about taking a Royalist officer to the dressing station. In all the confusion, who's going to stop and worry about a half-dead Cavalier?' His dull grey eyes lit up as he contemplated the clever stratagem.

'When we're safe over the bridge we'll split up. Until then, we go together. How's that sound, Major?'

'Very good Hale, very good,' Arbright breathed, beginning to form new plans of his own.

Why, with Slow Georgey up to his neck outside Newark, he might have a chance to pay Lady Winter and young Thomas a visit. He knew her sister's house in Wolverhampton, after all. He grinned down at the distressed Cavalier.

'Cheer up, son. We'll see you right, just as long as you keep your lip buttoned.'

In the event it all went absurdly easily.

Hale left his distinctive medical wagon parked beside the headquarters tents, transferring his essentials to a small, broken-down dog cart which had been abandoned by the master gunner. He then stripped off his bloody red and white band and tossed it in the bottom of the wagon. His equally distinctive bald head proved slightly more problematical. He would be spotted a mile off, if any of the jubilant Newarkers decided to poke their noses in. In the event he took his scalpel over to the temporary morgue behind the dressing station, inspected each mangled body until he found what he was looking for. He crouched down over the hairiest corpse he could find and carefully cut away the dead man's crowning glory. The sopping wig would do at a pinch – especially if he kept the bloody curls clamped in place beneath a good hat. The ghoulish surgeon completed his grim task, wiping his hands on his apron before taking it off and tossing it over his unfortunate victim's knife-mangled features. He then returned to the stark chimney breast and his dozing hostage. Telling blinked up at the demon barber, hardly recognizing his flushed features beneath the startling wig. Thin trails of blood trickled down Hale's sweaty brow. He wiped the cold blood away, jammed his hat over the mass of matted brown curls, and nodded.

'Right then, Captain, let's get you in the cart.'

Arbright ordered his men to form up, shouting and bawling as they took their places in the long column of nervous Roundhead foot about to march out of the Spittal. They left their muskets stacked behind them – bandoliers and match, powder and ball left out in untidy heaps for the triumphant victors. As well as four thousand stands of arms, the Roundheads abandoned eleven guns – one of them an enormous thirty-two-pound demi-cannon which had been hauled at great expense all the way from Hull – as well as two good iron mortars. The wondrous windfall had the Royalist quartermasters licking their lips in gleeful expectation. Enough weapons and powder to fully equip a respectable army, not bad for a day's work!

The best Sir John Meldrum had been able to negotiate was for the safe conduct of his men as far as Lincoln. The sole concession the poor old gentleman managed to wring from the remarkable Prince Rupert was his men's right to retain their drums and colours – they would run the gauntlet of the entire Royalist army armed with just their swords and polearms. Sir John protested – in vain.

'You have my word on the matter, sir,' Rupert told him with his customary gruff respect for a fellow soldier.

'I do nae doubt your word, Your Highness, but what of your men?'

'My word will do for all,' Rupert concluded, curt but firm. He had allowed Meldrum and his rebels more conditions than they deserved. They would either march out as arranged or fight on.

Having obtained as generous a treaty as he could, Meldrum set about organizing his army for the dangerous withdrawal to Lincoln. His officers busied themselves about the chaotic Spittal, organizing some semblance of order from the mass of frightened fugitives. The companies, regiments, and brigades eventually took shape, forming up behind their colours – blowing proudly in a stiff Royalist wind. The dour commanders sat on their horses a little way off, grimly reflecting on their fluctuating fortunes.

At last, all was ready. Meldrum took off his hat and nodded his tired head.

The moment the massed drummers beat 'march on', Arbright excused himself, making a great play of urinating against a crumbling earth wall. He glanced over his shoulder as his men began to file out of the main gate, slipped back down the ruined defences, and made his way to the rear of the virtually deserted fortress. He found a surprisingly hirsute Giles Hale standing beside the battered dog cart, nervously glancing over his shoulder like some thieving tinker. Arbright tilted his head in mock horror, studied the barber's vigorous new growth.

'By Heaven, Hale, you could make a fortune selling hats complete with a headful of hair,' he joked, his coarse features split by a filthy grin. Hale scratched at his outlandish headdress, careful not to knock the wig from his sinister bald dome.

'The bastard must have been alive with lice,' he cursed. 'They're all jumping on to me now.'

Arbright laughed like a drain, his sausage fingers busy untying his buff coat.

'Aye, I'd best lose this. I'll put my pistols and sword in the bottom of the cart – just in case things go awry.'

Hale nodded, anxious to be away.

Hugo Telling lay on his stomach on the bloody running-board, raising his head to stare at his filthy tormentors. Arbright grinned down at him.

'Got your arse-rags handy there, Hale? Good man. Listen to me, Telling. You fell on your sword, crossed your old scar for your trouble – but no worse. When we let you go, you can go and get it stitched and be as right as rain in a week or three. But if Hale drops his arse-wipe onto it, it'll fester like a five-hundred-year-old whore – and there'll be no cutting it out, not where it is. Now it's not the neatest trick I've ever pulled, I'll admit. But needs must when Rupert drives, so just keep it closed, eh? For your sake.'

His battered features seemed to blend and shift as he spoke, transforming him from callous butcher to avuncular superior and back to butcher once more.

Telling slumped on his splintered bed, too exhausted to argue with the mad brute. He hardly felt a thing as Hale whipped up the broken-winded nag, drove the cart down towards the trampled walls at the rear of the Spittal. He lay there, numbed with fatigue and weak with loss of blood, hardly able to focus on the fingers in front of his face.

A few minutes later Hale saw the first enemy troops moving cautiously through the orchard, hoping to be first over the wall of the abandoned fortress.

Telling was hardly even aware of them: all he could hear were their dim voices, getting further and further away with every maddening creak of the wheel. They seemed to be calling through a clinging fog of background noise, the gentle lap of the river beating like storm-driven surf on his feeble mind. He raised his head an inch from the bloody running-board, blinked over the wagon rim at the shadows moving like wraiths through a petrified forest. He was too tired to raise a shout of warning, even if he had recognized them.

The anxious Royalist musketeers watched the muddy dog cart rumble and bump down the scored track between the shot-blasted remains of the orchard, the driver waving a filthy scrap of white cloth in feeble token of surrender.

'We've an injured officer of yours – Captain Telling! Don't shoot, sirs!'

Major Arbright had taken off his buff coat and thrown off his helmet, stumbling along beside the cart in his blood-splattered shirt as if he had just escaped from Bedlam. An inquisitive Royalist musketeer raised his chin a notch, took a suspicious peek at the groaning Cavalier lying in the back of their filthy contraption.

'I thought you wuz s'posed to come out front way,' the musketeer enquired in a rich West Country accent.

'We'll go any way you reckon, mate, only if we have to get to the back of the bleedin' queue again, well, yer man'll be as good as dead. Who d'you say he was, Simon?' Hale called at his bogus assistant.

'Some captain o' that Princey feller's,' Arbright replied, playing the regimental idiot for all he was worth.

The distracted musketeer watched his mates hurry on through the deserted gate, obviously eager to get their hands on as much Roundhead loot as possible before their damned officers brought them to order. That wouldn't be too long either, with that hound Rupert in charge!

'All right then, on you go,' he waved his hand the way he had come, back towards the gently flowing river and the distant bridge of boats.

Meldrum's army marched out towards Lincoln, the hooting Royalist troops clustered about the miserable ranks – noisily intent on plunder and revenge.

Here and there angry scuffles broke out as the furious King's men set upon the shambling column, attempting to wrest colours or treasures from their bewildered enemies. Rupert galloped to and fro, berating his troops for breaking the treaty and handing the colours back to their defiant owners. The noise was indescribable, animals screeching, men shouting, pistols popping. Carts rumbled and hoofs drummed the trampled meadows.

Sir George Winter spurred along through the angry press of men, beating the more enthusiastic looters out of his path.

'Make way! Back to your colours, you malignant shits! Out of the way!' He gazed at the nervous Roundheads, scanning every face, searching every unit for his despised enemy: Miller Arbright. Where had the rogue hidden himself? He ought to be easy enough to spot, the great prickster! Company after company traipsed past, heads cast down as the Royalists hurled abuse at their bowed heads. The angry colonel pulled his horse up, turning the sweating beast through the cursing ranks. Where was that thrice-damned miller?

Hugo Telling heard none of it. He had fallen into a deep faint, his outstretched limbs waxy and cold. Giles Hale had divested himself of his red and white band and hidden his medical tools under some sacking in the back, but he still possessed a quick wit and a ready tongue, sweet-talking the musketeers who had been detailed to watch the bridge.

'Give us a hand here, lads, one of Rupert's horseboys, taken a bloody knock. You know what candle-wasting clods they are in the cavalry!'

'Aye, you'd think they'd won the damn battle single-handed,' one of the morose guards called back in a thick Irish brogue.

'They fuckin' well did, yer lousy arsehole!' one of his colleagues replied, earning a peal of laughter from the relaxed musketeers. Arbright had bent his back to the muddy cart wheel, helping to manhandle the wagon through the trampled filth. He kept his head down, staring at the mud as Hale engaged Tillier's men in a good-natured conversation.

The same men he had cheerfully hung a few short weeks before. If they recognized him they would undoubtedly tear him apart. He swallowed hard, let his lower lip sag like some over-grown cretin. The musketeers had assumed the casualty had been sent out from their own lines. Nobody seemed too bothered who the poor splinter in the back was, at any rate.

'Wait on there, uncle,' their sergeant called.

Hale froze on the running-board, the reins stiff in his sweating fist.

'Don't you mark him, Peter? That cocky little shite-hawk from Bridgnorth?'

The musketeers peered over the wagon at the swooning Cavalier. Telling could just see their faces, pale blobs swimming in his watery vision.

'That little turkey-cock as bossed us about, aye. Copped for one, has he? Good bleedin' riddance!'

Hale laughed. 'Well, whoever he is, he's a pal of Rupert's.' The musketeers could well believe it, arrogant little devil. 'Lend a hand to get us over the bridge, lads,' Hale called, winking at the idle loafers waiting by the bobbing pontoon.

'Aye, all right, then. We don't want that bastard round kicking up a storm over one of his own.' They stacked their weapons and leaned on, boosting the old cart over the tightly lashed ropes which restrained the bridge of boats.

'That'll do, boys! See you in London!' Hale called cheerfully.

'Aye! Won't be long now,' one wag called back, earning a burst of ironic laughter from his tired mates. Arbright shuffled on beside the creaking cart, breathless with anticipation. Over the island, across Muskham bridge, and they would be free.

Free to look up a few old friends.

'Well done, Giles, you're playing 'em for apes!'

'We've a way to go yet, Major, and if I were you, I'd wipe that bloody grin off my face.'

WEST MEON,

NEAR WINCHESTER, HAMPSHIRE,
26 MARCH 1644

Sir William Waller's army had been fortifying itself for months, absorbing contingents of new men from all over the South-east, training day and night so that the bawled orders of the officers were instantly obeyed. They had marched until the complex battle manoeuvres so necessary for their survival had become second nature, drilled until their new pikes and muskets were as familiar as their old tools from home, the newly turned stocks and staves worn smooth from constant use.

The troops in the newly raised regiments were anxious to prove themselves, to run the same risks as the boastful veterans from Waller's well-seasoned units and to try a fall or two with their mysterious brothers over the hill: Sir Ralph Hopton's equally fit field army.

An army they had never yet beaten in open battle.

Waller's men – green recruits and leathery sweats alike – were determined to get their revenge, to build on the small successes they had achieved at Alton and Arundel over the winter. They were thrown into an immediate fever of anticipation when the orders finally came round to strike camp and prepare to march. Sir William had assembled more than ten thousand men, well equipped, well trained, and well fed. The shrewd and timely distribution of a month's pay stirred even the most reluctant Roundhead's blood, and persuaded the rather unreliable London volunteer units to one further effort before they were rotated home.

The long winter lay-off was over.

*

Sir William finally ventured forth from his lair at Farnham, confounding hundreds of his newly sprouted soldiers, who had been confidently predicting an immediate descent on Basing House. But instead of taking the thrice-damned road towards Basingstoke, Waller marched his men towards the South-west, and an immediate confrontation with Sir Ralph Hopton's smaller but rather more experienced Royalist army, presently manoeuvring around Winchester.

The Night Owl had correctly judged that the Royalist field army – lately reinforced by two thousand veterans under the gouty Lord Forth – had to be dealt with before he could turn his attention back on the despised stronghold which had become such a thorn in the side of the Parliamentary cause.

'Ah, it's time that fat bleeder Essex got off his arse and had a crack at that shite pit,' Billy Butcher commented, pushing his hat to the back of his straw-coloured curls and spitting into the bristling hedgerow.

The Earl of Dartland's regiment had been shooed from its slumbers beside the insect-loud verge, waiting to take its place behind the boisterous London Trained Bandsmen on the track which wound down the valley. The road ran a stone's throw from the chattering river, overgrown with willows and fat ranks of bulrushes. The meadows and rolling slopes were bathed in sunlight.

To an army reared that winter on muddy enclosures and a few feet of snow, the lovely Meon valley might have been a spring paradise – if it hadn't been for the presence of seven thousand crack Royalist troops somewhere over the tree-capped horizon.

Waller's tired soldiers had marched miles – doubling back on themselves more than once as their general played chess with his opponent, attempting to confound his old adversary Hopton. Up and down, round and round, the armies hardly more than a few miles from one another, bivouacking within sight of one another's breakfast fires.

The veterans remembered the previous summer's campaign, those ever more dangerous manoeuvres which had resulted in the bloody fight on Lansdown. It wasn't an encouraging omen.

The troops had kicked up a storm of choking grit which bleached their newly repaired coats white, turning the warriors into pale wraiths. The rapacious wanderers had helped themselves to switches or walking sticks from the root-furrowed verges, adapted leafy branches to keep the clouding flies at bay. High-spirited individuals had swatted their neighbours with their improvised whisks, or lobbed pebbles at their comrades in front, enjoying the punishing march as if was a pleasant summer stroll.

Butcher snatched off his hat and beat the greasy felt over his arms with a curse.

'We've had three goes at that bleedin' dump – his lard-arsed buggers haven't shifted since Brentford!' he went on, warming to an all too familiar theme.

Colston Muffet nodded distractedly and wiped his chin. 'But we're not going to Basing,' he pointed out. 'We're off after Hopton.'

'I know that,' Butcher snorted. 'I'm just sayin', that's all.'

Muffet munched on a handful of bread, served up from Waller's well-supplied field kitchen that morning.

'That's why they've sent that Scots bleeder down with all them extra horse. They weren't doin' much good back up there with Essex, so they figured they might as well send 'em down here to help us,' the disgruntled musketeer called.

'I wouldn't go raisin' your voice too high, Billy lad. You know what those buggers in the cavalry are like for stroppin' up sudden.'

'Wasters the lot of them,' the musketeer mumbled, settling his hat back over his bleached hair.

The half-dozen or so drummers up ahead were sweating and panting over their stretched skins, forearms rising and falling as they rattled out the varying rhythms of war. An endless clatter to while away the miles.

William Sparrow hauled the big grey mare into the side of the lane and dismounted, dusting the worst of the road from his fine new suit. He fished in his breeches and relieved himself over a patch of dusty dandelions, taking an ever-alert look back along the files of equally bedraggled men. His experienced eye was drawn down an oddly picturesque avenue, a dappled tunnel formed by the overhanging branches of an early blossoming cherry orchard. The careless vanguard whistled and stamped under the delightful bower as if they were latter-day legionnaires – triumphantly following some great Caesar beneath a ceremonial arch. But instead of shield and pilum these soldiers carried matchlocks and pikes. Sparrow idly wondered how Waller's men would have performed against one of Caesar's legions. Would they have shot them to pieces or run a mile? He had read a little history in his youth, delighting in Livy's tales of civil war and endless conflicts with the Carthaginians. Somehow, this modern strain of civil war seemed to lack the glamorous honour of Livy's day, the silvery sheen of Roman arms replaced by the rusty glimmer of mass-produced weapons: one-size-doesn't-fit-anybody breastplates and carelessly hammered helmets lined with crude (and sometimes life-threatening) rivets.

He sighed, tucked himself back into his breeches, and wiped his hands on his thighs as the twin files of musketeers clattered into view, their bandoliers clinking merrily on their chests, grubby faces flushed red by the fine weather. Behind them came a stand of pikes, the long ash shafts knocking the blossom from the cherry trees, turning the dusty air above their heads bright pink. The petals floated down to alight on helmet and breastplate, coat sleeve and scuffed boot. The curious procession reminded him of a guard of honour at a fine town wedding, garlands and flowers hurled into the sky above the guests' heads.

Well, it would be different when they ran into Hopton's men, Sparrow thought sourly. The only things being hurled into the air then would be iron balls and lead bullets. Blossoming giblets would provide all the colour they could stomach, flying brains their pinky haloes.

'Come along, you sacks! You're dragging your feet as if you've marched 'undred mile!' he called, standing on the verge as the sadly reduced regiment shuffled by. He nodded at the veteran sergeants following behind, their buff coats wreathed in clouds of buzzing flies.

Sparrow climbed back into his saddle and sat there looking hot and bothered as Colston Muffet traipsed into view with his veteran marksmen, looking more like a rusty old serving man than a bold centurion.

'Morning, Will, warm enough for yer?'

Sparrow grimaced at the overfamiliar sergeant, picked a stray cherry blossom from his expensive doublet.

'Ah, morning, Elder Sergeant Muffet. You'd best make sure the daft buggers remember to take water when they can, this dust'll dry 'em out quick enough.'

Muffet had of course already warned the men to keep themselves well supplied. He scowled up at the big man on the twitching grey, giving his orders as if he had been born to it. Muffet remembered their first battles together in the dim and distant days of the previous summer. By Christ, they had come a long way since building that fort at Claverton, just down the river from Bath.

'They'll do. Course, you aren't sufferin' from the fouled air so much, sat up out of it on that bliddy donkey!' he observed, tipping his tired old hat to the back of his head. 'Mind you, all that sittin' around'll catch you out – fittin' yourself into those tight new breeches of yours!'

Sparrow sucked in his cheeks at Long Col's witticism.

'You ought to take softer steps, Sergeant, you wouldn't stir so much shite!' he breathed dangerously, urging the grey on with a supercilious thrust of his loins.

'Ah, and fuck you too, sir!' Billy Butcher piped up from the anonymity of the ranks.

Strong language wasn't encouraged in this man's army.

*

Sir William Waller had indeed been reinforced by a brigade of horse from the Earl of Essex's otherwise idle army – temporarily debilitated by a crippling bout of typhus in the Thames valley. For once, the lethargic earl had acted with some insight, sending Sir William Balfour with two thousand experienced horsemen to assist his despised colleague Sir William in Hampshire while his own men recovered their strength. The welcome addition of Balfour's brigade gave Waller a telling numerical advantage over his old friend and comrade Sir Ralph Hopton, an advantage he intended to exploit to the uttermost. His cavalry led the advance, leapfrogging forward from several directions, each armoured column aimed at the waiting Royalists. The foot, guns, and baggage followed along as best they could, finally arriving in their advance quarters in the winding Meon valley. Sir William's thrust sparked an immediate response from the ever-watchful Hopton. He sent the vanguard of his army to hold up his old adversary while he collected the rest of his forces. The two armies spent two days shadow-boxing, jockeying for the best ground before the battle which would settle the campaign one way or the other.

And that was where Sir William's grand design came to an immediate and demoralizing full stop.

An urgent express from London had stopped the army in its tracks – news from the North so profoundly shocking that the Roundhead general had been forced to drastically revise his plans.

Sir John Meldrum – whom he had last heard of about to force the surrender of Newark – had been trounced by Prince Rupert, forced to march off the field without his arms leaving his cannon, carts, and baggage behind.

The unexpected catastrophe had left the road to London virtually open, the heart of the rebellion laid bare to the mighty Prince and his irresistible Cavaliers.

*

The dumbfounding news ran through the camp, turning the men's bowels to water, their cheerful laughter to howls of bewildered agitation. A well-armed and efficiently organized Parliamentary army – not much smaller than their own force – had been obliged to lay down its arms and march off in disgrace. If Rupert had possessed the means of feeding such a horde, he might have taken the whole lot of them prisoner, instantly revising the long odds against the King. But Rupert's mushroom army had achieved its miracle – trying to cage upwards of six thousand men would have turned his lightning campaign into a murderous administrative fiasco. He had been content to take possession of Meldrum's arms, supplies, and cannon, and watch the dispirited Roundheads shamble off towards Lincoln, baffled by their own ill fortune.

Waller's men had already suffered more than one similar defeat, been forced to submit to the King's mercy at Roundway and Bristol. They were no strangers to bad news, but this latest calamity seemed to subdue even the most extreme Parliamentarian.

The men were given the bad news that night, relaxing in their bivouacs outside the tiny hamlet of West Meon. William was as stunned as the rest – the dreadful defeat robbing the men of their carefully accumulated *esprit de corps* in a moment.

Muffet and Butcher shook their heads in dismay, refusing to catch the Captain's eye. Poor Nicodemus burst into tears. Even Gillingfeather – the most fanatical soldier in the army – was utterly cast down, mystified by the mortifying details.

Meldrum's men had been allowed to march off in reasonably good order despite the unauthorized attention of some renegade cavalry units, quickly ordered back into line by an apoplectic Prince. Meldrum's army had only suffered a few hundred casualties – in addition to the usual crop of deserters, turncoats, backsliders, and malingerers – but Gillingfeather reacted as if each corpse they had left behind had been a sworn comrade, a brother in arms, his hands clenched into white-knuckled fists.

Sparrow finished reading the grim dispatch to his silent company, frowning at their shocked expressions but unable to find the words to soften the terrible blow. He felt weighed down by their shared sorrow, deeply depressed by the apparently pointless suffering. Another army demolished but still the war went on. When would it ever end?

The grim dispatches from Newark provoked a bitter debate at Whitehall. The devastating blow sparked a barrage of panic-stricken correspondence to the Roundhead field commanders, underlining the fearfully upset strategic situation. Essex was ordered to stand to, Cromwell and Manchester – about to coordinate operations with the Scots in the North – were instead told to fall back towards London. Sir William Waller, no stranger himself to bitter defeat, was singled out for some particularly piteous entreaties from the House. His army was the only force still intact which could move to protect the capital in time to prevent the gleeful Royalists from making a rapid march on London. The letters had lain an enormous burden on the conscientious general's shoulders. He was to be the bulwark of the southern front – without jeopardizing the northern or central armies. He was to push Hopton back without moving from the defensive: in short – win the war without losing it.

He read the gist of the gloomy letter to his officers that evening, his solemn gaze illuminated by a yellow lantern.

' "This account we have thought to give you, and you knowing we have no other reserve ready if your army should receive a blow, we assure ourselves you will be most careful not to engage in fight but upon such terms as . . ." Gentlemen, I feel I need not concern you with the rest.'

'Those whining dogs at Whitehall,' Colonel Birch rasped, 'they'll sink us yet with their faint-hearted orders! If they want us back there, why don't they say so!'

'They do say so, sir,' Sir William sighed, turning from the abrupt colonel to Sir William Balfour, the Scots professional whose recent arrival had prompted the ill-fated advance into Hampshire in the first place. The clumsily built cavalryman raised an enquiring eyebrow at the morose general.

'Sir, the committee feels your brigade at least should be rejoined to my lord the Earl of Essex's army forthwith.'

Haselrig was dumbstruck, snatching the document from the plain table where his commander had lain it to read the miserable instructions for himself.

'March back to London with all his horse! That would rob us of all our advantage over Hopton!' he exclaimed.

'Unless we beat him first, strike while we still can!' Birch leered. 'We could bring Hopton to battle on the morrow, aye, answer his damned challenge,' he suggested, referring to the Royalist general's recent letter, a charmingly insolent invitation to his old friend Waller to meet him with all his forces at an appointed time and place in the proper medieval manner. Waller had of course ignored the formal challenge, knowing his old comrade was merely daring him into the open, hoping to persuade him to fight without his usual advantages of ground, wind and sun.

The scurrilous Royalist news-sheets claimed Waller, that canny old Roundhead, wouldn't fight without them – Hopton, to his cost, knew better.

Sir William nodded, subdued by the confused appeal he had been sent by the newly created Committee of Both Kingdoms and at a loss as to which course he should follow. The committee had been set up to coordinate the plans of both Parliamentary and Scots armies, to direct their enormous war effort against the stubborn King. The anxious, beseeching tone of the letter, however, did not inspire Waller with confidence in their leadership. Birch was right, they could strike quickly, push Hopton back on his heels, and then retire on London to protect the capital.

No matter what his reservations, Waller was able enough to recognize that he dared not hazard Parliament's last field army in open battle unless victory could be virtually guaranteed. He stroked his nose, pondering this conundrum while his senior officers shuffled and muttered amongst themselves. The fiery Birch was for going on, driving Hopton out of Winchester and chasing him all the way back to Oxford if necessary. Haselrig was more cautious, reminding the others of the disaster on Roundway.

They had seemed guaranteed to triumph that day – and look what had happened.

Another Roundway could see them all in irons by the end of the summer!

Sergeant Major General Browne, in charge of the London contingents, was equally uncertain he could trust his brigades so far from their homes. They would fight like demons for the capital, but not for some questionable objective out in the counties.

'We're already banging up against Hopton's pickets!' Birch snorted. 'He won't let us march off without a fight, and we'll be giving up all our tactical advantages, trying to run out!'

'It's not a question of running out, man!' Haselrig, his superior officer, snapped back, his small, staring eyes intent on the thickset colonel. 'You have heard the orders, have you not? We must not hazard our last reserve!'

Waller raised his hand for silence. 'Sir Arthur is right,' he concluded, deeply subdued by the course he had decided upon. 'We needs must protect the capital. There will be plenty of favourable ground nearer London for us to fight Hopton,' he said heavily. 'Gentlemen, we have no choice but to order an immediate retreat.'

John Ruell rapped on the ribs of the muddy wheeled wagon and bent down to peer underneath. Major William Sparrow was lying out full length beneath the creaking wain, his hands crossed under his head as he stared at the splintered planking a few inches above his nose. He had lain there two hours, digesting the frightful intelligence from Newark.

'Ah, there you are, sir. Having a nice kip, eh?'

Sparrow glanced at the company clerk's cheerful face, oddly framed by the running-board. Regular meals had thickened the rogue's once skeletal features, lain layers of greasy flesh beneath his prominent chin. The clerk had joined them back in Penmethock, one of a trio of ringleaders who had become the unofficial spokesmen for Sparrow's mutinous raiders. They had practically taken over direction of the fight – once they had caught a whiff of Cruikshank's famous golden hoard. A hoard he had played a considerable part in helping to remove. But his fellow ringleaders hadn't survived the bloodbath to share his good fortune, and the suitably chastened Ruell had been on best behaviour ever since – dreading the day Sparrow might remember his treachery and have him put up against the nearest wall. He had taken to his new role with uncharacteristic enthusiasm, relishing the opportunity of pitting his fraudulent wits against the regimental accounting system. In short, he had made a typically efficient administrator – and prospered into the bargain, no doubt.

'What is it now?' Sparrow growled. He had been thankful the long winter's wait had come to an end, as eager as any to take the fight to Hopton. But the exhausting manoeuvring about the Meon valley had steadily extinguished his enthusiasm, and the debilitating news from Newark had shaken the entire army's resolve. He could sense it as he moved about the camps, listened to the anxious conversations beside their bivouac fires. Waller's army had marched out with a spring in its step, but had been reduced to sullen shuffling by a scrap of paper.

'Letter for you, Major Sparrow, sir,' Ruell reported. 'Came with the baggage down from London. Sorry it's a bit smeared, like.'

Good Christ above, what was it now? Had he been appointed to command the entire army or thrown out of the service altogether? The bewildered major hardly knew what to think any more. He was sick of the whole business, sick of the blood and the pointless sacrifice. How many more men were going to die before there was some kind of decision? The Roundheads had been celebrating a few months back, thanking God Byron and his Papist butcher-boys had been slaughtered up at Nantwich. They had been turning handsprings at the news the Scots had finally decided to join them, tipping the balance against the King.

Now it seemed His Majesty's trusted servant Rupert had upset the apple cart all over again, ruined their premature celebrations with his astonishing thrust across the Midlands. If neither side could finish the business then maybe the time had come to talk, to settle their differences at some kind of conference? Sparrow had wisely kept such heresies to himself, preferring to brood in his quarters than join his brother officers with a jar of ale. 'I've had my fill of bloody orders,' he growled, snatching the scroll from the clerk's fingers. He picked at the elaborate wax seal, tugged the document open and began to read the flamboyant script.

Given by Sir Gilbert Morrison, Colonel of Militia, by Chipping Marleward, 15 March 1644.

The merchant had found his way home, then! Sparrow grunted with annoyance at the thought of the slippery turncoat taking to the hills with a good portion of William's hard-earned cash. And he had restored all his old titles – no matter how fanciful. Colonel of militia, indeed!

'To Captain William Sparrow,' he read, 'lately of Colonel Tobias Fulke's regiment of foote, at the Mermaid, Lambeth, London.'

It was a miracle it had reached him at all, this far away from that damned dump!

William, fondly remembered companion and generous colleague, you will be gladdened to hear I have fulfilled my mission and kept the promise I made to you.

Chance would be a fine thing, William fumed. Running off to Chipping Marleward when he should have been . . .

Your wife Mary Keziah is as well as can be expected, and the babe is doing well. She has named the boy Callum after her great-father (you wouldn't remember Gregory's old gaffer, he used to run errands for me before . . .

Babe?

William sat up with a start, cracking his head on the underside of the wagon. He shouted with pain, grabbing the hurt while he ruffled the astonishing dispatch. His green eyes scanned the ragged handwriting, desperately seeking more news of his infant son. Surely it – he – had been born too early?

> . . . gave her the fright of her life, and she calved down on the spot, if you can believe it. God's bones, William, I wager your ears were burning, you could have heard Mary three furlongs off shouting and bawling and making a terrible fuss. Healthy babes don't grow from seed, although I suppose in a way . . .

Never mind the blather, what about the boy? William fretted, turning the letter over.

> . . . abilities recognized at last. It's obvious I made a good impression on His Highness when he met me outside Gloucester last September. He has clearly not overlooked my skilful operations before the city, sadly curtailed before I was able to achieve a more telling conclusion. He and I have high hopes we shall be able to raise a whole new regiment of men for the King's righteous cause.

What was the old fool dribbling on about now? It sounded as if the turncoat turned midwife had been busy earning the respect and patronage of Prince Rupert himself! He must have inveigled his way in with someone, to dare return to Chipping Marleward! William shook his head at this puzzling and unexpected development. Sir Gilbert back at home, lording it over the Mendips once again? Somebody must have pulled some strings for him somewhere.

> And so, William, I must, in all honesty and respect to my new position in the county, earnestly and sincerely urge you to resign your commission with that damned rabble and get yourself back to me as soon as you are able. His Highness has promised, or as good as, considering we're so frequently of the same mind, to forgive your previous errors and accept you utterly regret your former rebelliousness. We all look

forward to seeing you soon, your servant and friend, sir, Gilbert Morrison.

Sparrow reread the entire letter three times, flummoxed by its tantalizing disinformation. Callum? He closed his eyes and tried to imagine the infant crying on Mary's brown breast, but he couldn't bring to mind any image – any real idea of the child he had fathered.

'Everything all right, is it, sir?' Ruell asked. He got no answer.

An hour later the wagon was on the move once more, the great wheels squealing as it was manhandled through a particularly deep rut in the Hampshire roadway. The laden wain was crammed in a massive creaking traffic jam surrounded by a crush of cursing, muttering soldiers tramping towards the east. The dispirited Roundheads were retreating towards Farnham, their hopeful manoeuvres in the Meon valley called off by an urgent order from the top.

An hour after that, Waller changed his mind once more, and ordered the whole army to turn about and face the enemy. He wasn't going to leave the valley without a fight.

HINTON AMPNER,

They marched over the ridge that dawn, every man casting an anxious glance across the valley towards the dimly discerned blocks of troops chequerboarded on the opposite slopes. Some, lost in horrified contemplation of the enemy host, missed their step or ran the butt of their pike into the man in front. The long files of soldiers buckled, anxious troops colliding with their neighbours.

'Sort yourselves out, you damned pricksters,' William called, wrenching the grey mare around in a tight circle as the Earl of Dartland's regiment crested the long ridge, took its first faltering steps towards the enemy.

For a moment, the tightly packed ranks looked little more than a mob, a flock of frightened children herded towards the waiting gunlines. Muffet cuffed and kicked the worst offenders back into line while Goodrich and Jameson performed a similar function with the gawping pikemen, shoving the raw-boned farm boys and crab-handed fishermen back into a semblance of order.

'Stand straight in your ranks and files! Watch your dressings, you damned sheep!' William urged the grey along the jostling column, joined the nervous Earl of Dartland at the head of his men. Nicodemus Burke, his pinched features paler than ever in the early morning glimmer, stood beside the young colonel's fiery charger, the regimental banner hanging limp on its new ash pole. The boy looked glad to see Will, encouraged by the presence of so many friends coming up behind him.

William tipped his helmet back and squinted through the slowly lifting mist, but could make out little of the enemy units formed up across the shallow valley. The dark, regular blocks of Royalist horse and foot seemed to have positioned themselves each side of a steep lane which bisected their position. The sunken road ran down the hill between overgrown verges, dipping into a gentle hollow before climbing back up the hill towards the Roundhead position. William looked left and watched Sir William Waller's veteran cavalry units take up their positions in front of a clump of trees. Other units trotted over the ridge and took up station in front of infantry forming up on the hillside. They had a clear field ahead of them, a steep charge into the rather cluttered valley floor. Sir William had as usual chosen his position with some care, placing his army on far better ground than his old adversary. The Royalist army, on the other hand, had been forced into a rat trap of small fields and enclosures, its various bodies separated by thick and thorny hedgerows.

William felt momentarily cheered by their general's skill, his insistence on providing his army with every advantage of ground.

By Christ, they would need it.

Dartland tried to smile at his grim-faced major, turning his reins over and under in evident agitation. Ever since his ridiculous escapade with Grenville, the young nobleman had veered between bouts of depression and childish enthusiasms, tortured by self-doubt over his unlikely role. He was a boy in a man's army, a puny figurehead for the Western cause which had been lost the previous summer.

Dartland had been completely duped by the wily traitor Grenville, taken in as easily as a five-year-old by his cunning plots. Worse than that, he suspected every man in the army knew it. If it hadn't been for the quick-thinking Sparrow and his bodyguards, Dartland would have been languishing in Oxford Gaol by now. He was well aware he ought to be grateful, but he had reasoned excessive deference to his second in command might undermine his already tenuous hold over the men. He was colonel, after all, not Sparrow.

The awkward youngster had been unable to make up his mind whether he should be dropping to his knees to kiss Sparrow's

boots or adopting a frosty, superciliously superior air. In the event
he had veered between the two courses, slavishly seeking William's opinion one moment and snapping orders like a sawn-off
Wallenstein the next.

Sparrow had not taken kindly to his understandable confusion.

'Ah, there you are,' Dartland simpered, lifting his spyglass to
take a look at the Royalist position being revealed by the slowly
lifting mist. 'Hopton's thrown in some horse and foot look,
thinking we were retreating. The rest are some way off yet.'

William grunted. Up until a few hours ago, he had thought
they had been retreating too. And then they had been turned
around and marched back the way they had come. He gazed at
the Royalist troops on the horizon, wondering if they knew what
they were doing. There were more than enough of the buggers
already, for his liking.

The big man watched a squadron of Parliamentary cavalry trot
along the hill from their left, swing into position a hundred yards
to their front. They looked efficient enough on their well-
groomed chargers, their fluted helmets and sturdy backplates
gleaming in the dawn light. The only trouble with the Roundhead
cavalry was its dismaying tendency of showing its damned backplates to the enemy at the first onset. William shook his head at
their positioning. If they had possessed any musketeers at all,
those daft horseboys would have screened their fire – prevented
them from firing for fear of shooting down their own men. Not
that this drawback had stopped those rock-bollocked strunts in
the Westminster Trained Band. They had somehow managed to
fire on their own front rank at Basing House, shooting eighty of
their own men in the back! He narrowed his eyes, wondering if
the damn fool in charge of the stray horsemen had lost his
bearings. Dartland caught his glance and rolled his eyes at the
major's bewilderment.

'That's right, Sparrow. Sir William's posting his cavalry in front
of us.'

'In front? That makes a bloody change,' William thought
aloud.

The earl made himself comfortable, sitting up primly in the saddle as if he was waiting for his breakfast to be brought up on a silver tray. Dartland appeared unimpressed by the enemy forces, apparently determining on complete nonchalance and affecting a slightly bored air as he briefed his resented saviour.

'Sir William has given word we are to divide the men along the front, the musketeers to support Potley's regiment in the wood there.' He pointed the glass at the dark mass of Cheriton wood, a broad leafy plantation crowning the long ridge to their right. The wooded slopes fell away steeply towards the north-east, giving Waller a valuable flanking feature. The wily Roundhead had wasted no time in sending a thousand musketeers into the wood to secure it. They had already made contact with the enemy sharpshooters, and the men on the ridge could just make out the distant crackle of their musketry.

'Divided? Aren't we going to fight as a unit?' William asked, alarmed at the prospect of the regiment being sent into the battle in penny packets. All their training had prepared them to work together, pike supporting the musket, wings of shot advancing in line with the formidably armoured core of erect spearpoints.

Dartland sighed in exasperation.

'Ours is not to question Sir William's judgement. Potley might need reinforcement in the wood, so our musketeers will be detached,' he rasped. 'We won't need them anyway, with all our cavalry lined up before us!' Dartland declared.

Sparrow held his breath and rolled his eyes under the rusty rim of his helmet. He wished sometimes he'd let that rogue Grenville carry off the flabby little runt!

'As you say, sir,' he breathed. 'Muffet!'

The elder sergeant hurried along the hedgerow, his musket upside down on his shoulder to keep the early morning moisture from the gleaming grey barrel.

'Take yourself back down the column and find Captain Pye. You're to take the shot along the ridge there, report to Colonel Potley.'

Muffet considered this for a moment and then nodded like the good soldier he was.

'Very good, sir!' He hurried off, the anxious musketeers falling out as the pikemen marched out over the crest.

'We'll take up station between those battery guns down the slope there,' Dartland said crisply, pointing down the hillside towards the wide bowl formed by the diverging ridges. Waller had positioned several of his light and manoeuvrable leather guns on the slope, their three-man crews hurrying to prepare the pieces to receive the enemy. His bigger guns had been placed further back on top of the ridge.

Sparrow didn't like the look of the land, it was far too open, exposed to any gun the enemy cared to roll out. Without musketeers they would be virtually useless, simply plugging the front unable to fire – and at the mercy of every sharpshooter in the Royalist army. Their only contribution would be to roll down the hill at charge of pike, hoping to clear the slopes of scattered musketeers and get to grips with their opposite numbers as soon as possible. And if things went awry in the valley it would be every man for himself, getting back to the top of the ridge. He glanced down at Nicodemus, gazing fearfully at the big officer as he clutched the regimental standard. Sparrow grinned.

'You stick by us, lad, stay in the middle,' he advised. The young ensign nodded dumbly, tapped the sword he had strapped to his belt. Please God the boy wouldn't have to use it.

Half a mile along the ridge to their left, Colonel Archibald McNabb sat on his charger, watching his troopers trot into line with commendable skill and precision. Aye, and so they should, the time he had spent training the Sassenach bastards! The regiment had formed up in two squadrons, each divided into four smaller blocks, standing four men deep. There was barely a boot length between them but each troop moved like clockwork, fitting snugly in its assigned place in the line. The short blast of a trumpet brought the whole mass of men and beasts to a sudden standstill. McNabb raised his chin in satisfaction, glanced up the slope at the gaggle of senior officers who had collected in front of a small copse to watch the deployment of the left wing. With the right secured by Cheriton wood, the left – running towards the small hamlet of Hinton Ampner – might be the obvious place for a Royalist assault, and the best of the available cavalry units had been sent to beef up the line.

Waller was there in his dull black armour, surrounded by a coven of black-coated ministers and anxious commissioners. His enormous shirt collar was neatly arranged over his breastplate, giving him a paternal appearance at odds with his occupation. He wore a large plain black hat with a wide rim, which he took off every now and again to smooth his threadbare reddish hair. With him was a selection of his rather more grandly turned out senior officers. Carr, in charge of the dragoons, resplendent in fine Spanish cloak, the rich red fabric set off by a thatch of frosty hair, Haselrig, lips pursed as he watched the horsemen manoeuvre opposite, and Birch, smirking and joking with his captains with his usual high-spirited exuberance. He had won his point after all, persuading Waller to give battle despite the committee's dire warnings to the contrary. He had made sure his pickets had remained entangled with the Royalists, sent beseeching notes back to Waller urging him to march the army back to his support. Waller, regretting his previous decision to retreat, had finally responded.

McNabb spurred his horse up the slope and saluted, Waller nodding soberly at the formidable and eminently reliable Scot. McNabb had served with Waller since the beginning of the previous summer, sharing half a dozen adventures. As well as their military experience, the officers respected one another's religious views. Both men were moderates, unwilling to press their own opinions on others, but glad enough to discuss the thorny issues of the day. Presbyterian by persuasion, McNabb shared Waller's deep concern at the growing power and influence of the Independents. Men like Cromwell, already making his mark in the northern Midlands. These were worrying times, indeed, when you couldn't trust the men in your own army.

'Good morning, McNabb. Your men look ready for a good bang,' Waller greeted his old friend, nervously pulling his over-large nose.

McNabb grinned. 'Aye, sir. Rarin' to go, every man.'

His compatriot, the dour Balfour, was sitting on his horse a little way off, grimly surveying the enemy lines. His own cavalry had been positioned away on the far right – to support the musketeers holding the woody ridge. McNabb bowed his head in greeting, receiving a curt nod in return. Not only was Balfour an outsider amongst Waller's closely knit officer corps, but he held the same rank as the general himself. He had, however, put aside such petty quibbling until the battle was done, recognizing the pressing need of a united front. He didn't mean to let his hurt pride stand in the way of a crushing victory for the Parliament they all served. Balfour had been in arms since the beginning of the war. At Edgehill his steadfast courage at the head of the cavalry reserve had helped prevent the King from crushing the rebellion in a single afternoon. His experience and determination would more than make up for his chilly manners.

'It'll be a warm one, when the sun burns off this dreck mist,' McNabb observed. Haselrig nodded sourly, hardly daring to take his eyes off the enemy cavalry regiments trotting into place across the valley. He had watched just such a cavalcade on Roundway – shortly before his regiment of heavy cavalry were chased from the field and over the nearest cliff for their troubles. He felt a chill of fear clatter through his armoured shell at the memory. John Birch, who knew his superior as well as any, gave the nervous knight a broad wink.

'Ah, cheer up, sir, this is but a rub. We shall yet win the cast!'

Sir William Waller glanced at his cheerful officers, hoping to God they were right. He had only rescinded his previous order to retreat after a sleepless night of heart-searching and deliberation. He had hardly relished the prospect of an ignominious flight back to Farnham, but he couldn't help wondering if he had done the right thing, transforming his anxious rearguard into the vanguard for a renewed advance on the enemy. If he was to lose this army as he had lost the old one on Roundway ... the consequences did not bear thinking about.

'To your positions, gentlemen. May God look kindly upon us this day!' he said piously. There was a mumbled 'Amen' from the black-coated cluster about him, before the senior officers rode off to their various stations along the ridge.

The dismal clatter and bang of the musketry had built in a series of crescendos as more and more musketeers and dragoons had been fed into the vicious firefight in the woods to their right. The leafy glades were no place for pikemen, William thought sourly, but he would rather be in there under some kind of cover than exposed out on this damned hillside.

Dartland had stationed himself just behind the solid wall of pikes, a gaggle of captains, drummers, and whey-faced ensigns clustered about his horse as if it were a good-luck charm to fend off ball and bullet. William had sent his mare to the rear with the baggage, preferring to feel good turf under his boots than plunge about the field on a skittish horse. He stood just to the right of the pikeblock beside the marvellously calm cockney sergeants. Goodrich and Jameson were leaning on their halberds, conversing in undertones despite the battle popping and banging in the woods to their right. William stepped forward and peered along the ranks, the men standing at order, sixteen-foot pikes forming a dense thicket above their heads. There were three other regiments deployed to their right which would presumably turn about if the Royalists won through the woods, but he couldn't help worrying about the flank. Muffet and the musketeers were their eyes and ears, they were usually there to alert the more ponderous pikemen to the terrifying fluctuations to their right or left, any sudden alerts behind them. Ah well, it was no use fretting about that now.

303

'Take a drink while you can, boys,' he called, throat already parched by the nerve-stretching delay. It was all this damned waiting about that stole the men's courage, preyed on their imaginations and drained their martial ardour.

The Royalist artillery had opened up a sporadic barrage, balls whistling to right and left. The anxious pikemen in the front wondered if they had been altogether wise – belatedly wishing they had put a few more ranks in front of them.

'Steady, lads. They couldn't hit a barn in this muck,' Sparrow called, wishing it were true. He thought for a moment of Mary, safe back at Chipping Marleward with his little son. By God, he might never get to see him! She had carried the babe going on nine months already, since he had last seen her the night before Roundway.

An ear-splitting screech heralded the arrival of a culverin ball, the heavy roundshot digging into the turf and sending up a spout of clods and stones twenty yards to their front. The hot debris clanged and rattled off of their helmets as they hunched their backs against the sudden storm. The squadron of cavalry in front of them seemed somewhat discomfited by the sudden fire, drawing off to their left leaving Dartland's men isolated on the smoky hillside. A few degrees' elevation and the bastard gunners would chuck a round right through the middle of them! William tightened his helmet, peered along the battlefront towards the neatly arranged horsemen flung out on the green slopes to their left. He could dimly hear their trumpets through the mad ringing in his ears. He squinted, made out a regiment of enemy foot begin the advance. The dark block detached itself from the constricted Royalist line and moved out into the open fields. William waited for their dreaded cavalry to move off in support, idly wondered whether that slim-shanked clod Telling was with them. He had developed a strange affinity with the twitchy Cavalier, bumping into him on half a dozen battlefields as if their fates had been deliberately entwined by the cackling gods of war. As he watched, the enemy foot regiment marched down into the hollow between the armies, drawing dangerously ahead of its colleagues. As far as Sparrow could see, not a single cavalryman had ridden with them. It had to be some kind of trap, surely?

McNabb stood up in his stirrups, watched the Royalist regiment dress its ranks in the hollow a hundred and fifty yards in front of his position. What were they about, sticking their noses out so far? The Scot took a suspicious look at the open flank, expecting to see a horde of Cavaliers swarm up the hillside to spring their trap. But nobody appeared. The enemy commander must have lost his mind!

He whirled about in his saddle at the sudden blast of trumpets to his left. For once, Haselrig had not waited to ponder developments. His heavy cavalry, the fabulously armoured Lobsters, were moving down the hill at a steady trot, swords drawn, helmets closed. McNabb felt a surge of exaltation, drew his own sword with a fierce Gaelic oath. If the enemy horse moved out now he would lead his own squadrons around the Lobsters and take them in the flank! He swallowed hard, eyes filling with the salty sweat rolling down from beneath his elaborate Polish helmet.

The Lobsters picked up speed, five hundred heavy horses thundering down the hill at the horribly isolated Royalists. The hill shook, the long ridge pounded to its rocky core by the thunderous crash of iron and flesh. McNabb watched in awe as the enemy musketeers panicked, opening fire at extreme range. Puffs of white smoke obscured their upper bodies, left their legs dangling beneath a choking cloud. There was no time to organize any kind of defence, no cover to hide behind. Their pikes formed a bristling hedgehog, the musketeers taking cover within the armoured heart of the regiment. Their drums clattered the alarm, colours plunging above the mass of men. McNabb could hear their terrified screams above the titanic rush of the hoofs. In another blink the Lobsters were on them, squadrons overlapping the forlorn vanguard. Horses wouldn't be foolish enough to impale themselves on the dipping pikes, but the very weight of the charge drove the leaders head first into the quailing Royalists.

Riders were tipped off or run through by the long spears, horses screamed as the long points pierced their sweaty chests. But the momentum was too much for the straining pikemen. Broken weapons clattered to the turf, others were tugged in all directions by the impaled horsemen. One horse – frightfully skewered by a broken pike – went head over heels into the front rank, its thrashing legs smashing skulls and crumpling breastplates. The ranks packed in behind fell over themselves, the bristling hedge of pikes wavering like brittle grass on a windblown shore. The Roundhead horse needed no further urging, piling into the fight in an orgy of reckless revenge. They spurred their chargers straight at the wavering mass, slashing and kicking, stabbing and gouging a bloody path through the shattered formation. In another moment it was over, the survivors at the back taking to their heels or clinging at the remorseless horsemen like lone ants attacking a scorpion. The Lobsters raised their bloodied, armoured fists, smiting left and right, crushing skulls, opening chests. The cornet carried their green battle flag before them, a serene cloud and dropping anchor, splattered now in gouts of gore.

'Roundway! Remember Roundway!' The maddened horsemen remembered their disgrace well enough. They fought like demons released from the pit, hell-bent on slaughtering every last man whether he ran or fought or flung away his arms in terror. They cut this way and that through the fugitives, trampled their corpses, slaked their bloodlust in a riot of flying entrails. Their chargers looked as if they had waded a river of blood, splashed to their chests with shimmering gore.

Sir Henry Bard's foolhardy regiment had simply ceased to exist.

'By Christ, look at that!'

'Whatever did they think they were doing?'

'Give 'em what for, boys! Give 'em one for Roundway!'

Sparrow swallowed hard, watched the heavy cavalry trot back to their starting lines leaving livid red trails behind them.

By God, an entire regiment had been wiped out in a few minutes! The Royalist position was no more than a shambles, a stinking heap of corpses! The enemy seemed too stunned to move, their regiments entangled in the closely hedged enclosures about the lane. Their artillery seemed to have turned its attention to the Roundhead left, battering the defiant musketeers in Cheriton wood.

It wasn't even time for breakfast yet.

Five minutes later the enemy commander reacted to the sudden reverse, threw the first of his horse regiments down the cluttered slope. They moved off down the sunken lane, one troop at a time, two men wide. It would take them an age to deploy, funnelled down the overgrown tunnel towards the waiting Roundheads. The russet-coated Parliamentarians saw their chance, tumbling down the bloody hillside before they could move out. The converging forces disappeared into the hollow, they could sense the fearsome impact vibrate through the hillside. Sparrow could hear the appalling clatter of steel on steel, the mangled screams of horse and men as the Royalists tried to cut their way through the superior Roundhead force.

William wondered where Muffet had got to, wished the experienced musketeers were back with their friends in the pikeblock. It was no fun, sitting out the battle taking everything the enemy chucked at you whilst unable to fire more than a pistol or two in response.

'Will! Look!' Nicodemus pointed excitedly to their right. Sparrow spun around and squinted through the drifting smoke, spotting the movement in the trees. Hundreds of soldiers were running for their lives, fleeing the burning woods and racing off across the open slopes to the startled support units. Sparrow watched in horror as the stampeding musketeers disappeared into another hidden fold in the converging ridge. The Royalists had cleared the wood, driven their own musketeers out of their cover. The London men had broken – and taken his friends with them. There was no time to wonder what had become of Muffet and the others – they were old hands at close-quarter fighting, used to cutting and running when things got too hot.

'Stand straight in your ranks and files!' he bawled hoarsely. This was it, the King's men were coming for them now. He turned, straightened his helmet, and stared into the quiet hollow, still wreathed with ropes of acrid smoke. He couldn't see anything on the slopes or hedges beyond. Another five minutes dragged by, the musketry in the wood slackening off long enough for them to hear the distant throb of the drums, somewhere across the stony depression. No horse! No musketeers! William thought about ordering an immediate advance, jamming his men into the hollow before it was filled with Royalist sharpshooters. He balled his fists, drew his sword, and swung it through the smoke before returning it to its scabbard. He was no swordsman, and the eight-foot long partisan was far better for close-quarter fighting.

'Have a care!'

The black and white clouds lifted, blown by some evil wind back along the valley to reveal the difficult ground beyond the hollow.

It was packed with Royalist troops.

Skirmishers and dragoons along the treeline, flushing out Roundhead survivors from the ominously silent wood. A body of horse dashed and speckled with gorgeous silk colours, swords glittering as they moved up in support. And directly ahead of Sparrow's men, a brigade of Royalist infantry, tramping down the slopes full of their own brutal majesty. Dartland was sitting on his charger, mesmerized with terror and unable to do more than stare at the approaching enemy.

Sparrow opened his mouth but the order had dried up in his throat.

He thrust his halberd towards the tightly packed Royalists, stepped out in front of the wavering line. He coughed, licked his parched lips.

'Earl of Dartland's regiment!' he croaked. 'Advance your pikes!'

The trembling ranks raised their weapons to their shoulders.

'Prepare to march. March!' Left foot forward, right foot forward. Looking up from their boots they saw a dark mass of enemy soldiers, smudged faces like blobs of butter above their faded blue coats. They were moving faster now, pushed on by the pressing ranks behind them, stumbling down the stony slope. Sparrow watched the colour party move to the rear, Goodrich and Jameson using their halberds to keep the ranks straight. William gripped his polearm, closed in on the anxious-looking farm boy who acted as their left-hand marker. He didn't know his name. The two forces had reached the hollow at the double, the Roundheads knowing they would be slaughtered if they couldn't close quickly.

But not quickly enough.

The Royalist musketeers clustered on either flank opened fire. William felt the vicious sting of the bullets clip the air above his head. The slugs clattered off pikes, dented breastplates, and burrowed into cowering flesh. The pikemen recoiled in the face of the horrific storm, bodies tumbling out on all sides.

'Charge your pikes!'

The survivors lowered their weapons to shoulder height, right arms thrown back straight to balance the deadly points.

'Advance!' Sparrow bawled, stepping over a crying pikeman curled up like a baby and clutching his belly. Blood was seeping between his fingers in hatefully eager streams. Another volley. The front ranks quivered, the ill-aimed musketry pounding and splitting the turf, rebounding to crack shinbones, destroy knees. Men were screaming on all sides, clutching their wounds as their comrades pressed on, pressed past them. Sparrow saw the enemy pikeblock loom out of the musket smoke, close enough to see the burning smuts on a man's nose.

'Charge!' he yelled, as the bristling formations impaled themselves upon one another in a fearful clatter of wood and scrape of steel. Pikepoints jabbed at his face, clattered off his helmet and skinned past his thigh. A pike tore a hole in his sleeve, a glittering point creasing his left forearm. Another point cracked him on the ankle but was deflected by his stout leather boot. The evil spears thrust past him as he barged forward between the pressing men, his shorter but handier halberd ready. He jabbed the broad-leafed blade at the nearest body, coming at him shoulder first as if the Royalist had been squeezed out of his rank by the terrible collision. The man ducked, but could not avoid the punishing blow. He fell sideways, immediately crumpled up by the massive lung-bursting impact as the two bodies crashed together.

Sparrow was stuck between them, the halberd wrenched from his hands. He was dimly aware of their bad breath and sweaty, straining faces, their yellow teeth bared like wolves' fangs. A terrible crush which must burst the brains from the top of his head. He worked one fist loose, worked it under the defenceless pikeman jammed in front of him.

'Get off me, you whoreson rebel!'

Sparrow thrust the loose plate up with all his might, cracking the steel rim into the man's chin. The Royalist choked with fury, his bitten tongue bleeding profusely.

'Ah, you fuckin' bastard!' he slurred, squeezed aside, arms akimbo, by a sudden thrust from the Royalist pikemen at the back.

'Push 'em down the slope!'

'Hang on, boys!'

Sparrow hung on for grim death, felt his feet leave the ground as the pressure built up from the rear. Unable to advance against their deadlocked opponents, the front rank was instead propelled a foot or more into the air, their struggling bodies meshed together but unable to do more than blink at their enemy.

' 'Ello there, Will!'

William blinked at the contorted face rammed into his breast-plate. Rivulets of spittle had escaped from the side of the man's mouth as he tried to get a breath in the monstrous crush.

The man's helmet had been tugged to one side, revealing a crop of greasy black curls beneath.

'It's me, Zack! Zack Pitt!' the crumpled soldier called cheerfully over the groans of the men crushed in around him.

The middle of a bloody battle – what a place to run in to your damned brother-in-law.

'Hello, Zack,' William gasped.

The pikeman gave him a gap-toothed grin.

'Have you seen your Mary at all?'

He had a sneaking suspicion they were going to be there some time.

CHERITON WOOD,

Illiam, caught up in one of the sprawling logjams of pikemen in the hollow, had given up any hope of exerting any influence over the outcome of the battle. He could only grit his teeth and hold on to his halberd, repeatedly pushed up onto the tips of his toes by the ferocious scrummage about him. The pressure on his chest was tremendous, his lungs felt as if he had been tied up into a straitjacket of dirty blankets, an ever-tightening garrote which threatened to squeeze the last puff of wind through his clenched teeth. Just when the murderous embrace was about to choke the last of the life from him, a struggling pikeman to his right or left would be lifted from his feet and turned about, the sudden fissure in the rockwall of men allowing his comrades a momentary breathing space. They would jostle and buck into the narrowest gap, the hopelessly intertwined front ranks reduced to exchanging clumsy body blows now that their weapons were ensnarled in the bonfire of pikepoints ten feet above their heads.

Zack Pitt didn't seem inclined to do William any further harm, happy enough to exchange small talk with his scowling enemy while the bizarre war dance carried them back and forth like seaweed in a storm. The Somerset farmhand arched his back, keeping his face free from the stinking mass of men, gratefully gulping the sulphurous smoke weaving between the trapped sticks.

William, nose to nose with his former crony, couldn't see a thing beyond Zack's shoulder straps. He had no idea how long the brutal deadlock would continue, or how the wider battle was going. Their precious horse might have been pursued from the field by now, their friends taking to their heels while their lone regiment struggled blindly in this damned hollow.

He lost and found his courage a dozen times over, gnawing his lip and heaving for all he was worth, his bemused friend apparently content to be carried along an inch or two by his titanic, back-breaking efforts. Zack whistled, brows furrowed as another deadly heave from the back deposited the struggling men back where they had started.

William caught his breath, hanging on to Zack in a deadly waltz over the trampled ground. He felt another surge of panic.

They might be surrounded by teeming Cavaliers as they had been on Roundway! They might be jamming themselves down the hot barrels of the Royalist guns. They might be about to be taken in the rear by cleverly concealed musketeers, shot down one rank at a time as they ploughed their lonely, smoke-filled furrow along a tattered hedgerow. William spotted a gate manned by a squad of enemy musketeers, busy taking pot-shots at his stranded regiment.

Where was Muffet and his damned crew? They would have driven those devils off by now, if they hadn't been sent on some fool's errand into the wood!

'Well, Will, seems we're set to go roun' in zircles,' Zack gasped.

William closed his eyes and tried to ignore his bucolic observations, praying the viciously uncertain crisis would be over soon.

Whichever damned side pushed hardest.

Sir Ralph Hopton sat on his horse, high on the brow of the hill above the grievously disputed hollow. He could see very little more than William, and the few glimpses he did catch of the raging battle did nothing to relieve his troubled imagination. The Royalist commander who had acted with such speed and resolution in half a dozen previous engagements seemed to have lost his initiative, pummelled by the ghastly crescendos of battle.

He slumped over his saddle, head thumping, his barely healed body shrieking for rest, release from the terrible torment of sending his fellow men to their deaths.

The general was torn with all too familiar uncertainty. Emasculated by fatigue, confounded by the ridiculously complex command structure which had been foisted upon him, and baffled by an enemy who seemed to have discovered some previously unguessed reserves of grit and determination.

Instead of heralding an immediate rout, the loss of the wood seemed to have put extra spirit into the rebel centre. Instead of taking to their heels the moment one of his regiments had so much as poked their noses out of the narrow lane, Waller's armoured horsemen had descended on Bard's unfortunate vanguard and cut it to pieces in a blink.

The sudden disaster hadn't unduly troubled his co-commander.

The venerable Earl of Forth shrugged his padded shoulders, wincing with pain as he shifted his not inconsiderable bulk from one gouty boot to another.

'He's given us a bloody nose, but no matter, sir,' the ancient gentleman observed, grimacing as he tested his weight with the aid of a fantastically carved walking stick.

Hopton gazed towards his old comrade Waller, lost in the chaos of smoke on the opposite slopes.

'I doubt we'll tempt him up for another crack.'

Hopton frowned at the elderly earl's assessment.

'If you'll take my advice, sir,' Forth went on, 'you'll stand where you are, and face him out. I'll send Stowell down the hill, to dislodge those damned lobster-backs.'

Hopton nodded grimly as Forth touched his hat and limped off towards his waiting coach. He raised his glass and swung it this way and that, trying to find some kind of pattern in the swirling chaos, to identify the gravest threat to his extended front.

Surely the wood to his left was safe enough. And the hedge which ran the length of his centre had been lined with musketeers, backed by several reserves of pike and batteries of guns. Bard's regiment had been crushed into the grass like a bloody tick, but there were still men enough to hold the line, he thought grimly.

Hopton raised his head, slowly becoming aware of the rising cacophony from the disputed hollow. He imagined for a moment the hell to which he had sentenced his veteran regiments.

Lathered horses plunging and rearing, spiked and goaded beyond endurance by muzzle flashes and jabbing pikepoints. Riders, hurled from their saddles, groping for their arms as the nimble musketeers darted out of their pikeblocks with butt and dagger to finish them off. Cannons hurling fiery comets though the helplessly packed ranks, disembowelling whole files before the hissing balls buried themselves in the turf.

Hopton swallowed hard, mortified with shame to think Englishmen would spend such energies in pursuit of one another's lifeblood. He remembered his opposite number, Sir William Waller. His old comrade would surely be sharing his doubts, sickened by the pointless slaughter of his countrymen. He took off his hat and wiped his brow, refreshed himself with a gulp of bad-tasting water.

The middle of a battle was no place to wring one's conscience.

William hadn't moved more than five yards in any direction for at least an hour. He was gasping for a drink, his parched throat scorched by blasts of hot smoke. The pikemen pressing behind had run out of breath, leaning on like winter lumber. The musketeers had returned from their mad errand in the wood, swarming about the flanks of the stalled porcupine, jabbing at the enemy soldiers holding the line of the hedge. Sparrow raised his head a notch, realized they had been pushed back alongside the gate. The muddy approaches were potholed and rutted by cattle and carts.

'Hold, hold hard, you buggers!'

The exhausted Roundheads dug in their heels once more.

*

Further up the slope, Waller had re-formed as many of his fleeing musketeers as he could, and directed them down the hill to support his shattered pikeblocks. The crumbling front had stabilized and thickened, the crisis on his right flank averted for now.

Encouraged by the success of his heavy cavalry, the wily general had ordered Balfour to charge towards the wood, driving the Royalist intruders back into the trees and giving his startled foot a much-needed tonic.

Waller spotted a flash of silver through the tumbling smoke, and snatched his glass back to his eye. He stared intently at the narrow neck of the sunken lane which dissected the Royalist position, wondering what cunning deception his friend Hopton was planning.

A regiment of Royalist horse was descending the slope, no more than two men at a time urging their horses through a jumble of splintered pikes and punctured drums. The lathered horses reared and bucked as they caught the ripe reek of blood, the bloody shambles which marked the high water mark of Bard's hare-brained attack.

A feint, surely? Waller paused, wondering where the real blow would come next.

Gallopers spurred along the ridge, pointing back towards the burning wood.

Balfour had run into the elite Queen's regiment of horse!

A trap, as he had expected!

Waller cursed the smoke and scanned the flaming horizon, knots of unidentifiable musketeers hurrying this way and that with their weapons at porte. They seemed terrified they were about to be caught up in the raging bushfires, their bandoliers turned to flaming necklaces about their heads. He watched the great dark blocks of Balfour's squadrons roll across the greensward and disappear behind the burning wood.

A minute went by. He remembered Roundway, the punishing sense of shame and dread when his squadrons had been tumbled back over the downs by the hard-riding enemy.

Another minute. And another.

Waller chewed the end of his thumb, paralysed with doubt.

He watched a young cornet with a bloody rag tied about his head come spurring along the ridge, whipping his horse with his hat. The newcomer ignored all military protocol, wrenching the sweating beast to a halt before the assembled officers and saluting his bewildered chief.

'Colonel Balfour's compliments, my lord. The Queen's regiment has turned tail!' he cried. 'They're all Frenchmen, sir, no heart for the fight, sir, no heart!' he yelled, hoarse with excitement.

Waller tensed. 'And his foot?'

'Retiring through the woods, sir!'

Waller thumped his hand onto his armoured thigh, practically swooning with relief. Hopton's foot were giving ground now!

The last field army Parliament possessed between London and the King, holding its own against their most deadliest, never conquered foe!

Thank the Lord!

The Cavaliers spurred out of the stranglehold lane, desperately attempting to deploy on the common beyond. But for every two men who rode through the bottleneck, Waller could throw ten riders against them. The Royalists charged three, four, fives times their number, confident the careless courage and elan which had won the day on Roundway would break the Roundhead resistance once again.

But they were met with pistol and sword, held, and then ground back on every side, charged from both flanks at once and harried from the front by the heavier, fully armoured Lobsters. Locked up in close-quarter carnage, the lightly armoured Royalists couldn't make any impression against the steel-plated knights. Pole-axes rose and fell, goring heads and impaling tired limbs. The Lobsters spurred into the midst of the enemy squadrons, practically immune to the sword blows which rained down on their ornate helmets.

Haselrig's heavy cavalry relished their revenge, firing their pistols into screaming faces, hacking a bloody path through a forest of arms and legs.

One regiment after another rode down the slope, smashing itself on their pitiless ranks with suicidal fury. But not even King Charles' fanatical Cavaliers could prise a gap in the enemy formations, and the tattered survivors turned their horses back up the slope, riding into their comrades still hurrying down the hill to join the unequal fight.

Sir Arthur Haselrig lifted his helmet, peered through the drifting smoke as if he could not trust his own eyes. The enemy horsemen who had pursued his troops from Roundway Down, driving them over a precipice like so many sheep, were melting away a dozen at a time, spurring their broken-winded horses back towards the protection of the hedge. The valiant colonel was astounded at his own success, hardly daring to credit what he saw.

Colonel Birch was whooping with delight and shrieking thanks to God, pulling his horse in ever-decreasing circles as he surveyed the enemy retreat.

'There you are, sir! Did I not bid you 'twas but a rub!'

Haselrig grinned weakly, nodding in bewilderment as his excitable subordinate thrust his sword into the air in triumph.

'Send word to Sir William. The enemy appears to be retiring in good order on their supports . . .'

'Good order? They're running for their lives! By God, sir, we've got them!' Birch cried, pointing his sword at the milling enemy, desperately seeking gaps in the hedge to escape the carnage on the common. Haselrig was too stunned to speak, as if he might break the wondrous spell which had granted them victory.

'Well, sir? Will you order the charge?'

'Charge?' Haselrig exclaimed. 'Our orders, sir, were to hold the common. I do not recall Sir William—'

'But we must strike while we may, sir, if we let them regroup behind the hedge we'll never force them from their hill!' Birch cried, his features contorted with fury.

Haselrig peered over his shoulder, tried to spot Sir William's personal pennants further up the hill behind him. The summit was crowned with smoke. Various regiments of foot were waiting their turn, their officers trotting ahead to peer into the hellish valley.

'We must advance, sir, or we'll lose all we've won!' Birch insisted, turning his horse across Haselrig's path.

The knight lowered his helmet, tormented with doubt.

How dare he risk the last Parliamentary reserve between them and London in a madcap charge up a steep hill?

'I implore you, sir, remember Roundway! Their impetuosity won them the day, as we will triumph now! Order the charge, sir!' Birch had grasped Haselrig's bridle as if he was an elderly gentleman enjoying a leisurely ride about his park.

Sir Arthur swallowed, squinting at the filthy green smudge which marked the extent of the enemy-held hedges. The formidable barricade was doing a grand job of keeping the broken enemy horse at bay, let alone his own tired squadrons.

'There, sir, look right, the hollow!' Birch pointed his sword towards the chaotic dip, filled to the brim with a thousand and more struggling men. It was impossible to tell the frantic fighters apart, every regiment had disintegrated into a multi-coated mob.

'Those colours near the gate, they're Dartland's, sir, the turncoat spark himself!'

Haselrig shielded his eyes. He could just make out the tattered green rag which the young earl had carried past him that dawn.

'But they're stuck fast, man! And they've been at it three hours!' Haselrig objected.

Birch seethed with frustration, boiling with impatience to charge down the hill and win the battle by God's grace. He sobbed with anger, clinging to Haselrig's bridle as if it were a holy relic.

'But look, sir, they've pushed the enemy to the right, they've opened a gap for us, sir!'

Haselrig peered at Birch's fanciful gap, a muddy cattle wallow just in front of the leaning gate. Their pikemen had forced a Royalist foot regiment around and away from the formidable hedge, leaving a gap the size of a tennis court behind them. The ground was strewn with bodies and broken equipment, the rutted gateway running with blood.

'Dragoons, sir, call up the dragoons to open the gate, and we'll ride the bastards into the ground!'

Haselrig clenched his fist, looked down and wrenched his reins from Birch's grasp.

'Call up the dragoons, sound the advance!' he cried, hoping to God his desperate lieutenant was right. 'Follow me!'

Slowly, inch by remorseless inch, Dartland's reduced regiment had ground its opponents back, pushing them at right angles along the hedge. The pikemen were still meshed together like crabs in a rock pool, the darting musketeers caught up in a running firefight along either flank. The enemy musketeers had clambered up behind the hedge to fire down on their enemies, but Dartland's men had taken cover under the earth bank, firing through the privets and brambles at point-blank range, feverishly reloading while the Royalists replied with stinging volleys of their own.

William felt the subtle change in pressure, and immediately dug in his heels, leaning on with all his might. Zack coughed.

'Steady, Will!'

'Get out of it, you prickster! Give it up, give it up for God's sake!' William cried hoarsely.

'Shut yer gob, Roundhead!' Cully Oates called, ramming his shoulder against his wavering colleague as if he was plugging a hole in a dyke. He was an old hand, and he'd been caught up in collapsing pikeblocks before.

'Push, you slacks, you sister-fuckers!' he roared, finding his voice now the terrible crush had slackened somewhat.

Sparrow matched him, bellow for bellow.

'Earl of Dartland's regiment, heave!'

'God and the West!'

Oates felt the scrummage behind him take a step back. He dug in his heels, drool running out of his whiskered mouth as he tried to prop the sagging front.

'Push!'

'Heave!' Sparrow felt the sudden rumble beneath his boots, the tired hill vibrating like a drumskin as the cavalry charged home.

Charged home on whom?

'Heave, heave for the love of Christ, push!' he roared, his chest and lungs bursting with the effort.

It felt for one tiny moment as if his tremendous efforts had suddenly borne fruit. The enemy regiment gave ground, infinitely slowly. But once they had lost their footing they were forced upright, and once they were upright they couldn't hope to hold against a well-angled opponent. They took another step back. And another. And then the entire mob collapsed, the rear rankers dropping their pikes and scrambling up the bank as if their lives depended on it. Sparrow peered about, dazed and confused by the swirling horsemen.

He realized with a surge of relief they bore Parliamentarian colours.

The same colours he had borne on Roundway.

The dragoons had cantered up the hill behind them, hurling themselves out of their saddles in their haste to force the gate.

The enemy defenders rushed over to beat them off.

Sparrow spotted Long Col and his musketeers crouching beside a row of rabbit holes in the tattered hedgerow. The veteran sergeant realized what the dragoons intended, and immediately supported their charge with a deadly volley. Four Royalists struggling to haul the gate closed fell back into the brambles. Another dozen fled. Dragoons spurred their horses up the bank, cursing and yelling as they went. Others scrambled over the obstacle on their hands and knees or swung their muskets like clubs, torn and slashed by the flailing tendrils.

'Get the gate open!' Sparrow staggered out of the pikeblock and was immediately knocked to his knees by a panic-stricken dragoon horse which had torn itself free from its terrified holder.

William ground the butt of his halberd and prised himself to his feet, waving his milling troops towards the slowly widening gap.

The earl staggered up from the rear, smothered in soot and blinking like an owl, utterly bewildered by the punishing struggle. Sparrow grabbed him by the shoulder and propelled the dazed youth towards the questionable safety of the hedge. They threw themselves down into the trampled turf as the first squadron of Lobsters spurred up the hill, their heavy horses blowing hard as they negotiated the hissing, sucking mud.

'Charge, charge! Through the gate!' Birch shrieked, leading the tired pack through the wallow, beating his horse with the flat of his sword.

Sparrow was crippled with agony, his cramped limbs turned to beef jelly by the frantic press he had endured. He lay back in the smashed brambles, oblivious to the tiny pricks and cuts, paralysed with exhaustion as he watched the world thunder by.

He rolled over onto his aching belly, crossed his hands over his aching head as the dragoons clambered forward to manhandle the gate open. Musketeers hurried through the breach to clear the Royalist defenders from the hedge, closely followed by Sir Arthur Haselrig and a gaggle of officers, their clenched-fist colour snapping above their heads.

The heavily armoured riders swept past his narrow sanctuary, a riot of black and bronze statues on huge snorting horses. The ground shook as they cantered through the gate and found the drier ground beyond.

The pierced heart of Hopton's position.

'Charge! Onward, onward!'

Sparrow could hear Birch bellow above the din, and raised his head to peer through the demolished vegetation. The Earl of Dartland lay in the brambles beside him, holding his throat and gasping for breath.

'Is that it, we've won?' he growled, his shrill voice marvellously transformed by the punishing crush.

'I don't know whether we've won,' Sparrow croaked, flopping back down beside him and taking deep draughts of stinking smoke as if it were the freshest mountain air. 'But it doesn't look like we're losing.'

'Amen to that,' Dartland sighed, satisfied with Sparrow's brief reconnaissance over the parapet.

'Aye, amen,' Sparrow croaked, laying his head down and closing his eyes.

By Christ, the way he felt, trampled and mauled and spiked and spat on, there wasn't an awful lot between winning and losing.

ACKNOWLEDGEMENTS

The one thing my research has shown me in the four years I have been writing this series is that I could have based each book solely on real-life events. The Civil Wars abound with larger-than-life characters, and incidents like those described at the fictitious port of Penmethock occurred on an almost weekly basis up and down the coast.

As usual with the Shadow on the Crown series, the truth is stranger than the fiction: McNabb's letter about the abortive attacks on Basing House is based on various first-hand accounts of the battle. The Westminster Trained Band somehow managed to fire into the backs of their own front rank, killing about eighty men. One look at H. P. Smith's *History of the Borough and County of the town of Poole* or C. W. Cullingford's *History of Poole* will convince readers I have not exaggerated the vicious firefight at Penmethock.

Thankfully, there are historians as keen on recording their inspiring details as I am in incorporating their brave deeds into my stories.

My thanks must go as always to the Sealed Knot. Attending various musters up and down the country immediately rekindles my enthusiasm – there's nothing like a good pike push to sort you out after a hard week at the word processor!

Many members have carried out far more detailed research into aspects of the period than I have, but have always been glad to share the fruits of their research with me over a pint or three. They will hopefully forgive me distilling years of painstaking reading into soundbites for the more general reader.

Typical of these incredibly clued up gentlemen is Pete Minall, editor of our regimental newsletter and keen student of Civil War correspondence. Another is Stuart Peachey of the Stuart Press, whose fine set of pamphlets is available at Sealed Knot musters or from 117 Farleigh Road, Blackwell, Bristol BS19 3PG. Stuart also organizes genuine seventeenth-century banquets for Sealed Knot regiments, one of which I was lucky enough to attend (only in the interests of research!). For those wanting an overview, *The Civil War in the Midlands* by Roy Sherwood (Alan Sutton Publishing) is worth a look. *Going to the Wars* by Charles Carlton is packed full of pungent anecdotes. I also drew on John Tincey's account of the Farnham Greencoats and Mike White's brief chapter on Newark which appeared in the *Miniature Wargames* magazine.

For those wanting a slightly more general view of the Civil Wars and a good idea of uniform, tactics and weapons, look out for Philip Haythornthwaite's *English Civil War* (Blandford Press).

For the military minded who want the details on the many skirmishes and battles of the three civil wars, then Brigadier Peter Young and Richard Holmes' *The English Civil War* is essential reading.

Peter Young's *Civil War England* (Longman Travellers Series) provides a pungent guide to the best battlefields and castles to visit, as well as thumbnail sketches of some of the lesser known combatants.

C. V. Wedgwood's *The King's War* (Penguin) provides the full political and strategic overview of the conflict, and further details of the bloody struggles on the Continent can be found in her excellent *Thirty Years War* (Oxford University Press).

Details of the efforts made by the Royalists to organize themselves are recorded in Ronald Hutton's *The Royalist War Effort* (Longman).

The Osprey Elite series on infantry and cavalry of the civil wars provides good background on uniforms and organization, as well as including sets of excellent illustrations by Angus McBride.

While I have endeavoured to make the Shadow on the Crown series as historically accurate as possible, there are inevitably occasions when a little journalistic licence is required. Please forgive any unintentional errors as to when and precisely where certain events took place.

Nicholas Carter, pikeman and pamphleteer.